DANGEROUS WATERS

A warm breeze lifted Carrie's hair, and that familiar relaxing feeling the natives called Polynesian paralysis crept over her. *The Winsome Blonde* cut through the turquoise ocean effortlessly, her teak hull darkly contrasting with the almost transparent water around it. Carrie adjusted one of the anchor ropes and caught another glimpse of Alex's blond head.

"Let's lock the tiller," he called, "and go below . . ."

He came to her and kissed her, then again more intensely. She let him lead her down the hatch, into the privacy of the cabin. "I love you," he whispered as he lowered her to the bunk.

* * *

She awakened to the sound of waves smashing against the boat. The loud crackling snap of the sails told her they'd been surprised by a squall. She ran topside. The sky was black; the sea roiled in a black soupy mess.

"Alex!" she screamed. "Where are you?"

The storm raged around her; a gust of wind swept her across the deck, knocked her against the mast. The boat jibed, the boom swung, and she spotted Alex, flipped over the side of the boat as if he'd been a cardboard figure.

Horrified, she grabbed a life jacket and dove into the sea . . .

THE
SILVER DOLPHIN

DIANA LORD

ZEBRA BOOKS
KENSINGTON PUBLISHING CORP.

for Bobby—in memory of the romance in Hawai'i
for Fred—for teaching me Hawaiian history
for Mom—because your faith in me is never-ending

ZEBRA BOOKS are published by

Kensington Publishing Corp.
850 Third Avenue
New York, NY 10022

Zebra and the Z logo Reg. U.S. Pat. & TM Off.

First Printing: August, 1995

Printed in the United States of America

Of his bones are coral made,
Those are pearls that were his eyes,
Nothing of him that doth fade,
But doth suffer a sea change.
—*William Shakespeare*

One

"C'mon, Carrie. Dive!" Alex's golden hair flowed out behind him like a mantle as he bobbed in the water beneath the bow of their sailboat, *The Winsome Blonde.*

"They won't get out of the way." Carrie stood poised on the bow, a tall, platinum-haired goddess reflecting the Hawaiian sun like a gold coin. Her toes hung over the gunwale, her eyes focused on the bevy of dolphins surrounding her husband.

"They'll move. Just jump!"

She dove, the blue-green Pacific instantly swallowing her. One kick, then two, and she cleared the surface. Raising her face to the sun, she took a breath, then felt a smooth fin skimming her body like a caress. Although the dolphins had often swum with Carrie and her husband, each time one of them touched her or came close to study her with its warm, intelligent eyes, she felt a special thrill.

"That was one of the new babies," Alex called. "He wants to play."

Alex dove beneath the surface and a group of five or six young adults immediately dove with him, cavorting like puppies, bumping each other with their snouts, chasing and jumping over each other in an intricate game of underwater leapfrog.

When Alex and she had begun escorting tourists on whale-watching cruises, one of the things Carrie had loved most about their trips was the childlike innocence the dolphins brought out in anyone who saw them for the first time. It was a feeling, she realized, that never quite went away.

While Alex played with the babies, Carrie watched the biggest dolphin, the oldest male. She and Alex had dubbed him Silver. His moves were more deliberate and graceful than the others', almost serious. With a swift flip of his pectoral fin, he pushed one of the calves out of the way. Carrie could hear his sharp whistle, the sound she had come to know was his disciplinary tone.

Suddenly, she felt Alex's hands slide up her calves, then to her thighs, surrounding her waist before he popped up beside her. He shook his head like a seal, then his bright blue eyes followed her gaze.

"He's a good father, isn't he?" He nodded toward Silver, who seemed to be herding the younger dolphins away from Carrie. They often nipped her toes and, though she knew they only meant play, she had spent many hours bandaging her bleeding feet.

"The best." Carrie smiled, wrapping her arms around her husband's tanned neck and nuzzling his lips in a salty kiss.

People were frequently surprised to discover that she and Alex were married, for they looked like brother and sister, both tall, tanned, blond and wild. Alex, the original California surfer boy, still seemed a teenager despite his twenty-eight years. His shoulder-length hair was never combed or tidy, bleached by the same sun and saltwater which had burnished almost every inch of his body to a deep gold. His looks were the kind sought for commercials to advertise suntan lotion, but he wasn't conscious of the effect his appearance had on others. In fact, he always seemed surprised when Carrie commented on the number of women looking at him. The only thing that mesmerized him was the ocean—its whales, dolphins, and sea turtles—and the people whose lives revolved around it. Especially Carrie.

Alex swung around, creating a ripple in the glass-like sea. "You think I'm going to be as good a father as Silver?"

"Of course. Anyone would be better than mine . . ." As soon as the words escaped her, she regretted saying them. Alex's eyes shadowed and his mouth stretched into a straight, hard line.

"Are you ever going to learn to forgive and forget or are you going to be pissed off forever?"

"You just don't—"

A strong calf with spots still on its belly slammed between the two of them, then turned on its back, whistling happily, as if asking them to join in the chase. The intrusion was a welcome one, Carrie thought, as she swam in pursuit of the little one, joining him underwater for a whirling game of tag. She shouldn't have said anything about her father. It would only serve to ruin this special day, their anniversary, and anything was preferable to thinking about the wealthy Texas entrepreneur, Philip DeBary.

For more than an hour, they played with the pewter-colored mammals. Finally, Carrie announced, "I give up," and clambered aboard the sailboat to collapse on deck. After a few moments, she could hear Alex puttering about and opened her eyes to gaze at her husband, then past him, toward the disappearing Kona coast. With a contented smile, she sighed deeply.

Even after five years in Hawaii, she had still not gotten used to the beauty of the islands, especially the big island, Hawaii, and its volcanic majesty. She loved every inch of "my island," as she called it: the black volcanic lava beaches, the wild coast, the orchids blooming naturally everywhere, the old Western-style cities of Pahoa and Hilo, the warm, friendly people who were equally at home on the ocean and on the stunningly resplendent island they inhabited. She had easily been convinced there was nothing more refreshing than a Kauai rainstorm, nothing more spectacular than a Diamond Head sunrise, nothing more satisfying than watching a humpback whale give birth right off Maui's coast.

A warm breeze lifted the wet platinum strands of hair framing her face, and she let that familiar relaxing feeling the natives called Polynesian paralysis creep over her body. To the south, their port, the Honokohau Small Boat Harbor, was barely visible now, melting into the profile of the island like a grain of sand on one of Hawaii's black beaches.

The afternoon sky held the promise of a premier sunset, one of the gold and crimson masterpieces that artists perpetuated in oil or watercolor, yet which were never quite perfect, never quite complete, unless you were able to experience all of the sunset—the salty smell of the surrounding ocean, the warm taste of the Hawaiian air, the endless panoramic view of gold-tipped horizon and emerald mountains leading to a diamond-and-sapphire sea. A crisp, fragrant odor nipped her nostrils, a combination of the sea air and the white gardenias she kept in a vase in the sailboat's galley.

The Winsome Blonde cut through the turquoise ocean silently and effortlessly, its teak hull darkly contrasting with the almost transparent water around it. Her father had designed the boat and had it built in Norway by master boatbuilders as a gift to her mother, Simone, upon the occasion of Carrie's birth. Together they named it *The Winsome Blonde* as a tribute to the exquisite, platinum-haired baby, their first, and only, child.

The boat was the only possession, beyond their clothes and personal items, that Carrie and Simone had retained five years ago when they left Philip, their Texas estate, and their society-filled lives for the peace found in a simple beach house on the Kona Coast. After more than ten years of suspecting her husband of adultery, Simone had finally come face-to-face with the truth when she found Philip *en flagrante delicto* with the mother of one of Carrie's friends.

Less than six years ago the words "special occasion" meant countless trips to the dressmaker, chauffeured Rolls Royces, hobnobbing with celebrities. Now, an outdoor barbecue served quite nicely. And Carrie didn't miss her old life at all. In fact, she never wanted any part of wealth ever again, and she knew her mother felt the same way.

Hawaii had lived up to its nickname, Paradise, in more ways than one, Carrie mused as she adjusted some of the anchor ropes and caught another glimpse of Alex's tousled blond head. She had found true happiness here, shedding the affectations that were almost necessary in order to be part of Houston's society, letting loose of all inhibitions, even to the point of leaving her hair long and free, allowing it to become sunstreaked and tangled instead of neatly barretted behind her ears. She pushed a waist-length strand back from her face, wishing she hadn't washed it this morning before leaving. It was so fine, even the best barrette wouldn't hold it in place just after a shampoo. But Alex liked it loose and swishy, a platinum frame around her bronzed face, he always said. His Golden Mermaid, he called her.

She could hardly believe that, as of today, February 25, 1995, they had been married for a full year. A seaside wedding, complete with fragrant orchid leis, Hawaiian love songs, Aunty Mariah's hula girls, a few special friends, *Maman,* and, of course, Alex Madison, the marine biologist who had asked her to share his life. They had sailed into the sunset that day, just as they had today, and Carrie would never have believed it if someone had told her then that her first anniversary would be even better than her wedding day.

As she bent her head back, stretched luxuriantly, and raked her fingers through her hair, she glimpsed a flash of silver off the starboard side and smiled to see the family of spinner dolphins frolicking alongside.

She called out to Silver, clicking and chirping to him as the dolphins did among themselves. He stopped momentarily, then lifted his head to look straight at her, his sleek snout shining like a new dime.

"What a lazy sailor you've become," Alex murmured in her ear.

Carrie jumped, startled out of her reverie. "There's nothing to be done," she protested. "Everything's calm . . ."

"So it is," Alex's bright blue eyes sparkled. "But whenever there's dolphins around, you can be sure Caryn Madison gets no work done."

Leaning toward her, he licked her lips gently with his tongue, sending shivers clear down to her pink toenails. "Let's lock the tiller and call it an afternoon," he whispered.

She didn't need to consider his suggestion for more than a moment before she turned back to him, her arms immediately encircling his neck.

"What about the genoa?" she murmured. "We really should take the sail down, just in case . . ."

"I've got something more interesting to do right now. I'll come back up later," he replied.

Their next kiss was longer, more intense than the one before.

"Happy anniversary, Mrs. Madison," Alex said when they finally pulled apart.

"Happy anniversary to you, too. . . . And it's Ms. not Mrs."

She was still giggling when he pulled her down the hatch, through the galley, and toward the compact bunk in the rear of the cabin. Her fingers already tugged at his shorts as he untied her bikini top and slid his hands over her hard nipples. Within seconds, their scanty clothing fell into a small pile at their feet.

She felt Alex's whole body, tense and hard, against her, his knee slipped in between her legs, his chest pressed to her breasts, the curve of his hip echoing hers. They fit perfectly, as if a seamstress had designed a pattern for their two bodies, carefully measuring and fitting the pieces together like a finely tailored suit.

Alex raised his head from her breasts, his face serious, his eyes the color of high-summer Texas bluebonnets. "I've missed you this week," he said. "I don't think I can wait much longer."

"So, go for it. What are you waiting for, an engraved invitation?" Carrie's hand guided him to the spot where she knew she'd lose all connection with the earth and just float, suspended in true contentment.

He moved quickly, comfortable with her body, immediately into her rhythm. Supporting himself on stiffened arms, he watched her face as she went from initial stomach-tingling surprise to full, satisfying release, never taking his eyes from hers, seemingly absorbing the passion he aroused in her body, then feeding it back to her again. And only after she stopped throbbing did he allow himself his own pleasure, closing his eyes and groaning low and soft before lowering himself onto her.

"I love you, you beautiful *haole,* you."

Carrie stroked his shoulder lazily, smiling softly at his use of the Hawaiian term for white people. "I love you, too, Alexander Madison."

She awakened to the sound of waves smashing against the side of the boat, the violent rocking sending her flying to the edge of the bunk. The loud crackling snap of the sails told her they'd been surprised by a squall, and Alex was not in his place next to her.

Shocked, she struggled into a T-shirt and shorts, then shoved her feet into a pair of docksiders and ran topside. The dark sky ominously obliterated any vestige of a sunset and the sea roiled in a black soupy mess. Nowhere could she see the clear blue tranquility she had enjoyed earlier.

She winced as the sting of sea spray hit her face. How could this be? No storms had been forecast and sea squalls usually didn't come up so quickly off the Kona Coast. How long had they been asleep? An hour? More?

"Alex!" she screamed. "Where are you?"

The storm raged around her as though the Hawaiian god Pele had caused a sea volcano to erupt beneath them. Carrie grabbed one of the lines and guided herself blindly.

"Alex!" Her feet slipped on the wet deck.

"Here!" he answered, standing up from where he struggled to get the genoa under control. "Come here, I need some help . . . get . . . sails down."

She headed toward him, holding her arms out to the side to steady herself. The wind whipped her hair against her face, slapping it soundly on her cheek. The sound of the storm, angry and powerful, roared through her ears and loose lines clanged against the aluminum mast, their noise as shrill as a fire bell. Her clothes stuck to her skin like sheets of wet paper.

Another gust of wind swept over the deck, knocking her against the mast. The halyard cleat bit into her lower back. She cried out, pushed herself erect, then looked up to see the genoa flapping wildly and Alex struggling with it, trying singlehandedly to control the whipping sail. Suddenly, it ballooned freely, and she saw the winch head snap. The boat jibed, knocking her off balance. She fell to her knees, lifting her head in time to watch the boom sweep across the deck, hit Alex and knock him down. Although it was only seconds, it seemed hours as she helplessly watched him struggle, the genoa sheet tightening around his right leg. Then the boat jibed again, the boom swung, and this time it flipped Alex over the side as easily as if he'd been a cardboard figure.

Frantic, she slipped over to where she'd last seen him and screamed his name. For several long seconds, she could see nothing but the surge and fall of the waves, then there! A blond head bobbing ten feet astern. Without pausing for a single precious moment, she kicked the anchor chuck, slipped her arms through the life-jacket kept in the starboard bow, and dove in.

Diving beneath the choppy surface again and again, she came back up for air only to scream Alex's name into the bawling roar of the storm. Even though she couldn't hear her own voice, she kept calling, over and over and over. More than once she gulped a mouthful of stinging saltwater, spat, and coughed it up, only to scream for Alex once more.

After what seemed like an eternity, she felt a strong, slippery body brush against hers and realized the dolphins had come back, surrounding her, pushing her, trying to help her. She dove with them, and finally found Alex's arm. As she pulled him to the surface, the dolphins pushed. The sea around her seemed full of them. To her right, Silver rose within inches of her face and met her eye to eye. She gasped, wiped the burning water from her eyes, and tightened her grip around Alex's chest. The dolphins edged closer, buoying her and Alex, chirruping among themselves.

She tried to gauge how far she had swum from the boat. There, only ten or twenty feet away, yet in this turbulent sea it seemed miles. She hugged Alex close to her and stroked with her left arm, amazed that the dolphins were slowing their pace to keep Alex and her within their protective circle. So far, Alex hadn't moved or coughed, and out of the corner of her eye she could see red-black blood streaming down the back of his head. Using every ounce of energy she had, she fought the waves, the pull of the water, and Alex's weight, keeping her eye on the dark teak hull. She was tired, and the dolphins seemed to sense it, crowding even closer, nudging her from beneath as well as from both sides.

Carrie didn't pause to think of the miracle the dolphins were performing or to thank the gods they were there to help. She only wanted this nightmare to be over.

"Don't panic," she warned herself aloud. "Just get to the boat. Don't panic."

With a burst of energy, she swam with strong, sure, one-armed strokes, her adrenaline serving as her strength to get Alex to the rope ladder slung over the transom. Holding herself against the ladder with one hand, she wrapped her legs around him, keeping his chin above the surface while she slipped the jacket off herself and onto him. The dolphins seemed to understand her efforts and kept their distance, their heads above water, their black eyes watching her intently. She grabbed a loose line and tied it to the jacket.

"You'll be all right, sweetie," she whispered hoarsely as she secured the line. Leaving Alex below, she scooted onto the deck. The boat rocked with each surging wave, smacking Alex against it, and the dolphins kept away, some now diving beneath the waves, to calmer, safer waters.

Carrie pulled the line in slowly, inch by inch, her arms aching and her back screaming, determined to get Alex on board no matter what amount of pain it took. She was crying, moaning into the wind, begging whatever gods were listening to help her, give her strength, keep her sane. Save her husband!

As the last of the dolphins disappeared under the dark and choppy water, she wound the line around a cleat, until she could finally reach Alex's arms to drag him aboard. It took all of her might to pull his dead weight on deck, all of her control to stop crying, and all of her concentration to lower her mouth to his. This time the kiss was a calculating one, a life-giving force, a desperate plea for some kind of human animation. She pinched his nostrils with her fingers and breathed into his mouth again.

"Alex, you have to try. Please, babe, don't go on me now. Try, Alex. Breathe, dammit!"

Two

For two hours, Carrie fought ten to twelve foot waves, dancing with the ocean, moving with the waves rather than against them, knowing with every fiber of her soul that the power of the sea was indisputable, that she could lose control of the boat too easily. But every time she looked at Alex's pale face where he sat lashed to the mast, she felt a cold knowledge that if she didn't ride with the wind, didn't get back to port as quickly as possible, she might never again feel him warm against her.

Her mind raced as quickly as the wind whining around her. Her sure-footed and swift cutting of the sails made the *Blonde* behave as though it were one with her, and, despite her fear and anguish, she felt the odd combination of absolute fear and pure exhilaration she had read about long ago in Thor Heyerdahl's *Kon Tiki*. Every piece of sailing knowledge she had ever learned was tested. Every muscle in her long, lean body was used. More than once she found herself grateful for having sailed from Galveston to Hawaii with her mother. The trip, though a fairly uneventful one, had given her the opportunity to experience more of the ocean's mercurial changes than most sailors encountered in a lifetime.

When she finally pulled out of the storm, into a calm, clear view of the Kona Coast, she realized it had taken her more than double the usual time to reach shore. Her attention turned once again to her husband. Alex's eyes were closed, his lips purple. She kneeled before him, a strange pressure bearing down on her chest. He had obviously lost a lot of blood and had not regained consciousness since going overboard.

She held his head against her breast for a couple of moments, whispering reassurances in his ear, trying to get some reaction from him. All the while, her eyes focused on the sloping green and beige mountains on the starboard side. No other boats on the horizon. Not close enough to see signs of life on shore. Yet everything seemed so normal. Just the same as they had left it. Had it been only this morning?

Finally, she knew she must go below, and, with shaking hands, she held the radio's mike to her mouth. At first, her call letters simply wouldn't come to mind. Damn, she thought, how can I be so stupid? I've repeated those damn letters a zillion times. Then she looked at the radio and the call letters Alex had pasted on to its metal side less than a month ago.

"Bless you, babe," she whispered, a knot in her throat. All business, she radioed port and sent a silent prayer that Matt Kamehea would be in the office to answer her call.

"What's up, you ol' married *wahini?*" Matt's cheerful voice crackled through the small cabin. "You tired of the big *kahuna* already? Wanna come home and have a cold one with Bruddah Matt?"

"Maybe more than one, Kamehea," she answered,

her voice a lot brighter than she felt. "There's been an accident, and I need your help."

Quickly, she explained Alex's condition, knowing that, with every word she spoke, every moment wasted, Alex was losing more blood. All the while, she fought to keep her voice from shaking. She'd be no help to Matt, or Alex, if she started flipping out now.

Matt's voice was calm and soothing, though she knew the edge to his clipped questions meant he was as worried as she. Nothing much flustered her Hawaiian friends, which was one of the reasons she loved them. No matter what happened, their smiles always returned. She wondered if her own would.

"You just take it easy, Caryn," he concluded. "We'll meet you at port."

She signed off and climbed back up the ladder. Matt must know how serious it is, she thought. He never calls me Caryn.

The realization didn't help to calm her.

The first thing Carrie saw when she finally reached Honokohau Harbor was Matt Kamehea's worried face. A native Hawaiian whose family was proud of its pure heritage, Matt and his mother had sheltered Simone and Carrie when they'd first come to the island. He knew almost as much about whales as Alex and had quickly become part of Alex and Carrie's whale-watching business on their other boat, *The Big One*, as well as their best friend.

Matt's stocky body loomed in front of her. The shark's teeth he wore around his neck dangled before her eyes as he bent over the gunwale to help her secure the boat.

"Wikiwiki! Wikiwiki!" he yelled over his shoulder to the white-coated ambulance attendants, urging them to come as quickly as possible. "Where's Alex?" he asked Carrie, not waiting for an answer before he spotted his friend and pushed past her to begin loosening the ropes which held Alex's limp body to the mast.

With a sense of relief, she watched Matt take over as she shrugged out of the safety harness she didn't even remember putting on. The blood on the back of Alex's head had finally congealed. Thank God, she thought, knowing that meant the bleeding had finally stopped. She shivered uncontrollably, then stood aside as the paramedics lifted Alex onto a stretcher.

Seconds later, Matt stood next to her, his large body warm and comforting. He mumbled words she couldn't understand, as the ambulance pulled away, lights flashing, siren wailing. In a daze, she let him lead her to his black Camaro, the car she and Alex had teasingly dubbed the "lean-mean-speeding-machine." She sunk into the seat, as they raced behind the ambulance to the hospital, thankful for once that the car was one of the fastest on the island.

She didn't really hear Matt's questions, couldn't answer if she had, felt only a numbing certainty that, should Alex die, she would, too.

Matt watched Carrie's face silently for a moment before heading out into traffic and was reminded of a puppy he'd found on the side of the road long ago.

Was he ten or eleven? Didn't matter. The puppy's leg had been broken, probably from being thrown from a car, and its eyes had seemed to beg Matt for an answer to why it had been abandoned. He couldn't answer the puppy's questioning eyes and simply took it home.

The same why-have-I-been-abandoned expression lingered on Carrie's shell-shocked face.

Don't ask me why, Matt silently begged her. I don't have any answers.

He turned away, wondering whether she knew Alex's blood was spattered all over her T-shirt or that her hair was tangled and unkempt, her eyes wild, unfocused. Not like Alex's Golden Mermaid at all.

A beige station wagon pulled out in front of him, and he caught himself in time to swerve, both hands and feet working simultaneously to control his car. Carrie didn't even notice.

"Don't need *us* going to the hospital, too, do we, Sistah?" he asked Carrie, trying to put a chuckle into his voice. But his question fell like a tree in an empty forest. He stole another glance at her, alarmed at the pale skin and lips beneath her tan.

Oh, man, don't let anything worse happen, he prayed as he pressed the accelerator to the floor. I'm not equipped to handle shit like this.

They pulled into the hospital parking lot at the same time as Carrie's mother. Although Carrie recognized the smoke gray Honda Prelude instantly, she didn't wait for Simone to get out of her car before running into the emergency room, leaving both Matt and Simone behind. All that mattered was Alex.

She spotted the attendants wheeling the stretcher into one of the examining rooms and caught up with them, wiping the tears off her cheeks before bending over her husband's still body.

"Alex? Can you hear me? Babe, you've got to hear me! You've got to come out of this! Don't leave me . . ."

A strong hand held her arm and gently, but forcefully, pulled her away. "I'm sorry, miss," the attendant said. "You can't come in here."

"But he's my husband!" She fought the hand that held her, amazed that he didn't seem to understand how important it was that she be with Alex. Alex would want her there. Alex needed her.

"I'm sorry."

"Caryn, come with us, *chérie.*" Her mother's small hands replaced the attendant's and pulled Carrie away from the door and to a couch in the waiting room. "Let them do their job. There's nothing we can do now but wait."

Although she towered over her petite, auburn-haired mother, Carrie collapsed into Simone's arms like a child, sobbing uncontrollably, trying to tell her what had happened. All Simone seemed able to say was, "That's good, darling. Let it out. It'll be all right. It'll be all right."

That was all Carrie needed. For now.

Behind them, Matt paced with the dedicated ferocity of a caged panther, his wide bare feet making slapping sounds against the linoleum floor. "How could this happen? He's a first-rate sailor. The *kahuna*. He knew all there was to know about that boat."

Carrie lifted her head, hating Matt for pinpointing the guilt she felt all along. "We didn't take down the genoa when we went below. I know we should've, but Alex said he'd come up later. I should've insisted, Matt. But the storm came up while we—Oh, *Maman,* why didn't I make him do it?" The tears started all over again. From the corner of her eye, she saw Matt's face fall and his shoulders slump as he looked at Simone and shook his head.

For a long time, Carrie lay on the waiting room couch, her head in her mother's lap, reliving the accident in her mind over and over again, as they waited for word from the doctor who had followed Alex's stretcher into the examining room.

Why didn't I insist he check the sails? she repeatedly asked herself. Why didn't I check them myself? Why? Why?

Finally, the doctor, a small Indian man with serious dark eyes, whose white smock was covered with blood, Alex's blood, came toward them.

"Mrs. Madison?"

"Yes? Is he all right? Is my husband all right?"

Please tell me he's fine, she thought. Please tell me this is all a bad dream, that Alex was only knocked out and is in that emergency room charming all the nurses with that crooked smile of his. Tell me I can go in and take him home now.

But the doctor's face remained serious, not even a hint of a smile behind his black eyes.

"I'm afraid we'll have to operate immediately," he said, reaching a rubber-gloved hand in Carrie's direction as if to prevent her from fainting or crying out. "He damaged his back somehow when he was flipped out of the boat, but we can't be sure how badly until we operate. I suggest you go home and we'll call you—"

Carrie shook her head violently, her blond hair flying around her face. "No. No way. I'm staying right here."

The doctor looked from Simone to Matt, then back to Carrie, realizing any argument he might make would fall on three sets of deaf ears. Finally, he nodded and walked away, leaving them in shocked silence.

Matt let loose a ragged sigh and looked down at his large hands, turning them over, rubbing them against each other. "Maybe I should get us some coffee," he said. "Looks like it's going to be a long night."

Shifting slightly, Simone reached a hand across Carrie and patted Matt's knee. "Why don't you do that? And call Kenny Meyers to take over the whale-watching trips for the next couple of days. He has the keys to the office, doesn't he, Caryn?"

Unable to do much else, Carrie nodded her head. The last thing on her mind was her business right now. Thank God *Maman*'s here, she thought.

They sat in the small waiting room all night, taking turns buying coffee, keeping each other occupied with stories of Alex's escapades.

Matt remembered the time a birthing sperm whale almost totalled their whale-watching catamaran. Alex had come out laughing, more excited about seeing a calf birthed than worried that the boat had suffered major damage to its hull.

And the Molokai to Oahu canoe race. Alex and Matt, drunk and singing old Beatles tunes after winning. They would've been arrested, Matt still insisted, if the police officer who finally caught up with them had been anyone other than Matt's second cousin Petey.

Simone talked quietly of the many sick animals Alex kept bringing home to the holding tank he had built next to the place where they moored *The Big One*: the dolphins with shark bites on their sides or missing flippers from accidents with big boats, the blind sea turtle they had named Helen, the baby shark whose wild antics wrecked not only their nets but Simone's favorite *mu'umu'u*.

Carrie listened to their stories halfheartedly, trying to laugh when they wanted her to, but unable to concentrate on anything except the treasured memory of lying in bed with Alex shortly after they were married. He'd thought she was asleep and had lazily traced the curve of her shoulder with one finger, whispering, "I love you," with such passion that she knew, even without opening her eyes, he'd been overcome with emotion. For long moments, she had lain there, feeling her heart swell with such love for him that the thought of even trying to express it seemed impossible. When she finally turned over to encircle him with her arms, she realized what it meant to have another person make you whole. She savored that feeling now, letting it push away the guilt and the pain.

Coming out of her daydream, she heard Matt begin another story. She reached over to place a single finger on his lips.

"Don't," she whispered. "This isn't a funeral. Alex isn't gone. Don't eulogize him. Please."

Matt nodded, closing his eyes for a second, as if the pain of that thought were too much for him. Then he opened them with a start when they heard muffled footsteps in the hallway. As they had many times that evening, all three waited expectantly for the doctor to appear in the doorway.

Almost ten hours since I docked the boat, Carrie figured, after glancing at the waiting room clock. Ten of the longest, most anxious hours she'd ever spent. She doubted she could let another go by without letting loose with a primal scream.

But she wouldn't have to, she realized, when the footsteps stopped and the doctor slipped off his gloves and untied his surgical green face mask before sitting down beside her. His black eyes down, a look of consternation on his face, he paused a moment as if putting together a presidential speech. She held her breath, terrified he was going to tell her Alex was dead.

"I'm afraid your husband's injury is more serious than we feared," the doctor began. "It will be a long, long time before he is even able to go home."

Matt swore vehemently, slapping his fist into his palm. Simone tightened her grip on Carrie's hand. Carrie felt her shoulders slump with the relief of knowing Alex was still alive. Then the doctor's words repeated themselves in her mind, and she looked at him more closely.

"What is it exactly?"

The doctor's face screwed up as if he was going to speak, then he swallowed hard and tried again. She got the impression he hadn't had much practice passing on this kind of news and wondered briefly how long he'd been a doctor. Had he done his best with Alex? Could someone else have done better? Would the news be more optimistic?

"Tell me. Please!"

"When your husband fell, he. . . . Well, he has a cervical fracture with cord compression."

"Which means?" She dug her fingernails into her mother's palm and heard Simone's involuntary gasp of pain, yet was unable to let go.

"He has damaged the cord in his neck. From what you've told me, it must have happened when he hit the boat's guardrail. The spinal cord has swelled, causing paralysis."

She heard Matt swear under his breath again and looked up at him sharply. He turned and walked away, which didn't surprise her. He'd never been able to take bad news, didn't want to deal with any catastrophes at any time. Everything always had to be bright and optimistic for Matt. And for me, too, she realized. She grasped her mother's hand even tighter and pulled herself up straight, as if being rigid would help her cope with the answer to her next question.

"Complete paralysis?"

The doctor gazed steadily into Carrie's eyes. She could see his compassion, but she wanted more than compassion. She wanted a replay. She demanded yesterday, and Alex, both back, both in one piece, the way they had been, the way they should be.

"I'm sorry, Mrs. Madison. . . . The chances of your husband walking again are extraordinarily slim. I wouldn't even dare extend that hope to you. Most people only have use of one hand after an accident such as this, if they're lucky. And their speech patterns are often disrupted. In fact, I've never heard of anyone completely regaining full mobility. I'm not saying it won't happen . . . eventually. Miracles do occur. But, please, Mrs. Madison, don't get your hopes up."

The world seemed to stop. Although she heard the tinny voice of the hospital's paging system and felt the waiting room's bright lights burning into her eyes and the odd squareness of Matt who had come back to stand behind her, Carrie felt disconnected. The doctor continued to talk. She could see his lips moving, could feel her mother beside her, asking the doctor questions, but she couldn't make sense of what they said. All she could hear were Alex's assurances that they would spend all of their tomorrows together, that they would build the whale-watching business into the best on the islands, that once they had some money in the bank, he would build his own oceanography institute, and she could have a child, as she'd wanted from the first moment she had met him. ("Jonathan, if it's a boy," Alex had said. "Melissa, if it's a girl.") And their child would grow up tanned and strong, free to enjoy the beauty they had found in their paradise.

Paradise. Nothing could've felt further from paradise than what she felt at that very moment.

She stood and forced herself to move toward the door. Ignoring the voices she knew were Matt's and her mother's, she ran, faster and faster, slipping outside into the now quiet, moonless night and gulping the fresh air as if breathing alone would make her heart stop pounding and bring back some sense of reality to the jumbled thoughts in her mind. She wanted to run forever, away from the antiseptic smell of the hospital, the doctor's nasal voice, the vision of Alex's still body, his head covered with blood. Away from the thought that life had suddenly played the meanest possible trick on her by stealing every last bit of her happiness.

Staggering into the almost empty parking lot, she found a cold, steel lamppost and pressed her forehead against it, repeating Alex's name over and over, as she had out on the ocean, and found herself wishing that they had both drowned during the storm.

Three

Simone watched her daughter leave the emergency room, her heart as torn and bleeding as Carrie's. But her thoughts were furious and her fury was directed toward Philip DeBary, her former husband, the man she had loved more than any other, the man who had subsequently stolen her pride, her passion and her *joie de vivre*. She blamed him for all the crises she and Carrie had had to endure since leaving Texas.

She swore silently as she watched her only child run through the hospital's glass doors. He will never again hurt my daughter.

"She'll be back," Matt said, watching the emergency room doors as intently as Simone. "She won't be able to leave Alex for long."

Simone nodded, her mind racing in French, her native language, as it always did when she was worried or troubled. "I should never have given her the boat. It's been cursed from the very beginning. *Anything* Philip touches is cursed."

Matt shifted. The plastic seat crackled beneath him. "She loves *The Blonde*. She needed to have it when she first came to the island. It was her freedom."

"It was mine, too, a long time ago," Simone whispered, remembering how *The Winsome Blonde* had also served to remind her that her marriage was not what she had imagined it would be. When she was growing up, Simone had watched the close partnership her parents had had and had dreamed of some day having that type of relationship. Philip DeBary had embodied the fulfillment of that dream, until his ambitions had overshadowed her ideal of a close-knit family who spent time together, who cherished each other, who loved each other completely, forever.

"I used to sail off Texas's Gulf Coast, racing the wind, braving summer hurricanes, simply to escape the knowledge that I had married a man who would never be satisfied with one woman. Yet that escape was never complete. Philip was always there when I got home, his handsome face covered with a brilliantly toothy smile he seemed to generate for me alone . . . *pour moi*. And I so desperately needed to believe in the facade he created—that he loved me, that we could solve our marital problems, that he would eventually appreciate the stability I could offer him, that he would once again make me feel desirable and beautiful as he had when we first met in Europe . . . that he would appreciate the sweet child we'd created and that he'd want to remain a family. But I ignored all the signs that our marriage was disintegrating. How naive I was!"

Simone gazed into the distance, caught up in her angry memories, yet all too aware of how uncomfortable Matt had become. In the time they'd known each other, she had never shared much of her life. Besides, he was a child, and most of her time had been spent with his mother, Pudding. As intensely private as Simone was, she had told Pudding everything. Somehow she knew she could tell Matt, too. Especially now when those memories were so close to the surface.

She reached over and patted Matt's big knee, the gesture giving her as much comfort as she attempted to give him.

"There are two types of people in this world, Matthew," she continued, "the givers and the takers. Philip was a taker. He was more concerned with his business than his family, so Caryn and I consoled each other. We spent all our time together and became so close . . . so close . . . that I can feel her pain as intensely as she does." Unexpected tears rose in her eyes and she turned to dab at them with a scented lace handkerchief she always kept in her purse.

To be married to a man unable to move, *mon Dieu!* Ah, *ma petite* Caryn, no amount of kissing the hurt will relieve the pain this accident has caused.

She closed her eyes, remembering Caryn's innocent, wide-eyed, eight-year-old face when she'd come to her, arm limp and bleeding after a fall from her favorite horse. "That beast," Simone said, "doesn't it know it's carrying a special package from heaven?" And Caryn smiled through her tears, bravely wiping them away with the back of a dirty hand, putting her complete trust and faith in her mother to make all things better.

"It wasn't that Philip was a horrible person," she said. The need to talk enabled her to stay in her chair, kept her from following Caryn. "On the contrary, he was often quite generous, possessed a charming wit and an extraordinary patience, especially when he was teaching Caryn to ride. We just came from two different worlds, and as hard as I tried, I could never fit into his."

However, the early years, before Philip had made his fortune, had been heaven. In fact, she couldn't remember ever feeling happier or more loved. But as time passed, the business became more and more important, and Philip wanted her to be the perfect corporate wife. It was difficult to keep up with the tightly knit Texans. She couldn't withstand their endless gossiping or the wife-swapping, which seemed *de rigueur.*

Having Caryn provided an outlet which she desperately needed, and she indulged her daughter totally, even though Philip never seemed able to find the time to do the same.

When he'd come back from business trips, Caryn often hadn't recognized him and Simone hadn't pushed her toddler to accept Philip. Often she pleaded with him to stay home for a while, to spend time with his family, and, at first, he did. But his attention always seemed elsewhere, and after a while, she simply gave up.

How could I have gotten such a wonderful child from such a marriage? she wondered, thinking of Caryn, alone and grieving, out in the parking lot.

Sitting there in the cold, white waiting room, Simone suppressed a chill and pulled her brightly colored *mu'umu'u* tightly around her. For the first time during her years of motherhood, she felt inadequate.

"Should I go find her?" Matt's gruff voice startled Simone out of her reverie.

"What? No. No, dear one. Let her grieve. When she disappears like this, she desperately needs to be by herself. She doesn't want others to follow. In fact, it only angers her. A few moments alone always allows Caryn to compose herself. We will simply wait for her."

"What about Alex? Do you think I should go see him?"

Simone shook her head. "Allow Caryn to be the first. We'll go in with her, to give her support and love. That's all we can do for now. Give her support and love."

Even though it had been almost two weeks since the accident, Carrie was still unused to seeing Alex's pale face quiet and drawn against the hospital pillow. She fingered the crisp, white, hospital sheet and stifled a yawn. His normally windswept blond hair, now unwashed, dark and greasy, clung to his forehead. The shadow of a beard covered the lower half of his face and his body lay still and useless under the sheet.

The shock was gone, replaced by bitter reality. She'd had time to think about what Alex's paralysis would mean to their lives, had dealt with all of the anger, denial, and guilt, and had begun to make promises to herself. And to him.

I won't let you down. I'll always be there for you, babe. Just like you would be for me.

"No matter what, remember?" she whispered to Alex's still sleeping face. "Together forever. Just you and me."

She stifled another yawn, tempted to close her eyes, but soon it would be time for lunch, and the nurses would come in to wake Alex up, turn him over, get his blood flowing, then Carrie would spoon feed him whatever pablum they brought from the cafeteria.

When Alex woke, she could tell from his eyes that he was still baffled by all that was going on around him, but he couldn't speak, though the doctor promised her that was only temporary. The shock of the accident caused it, he'd said. The shock and the injury. The injury which might render him crippled forever.

Still, she waited every day for Alex to awaken again, for the possibility that he might speak, for those moments when she could talk to him, to tell him how much she loved him and how she wanted him to get better. But mostly she wanted to hear him say he loved her too.

"Chérie? Are you awake?" Simone had come in quietly and stood at the end of the bed, her pumpkin-colored *mu'umu'u* a bright contrast against the white sheets. She held a P.D. James mystery under her arm, her finger holding her place.

Carrie smiled. Her mother had never been without a book as long as she'd known her. They flooded the tables in her little immaculately white house, several were always tucked into the glove compartment of her car, and she never went anywhere without one in her pocketbook. Simone had always said reading helped her feel that waiting wasn't a waste of time, but Carrie knew the truth. Her mother clung to her mysteries because they kept reality at bay.

"It's almost lunchtime."

"I know, *Maman.*" She stretched and yawned once more. "But I want to be here when Alex wakes up."

"Come," Simone held out her hand, "how are you going to keep up your strength if you don't eat? You haven't left his side even for a moment. I'm sure the nurses can take care of him while you have some lunch."

Carrie smiled meekly, too drained of all her energies to resist any longer. Taking her mother's hand, she followed her into the hallway, feeling, as she always did, gawky and too tall.

Who would know we're mother and daughter? she wondered, gazing down at the top of her mother's silver-streaked auburn head. Often as a child, Carrie had fantasized she'd been adopted, that petite, sophisticated Simone had found her abandoned on the side of some Texas highway and brought her home. Carrie used to imagine Simone was able to convince everyone they were mother and daughter because Carrie resembled Philip. "She's inherited dear Philip's traits. They must have been the dominant genes," Simone would have claimed.

Philip's traits. Carrie knew she looked like her father. Nobody could deny that the slight point to her nose was his, the almond-shaped brown eyes were a carbon copy of his, the arrogant way she tilted her chin, and the broad, toothy smile. And she resented it. She wanted Simone's small, pretty feet, her gray cat's eyes, her naturally regal carriage.

Matt's mother, Auntie Pudding, still held to the belief that Simone had royal blood, and no amount of proof that Simone had been brought up in a small farming community in southern France could convince her otherwise.

Sometimes even Carrie believed in Auntie Pudding's fantasy about her mother. Even now, fifty-one-year-old Simone, dressed in the colorful, loose-fitting *mu'umu'u* most Hawaiian women wore, seemed to be holding court, nodding to each nurse or attendant they passed, holding her head high, shoulders erect. And though Carrie knew her mother's posture was born of a deep desire to be taller, her carriage simply made her appear even more sophisticated than everyone else around her.

As they walked, still hand-in-hand, into the crowded hospital cafeteria, Carrie felt a twinge of guilt that Simone had given up her cherished time at the Waimea Bay Art Gallery, where she worked four days a week, to be with Carrie and Alex. Simone could not afford to be out of work. And neither could she. In fact, Carrie knew she'd have to go home soon, check on her messages and mail, then visit Matt at the marina, where he was handling their whale-watching cruises alone. But she couldn't leave Alex yet. Not before he spoke.

"Caryn?"

"Oh, I'm sorry, *Maman*. Guess I was daydreaming."

"I asked if you wanted chicken or mahi-mahi."

Carrie shook her head. "I'm really not hungry."

Without another word, Simone put a plate on Carrie's tray and motioned the cook to fill it with mahi-mahi, then continued down the line, pulling both Carrie's tray and her own. Carrie smiled slightly. Why did *Maman* bother to ask? she wondered.

The cafeteria's din seemed almost a comfort to Carrie after the deathly silence of Alex's hospital room. White-jacketed doctors and nurses laughed and talked, seemingly relieving the tensions their stressful jobs caused. She recognized a few of the nurses from the Intensive Care Unit and nodded at them, trying for a smile but failing miserably.

Long nights spent on hard hospital beds, waking every hour or so to listen to Alex breathe, had begun to take their toll. She had noticed just this morning as she was washing her face, that her normally clear eyes were cloudy and that black circles had formed beneath them. She wondered if they'd ever go away.

Only if Alex gets better. Only if he starts acting like my "Water Baby" again.

She settled her tray next to her mother's and sank gratefully into the hard plastic chair, then stared at the unappetizing food on her plate. Out of force of habit, she picked up the fork and started mechanically stabbing a piece of food, putting it into her mouth, chewing and swallowing. Then she did it again. And again. She hadn't realized how famished she'd become.

"Très bien," Simone nodded and smiled, gesturing with her fork that she was pleased to see Carrie eating.

Catching her mother's eye, Carrie felt her throat close up, as it had so many times during the past couple of weeks.

"Maman, how am I going to pay for all of this? How am I going to manage? Take care of Alex?"

"We'll manage." Simone reached across the table and grabbed Carrie's hand. "No matter what happens, we'll manage. And Alex will be fine. You'll see, *chérie.* Everything will be fine."

But Carrie could tell by her mother's eyes that even Simone wasn't sure everything was going to be okay.

"I think you need to go home this afternoon."

"But—"

"No arguments," her mother insisted. "Go home to your apartment, make your phone calls, pick up your mail, take a nice bubble bath, and a long nap. I'll stay with Alex and I'm sure Matt will come by again tonight. You need to keep your strength up, my darling. For Alex, if not for yourself."

Despite the urge to argue, Carrie found herself nodding. Lord, how wonderful a hot, rose-scented bath would feel right now. And to sink into her waterbed, to snuggle with the pillow, which probably still had Alex's fresh scent on it . . .

"Maybe you're right, *Maman*. But I'm not going until after I feed him lunch."

From across the table, Simone gave Carrie what she'd always called her Gallic smile, the satisfied look which said, I'm right and I know it, but now you know it, too.

For the first time in almost two weeks, Carrie laughed out loud.

When Carrie got back to the room, it took her only fifteen minutes to spoon some oatmeal between Alex's trembling lips. Then he fell back to sleep, and she stood, watching him for a moment, torn between the need to stay and the urge to get out of the stuffy hospital room, to breathe the fresh Hawaiian air.

"Go," Simone urged. "Come now, you promised."

The drive to her apartment seemed to take forever, even though it was only a few miles away. Everything seemed different, more intense, the details clearer, sharper. The hibiscus bloomed in several colors, red along the highway, pink next to one house, yellow alongside another. The afternoon sky seemed incredibly blue; the breeze which always bathed the islands washed over her face like a gentle hand, wiping the lines of tension from her brow and easing the tight muscles in her neck and shoulders. The smell of the ocean permeated the car, erasing the antiseptic hospital odor she'd been breathing for far too long.

By the time she reached the apartment, she had turned on the car radio and caught a bit of the news. She felt as if she'd been out of touch for years instead of weeks. She listened to the broadcaster's voice with an intensity she thought necessary for her own survival. She must know what was going on. She should be able to tell Alex what he missed. She needed some connection with something beyond Alex, the accident, her mother, Hawaii. She thought briefly of Texas and of how more attuned to the rest of the United States she felt there, then, just as quickly, turned her thoughts to the here and now.

The pile of mail jamming her mailbox seemed to consist mostly of bills. With a groan, she dumped them on the overstuffed, rose-colored chair in her cramped living room and headed for the answering machine. Its blinking red light signified the tape was full.

The first couple of calls were Alex's friends, obviously messages left before the accident. Ryan wanted to know when they were going diving again; Jimmy Kailua, one of Carrie's least favorite people, left a message about wanting to borrow money from Alex.

"As if we have any to lend," she mused to the machine.

As the messages slowly repeated themselves, the voices became those of bill collectors. Last month had been a slow one for the whale-watching business, and Carrie hadn't been able to make the car payment, the rent, or either of Alex's school loans. Now, they were beginning to threaten repossession.

"Just what I need." In disgust, she rewound the tape and turned the machine back on answer. For a moment, she considered shutting it off completely, then reconsidered since the hospital might need to get through.

"Let those damn bill collectors find me," she muttered as she swiped at the dust on her kitchen counter. "I have more important things to worry about."

For a moment, she stood in the kitchen, bone-tired and confused, unsure of what she wanted to do next. She poured herself a glass of wine. The house seemed unusually quiet, stuffy, and empty without Alex's voice. The living room's pinkish gray walls and matching overstuffed furniture seemed muted without Alex's constantly moving body going from one project to the next, denting each of the chairs with his almost frenetic energy. If he were here, she thought, the stereo would be on full blast and he'd be singing off-key to "Stairway to Heaven" or some new rap song. If he were here, he'd be bumping into the furniture, making a mess in the kitchen, tackling her on the floor for an "afternoon delight." The dust motes wouldn't get a chance to float lazily down to the dark koa wood coffee table as they did now. The books now resting on their shelves would be scattered helter-skelter while he tried to find some obscure information he was sure he had seen someplace. The phone would be ringing with invitations to go surfing ("Waimea Bay is up, Golden Mermaid; we gotta go!"), and Alex would spend his evenings planning their future, reading his books on marine biology while she rested, head on his stomach, staring at his serious face.

She felt her throat close up again and shook her head violently.

"No more," she whispered. "It's time to stop crying and to start accepting." Balling her hands into fists, she took a deep breath and cleared her eyes. "No more crying. No more crying."

Alex was alive. Hurt, but alive. That was the most important thing. And she needed to be whole and strong to help him. He would've done it for her. That's what it's all about. Love doesn't mean a damn if the marriage commitment isn't there. Like Grandpa De-Bary used to say, "If you can't handle the mare, stay off her back."

"Well, I can handle this." Carrie's words fell into the silence of the kitchen, unanswered. She loosened her fists, then flew around the small apartment, opening windows to let in the afternoon breeze, wiping the dust off of counters and tables in mad, flying swoops. When done with the cursory cleaning, she whipped off her Smithsonian Institute T-shirt and khaki shorts, dropped them on the kitchen floor, and headed for the bathroom. Within moments, she sank into a bathtub full of soapy water scented with a full bottle of wild ginger cologne.

Her eyes had just closed and her muscles had loosened when the phone broke the silence. Her instant reaction was to get out of the tub, but the answering machine picked up the call before she had one foot over the side. She paused, mid-air, and cocked her head to listen to the message before going any further.

"Darling, Alex has woken up," Simone's French accent piped through the machine. "Call me immediately."

Four

Carrie didn't hesitate long enough to wash the soap-suds out of her hair before jumping into the truck and gunning it down the highway. With the worst of scenarios ripping through her mind, she sped down Hualalai Road, took the right on Kuakini Highway, then gritted her teeth as she passed the curve where the state troopers' unmarked cars usually waited for speeders like her. When she took the right into the hospital's parking lot on two wheels, she prayed her mother's urgent phone call did not mean Alex had taken a turn for the worse.

As she sprinted through the lobby, she ignored the startled looks she got from tightly grouped families, then impatiently waited for the elevator, tapping her sandalled foot against the tile floor.

The elevator finally opened to reveal a group of doctors surrounding a frail old woman on a gurney. Carrie skirted the frustration she felt and ran down the hall.

"Where're the stairs?" she yelled to an attendant. He pointed to her left, and she didn't even stop to thank him before skimming the three flights to Alex's room.

By the time she threw open the door, she was out

of breath, her sleeveless jersey dress was soaked with sweat, and her normally silky hair matted and tangled against her head.

Simone sat beside Alex, her hand on his arm, a warm smile lighting her delicate features, looking as serene as a Christmas card portrait of the Virgin Mary, Carrie thought.

"Chérie, I didn't expect you here so quickly," Simone began, but Carrie paid no attention. Her eyes were on Alex's pale but smiling face. He had been awake before, but never in tune with what was going on around him. For the past two weeks, Carrie had had the distinct impression that Alex spent most of his days drifting in and out of a fog, some of which was induced by the medication, she was sure. But she'd found herself wondering whether his dazed expressions were going to be permanently fixed upon his features. To lose Alex's brightness, his quick wit, and zealous curiosity for life hurt her more than the thought that he'd never walk again.

Now, it looked like the old Alex was back. He was definitely awake, fully aware of what was going on around him. Her lips stretched into a smile.

Ignoring her mother and Matt, who stood in the corner like a dark Buddha, she slid onto the bed and touched Alex's face gently with her hand.

"What took you so long?" he asked. "Did you bring my pizza?"

For a moment, Carrie couldn't speak. She stared at Alex, unable to believe it was his voice she was hearing. What if this really wasn't happening? What if she'd really fallen asleep at home? What if this scene was merely the result of slipping into a warm bathtub after the wine she had been drinking?

She swallowed and blinked. Yes, she had to admit, Alex's crooked smile was the same, the intelligent light in his eyes still focused exclusively on her, and the gravelly, little-boy voice still did excruciating things to the cartwheels sleeping in her stomach.

"Alex? You can talk!"

Although his chuckle was a feeble one, it was undeniably his. He nodded, telling her more with his eyes than he'd been able to reveal since the accident. His eyes, those wonderful ocean-blue eyes, said he loved her, he trusted her, he wanted no one but her beside him. Finally convinced, Carrie took him into her arms, laughing and crying and talking all at once.

"I can't believe it," she said, when she could pull herself far enough away to look into his face once again. "I kept hoping and hoping that you'd talk, but I guess. . . . I guess I was just kind of . . ."

"You better not even think of giving up on me," Alex said. "What'd you think I was going to do, just let you keep on doing all the talking? You know I can't stand listening to you ramble on about nothing and nobody like you've been doing for. . . . How long has it been? How long have I been here now? And, by the way, when am I going to get out?"

Carrie exchanged a glance with her mother, sitting slightly behind Alex's right shoulder. Simone shook her head warningly. Carrie lowered her eyes.

"Well, do you really want a pizza? Are you sick of this hospital food?" she asked brightly, straightening the sheets on Alex's bed.

Oh, God, she thought, as everyone started talking, how in the hell am I going to tell him?

Questions flew back and forth among the little group. Simone wanted to make sure Alex was comfortable, warning him not to tax himself and urging him to eat a full, healthy meal.

"I never believed in intravenous," she said. "Who knows what kind of chemicals they've been feeding into you."

Matt, usually quiet, seemed nervous and uncomfortable. Although he usually contributed little to the conversation, answering questions with nods and eyebrow raises, now he chattered about the weather, the ride to the hospital, anything, it seemed, as long as Alex would talk back.

Alex acted like an uncorked champagne bottle. Questions bubbled forth and escaped into the air unanswered because everyone was talking at once. He didn't seem to care, just continued to ask questions, not pausing to take a breath.

Only Carrie remained quiet, though she couldn't help laughing when Matt began imitating a tourist from the mainland seeing her first whale.

"Aw, man, I wish you'd been there," he said. "Here she stands, this ancient *wahini* bogged down with ten *leis* and a straw hat the size of Mexico. She had these fancy white opera glasses she had brought along to spot the whales, and she thought she was all set. Every time she'd spot one, the glasses and hat would go flyin' and she'd go, 'Oo, oo, oo.' " He flapped his arms and screwed up his face. "I tell you, I thought we were going to have our first tourist overboard. I had to personally usher her off the boat when we came into the harbor. I bet she *still* hasn't recovered from when the big humpback breached alongside the boat."

"Navajo?" Alex asked.

During the past five years, he and Matt had photographed the returning humpbacks, learning to distinguish them by the unique markings on their flukes, then giving each a name. Alex had told Carrie when they first met that a whale's flukes were as identifiable as a human's fingerprint. She remembered the long-ago conversation in detail as she sat on the bed watching Alex's animated expressions as he talked with Matt.

When he'd met Matt, Alex was doing his senior thesis on Hawaii's whale population. He needed a local to show him around the islands, and Matt was the perfect choice, an unemployed Hawaiian-born surfer with a Bachelor's degree in Asian philosophy and an incredible respect for the marine life that filled the oceans surrounding his home. The two had hit it off immediately, and Alex soon took up residence in the Kamehea household. Since Simone and Carrie lived only two houses away, it was inevitable that Matt would introduce Carrie to Alex.

To this day, she would deny believing in love at first sight, but it had been that way for both of them. Carrie had thought Alex one of the most beautiful men she had ever seen.

She watched the two friends now, teasing and sharing quips. Impulsively, she leaned over to kiss Alex on the mouth, catching him unawares. He smiled up at her, his eyes twinkling. How could she have spent the rest of her life without hearing his voice? It would have been literally impossible. When she pulled away, he pulled her back and held her tight.

"Pizza's here!" Matt announced. "Sorry guys, but the wedded bliss is going to have to wait. It's chow time."

Reluctantly, she broke away, avoiding her mother's eyes. I know, *Maman,* she thought, but I don't want to tell him right now. Let me enjoy a few moments with him first.

As she watched Alex devour the pizza, Carrie vacillated between elation and despair. Although Alex had full use of his arms and hands, he was still too weak and full of medication to notice he couldn't move anything below the waist. Sooner or later, he would realize it, she knew. But when? And how upset would he be to discover his chances of walking again were practically nil? More importantly, how angry would he be with her for not telling him right away?

It didn't matter. She'd endure his anger just to have a few more moments with him like this, watching him enjoying his pizza, exchanging quips with Matt, looking at her the way he had before the accident—full of life and love. There would be plenty of time for the pain. Too much time.

"Now I can't call you Sir Sleeping Beauty anymore," Matt was complaining. "I'll have to think of a new name for you, like, let's see . . ."

"Don't get any ideas, *Br'a,*" Alex countered. "I'll be out of here in no time, then you'll have to pay for all your wisecracks." Alex took another bite of his pizza, unaware of how quiet the room had become.

Simone reached over and grabbed Carrie's hand, giving it a quick warning squeeze, before turning to Alex. She pecked him affectionately on the cheek and wiped a strand of hair away from his eyes.

"I must go, darlings," she said, motioning to Matt that he should come with her. "Visiting hours were over long ago. I'll see you again tomorrow." Pulling Carrie to the door, she whispered, "If you need me, I'll be only a phone call away. Please, *chérie,* take care . . ."

Carrie fought a lump in her throat and leaned into her mother's embrace. "How am I going to tell him?" she said. "Oh, *Maman,* I can't do this."

"You must," Simone said as she pushed Carrie away. "You must." She held Carrie by the shoulders and looked deeply into her eyes as if trying to impart some of her wisdom, some of her age, into Carrie's younger body. "No one but you can do this. Be strong, *chérie,* for Alex."

Behind them, Matt's guffaw filled the room, then he, too, began moving toward the door. "Long day tomorrow, *Bruddah.* Got to go swab the decks and all that sailor stuff. No one else to help me now. And the boat's got to sail or none of us will make any dough. Those whales are doing great tricks for the *haoles* these days. Gotta make hay, y'know." He winked at Carrie as he passed her and squeezed her arm. "Call me later," he murmured. "Let me know what happens."

Carrie nodded and watched Matt and her mother walk down the hall, their heads cocked toward each other, talking seriously. Anyone who saw them would realize that, despite their ages, they were lifelong friends. Matt towered over tiny Simone, but somehow Simone seemed the stronger of the two, the leader.

Carrie turned and smiled at Alex, who lay in the bed, looking at her expectantly. As she walked the few steps which separated them, she thought about what she should say and fought the urge to follow her mother and Matt down the hall, to pull them back into the room and force them to be part of this, the hardest moment of her life.

"C'mere," Alex said, reaching out his hand to her. He wore a half smile, the kind he gave her right before they were about to make love. She took his hand and sat on the edge of the bed, then buried her head in his shoulder, letting him kiss her neck and nibble the most tender part of her ear. She could have sat like that for hours, ignoring what she must do, but in between nibbles, Alex talked about what he was going to do to her when they let him go home.

Home. She had to tell him he wouldn't be seeing home for quite a while. And that what he was threatening to do to her might not be possible. Ever.

"You never did answer me," he said. "How long have I been here and when are they going to let me leave? What happened anyway? The last thing I remember is trying to get the genoa down."

Carrie took a deep breath and sat up. "You can ask Dr. Karachi that question when he gets here, which should be anytime, *Maman* said."

Alex nodded, the distinct and urgent question still hovering in his blue eyes. "But you're going to tell me what happened before he gets here, aren't you?"

"Well, I really think we ought to wait for him . . ."

Alex seized her by the forearms and drew her to him, his eyes growing dark, almost black. She had only seen him this angry once, when they'd seen a school of dolphins caught in seine nets off the north coast of Oahu. Alex had immediately dived into the ocean, trying again and again to free the squealing mammals, and when the fishing trawler responsible for the net arrived, Alex climbed aboard, furiously demanding to see their fishing license. The captain refused to turn it over, and Alex, after more than an hour of trying to talk to the man reasonably, then unreasonably, finally lost control and hit him, knocking him off the boat and into the water. Once back on _The Winsome Blonde_, Alex refused to deal with Carrie's fear when the fishing boat's crew began to threaten him. He simply raised sail and calmly headed past the boat ignoring the men screaming obscenities after them.

She couldn't really blame Alex for being angry then, and she couldn't blame him for being angry now, either. She had to be honest with him. He expected the truth. And he had a right to it.

"How much do you remember?" she asked tentatively.

"I know I went up for the genoa, after I realized a storm had come up. I remember fighting with the lines, but that's all." He pushed his hand through his hair, then blinked and stared straight at her. "What happened then?"

Carrie ran her tongue over her teeth and squared her shoulders. Okay, she thought, if I have to do this, I might as well get it over with.

"The genoa whipped up," she began, "then the boom came loose and swept the deck. I dove in after you were knocked overboard, then the dolphins were there . . ."

* * *

Simone stumbled slightly getting out of the deep seat of Matt's Camaro, then stood outside and waved to him, a bright, cheery flick of her fingers, before heading up the volcanic rock path which led to her little white house. The closer she got to the house, the stronger came the gardenia smell wafting through the air. Her roses, also in full bloom, were a pleasant sight, she thought, especially since she'd been away from the house for a while. She took a deep breath, inhaling the headiness of their mixed scents. In the deepening twilight, the house's white exterior softened, taking on the darkening colors quietly, subtly. Her front yard, edged with a lava rock driveway, had been a disaster when she had first moved in, but through years of loving care and cultivation, she had coaxed hibiscus shoots into full-blown bushes, had trained several types of roses to frame the small house like an English cottage, and had made a point of adding a new plant every year on the anniversary of her arrival in Kona. She never would have believed seven years ago that the house was salvageable; in fact, she had spent many of those first days wondering why she had ever thought she could do anything with the cottage short of burning it down. Now, she wouldn't dream of living anywhere else in the world. Even back in France.

She meandered up the curved path leading to her front door, thinking of the day's events, picking a dead leaf off here, plucking a shoot there. All the way home, she had imagined the words which must now be passing between Caryn and Alex, and she longed to be with her daughter, though she knew it was not her place. Caryn was an adult now, with adult problems, married problems, problems most families never should have to face.

Certainement.

It was hard not to blame herself, and Philip, for all that had happened to Caryn. There had been a time, long ago, when it seemed nothing could go wrong, that she, Simone Mitterand DeBary, was leading a charmed life.

But those days were over.

Since leaving Texas, life had been a constant struggle—no money, no family except for each other, no job. She struggled to keep them together, struggled to explain to Caryn why her father's actions had destroyed their family, struggled to help Caryn make it through her teenage years in a new home, one so unlike the one in which she'd grown up there was simply no comparison, struggled to make ends meet when the little money she had brought with her ran out. Her pride had kept her from asking Philip for help, so she had tried to find a job, only to discover that the arts background she'd been so proud of was a deterrent rather than an asset. When she had finally convinced Mr. Rossner at the Waimea Bay Art Gallery to let her come in a couple of days a week, she went home that night and cried from sheer relief.

Perhaps, she thought, struggle is good. Maybe it will make Caryn strong. Perhaps it'll bring her and Alex closer. Certainly, their relationship has been strengthened by the tests they've already undergone. Yet, I thought Philip and I had a strong relationship, and we would never have been able to endure a tragedy like this.

Simone opened her front door, anxious now to get

into the house. She wanted to open the windows and let in the ocean breeze, which would bring her garden's smells into the cottage's compact rooms. She'd been home so seldom lately that the house had begun to get that faintly moldy odor Hawaiian houses got when they were closed up during long periods of rain.

Even though the cottage was designed with no interior doors for better ventilation, Simone still insisted on having exterior windows and doors open. If she could have lived outside, she would, but if she had, she would not have wall space, and that would mean she wouldn't be able to hang the vibrant Hawaiian paintings which had become part of her life.

Who would have believed, she mused as she opened one wide window after another, that she, a true *Française,* would appreciate the childish impetuosity of a Hawaiian watercolor of a hula lesson or one of marine painter Wyland's dynamic oils of underwater life? She couldn't imagine Wyland's specially created portrait of a humpback whale and her calf hanging on someone else's wall. It was hers. The artist had consulted her every step of the way. And she, in turn, had consulted with Alex, making certain every detail was anatomically correct.

She reached up, touched the painting's frame, and straightened it. Through the window to the painting's right, she could hear the ocean slapping against the black volcanic cliff at the end of her road. Her view of the ocean was not the best on the island, but she didn't care. All that mattered was that she was near it, could smell its spicy tang when she opened her window and hear its rhythmic waves before going to sleep. How could she have ever lived in such a vast, ocean-poor state as Texas? She straightened the painting again, knowing the answer to her question—escaping to the Gulf Coast to sail on *The Blonde* was the only way she'd survived Houston. But that was the past, she reminded herself, and this is now. This is Hawaii.

Although the Kona Coast was traditionally drier than the southern coast of the Big Island, for the past month they had endured more than their share of precipitation. The rain had helped her plants, as well as the weeds, and normally she would have welcomed it. But for the past month she had been either at the gallery or at the hospital. She hadn't had time to keep up with the garden. She hadn't even had a chance to finish the latest Sue Grafton mystery. But now was the perfect time to read the ending she'd already imagined. After supper, she promised herself.

A breeze was wafting through the house, a soft Hawaiian melody floating on the air, and Simone's knife cutting easily into a fresh papaya when she heard a soft *rat-tat-tat-tat* at the door. She knew immediately who it was.

"I almost forgot," she said, opening the back door to Jerry Kahala, who stood patiently outside, a spray of white gardenias in his hand. "You must forgive me."

Jerry's compact, wiry body slipped easily through the door, and he gave Simone a curt bow before handing her the flowers. His formal manners endeared him to her. They were a Japanese habit he maintained, even after almost thirty years on the island.

Jerry, one of the best engineers in Japan, had given up his life there to settle in Hawaii after his wife had died. He'd told Simone that he had believed his career the most important thing in his life until Tashimu passed away, leaving him totally alone. Then he realized he hadn't been taking a long, hard look at what really made life matter. His position as head engineer for one of Japan's major electronics firms was a prestigious one, and the company fought long and hard to keep Jerry on the payroll, offering him a raise, a promotion, even vice-presidency of the company. But he'd turned it all down, knowing that his life there was empty without his wife. They'd never had children and his sisters and brothers were now scattered throughout the country with families of their own. He had no ties, nothing to keep him there, so he started looking at other options. During a trip to Hawaii, he fell in love with the peacefulness of the state. He moved there three months later, leaving the past behind.

For the first ten years, Jerry had toyed with different approaches to life. For a while, he taught karate, but he soon grew tired of giving the neighborhood children the means with which to fight each other. Then he opened a small restaurant, but it failed because he didn't have the culinary talents necessary to sustain it. Finally, he retired to his cottage, just a few houses down from Simone's. He was one of the first people she'd met on the island.

Although most of the people on the Kailua-Kona Coast knew Jerry as an expert gardener, few realized Simone had taught him all he knew. At first, he hadn't even known which plants were perennials and which were weeds, but through Simone's patient tutelage he had learned quickly and soon shared his newfound knowledge with everyone in the neighborhood. They all agreed Jerry was the best of neighbors, the kind of person you wanted around for advice or to offer help during a crisis. He was the antithesis of Philip DeBary, Simone had thought when she'd first met him, and she thought it still.

Where Philip had been thoughtless, Jerry was considerate. Where Philip had misunderstood, Jerry was wise. Philip had money; Jerry had faith. Some women would have opted for Philip's wealth and worldliness. Simone treasured Jerry's sincerity.

"How is your daughter? And her husband?" Jerry asked quietly, his voice as hushed and reverent as the breezes which drifted through Simone's open windows.

Simone returned to the kitchen counter and took up where she had left off. Jerry, with the easy habits of an old friend, settled into a chair at the lace-covered kitchen table and patiently awaited her answer.

After a moment, Simone considered the sliced papaya, then turned to face Jerry. "I do not really know," she said. "When I left the hospital, Alex had just begun to speak—"

"Oh, that's wonderful—"

"But he doesn't know what's wrong yet."

"Not so wonderful." Jerry shook his head and adjusted his square, wire-rimmed glasses, which always seemed ready to slide off his tiny nose. "What is Caryn going to do?"

"Ah, *mon Dieu,* I do not know. It will take a formidable strength to come through this ordeal, a formidable love to keep them together. I wish I could do more. I wish I could help her."

With as much vehemence as Simone ever mustered,

she slapped the knife down on her cutting board and swiftly crossed the kitchen searching for a wooden salad bowl. She fussed with the plates and bowls in her closet, clattering them, stalling for time. Behind her, she heard Jerry running water into a vase and knew that he was doing his usual magic with the flowers she had yet to thank him for. She closed her eyes and leaned against the door for a second.

"Matt thinks I should call Caryn's father," she said. "He said that since I called Alex's family, I should call Philip, too." She looked up, expecting her answer in Jerry's eyes, but he stood in front of the door, looking out into the night, his back to her.

"When I called the Madisons, right after the accident," she continued, "they said they could do nothing except wait for additional information. Mr. Madison is too old to travel and his wife. . . . Well, they are simply too poor to take the trip down here. And I am sure Alex will understand. On the other hand, Philip has the means . . ."

Simone brought the bowl back to the counter and absentmindedly tossed the salad, remembering Caryn's face in the hospital, the wonderful lightness that had spread over it when she had realized Alex had finally spoken. Despite the happiness of the moment, there had been an undercurrent of barely contained hysteria. The room pulsated with it. Simone had watched Matthew's eyes flicker from Caryn to Alex and back again. At the same time, Simone sensed Alex's mind traveling at light speed, unable to keep up with the questions. His speech had been broken, as crippled as his body, Simone thought, until Caryn had walked into the room.

Caryn. Her wet hair had clung closely to her forehead, framing the pale violet circles under her eyes;
stress was beginning to take its toll on her. No matter
how happy the news that Alex had begun to speak
again, the tragedy was far from over. Carrie's pain
might last for months. Years.

Simone didn't know what else to do.

Jerry sauntered away from the door and into her
line of sight, startling her back to the present.

"Maybe you should," he said.

"Should what?"

"Maybe you should call her father."

Simone hesitated for a moment before allowing herself to walk into Jerry's arms. It was the first time in
weeks. She burrowed her head into his clean-smelling
shirt and held tightly to his sinewy back, treasuring his
warmth and his hug, stealing some of his practiced se-
renity, before releasing him.

"Not yet," she said with a determined shake of her
head. "Not yet."

"Matthew! You need to talk to your brother. Hurry!
There's not much time. You must come now!"

"Slow down, Mama. What you so upset about?
Chill out!" Matt stood with one foot still in the
Camaro and one out. His mother, panting and obviously worried, stood in front of him, her *mu'umu'u*
clinging to her like a soaked tissue.

"Isaac," she wheezed. "Isaac!"

Matt felt his chest fill with anger. Goddamn little
brat, he thought. Why does he have to go and get

himself mixed up with that friggin' bunch of trouble-makers? Especially now.

"I got better things to do than chase that little—"

Matt's mother had caught her breath; now she caught his arm and held it in a viselike grip. Years of working with her hands had made her fingers the strongest he'd ever known. When they were kids, she'd had a habit of poking them in the chest when she wanted to make a point. Many times Matt or his brothers and sisters would go to school the next day with a round black and blue bruise from where Mama had poked. She poked his chest now, and he had to steel himself to keep from wincing.

"He's your brother," she warned, her eyes dark and squinted, her voice deep and hoarse. Family was important to her. Very important. All of her kids had been raised with a loving patience and skill few parents could boast, and she had been like a single mother for so long that Matt and the rest of her family didn't know what it was like to be disciplined by their father, a fisherman who never stayed around long enough to leave his imprint on one of the parlor chairs. If just one of her children fell short of the mark she expected them to reach, she fought like a threatened mother blackbird to get them back into line.

Though most people knew Mama Kamehea for her almost uncanny calm, now her voice grumbled like an active volcano. "You go find him. You find my son and bring him home. Get him away from those bad boys."

Matthew stood with his eyes downcast. This was the sixth time in a month that he'd been sent out to look for Isaac. And he was tired. Tired of babysitting for a full-grown boy and tired of working sixteen-hour days, running the whale watches by himself, taking the calls and reservations, tired of dealing with tourists who expected wild mammals to perform like trained sea lions, tired of swabbing down the decks and the boat's hull after dark. When all of his chores were done, Matt ran to the hospital and spent a half hour or so with Alex and Carrie. He didn't remember the last time he'd slept past sunrise or gone to bed before midnight or eaten at the kitchen table with the rest of his family.

He felt his shoulders droop and didn't have the energy to push them back. Sagging against the car, he regarded his mother almost sullenly and heard himself whine, "Ma, I really don't want to. The kid's old enough to take care of himself. Why do you keep wanting me to chase after him? If he gets into trouble, we'll find out soon enough."

"Matthew!"

With a huff, Matt got back into the Camaro and gunned it loudly before pulling out onto Kaiwi Street. The first place he'd head was the shopping mall at the Hotel King Kamehameha. That's where he'd last seen Isaac on Tuesday, selling dope to the *haoles*.

"No way! You're wrong! You're absolutely, positively out of your mind!" Alex's face turned scarlet and his fists pounded up and down on the bed. The monitors hooked up to his chest and arms beeped and sputtered like a crazed computer game.

Dr. Karachi glanced at Carrie in dismay and motioned her out of the room. "Mr. Madison, please calm down," he warned. "Getting upset will only make matters worse."

Carrie stood at the door, watching the nurses hold Alex's arms down and administer a tranquilizer. Hot tears burned her eyes. She crossed her arms over her chest, trying to hold back her emotions for Alex's sake.

Alex had been all right when it was just the two of them in the room, and Carrie had been proud of herself for remaining calm throughout the retelling of the accident. She had even managed to smile a few times, to chide Alex for making her work so hard, for scaring her. And he'd promised, with his crooked grin, that he'd never do it again. He'd never forget to take the genoa down again.

It had been hard for her not to fall apart when he'd said that, not to burst right out and tell him he'd probably never get the chance to sail again. He wouldn't have to worry about the genoa. But she'd kept herself in check, had maintained some semblance of control. And she probably would have been able to explain everything, if the doctor hadn't come into the room immediately and begun telling Alex about his injury and the paralysis he'd have to get used to.

For the first few seconds, Alex had been quiet. All color had drained from his already pale face. His lips had turned a sickening light purple, then gray, until they had matched the rest of his skin. Carrie had reached for him then, whispering, "I love you, Alex, we'll make everything all right. Don't worry, sweetheart, I'll be here for you . . ."

Then he'd screamed, a loud, long, wail—

"Noooooooo!"—and half the nurses on the floor had come running into the room to see what was going on.

The doctor had tried to talk, to tell Alex how lucky he was to have his speech and control of his arms, how many people with this type of injury didn't have even that, but Alex had flailed at him with all the strength in his beaten body, trying to hit him or reach him. Surprised by his patient's reaction, Dr. Karachi had taken a step back, then had barked a few short commands at the nurses. Carrie had heard valium ordered and only seconds later the nurse had jabbed Alex in the arm.

Now the tranquilizer started to take effect. Alex's screams turned to moans, his face screwed up into pitiful mews, and his cheeks were covered with tears. Carrie pushed past the doctor and nurses to sit on the bed, taking Alex's clenched fist in hers.

"I didn't want it to happen like this," she whispered, as she stroked his damp head. "I wanted to tell you myself, but I just couldn't . . ."

"Why?" Alex asked, looking at her with vacant eyes. "Why me? Why?"

Five

Carrie reached the phone on the third ring, the mail still in her hands and a small bag of groceries on her hip. It was another bill collector. Her shoulder muscles stiffened.

"My husband's in the hospital, and I've been out of work for over a month," she said. She threw the bills on the coffee table and paced with the phone, trying not to pull the cord out of the wall but not caring if she did. At least it would stop the man's contemptuous voice.

"Well, when are you going to send us a payment? You haven't sent a penny for the past three months. Didn't you say your husband has just been in the hospital a month?"

"We'd been having some money problems . . ."

"How are you paying for the hospital?"

"I'm not." She coughed, then tried to ignore the nagging tickle in her throat.

"Don't you have someone you can borrow the money from?"

"My mother's just as broke as I am."

"How about a friend?"

Carrie was silent for a moment, then she replied

evenly, "Can't you understand that I'm having a hard time right now?"

"We're talking about a big loan here, Mrs. Madison. An auto loan. Do you need the vehicle?"

"Yes, of course I need the truck."

"Well, then, you'll have to make payment arrangements or we're going to have to repossess it."

Carrie's face prickled as the blood left her cheeks. "Repossess it?"

"We can't carry you any longer, Mrs. Madison. Either send a payment or we'll take the truck back." The man's voice cut through the telephone wire like a razor.

Frantically, Carrie tried to think of something saleable, something she could pawn which would give her enough money to pay for the truck. Her simple silver wedding band wasn't even worth $10, and even if it was, she'd lose the truck before she'd sacrifice the only piece of jewelry Alex had been able to afford to give her. She looked around the living room. The stereo system was one Alex had brought with him from the mainland, and it had been old then. Even at a yard sale, she'd be lucky to get more than $15 for it. Their travel posters were tattered and inexpensive, their collection of paperbacks took up less than half a shelf on the wall which held the television and stereo, and Alex's college books were invaluable to him, he'd never give them up. Their furniture cried of loving wear and tear, nothing anyone would want.

She felt a fist of panic grip her chest.

"Hello, Mrs. Madison? Are you there?"

"I'm here." Her voice became small and doubtful. "I just don't know what I'm going to do. I don't have any money. I don't even have anything to sell to get money."

"What about your business? My records here say you own a whale-watching cruise ship business. If you're out of work, what's happening with that?"

"Our first mate is taking care of things while my husband is in the hospital."

"Oh, and are you paying him?"

Her fear turned to anger. How dare this man ask such personal questions, then make her feel like a criminal? "No, as a matter of fact, I'm not. The business is in a down season right now. It's not even making enough to pay my overhead."

The bill collector's sarcastic laugh made the hairs on the back of Carrie's neck stand straight up. "Right. Well, Mrs. Madison, if you want to keep your head above water," he laughed again, as if pleased with his pointed pun, "then you'd better think about how your business can help you. Maybe you can sell your boat?"

Carrie hung up and sank into the closest chair. The boat. Sell the boat. But it wasn't the whale-watching catamaran she was thinking of. It was *The Winsome Blonde*.

And that thought made her double over in pain.

Before the phone could ring again, Carrie put the bottle of Coke she had bought into the refrigerator and ripped open the bag of chips, her supper. In less than half an hour, she showered, scanned the rest of the mail, drank a full glass of Coke, ate half the bag of chips, and threw some fresh clothes into an overnight bag, then she scooted out the door and drove back to the hospital.

It had been over a month since the accident, but Carrie figured she still needed to be with Alex every day, especially since he had sunk into a deep depression. She fought to bring him around, telling him news from the harbor, gossip of any kind, anything to get his interest, but she never told him about the pile of bills she found in her mailbox every time she went home or about the threatening bill collectors. It had gotten to the point where she knew that the "hang ups" on her answering machine were her creditors, and she had even become devious enough not to answer the phone until after the machine did. That way she knew who was on the other end.

None of the collectors seemed to sympathize with her plight, perhaps because Alex and she had been having financial problems even before the accident. Now they were downright rude. And soon they'd be repossessing the truck.

She wouldn't tell Alex about that, either.

Matt reported on a regular basis that business was slow, as she had told the auto finance man; the whales were heading back up north, as were the tourists. Still, she needed to make sure she kept up the payments on the whale-watching boat, as well as their small office space in the harbor. *The Winsome Blonde* was the only thing she owned free and clear.

She thought about her childhood and her lack of concern with money or the things it bought. Not once had she ever asked for anything, yet there were always gifts when her father came home from one of his trips: a new pony when she was five, a motorized, mini-Corvette when she was seven—and how that thing moved when she pressed the pedal! Her mother still said the reason why Carrie drove so fast was because of that introduction to the world of speed. Carrie knew she had been pampered. She had never known the word "budget," had never seen her parents struggle to stretch a meal, had never seen her mother even pick up a dustmop to clean the floor. When she grew older, she knew the bills had been paid by accountants and that her mother had an allowance which was so large she never spent it all before the next month's allotment. That leftover allowance had paid their way to Hawaii and bought her mother's little white house.

It had taken some time for Carrie to get used to not having everything she needed, but the hardest part had been learning how to balance the meager budget she and Alex created when they married. Their different backgrounds had prepared them for totally opposite life-styles, but that was all right, Carrie thought. To her surprise, she never missed the expensive clothes and cars, the winter vacation in Switzerland, the summers in St. John. It was enough that she and Alex had each other.

Except I could really use some of that money now, she thought.

That afternoon, as she straightened the sheets on Alex's bed, she chattered aimlessly about Mrs. Whitman in room 221, the old lady in the wheelchair who never failed to visit Alex on her forays down the hall. Despite her illness, she always had a smile and an optimistic outlook. Alex, on the other hand, showed no interest in the progress he was making or the therapy program the doctors were now planning. His face seemed chiseled into an uncharacteristic frown. Carrie peeked at him now, hardly recognizing him.

"Don't do that," he said.

"Don't do what?" Carrie straightened, wiping a sheen of sweat from her brow and wishing she didn't feel so woozy. Stifling a cough, she came around to the other side of the bed.

"Don't tighten the sheets so much. I can't move my hands."

"Oh, sorry." She ducked her head and coughed strongly into her fist, then turned away, wincing as yet another spasm gripped her chest. I'll have to borrow more money from Matt to get another bottle of cough syrup, she thought. That last one just wasn't strong enough.

" 'Star Trek' is on," she said when she could finally speak again. She reached for the remote next to Alex's hand, but before she could put her fingers on it, he grabbed it and flicked the "on" switch.

"I can do it," he growled. "I'm not completely incapacitated."

She shrugged and let him flip through the stations. The only time she got any pleasure these days was when she could rest her head against Alex's knee and immerse herself in the voyages of the Starship Enterprise. It had been one of Alex's favorite pastimes before his accident, and they had always made it a point to be home the evening when the program was on.

One of her fondest memories was of the night they had gone to see *Star Trek: The Voyage Home*. The movie, one of her all-time favorites, had been spell-binding, but the best part of the evening was when Alex had surprised her by taking her to Giuseppe's Italian Café for a bottle of chianti and a pizza afterward.

Carrie nestled against Alex's knee now, a smile on her face as she remembered the long conversation they had had that night about their future together, about the family they would raise, the places they would go, the things they would do.

After they had left the restaurant, they'd walked down to the Kailua Pier. It had been quiet, the only sound the water slapping against the boats in their slips. Above them, the sky was full of shooting stars and the moon hung, clear and yellow, a slice of lemon against the deep purple sky.

"I never want to stop feeling like this," Alex had said. "I never want to stop loving you and feeling like the world is a gorgeous place to live in. I want to always believe that there are new adventures to have and new discoveries to make. You know, when I was a kid, I thought the world revolved around the farm. Everything in my life was determined by what happened to the land and the animals. If a cow gave birth, it was a celebration. If the hay came in nice and dry, we had a special dinner. If the corn grew higher than my head, I knew I'd be able to get a new pair of school shoes. *Everything* depended on the land. I never even knew what an ocean looked like until we went to California during my senior year. But once I saw it I was hooked. I finally realized there was more to the world than what I knew in

Wisconsin. And I was right, wasn't I, my Golden Mermaid?"

He had dipped his head to hers, capturing her mouth with his, kissing her deeply and completely, until she'd thought nothing could ever make her happier, that she had just experienced the most perfect moment of her life.

Yes, it had been special, she admitted. But there had been other nights, and days, and they would have more. At least she hoped so.

The familiar theme song came on, and she glanced sideways at Alex. He leaned back against the pillows, a different man from the one she had just been daydreaming about. His cheeks were sunken, pale caverns against his once tanned skin. His eyes, lifeless and dull, focused on the television affixed high against the wall. Even "Star Trek" couldn't bring back the spark she used to see in him. She sighed and started to watch Captain Jean-Luc Picard and the crew of the Enterprise, but a cough caught in the base of her chest and worked its way upward. By the time she got it under control, the show was almost over and she was drenched in sweat.

On the way out of the hospital that night, Liliani McSweeney, who worked in the business office, caught up with Carrie and walked with her to the parking lot.

"I hear Alex isn't taking it too well," she offered, flipping back her thick black hair and adjusting the pocketbook she had slung over her shoulder. Carrie knew Liliani through Matt, who dated her occasionally. The two women had become friends, though they weren't as close as Liliani seemed to want. Liliani, who was a bit of a gossip, seemed to sense Carrie's first loyalty was to Matt.

"No, he's not really taking it well at all," Carrie said politely, her eyes straight ahead. "Alex isn't used to sitting in bed all day long. He'd really like to be up and around."

Liliani lit a cigarette and blew its smoke into the sky. "Can't say I blame him. Poor guy'll probably have to be wheeled around the rest of his life. Got to make you think how lucky you are, y'know? You got out of the storm okay."

The smoke drifted Carrie's way and tickled her throat. She fought the urge to cough but wasn't strong enough. When the spasm stopped, she stood, still clutching her chest, waiting for the pain to subside before turning back to Liliani.

"I know how lucky I am," Carrie wheezed. "I'm lucky to have him around. I'm lucky he's alive."

"Yeah, but *you* don't sound so good!"

Carrie shook her head, stifling another bout of coughs. "Don't feel so good either—" The ripping spasm took over, and she doubled, leaning against a car until it stopped.

Liliani stood back as if afraid to catch whatever Carrie had. She puffed on her cigarette, then pointed the lit end at Carrie. "Y'know, I've been wondering whether I should tell you something or not."

"What?"

"Well, you know I send out the bills and every-thing."

Carrie nodded, afraid to speak for fear it would send her into another coughing fit.

"I know you guys are having money problems, but maybe you should know the office is thinking of asking you for something on Alex's bill."

"Before he even gets out of the hospital?" Carrie sputtered.

"Well, the bill's almost $20,000 already." Liliani sounded defensive. "You don't have any insurance. How do you expect to pay for all of this?"

All the anger Carrie had been controlling for the past month exploded. "How dare you dump this on me when my husband's still up there in bed paralyzed? Does your boss know you're talking to me? Do you think you'd keep your job if I said something?"

Liliani took a couple of steps backward, a look of surprise on her fleshy face. "Hey, I'm sorry. . . . I just thought you ought to know, y'know, friend to friend. I was just trying to help."

"Go help someone else!" Carrie screamed, then lost her breath as yet another coughing spell wreaked havoc with her body. By the time this one had abated, Liliani was gone, and Carrie was sure she'd cracked a rib.

The ride down Route 11, Kona Coast's main highway, was quiet at this time of night. The only thing Carrie passed was a truck loaded down with surfboards and furniture. She looked after it wistfully, knowing that the kids in the truck's cab were probably full of plans for finding the perfect wave, nothing else.

She drove straight to the harbor, hoping to see a light in her office window. Sure enough, Matt was still there. She found him on the pier, where he'd just finished cleaning the boat. He seemed surprised to see her.

Although night had settled on the small harbor, there were still pockets of activity around several of the larger boats. Carrie leaned against the truck, watching one crew dismantling a large outboard motor as Matt walked toward her, a loop of heavy rope slung over his shoulder and a pail and mop in his hands. He looked as exhausted as she felt.

From here she could look past Matt's head and see *The Blonde's* main mast bobbing in its place in line. She turned away quickly, remembering what the bill collector had said about selling it, then lifted her face and breathed the warm ocean breeze into her lungs. It was the first time she'd been able to take a deep breath all day; every time she'd tried before, all she could do was hack for at least an hour afterward. She pushed the muscles of her shoulders up against the truck door. Every joint in her body was sore. She felt like she'd aged forty years.

"What do you say we go out for a quick bite?" she asked Matt. "I have a coupon for free fries. We could make the Jack-in-the-Box before it closes."

"Just in time. I'm starved. Haven't eaten all day," he huffed, as he stored the rope and cleaning equipment in the small shed next to the office. "Let me lock up here."

"Not yet," she answered. "I want to go through some of the mail."

"Nah, that's really not necessary. You can do that anytime." Matt positioned his large body in front of the door so she couldn't get by.

"Matt, come on, I haven't been to the office in weeks. I want to see what's going on."

"You don't need to know. You got enough going on right now. I'll take care of things here," he replied, putting his hands on her shoulders. "Let's just go get some chow. We can worry about all this later."

His hands weighed heavily on her. Although she wanted to get into the office, felt she should, she found herself agreeing with him, especially given the type of day she'd had. Still, there were bills that needed to be paid, and she was the only one who could sign the checks.

"Let me at least pay the rent and the phone."

Matt still seemed reluctant, but he slipped aside and let her into the tiny office. She collapsed into the chair and looked helplessly at the piles of paperwork on the desktop.

"I don't know where to begin," she groaned.

"Here, let me help." With a flourish, Matt shoved one pile aside, then rustled through another. "Here's the rent bill, and there's the telephone. Satisfied?"

He waited by the door while she penned the checks. The checking account balance was pitifully low. Although she hated to admit it, she realized they wouldn't be able to meet expenses next month without approaching the bank for another loan. And if the bank even thought about checking her credit, there would be no loan. If only they were going into high season instead of the slowest time of the year. If only . . . if only . . .

She put the checkbook back into the drawer and looked around the office quickly, not knowing what she was looking for.

"Maybe I ought to take Alex some magazines," she said, then stood to reach for the pile on the opposite corner of the desk. Suddenly, the room spun before her. She momentarily lost her balance and gave a weak laugh as Matt jumped to catch her.

"Guess I'm overtired," she managed before another spasm of coughing forced her back into the chair.

"You don't need Jack-in-the-Box," she heard Matt say. "You need some of Auntie Pudding's special soup."

"Does Simone know how sick you are?" Pudding spooned steaming vegetable soup into the bowl in front of Carrie.

Carrie shook her head. *Maman*'s been at the shop the past couple of days. I told her she needed to go back to work. No need for both of us to be at the hospital all the time."

The chickeny mist drifted into her nostrils, and she breathed it in gratefully. Every bone in her chest ached and burned. Every muscle in her body felt as though she had stretched it to its maximum. She wanted nothing more than to sleep a whole night uninterrupted by coughing spasms. She tried to take a deep breath, but it hurt too much.

"You know, little one, if Mama Simone knew you were here instead of home in bed, she would come and take you out of here by your ears. You do too much! Let the doctors and nurses take care of Alex for a day or two. I'm sure he'd understand if you stayed home in bed. Who knows, you might be contagious and you wouldn't want to pass this on to him, now would you?"

Carrie spooned some of the soup into her mouth and shook her head.

Auntie Pudding crossed the little kitchen and stood behind Carrie, gently stroking her hair and massaging her neck muscles. Carrie could have fallen asleep right there, her face in her soup, but the tightness in her chest reminded her another cough might attack at any moment.

As she talked, Auntie's chubby fingers found all the sore spots in Carrie's shoulders, caressing them until the tension eased away and her sore muscles relaxed. Soon Carrie wasn't listening anymore, just longing for her bed and for Alex's strong arms around her.

She had no idea how she got home that night.

Simone closed Carrie's bedroom door quietly and walked back into the living room where Jerry sat stiffly on the couch, a worried expression on his sharply angled face. They had picked Carrie up at Matt's less than an hour before. She'd been soaked to the skin and shaking by the time they put her to bed.

"Is she all right?" he asked.

Simone nodded. "She's finally asleep. If Mama Kamehea hadn't called us, I never would have known."

Jerry motioned her over to the couch. She sank into it and leaned against his shoulder. "Not to blame yourself," he said into her hair. "Sometimes these colds come on overnight."

"I think it's more than that. *Mon Dieu,* the poor girl cannot even breathe without coughing."

"I will prepare some ginseng and pineapple tea for her when she wakes."

A cough rang out from the bedroom. Carrie cried out in pain, then all was quiet again. Simone started to get up but stopped when she realized Carrie must have drifted back to sleep. Her eye caught the blinking answering machine and the pile of mail next to it. Restless, she disengaged herself from Jerry's arm and wandered over to the telephone table. She straightened the pile of mail, noticing that each one appeared to be some kind of bill or disconnect notice. She shook her head, half listening to what Jerry was saying to her, and turned the answering machine on, a pen in hand so that she could take Caryn's messages for her. By the third message, she realized Jerry had stopped talking. Glancing up, she realized he had come to the same conclusion she had. All of the messages were from bill collectors. It was obvious Caryn had gone over the edge financially.

Another cough came from the bedroom. Simone froze. This spasm had no intention of stopping and the wheezing, ripping sound made her run to Caryn's side. This time she was completely awake, her face distorted with pain, her hands clutching her ribs. When she finally stopped coughing, Simone slid an arm under her daughter's back and eased her up gently. As she lifted her, she noticed the spots of blood staining the pillow.

"I can't breathe, *Maman,*" Carrie said. Her body was soaked with sweat.

Simone stroked her daughter's head and barely realized Jerry was at her side.

"We have to take her to hospital, Simone," he said firmly. "Coughing blood very bad."

Simone nodded, murmuring reassurances into Carrie's ear.

"And you have to call her father," he stated. "It's time."

Six

May 7th. Spring. It didn't seem possible. More than two months after the accident and Alex was still in the hospital and would be for a long time.

Carrie looked out her hospital window at the imperial palms surrounding the building, their majestic heads swaying in the afternoon breeze. She shifted in her bed, wincing with the pain of four fractured ribs. Viral pneumonia, the doctor had said when he'd checked her in a week ago. She had thought she was going to die, had even had hallucinations about it. But after six days on intravenously ingested antibiotics and vitamins, she finally felt better. The doctor promised he'd let her go home in a couple of days if, and here he made her promise, she'd take it easy.

"No more traipsing to the hospital to see Alex twice a day. I want you to get out in the sun and fresh air. No working. No hard socializing, until I say so. Okay?"

Dr. Karachi had become a good friend and practically the only person she still saw on a regular basis. Now that she thought of it, she hadn't seen Matt almost all week and her mother had been working at the gallery. Although Carrie understood Matt was occupied with booking the whale-watching cruises and handling the business alone and had the added stress of trying to straighten out his younger brother, she still missed having him to talk to.

Alex sent her an occasional note via the nurses, but he was still too weak to visit. And so was she. The nurses told her he had his good days and bad. Carrie could tell by the way they averted their eyes that Alex had become the least favorite of their patients. She tried not to let the knowledge bother her and told them poignant stories about Alex—how romantic he was, how he made her laugh and was so sensitive to her needs, what he was like before the accident. But even she was beginning to have a hard time dealing with the disgruntled, obstinate man he'd become. To think of him any other way besides rude and inconsiderate took a lot of effort.

She checked her watch. Almost time for her mother's after-work visit. Carrie smiled. *Maman* would be happy to see her finally sitting up and with a little makeup on for the first time in days.

She heard footsteps in the hall and reached up to smooth her braid. Sitting up straighter in the bed, she realized the footsteps had the distinct heavy fall of a man's weight, not her mother's light clips. She didn't recognize the walk and sank back against the pillows, disappointed. Her attention drifted back to the television's drone, and she didn't notice that the footsteps had stopped at her door.

"Hello, darlin'," a familiar voice drawled.

Carrie could hardly believe her eyes. "Dad? What are *you* doing here?"

Philip DeBary strode into her room, his presence filling the tiny space with electricity, as it always had.

It immediately irked Carrie that he knew he made the air crackle with anticipation. Perhaps the effect was necessary when dealing with the international clients he met on a daily basis, but she'd always wanted a father who paid more attention to his family than his multimillion-dollar businesses. Her eyes flicked over him disdainfully. He wore an exquisitely tailored, double-breasted, navy-blue pinstripe suit, a light blue silk shirt and a red tie. When he leaned forward to give her the bouquet of pink and yellow roses he held in his hand, she could see that he'd taken to wearing banker's suspenders.

Very dapper, Daddy, she thought with a bristling sarcasm. Is this the "power business" suit this season?

"Your mama called to let me know what happened to you and Alex."

His lips lightly brushed her forehead. She instantly recoiled. His good ol' boy manner had often been used as a ruse against his competitors. He thought, quite rightly, that if he kept his country accent, his business contacts would think him "dumb as a rock." How wrong they were! Philip DeBary's mind for mathematics often put Harvard economics majors to shame, and his ability to read people was legendary. In another era, he would have made an unbeatable gambler. And it was in that type of position Carrie always imagined him. It had been extremely difficult to have respect for someone she knew so well and saw through so clearly. How could she believe he was being honest with her when he had never been so with anyone else, including his wife?

"Why should you come now? You didn't have

much of a problem staying away when we lived in Houston," she snapped.

Philip straightened and shook his head sadly. "My Lord, sweetheart, how could I stay away?"

He straddled the chair beside her bed, his pants rising to reveal handmade stenciled leather cowboy boots. About $1,000 a pair, Carrie calculated. She suddenly remembered hiding in his closet at age six, trying on what seemed to be hundreds of pairs of boots, boots for every occasion. He had caught her that day and chuckled at her tottering strut, both boots on the wrong feet and many sizes too big for her. Now she'd come to loathe them and all they symbolized.

If Alex ever decides to buy a pair of those ugly things, I will personally remove the boy's feet, she thought.

"Now, Carrie, I didn't come thousands of miles to argue with you," Philip continued with the patient tone she had come to hate. "You look horrible, darlin'. Aren't they taking care of you?"

"I'm fine, Daddy. Why are you *really* here?"

"I told you—"

"Maman asked you for money, didn't she?"

"And if she did?"

"I don't want any of your money."

"Carrie, sweetheart, you were always so stubborn. Why don't you just let me help you?"

"I don't want your help. In fact, I don't know why *Maman* even called you. I can take care of myself." With her last word, she suddenly wheezed and fell into the first coughing spasm she'd had for well over two hours. Her father kept on talking, as he always did.

"Should I call a nurse?" he asked, when her coughing overpowered his voice.

She shushed him with her hands, wishing she had enough strength to get out of bed and usher him out the door. How dare he sit there looking concerned now? How dare he come to Hawaii, where she'd always felt safe?

"I've missed you," he drawled. "I've wanted to come see you for an awful long time. It's really a shame it has to be your illness that brings me here."

She ignored her shaking hands and the need to tell him, as much as she hated admitting it, that she'd missed him, too. "How long ago did *Maman* call you?"

He paused, one impeccably manicured hand stroking her arm. "Well, I was in Paris last week when I got the call, then I went back to Houston, tidied up things there—"

"Didn't exactly rush to get here, did you?" Carrie swallowed hard, forcing another cough to remain in her chest.

"Now, honey, you know how things—"

"All too well," Carrie interrupted. Without giving him a chance to answer, she continued, "As long as you're here, let me ask you something that's been bothering me for a long time. We all know that little girls fall in love with the first man to take care of them, their father. Only I never really knew mine since he was too busy taking care of all his businesses. Then you went and spent most of your time with someone else. Weren't *Maman* and I good enough for you? Weren't you happy with us?" She swallowed hard. "Didn't we love you enough? No, don't answer that. I don't even know why I ask—"

"That wasn't it at all, Carrie, and now that you're old enough, you should under—"

"No, it wasn't enough! You needed more. You needed the businesses, the travel, the women, the money, the power . . . but not a family. Never just us. How do you think that made us feel?"

"But, I did care—"

"Bullcrap." Carrie pulled the sheet up around her and bunched it tightly in her fists until her knuckles hurt. "Bullcrap! If it wasn't for *Maman* and Grandpa DeBary, I wouldn't have known what family was all about."

A spasm finally reached up and grabbed her. She let the cough take control, unable to stop it any longer. When she finished, her father had his arm around her shoulders and was forcing her to take a sip of water. She took the glass gratefully, then handed it back to him and shrugged his arm off her body.

"So, how dare you come here now and pretend everything's okay?" she continued hoarsely, unwilling to let the argument, which had lain dormant inside of her for so long, die.

Philip exhaled, a sure sign he was losing his patience. "I'm not pretending anything. I came to talk. To help, if I can."

"Help? You mean you want to give me money. I don't want your money. Money doesn't fix everything. Maybe you thought it made me feel better when I was a kid, but it was just a facade. The fancy toys, the clothes, the birthday parties with hundreds of people—all I wanted was two people. Just *Maman* and Daddy. But Daddy was never there. I didn't want all your excuses then, and I don't want them now."

"Carrie, you don't understand what it was like then. I had a business to build, a future to carve for you and your mother. If I had ever realized that being away so much would push you away from me . . ." He sighed. "Be sensible, sweetheart. Whether you want to admit it or not, you're in a tight fix, and I can help. Let's let bygones be bygones. We're both adults now. We can start over." He reached for her hand. She let it lie limply on the bed. "Let me help," he pleaded. "Let me help you and Alex. It'll be the first good thing I've done with my money in quite a while."

For a moment she almost believed him. She wanted to believe him, but she turned away, hating for him to see the tears which had traitorously begun to well in her eyes. "You didn't even come to our wedding."

"I wasn't invited."

Silence.

"I don't want your money," Carrie repeated.

"Now, don't you think it's *you* who's being selfish? What about Alex? From what your mother told me, you're not going to be able to keep up with all the special nurses and therapy that boy's going to need. Can you carry all the weight, pay all the hospital bills, take over the . . . what is it? A fishing boat business?"

"Whale-watching cruises."

Philip's eyes widened and Carrie felt an odd sense of satisfaction that she had managed to catch him off guard.

"Whale-watching . . ."

"Yeah, those big creatures your tuna fleets kill on a regular basis."

Realization dawned on his face. "So that's it."

"What do you mean?"

"You don't want to take my money, because I earned it doing something that goes against your beliefs—"

"I know your money doesn't come from *just* the tuna business."

"But that's the only one you want to associate with me, isn't it? You conveniently forget about the banks I've opened, which helped Texas's economy, and the homeless shelters, the radio stations, the television station. It's just like you to focus on the one thing that affects *you* rather than trying to understand the whole picture."

Carrie paused, letting his comment sink in and feeling the old anger rise once again. But was he right? Was that part of the reason? Yes, she had to admit, of course he was. She read about Ocean Fresh in the newspaper every once in a while and the news was never positive. Less than six months ago, one of her father's fleets had captured over a hundred dolphins with the invisible seine nets the company used to fish for tuna. The news had infuriated Alex. She remembered sitting at the kitchen table with him that evening, listening to him fume and fuss and feeling almost as responsible for the slaughter as the person who had ordered the boats to fish that area, her father.

"Maybe you're right." She turned to face him squarely.

"I'm trying to change the industry, Carrie. Believe me, it's just not something that can be done overnight. You know, back in 1960 those old boats and their big nets did a lot of damage, and we never worried about whales and dolphins." He shrugged, as if the whole horrid mess had caused him no more than a night of worry. "I felt out of task when I started realizing things had to be changed. Pronto. But the job is gargantuan, Carrie. You don't realize—"

"Oh, but you're wrong. I realize all too well how out of proportion it's become. I see dolphins and whales every day. You seem to forget that's what Alex studied in school. In fact, Alex and I swim with them, and we see their scars. We spend a lot of our time rescuing them from those damn nets, and sometimes we've watched them take their last breath."

Her voice caught, but she covered it and shot her father a scathing look. She felt a sense of power over him now. Lines creased the outer corners of his tired eyes. His shoulders slumped just a little in the expensive suit.

"You always did have a real pretty way of explaining yourself, Daddy, but I don't want to hear it anymore. I can see through you now and I really don't like what I see."

Philip's chin hardened. He had had enough, she could see. "You're closin' yourself off, darlin'. I'll always be your daddy. I'm here and willing to negotiate. Can't we try to talk about it, patch things up?"

For a moment, Carrie was caught up in the fantasy that her life might have a happy ending, tempted by the thought that her father would be hers again, rather than belonging to the stepbrother she didn't know. But then she realized he was doing it again. He always managed to paint a beautiful vision, but she knew the reality. She knew Philip DeBary all too well.

"No," she said. And she didn't regret it for a heartbeat when he walked out of the room, defeated.

* * *

"She's still very angry, Simone. Can't you do something about it? Can't you talk to her?"

Philip had gone directly to the Waimea Bay Art Gallery. Now he paced back and forth in front of her, in more turmoil than she had ever seen him experience, no matter what kind of business deal he was trying to negotiate. As much as she hated to admit it, his actions served to prove that he still cared for his daughter. Even if Caryn didn't feel the same.

Simone watched him, feeling a mix of emotions as powerful as the tides which changed every evening. On the one hand, she sided totally with Caryn, knowing exactly how furious her daughter was when Philip abandoned them. But on the other hand, this was one time Caryn needed to put aside that pride and accept the help she so desperately needed.

Money. The power of someone who controlled it over those who didn't have it. Well, given the choice, Simone decided at that moment, she'd rather be on the plus side than the minus. She had had it both ways and there was definitely something to be said for not having to worry about whether one long-distance phone call would put you over your budget for the month.

And to look at the man in front of her, the man she had lived with, had shared her most intimate secrets with, had allowed into the most private areas of her heart, to see him, still handsome and vigorous well into his fifties, only served to remind her of what had drawn her to him in the very beginning.

Just that morning, knowing her ex-husband was coming in on the eight o'clock mainland flight, Simone had taken special pains with her makeup and had discarded dress after dress before choosing the Delft blue *mu'umu'u* Mariah Redmond had created for her last year. Still, she felt dumpy and old standing next to the tall, magnetic Texan.

But he wasn't even paying attention to her. He strode around the gallery, touching a frame, studying one of the sculptures hidden in a corner. He seemed preoccupied. As usual, she thought.

"Caryn's an adult, Philip. She can make her own decisions."

"Doesn't she listen to her mother anymore? Children never get too old to listen to their parents, Simone. You, of all people, should know that." He looked down at her disdainfully, dismissing her as he would a lowly receptionist. She suddenly felt the urge to slap his face, not only for herself and all that he'd done to her but for what he'd done to Carrie, and to all the lowly receptionists in his life.

"I do know," she replied with vehemence. *"I'm* the one who kept telling you how important parents are. *I* was the one who acted as parent when *our daughter* went through her most difficult stages. *I* was the one she woke at night when she had a nightmare. *I* was the one who sat with her when she didn't have a date for her senior prom." She pulled herself up to her full height and raised her head haughtily. *"I* was the one who gave her away when she got married."

The comment stopped him and he finally turned to face her. "Touché. You got me. But still—"

"Obviously, I made a mistake asking you to come here, Philip. Maybe you should just leave." She walked toward the door, intending to let him out. Why had she believed things might have changed? Why had she put Caryn in such an uncomfortable position? Desperation, she thought with a rueful smile. It'll make you do anything.

"I figured I'd never hear from you again," Philip said quietly. "When you called, my heart stopped." The look in his eyes was the same one he had given her the first time she'd faced him with proof of his infidelity. "All I could think was that something horrible had happened. And I was right." He stepped in front of her, blocking the door. "Let me at least try to do something for Carrie. Allow me that much. She can go to my chalet in Monaco to recuperate. I'll pay for the best physical therapists in the world to come here to treat Alex. I've got to do something, Simone . . ."

Something wan and pitiful in his voice made Simone lean her head back and look into his bottomless brown eyes. Caryn's eyes. Although his face was tanned, deep lines knifed his cheeks and his eyes looked tired. The creases around his mouth, which she had often traced with her finger while he lay sleeping, had deepened. He was getting old. The fast life he had led for the past twenty-five years was finally taking its toll. She felt a surge of pity for him, then brushed the feeling away, remembering that, as one of the richest businessmen in the northern hemisphere, he didn't need her pity.

"If I let you do anything now," she managed shakily, trying with her last ounce of energy to be circumspect, "I'll lose Caryn's respect. No, Philip, go home to your wife and your new baby. Caryn and I have been able to take care of ourselves. We shall survive this as well."

Philip's sharp eyes clouded and his lips tightened. Simone recognized the look of resignation. She had often seen it mirrored on Caryn's face in the past couple of months. But she was surprised Philip had given in so quickly. Perhaps he had changed in the last seven years. She certainly had.

"Allow me to at least pay her hospital bill."

Simone hesitated briefly but figured it was the least he could do. After all, he was Caryn's father. And there were so many other bills to pay.

She nodded, then stood back to let him leave. He didn't say another word, just climbed into the waiting silver limousine.

Simone stood at the gallery window for a long time, watching the powerful car carry him away. She had always hated limousines. They represented loneliness and desertion to her. She had watched far too many of them leave her behind.

Expectantly, she waited for the familiar stomach-burning anger to appear, but all she felt was a muscle-weakening defeat. She watched the car until it disappeared and all that was left on the horizon were the high white clouds and bright blue sky that she counted on to heal her soul. For a long time she leaned against the glass, motionless, waiting for the solace to come.

When it didn't, she turned away, with the full realization that she hadn't recovered from the impact Philip DeBary had had on her life.

Seven

Matt heard the brisk sneakered footsteps even before Carrie rounded the corner of the building and strode into view like a proud Amazon princess. He eyed the men in the boatyard as they watched her slap her knapsack on the ground next to him. Old and young, married and single, none of them could tear their eyes away from her, all did the standard eye sweep from the top of her platinum head to the bottom of her tanned feet. Matt grinned, knowing by the set line of her mouth that she, too, felt the stares. And she hated being the center of attention. Matt had even known her to whip her head around and set her braid flying, to demand, "What in hell're you looking at?"

"Where's Isaac?" she asked, squatting down beside him.

"I got him swabbing *The Blonde*'s decks. Do the boy some good to work hard for a change."

It had been Carrie's idea to give Matt's younger brother a job, and Matt had agreed wholeheartedly that having Isaac around the harbor would keep him away from his pot-smoking buddies and under Matt's watchful eye.

"When will she be ready to sail?" Carrie shaded

her eyes with her hand and peered out to where *The Blonde* was berthed.

Matt followed her gaze and shrugged. " 'Bout fifteen minutes, I guess."

"Okay, I'm going in the office and catch up on some paperwork." She glanced at her watch. "What time's our first trip today?"

"Only one trip is full—the 4 P.M. The Hyatt's sending a tour group over, probably a bunch of blue haired ol' *wahinis*. That's all they seem to be gettin' over there lately."

Carrie rolled her eyes. "Oh well, they pay the bills."

"Sometimes." Matt hated himself for the quip the instant he saw the flush creep up Carrie's neck.

"I can give you a week's pay as soon as the Hyatt pays me," she said.

He rose to give her an apologetic hug. "Don't worry 'bout it," he said. "Guess Isaac's just getting to me. He's always bitching about being broke."

Their eyes met and held, two old friends who wordlessly realized it was probably just as well Isaac didn't have any money. It would keep him out of trouble. Carrie squeezed Matt's strong forearm and smiled before turning to disappear into her office.

When she came back out almost an hour later, the harbor had quieted down a bit. Those who wanted to sail had already headed out to open sea to take advantage of the morning winds. Those who had chores were done for the day. The only people still wandering the docks were those who ran fishing charters or who, like Carrie and Matt, catered to late-rising tourists interested in chasing the whales that wintered between the Kona Coast and Maui.

"You ready?" Matt asked Carrie, trying to act casually interested rather than concerned. He knew she had chosen to take *The Winsome Blonde* out because she'd put the sailboat up for sale the day before. This could be her last sail. And selling her prized possession was a touchy subject, one that even he wouldn't broach.

Isaac moved aside as Carrie hoisted her knapsack up onto her shoulder. "Yup," she said with a bright smile, "I'm ready as I'll ever be." She winked at Isaac and punched Matt playfully. "Keep an eye on things for me, huh? I'll be back before four."

As she strutted down the pier, Isaac caught Matt's eye. "You ask her about the money?"

The boy has about as much class as a wedding-party crasher. Matt gave an exasperated huff and turned on his brother. "Don't you ever listen to what I say? She's broke, man. That's all there is to it. We'll get paid as soon as she does."

"That's not what I hear. Her old man's worth millions."

"Yeah, but she's not."

Isaac snapped his gum and leaned against a piling, flipping the quarter he held in his hand. "Why didn't she take her old man's money when he was here? She's nuts to turn that kind of offer down."

"Not her style," Matt replied.

Carrie had reached *The Blonde,* and he watched as she slung her knapsack aboard, jumped in, then loosed the anchor ropes. "Don't worry, we'll get paid. What you worried about anyway? You get fed. You got a roof over your head. You ought to consider yourself lucky. Look at Carrie and Alex. He's in a nursing home now, and she's just about making enough to feed herself. What kind of life they gonna have when he comes home? *You* got nothing to complain about, *Bruddah."*

"Yeah, but a guy's got to take care of his girl, y'know."

"What girl? You don't have a girl."

Isaac stepped away from the piling and pretended to busy himself straightening a mess of mops. Matt watched him, wondering what was going through the teenager's mind. He remembered Isaac only a couple of years ago, a curly-haired kid with a quick grin and a passion for surfing. Where was the surfboard now, Matt thought. Where was the kid who used to idolize his older brother?

As he watched *The Winsome Blonde* slowly wend its majestic way out of the harbor, Matt wondered how much longer he'd be able to let everyone lean on him before he, too, would begin to bend under the strain. He nodded to Isaac, indicating that it was time to get back to work, and soon was lost in plans for what had to be done before the tour group arrived.

Carrie pushed a long strand of hair behind her ear and tried to concentrate on controlling the mainsail rather than giving in to the memory of a battered and bleeding Alex lying on the sailboat's deck. The day of the accident had been the last time she had taken *The Blonde* out. How ironic that today would be the last time she'd sail the magnificent boat. Ever.

Open sea greeted her in every direction, beckoning her. She gave in to the call, feeling the surge of salt air slowly fill her nostrils and veins with its intoxicating wine.

It had been too long, much too long.

With the natural ability of one born to the sea, she handled the tiller joyfully. *God, how can I let her go? How can I turn this gorgeous beauty over to some stranger, some weekend sailor who doesn't know the language of her polished teak hull, the satisfied creaks and groans she makes when under full sail? Who else would care for her as we have? Love her as Maman and I do?*

Maman. Another unpleasant memory forced its way into her thoughts. Though her mother would never admit it, she'd been devastated when Carrie had explained her plans to sell *The Blonde*. If Carrie had not been looking directly at her mother's face, she might have missed the flicker of eyelashes, the ever-so-slight jerk of her head, the dainty folded hands which clenched so tightly their fingernails turned white.

"Is there no other way?" Simone had asked.

Carrie had had to turn away. "No," she answered. "I've tried everything. You know none of the banks will give me a loan, all of our credit cards have been taken away, my landlord is threatening eviction, the finance company has already tried to repossess the truck. . . . Matt had one of his friends paint it yesterday so that it looks different. That'll throw them off for a little while, but not forever. And, worst of all, Alex's nursing home wants a substantial portion of their fees up front. Every month."

"What about your insurance?"

"Cancelled. I wasn't able to make the premiums."

With that, Simone had risen, a grim look on her face, and forced Carrie to meet her eye-to-eye. "Your father will help you. Call him. Please."

It had taken great restraint not to lash out verbally, as she had the day her father had visited, but Carrie had managed to keep her temper in check. "I've already told you I won't call him. He paid the hospital bills. That's enough. In fact, that's much more than I ever wanted from him. *Much* more. And you know that."

Simone had stepped back, certain she'd been soundly defeated.

"Are you sure you want to do this?"

"Yes."

"Then, *bonne chance.*"

Carrie looked out over the bow, forcing aside the guilt she felt. *The Winsome Blonde* had been her mother's long before it had been hers.

"I have no choice," Carrie said into the salty spray from the waves that broke alongside the ship. "And, someday, *Maman,* when this is all behind us, I'll tell you about my last sail, about today, about how perfect the ocean is, about how warm the air feels and about the diamond blue color of the water."

She let the serene feeling she always experienced when sailing wash over her and sat, her right hand on the tiller, her left holding the jib line. Her mind drifted, from the past to the present to what might be in the future, but she felt no passage of time. She didn't even notice the spinner dolphins frolicking beside her or the humpback whale breaching in the distance off the starboard. She wouldn't have seen the large, battered ship pulling up astern if the skipper hadn't hailed her, loudly.

Jerking her head around, Carrie was shocked to see the skow coming straight for her. With a few quick movements, she tacked, caught a good gust, and sailed smoothly out of the other boat's path. With her heart still pounding, she turned as the skipper once again hailed her.

"Ahoy! You in the sailboat. You all right?"

She raised a hand to her forehead trying to shade out the sun, but it was no use. He was standing directly in its blinding rays. All she could see was a black shadow.

"I'm okay," she yelled back. "Just caught me daydreaming, I guess."

She thought she heard a chuckle and squinted, but still couldn't see him. The side of his boat was painted with what appeared to be a rainbow.

"Well, you'd better keep alert," he yelled. "There's a lot of action out here today."

"What do you mean?"

Both boats had moved, and if she stood just right, she could make out the skipper's profile. Greek, she guessed, or Italian. Dark, curly hair, and the physique of a man used to strenuous labor. A fisherman, probably.

"Tuna boats about a mile out. They're laying seine nets." The disgust in his voice was unmistakable.

"They're too close to shore," Carrie protested.

"We know. That's why we're here." The skipper's voice drifted now. Although he was farther away, she could see him clearly now. And she could also read the name emblazoned across the boat's bow: *The Rainbow Warrior.*

"Greenpeace," she whispered and plunked down next to the tiller.

If Greenpeace was there, then the dolphins were most definitely in trouble, more trouble than anyone on the islands had been led to believe.

"You'd better go back to harbor, *Winsome Blonde.* There might be some commotion out here."

She cupped her hands to her mouth, anxious to ask one more question before he motored out of earshot.

"Which company is laying the nets?"

"Ocean Fresh," he replied.

Somehow, the knowledge that her father wasn't physically navigating one of his own tuna boats did little to quell the surge of anger Carrie felt when she heard the company name.

Ocean Fresh. What an anomaly!

She maneuvered *The Blonde* to catch the breeze coming out of the northeast, juggling sails and wagging the tiller so hard it sounded almost like a motor. Out of the corner of her eye, she kept a fair amount of distance between *The Blonde* and *The Rainbow Warrior.* No need to have a collision before they reached their destination. She wanted to follow the Greenpeace boat, though she had a feeling the captain would object.

Now she could see him shouting in her direction, but she couldn't hear him. And she wanted it that way.

Her heart pounded as it had when she'd been riding and her horse had cleared an abnormally high hurdle.

Every fiber of her body strained against her skin, screaming with the stress and strain of being put to the ultimate test—racing the sailboat against a much larger boat, and one with a motor to boot. She immediately felt the toll her bout with pneumonia had taken on her body and almost turned back. But suddenly there was nothing more important than for her to defeat her father. Ocean Fresh symbolized Philip DeBary and everything she couldn't stand about him, more than any other company he owned.

Another gust of wind, and she came abreast of *The Rainbow Warrior.* She could see the tuna boat in the distance, barely an ink blot on the horizon, but it was there, and the reality that she was going into war, into forbidden territory, against one of her father's boats struck home. For one instant, frozen in time, she paused, back straight, legs spread apart on the deck, head up, and felt more empowered than she ever had in her entire life.

She was profoundly aware that a pod of dolphins was swimming next to her boat, happy clowns who lived such a peaceful life they didn't react fearfully when large, foreign vessels entered their territory. If only she could tell them to turn back, teach them how to be wary of strangers, as her mother had taught her.

"Go home!" the Greenpeace captain yelled at her when she was within earshot. "*Winsome Blonde,* go home!"

His voice reached her as if it had been delivered through a tube connected to her eardrum, and she reacted as though she'd been slapped across the face.

"Like hell I will," she muttered.

Then suddenly she was racing again, *The Blonde*

skimming the water effortlessly. The wind pulled at her hair like a clawing cat. Her arms shot out like pistons as she fought to maintain control of the straining sails. She had an absurd vision of herself in full Viking armor, poised on the bow of a battleship, ready to die with honor. A gurgle of free and hysterical laughter rose through her chest, out her open mouth, then whisked away with a particularly strong draft. She felt powerful, invincible, yet, somehow, slightly ludicrous. And totally, absolutely, insane.

The closer she came to the tuna boat, the more she realized she didn't have a snowball's chance in hell of doing anything to stop Ocean Fresh. *The Winsome Blonde*, at forty feet, was hardly a dinghy, but even its majestic stretch was not a match for her father's vessel. For an instant, she felt the same kind of intimidation she experienced every time her father came near. That feeling was quickly replaced by an uncontrollable fury when she sailed close enough to the boat to spot the almost invisible seine nets the boat was dropping.

Quickly, Carrie tried to judge how long the net was. Some companies were known to stretch the dangerous netting for miles over open ocean, trapping every living creature in the vicinity, most of them maimed or physically damaged in some way by the strangling nylon net.

Carrie remembered diving to loosen a large tortoise from a driftnet only a few years before. Alex had figured the old fellow to be at least a hundred and ten. "Imagine how many miles he's traveled," Alex mused. "How many changes he's seen. And this is the way he dies. Suffocated by a huge death-net that wasn't even meant for him."

Now she was close enough to notice that the waters near where the net had been laid were alive with action. Pods of dolphins rose and dove, then quickly rose again. Their chittering patterns quickened, forming the calls Carrie recognized as their distress signal. They were beginning to panic. Soon they wouldn't be able to find their way out of the baglike net used to get the dolphins and other fish out of the way, so that the fishermen could get at the tuna swimming below.

She jibed smoothly, then studiously followed the net's line for several hundred feet, watching for animals who had become entangled, before heading back in the direction she'd come—straight for the massive Ocean Fresh boat.

As she drew near, she spotted figures on deck, but no one seemed interested in her. They all concentrated on the job at hand. All the men, and there appeared to be at least a dozen on board, were talking to each other at the same time, yelling instructions or warnings. For a moment she paused, wondering what she'd say or do when they finally saw her.

"Hey! Hey you! What the hell you doing here? You gonna get hurt!" one of the men on deck yelled. "Back off!"

Giving the man a cocky salute, Carrie replied, "I'm not going anywhere until you move your net. In fact, I might just get a little closer."

With that, she maneuvered *The Blonde* so that she was in line with the tuna boat. A strong, fishy stench floated over her bow and Carrie wrinkled her nose, fighting the urge to gag.

"I don't think that's a good idea," the fisherman sing-songed in her direction. Then he swaggered toward the others, motioning down toward her with almost drunken gestures. He seemed to think the idea of one sailboat stopping an international corporation's state-of-the-art fishing vessel was some kind of a joke.

She didn't blame him. Now that she was next to the ship, whose hull rose high above her, she began to realize how futile her efforts really were.

But someone had to do something. What Ocean Fresh was doing, fishing this close to the coast, was absolutely against the law. How could they even think they'd get away with it, especially using driftnets?

She heard a familiar voice shout, "Ocean Fresh! Greenpeace International demands you comply with the fishing regulations that govern these waters." *The Rainbow Warrior* drew up alongside her. The loudspeaker its captain held spit and snarled, but he continued. "You are more than half a mile within the no-commercial fishing zone. And you realize, of course, that it's against the law to sell any fish caught with the use of driftnets. So, pick up your nets and move. Now."

The Rainbow Warrior meant business. She'd heard how strongly Greenpeace reacted when pitched against corporations like Ocean Fresh, but what she'd read didn't make half the impact of actually seeing a face-off in action. And here she was, sandwiched between them.

Ocean Fresh's crew hung over the railings of their boat, hooting and hollering and laughing at the prospect of not one, but two, silly little boats trying to stop them. In her mind's eye, she saw them as they saw her—one woman in a fancy, elegant, somewhat antiquated sailboat—then she looked at the cumbersome, wholly unattractive boat painted with a rainbow and the scowling, dark-haired captain now pacing the bow. She felt that, had he been able, he'd jump the distance to Ocean Fresh's deck and personally pummel anyone else who so much as tittered at *The Rainbow Warrior* and its mission. She got the impression the captain was unlikely to let much of anything get past him.

For three long hours, the face-off continued, with each boat matching its opponent's every move, every degrading comment answered in kind. They argued about marine law, insulted each other, tried to reason with each other, then, ultimately, threatened each other. Carrie admired *The Rainbow Warrior*'s daring and intelligence. With each maneuver, the captain managed to move his boat closer to cutting the Ocean Fresh off, perhaps even slicing her nets. But it appeared he had decided to work out all possible options before doing any harm. Carrie respected him for that.

Finally, she could wait patiently no longer.

"Listen, you two jackasses," she yelled. "While you're out here arguing, innocent animals are dying underwater."

In the moment of stunned silence that followed, she pitched a quick plea. "If the nets are not raised and moved, or at least *started* to move, in the next fifteen minutes, I'm going down to free the trapped animals . . . even if I have to cut huge holes in the net to do so." She held up the large razorlike knife she kept on board for fileting fish and let it flash in the midday sun.

"Oh, c'mon, lady, all we want is to do our job and go home," the fishing boat's captain snarled. "Now why don't you just go back to harbor and leave us with *The Rainbow Cripple* here?"

Carrie turned and caught the Greenpeace captain staring broodily back at her, shaking his head slowly, as if convinced she'd completely blown his chances of any civilized agreement.

It was one of the most uncomfortable moments of her life. She glanced from one captain to the other, her face burning, then dove straight down into the water, where no one could see the red blotches she felt high on her cheeks. One of these days, she'd learn what caused her to blush so easily, and how to control it.

The cool water closed over her head. She swam strongly for a few yards in what she hoped was the direction of the driftnet. When she felt one strong, sleek body pass on her right, she knew she was close, but before she could do anything, she needed some air and her bearings.

She surfaced and could almost touch the Ocean Fresh's hull. Someone yelled, then someone else, but she couldn't understand them and dove again.

Getting the first dolphin untangled was easy. Two slices through the net and she'd made a hole large enough for him to escape. Several more quickly followed him through, and she knew they'd signal to the others.

The second dolphin made her dive again and again. He thrashed against her violently each time she swam near. He's hurt badly, she thought, trying to anticipate his moves so that she could get close enough to loosen his flipper from where the nylon net cut into him like razors. On her sixth trip to the surface, she gasped for breath and forced herself to float calmly for a minute, before once again diving below.

Was it her imagination or had the boats moved? Perhaps she'd just swum further along the wall of net than she'd thought. She forced herself to concentrate, then took another deep breath and gave a powerful kick, propelling herself to where the dolphin had momentarily given up his fight with the net. He hung like a silver plane in the water below her.

She circled slowly, deciding to come up from under him so that she could get near before he panicked again. It worked. She cradled her arm around his stomach, getting close to him, holding him still while she worked at slicing the net, a little more. There!

In a swooping motion, the dolphin slipped away, spinning through the hole she had made, swimming to a deeper, safer part of the ocean. With a sense of relief, she pushed for the surface.

"Are you all right?"

Carrie gasped for air, then spun around to look directly into *The Rainbow* captain's eyes. He leaned over the edge of an orange dinghy, marked with the Greenpeace symbol. Another man was with him, steadying the boat from the other side.

"Are you okay?" the captain asked again. "You were down there an awful long time. We were about to go after you."

She sputtered and shook her head, still out of breath and unable to speak.

"Here, let us at least give you a ride back. After all, you did *our* work today." He gestured starboard. She followed his eyes and saw Ocean Fresh's fishermen reeling the drift net back in. An indescribably delicious feeling of success propelled her out of the water.

"It worked!" she shrieked.

The captain reached his hand toward her with a pleased, and quite sexy, smile. "Oldest trick in the book," he teased.

She grabbed his hand in hers and let him pull her into the boat. "Then why didn't *you* think of it?" she asked breathlessly when they finally stood nose-to-nose.

Eight

Jack Briskin was not at all the type of person Carrie expected a Greenpeace activist to be. She waited for the sing-song California "valley boy" voice but, instead, heard one that was sharp and businesslike. He had the habit of leaving words out of his sentences, almost as if he didn't have enough time to insert them. And she'd been wrong when she'd first guessed him to be Italian or Greek.

"Uh-uh," he said with an emphatic shake of his blue-black curls. "Black Irish. My mother's name was Foley. Mary Sullivan Foley. Gave me both my curly locks and my temperament."

His first mate, who'd been introduced simply as Bob, let loose a whoop. "That's not saying much for your mother, old man."

Bob had a distinct Australian accent and the sandy-brown skin of someone used to spending his life in the sun. Now he, Carrie thought, fit her image of the typical Greenpeace activist. She also figured him to be a part-time surfer and found herself dismissing him the moment he spoke. The captain was much more intriguing.

Carrie's instant, on-the-spot assessments of people were legendary at Miss Kiki's Ranch. All the girls used to count on Carrie when a newcomer tried to join their group. Her gut reaction always hit the mark, and the girls would come back to her weeks, months, sometimes years, later, demanding to know how she'd known. No big secret, she thought. Anyone with eyes can notice whether a person is lying by the way they stand or sit. And if you can't read someone's personality after a few moments of talking to them and watching their eyes . . . well.

She'd felt like that when she'd first met Wanda Firthmore, daughter of Milton Firthmore of Firthmore's Fine Liquors, heiress to the oldest, most respected liquor distilleries in the world, and Daddy was a duke to boot. The halls had buzzed for weeks before Miss Wanda's first appearance on school grounds. Even Carrie had had to admit her opinion of Miss Wanda, as they had dubbed the heiress, was partially formed before her first glimpse of the girl.

It had taken exactly seventeen hours, thirty-two minutes, and four seconds for Carrie to see through good ol' Wanda's scam.

"She's not a Firthmore," Carrie whispered to Lorilene, her best friend, and Miss Kiki's daughter, late that night, hours after lights out. "She's a phony."

"You're nuts, Carrie DeBary," Lorilene swore. "This time you are *definitely* wrong."

When the state police had come to pick up Donna Farren, alias Wanda Firthmore, nearly three months later, Carrie had stood with Lorilene on the main house's front steps and merely held out her hand, palm up.

"Okay, you win," Lorilene had said, forking over a ten with a grimace that had made her freckles seem to run together. "I won't ever doubt you again. You're the best."

Carrie's reputation had grown as her uncanny knack for instantly judging a person's true intentions far outshone any other of her talents. She had always hoped for large groups of friends, wished she could be one of the blue ribbon riders at the ranch or the chairperson of the debating team or president of the Spanish club. Anything. But all through the four years at the ranch, Lorilene had remained her only friend and, to make matters worse, the highest grade Carrie had ever gotten was a B minus. Finally, she had decided that if this first-impression gift was the only one she was going to have, well, then, she'd become the best "bullshit sniffer"—as Lorilene had so daintily put it—that Texas had ever seen.

Carrie stood on deck and put her gut impression instincts to work on Jack Briskin. As far as she could tell, he was a no-bullshit type of person, but that was about all she could tell. He seemed a contradiction in terms. She had witnessed his loyalty to his mates and knew he cared strongly about the ocean's mammals or he wouldn't be part of Greenpeace. Yet she could sense a very strong will and his comment about his temperament gave her reason to suspect a fairly virulent nature.

"You know," she said when the dinghy pulled up beside *The Blonde*, "back home we'd call this a day worth crowin' about. I must admit I enjoyed myself tremendously." She bowed slightly to Jack before he offered her his hand so that she could make the jump to her boat.

"Let's hope the next time we meet, it'll be under more stable circumstances," he said.

Something in Jack Briskin's voice made her look back at him. Although he stood less than two feet away, she found herself quickly appraising his body, something she hadn't done since before she'd met Alex. About thirty-two years old, she figured, in great shape.

Yes, she thought, I was right. He's used to being alone and he likes it. Yet he really doesn't seem aware that the combination of his raven hair and those sassy green eyes could make a lonely woman think of how much she'd like to have someone to talk to . . .

Mentally she pulled in the reins, then physically she yanked her hand away from his.

Whoa! Where the hell did that come from?

She thought of Alex and realized she would see him before the day was over. Sobered, she averted her eyes.

"I enjoyed meeting you," she said sincerely. "Thanks for the ride and best of luck. I hope you can keep chasing those guys out of these waters."

"They didn't leave because of us, they left because of what you did. I don't think they expected to find Wonder Woman in this part of the ocean." With a chuckle, he raised his hand in salute, as Bob raced the little dinghy back to where *The Rainbow Warrior* waited.

As she watched them, Carrie's intuition told her that he was one man who wouldn't have any problem at all reading her.

The thought made her immensely uncomfortable.

* * *

The sun drifted slowly behind the mountains, leaving only burning slivers of memories to prove it had existed. Carrie sat in the boat daydreaming, as she had since docking more than half an hour before. Fascinated, she watched until there were no flaming tracers left anywhere in the sky. She knew that she was stalling, drawing every last second out of every last minute of the time she could spend on *The Blonde* and that, in doing so, she was simultaneously putting off visiting Alex. But she couldn't help it.

Finally, she stood and stretched, grabbed her knapsack, and headed for her truck. Time for the nightly visit to the nursing home. Maybe this time she could drum up enough courage to tell Alex about selling the sailboat. On the other hand, maybe it would be easier if she didn't say anything at all.

She walked slowly and deliberately toward the truck, inventing excuses to go straight home. Each one sounded lame, even to her.

A leftover feeling of euphoria about the earlier part of the day crept over her. That's the way I'll do it, she thought. I'll tell Alex about what happened today. Maybe he'll have some kind of positive reaction. Something. Anything.

Maybe once they started talking, she could tell him everything else. About the boat and the bills and her father and her mother and the business and Matt and Isaac . . . and everything they hadn't been able to talk about since the accident. About her life.

She climbed into the truck and turned the key, pumping the gas a few times, praying that the motor would turn over, as she'd been doing for the past month. Matt had said it was only a matter of time until the transmission quit, but this time the engine caught. Safe once more, she thought as she turned on the headlights and leaned against the steering wheel, suddenly exhausted.

On the other hand, what difference would it make whether I go see Alex or not. The only people who ever notice I'm there are the nurses. Alex hasn't even looked at me in weeks.

Jack Briskin's friendly, sexy face popped into her mind. Determined to stay on track, she swore aloud, jerked the truck into drive and headed home. No matter how bad things got, she reminded herself, she wouldn't be like her father.

I won't do that to Alex.

Carrie pulled the truck into her mother's driveway and parked. She wasn't sure how she'd gotten there. She didn't remember heading in this direction after leaving the meeting with Larry Chase, but here she was, a bill of sale in her pocket for *The Blonde* and a cloud over her head the size of Idaho.

She sat in the truck a moment, hesitant about going in, but the lights from her mother's lanai were warm and welcoming. She walked toward them as though in a trance.

When she came into the backyard, she halted and watched in silence, admiring her mother as she performed the ancient Oriental martial art t'ai chi with Jerry. Their shadows cast perfect silhouettes against the wall of foliage separating Simone's property from

Hannah Lanaki's. It always awed Carrie when she saw her mother moving so gracefully and effortlessly through the slow, majestic movements that Carrie knew from experience were arduous and difficult to learn. A body had to be incredibly strong to endure the two-hour session of stretching, posing, and meditating that was t'ai chi. She had tried to learn the art a few years before and even her strong, young limbs couldn't withstand the sustained statue-like positions. Yet, as she watched Jerry and her mother, she saw no strain on either of their faces, just a complete concentration, almost mystic. An enviable peace.

When they finished, Jerry nodded to Carrie. After asking about Alex, he slipped out into the night, seeming to sense her need to be alone with her mother.

"You told him about *The Blonde,* didn't you?" Carrie walked over to the patio table and sunk into an overstuffed wicker chair Simone occupied when reading her mysteries.

Busying herself with a pot of herbal tea, Simone murmured something Carrie could not quite hear. She waited for her mother to come back to the patio, but after studying Simone's serene profile, decided against asking what she'd said. Talking about it would only make it worse for both of them, she decided.

They sat on opposite sides of the table, each cradling her warm cup near her nose, inhaling the heady wintergreen fragrance. The tea relaxed Carrie completely, and she sat back listening to the night sounds. The geckos started their evening serenade and she spotted one of the perky green lizards shooting up the railing. He stopped abruptly, twisting his long neck forward, intently watching something on the roof before scampering after it. She envied him his freedom and longed to give up everything that had become her life so that she could follow the foolish lizard up the trunk of the nearest palm tree.

"Did you see Alex tonight?" Simone asked. "Did he see the therapist today?"

Carrie placed her cup on the table. "I didn't go."

She made her comment quietly, knowing that her mother would disapprove, but she couldn't lie to her. Simone had taught her lying wouldn't get her anywhere, and she knew her mother was always right.

"Oh."

Simone's one word statement fell like a bomb between them.

"It was too late once . . . once Chase and I settled on a price for the boat . . . and everything. I just didn't feel like I could visit after that. Alex will understand."

They fell silent again. Simone looked up at the brilliant map of stars above them and sighed. Carrie knew she'd never again mention *The Winsome Blonde*.

Neither of them would.

Nine

"You mean add another cruise?"

Matt straddled an office chair like a cowboy, his attention focused on the June schedule sitting on the desk between him and Carrie. Her eyes focused on him as she leaned forward, tension through her shoulders, a burning sensation behind her eyes. She'd had little sleep the past week, no rest even when sleep came.

The reality was she needed $3,000 a month to keep everything running, and to make the payments to the physical therapy center in Hilo. She'd transferred Alex from the nursing home after he'd loudly complained that he wasn't "over the hill yet" and didn't like being housed with a group of senior citizens "waiting to take their last shaky breath."

With a few quick calculations, she'd figured she could cut some of her overhead by giving up the apartment and staying in the back room at the office. She had placed her belongings in storage until the time came when she could get all the bills back to a reasonable level. Maybe Matt was right—if they could add a couple of cruises to their schedule . . .

"We can do it," she answered Matt, a determined glint in her weary eyes. "I'm going to stay here anyway, and between the two of us, we can train Isaac so he can work with us on the full trips. He can do all the cleaning you've been doing and that'll free you up to help me handle more trips. *Maman's* going to be working the office at least three days a week. That'll give me time to do some of the trips you can't. It looks like it'll work. It'll take a lot of time and energy, but it'll work. I'll stake the business on it."

Matt seemed to be catching on to her enthusiasm. It was the right time. Whale-watching cruises had become more and more popular. *The Big One* had been booked to eighty percent capacity last month and this month looked even better. The only reason they hadn't scheduled more trips was because Matt couldn't do it all alone.

"I think you're right." Matt nodded and tapped his pen against the schedule. "I know just the kind of trip that'll bring in more customers." He stopped tapping and raised his head. "But I don't know whether you'll go along with this—"

"I'm up for just about anything, short of turning this office into a bordello. Shoot. Give it to me."

"Well," he'd began, stretching his large frame, "the hotels that do nighttime harbor cruises never take out empty boats. Have you noticed? All they do is offer their passengers a couple of glasses of wine, show them a perfectly free, perfectly perfect sunset, then take them back in and everyone eats it up. They even pay seventy-five dollars for the privilege. That's thirty-five dollars more per person than what we get."

"So, what're you saying? That we should get into harbor cruises now and out of whale watching?"

"No, that's not where I'm going at all. If you could just keep quiet a minute, *Sistah,* I'll tell you."

"Oh, don't get your feathers in an uproar," Carrie yawned. "Just talk to me quick before I fall asleep on this table."

"I've been trying to tell you I think we should schedule that additional trip at sunset. Bring the *haoles* out to see the whales then, or even at night. There's nothing like seeing a humpback breach by full moonlight. And if you throw in a glass of champagne, make the tourists feel like the trip's special, we can add on another twenty to twenty-five bucks per head. At one-hundred percent capacity that's . . ." he multiplied quickly, "twelve hundred and fifty bucks more than we're making now, not counting the additional money from just putting on an extra trip."

Carrie listened closely. She had to admit Matt had a great idea, and, as far as she knew, none of the other whale-watching boats were doing it. It would be the perfect thing to bring the business out of the hole.

"Do you really think we need to serve drinks?"

Matt grinned. "I don't think a glass of champagne would do any harm."

"Maybe it would have been wiser for you to have come alone, Caryn."

Simone shifted the stack of magazines and books she was carrying to her other hip and looked up sharply at her daughter. They walked side by side down the long, sunlit passageway between the therapy center and the main house where the patients, including Alex, lived.

Terry McElroy, the center's director, had earned

worldwide recognition when he'd opened it only five years before. His unshakable beliefs in the combined powers of the mind, nutrition, and environment in healing the body had won him acclaim and undaunted support from his celebrity following. No "unsolvable" medical problem had defeated McElroy yet, and when he'd heard about Alex's accident and paralysis through the tightly knit island gossip network, McElroy himself had come directly to the hospital. At first, everyone, including Alex, was skeptical that the center's natural healing cures would work. Dr. Karachi had intervened, talking to McElroy for hours before allowing him to see Alex. After McElroy had left, Dr. Karachi, Alex, Simone, and Carrie had met for a somewhat emotional meeting, which resulted in the group basically agreeing that McElroy's techniques had not been accepted by the medical community. Dr. Karachi had suggested they forget about McElroy's offer for the time being.

Less than two weeks later, Carrie had followed Dr. Karachi's advice to put Alex in the Leilani Nursing Home, but only a week after his arrival, Alex's complaints had risen to sonic boom level.

"I'm not seventy-five years old with cancer of the colon or some other gross and disgusting disease!" he yelled at Carrie as she'd pushed his wheelchair down the hallway. "Get me the hell out of here!"

Beneath Alex's explosive anger, Carrie had heard the plea of a scared child. She'd sympathized but had felt like taping his mouth shut, as she would have been tempted to do to a mouthy teenager. It had seemed Alex had absolutely no pride then. He'd said whatever he wanted, whenever he wanted, no matter who he embarrassed.

That night, she'd remembered Terry McElroy's challenge. "Let me take Alex and work with him. You don't have to pay me a dime. Just let me prove I can get him up and moving again."

Carrie had to admit she'd lost her fantasy that Alex would ever walk again—he wouldn't even try to move his toes—but if the staff at McElroy's Center could at least teach Alex how to take care of himself and give him someone to talk to besides a 95-year-old roommate with Alzheimer's, then Carrie was all for it. If there was even the slightest chance McElroy's fantasmagorical cures could work, she wanted to take it. All she cared about was getting Alex back to some semblance of normality.

Although she dreaded the twice-weekly drive to the oceanfront center in Hilo, at least she was free to work on the cruises the other five days of the week. Now she only had to rely on Matt to cover the two afternoons she visited Alex, and she found she was actually beginning to see some benefits from her long hours at the office. She'd finally caught up with the truck payments, so she didn't have to worry about repossession anymore, and without the apartment rent to worry about, she'd been able to pay the office telephone bill. Her mother had urged Carrie to live with her, but it had seemed a half-hearted attempt, so Carrie had declined, knowing that her mother reveled in being able to go home to her quiet cottage, and to Jerry. Besides, she wasn't so sure the two of them could live together. Carrie really didn't want to have to tell her mother what time she was coming home, and she knew her mother would certainly ask!

Glancing back at her mother, Carrie considered taking some of the books Simone carried, but her own hands were full with the bowl of fruit Simone had insisted they take and some paperwork McElroy had asked her to fill out.

She kept an eye out for Dr. Karachi. He'd called the night before to make arrangements to meet her at the center. He wanted to keep a close eye on Alex, and Carrie suspected he was more than a little curious about the physical, mental, and nutritional therapies being used. The thought that Alex was being evaluated so soon after coming made Carrie nervous, which was why she'd asked Simone to come.

"What if the doctor wants Alex to go somewhere else for treatment?" she worried aloud. "How am I going to manage it? I'm already working *The Big One* so much I'm probably going to have to get the engine overhauled pretty soon. And I can't keep up with the bills as it is. If I have to move Alex again, they're going to want money . . ."

The women stopped in the open lobby, which led to the maze of therapy rooms, whirlpools, saunas, gardens, and offices that made up the heart of the center, the "healing heart," as McElroy's brochures described it. Soft guitar music floated through frangipani-scented air. None of the medical personnel wore white, and everyone seemed to sport a permanent smile, especially the receptionist. Carrie checked in with her about the conference rooms, then headed in the direction she pointed.

Without thinking, she put her hand on her mother's elbow, propelling Simone forward.

"Now, *chérie,*" Simone paused at the door, "whatever the doctor decides, we'll work it out."

"I'm tired of working it out." Carrie stalked into the conference room.

Less than fifteen minutes later, Carrie and Simone were back in the same hallway, but this time, they headed toward Alex's room. Carrie led the way with long, loping strides.

"Okay, mister." She stood, panting, beside Alex's bed. "What the hell is going on with you? I'm getting sick and tired of this noncooperative bullshit. If anyone ever treated you the way you're treating the people who've tried to help you in the past couple of months, you'd think they were the biggest jerks you'd ever met."

Alex's face paled, and he shifted his eyes to the side, stunned and unwilling, or unable, to defend himself.

"You know, I've really been kind of ashamed of you, Alex, and I haven't said anything because I felt sorry for you. Well, I don't feel a damn bit sorry for you now. You've just thrown your spoiled little boy trick once too often. Now, enough is enough. You'd better start acting like the old Alex . . . or . . . I'm not coming to see you anymore."

The threat lay heavy in the air between them.

Simone stepped forward and gingerly laid the stack of books and magazines she held on Alex's bed, then shot Carrie a questioning look. Alex looked at the pile, then blankly back at Carrie.

"You don't know what it's like," Alex said. "You don't know how I fe—"

"I know exactly how you feel—sorry for yourself. And it's damned unattractive."

Some of the color came back into Alex's cheeks. "I didn't ask for this. Don't come here if all you're going to do is yell at me."

Carrie gave a harsh laugh. "You've been yelling at anyone within earshot, but now that the tables are turned, you don't like it." She looked down at him and found tears welling in her eyes. "I can't stand to see you like this," she continued, more quietly. "The Alex I knew wasn't someone people would turn away from. You were never the type of person to start trouble, and you weren't the kind to give up. Or at least that's what I *thought.* Was I wrong?"

Simone watched them look at each other and saw the pain within Alex's rigidly held shoulders and hidden beneath the hurtful words Carrie spat. Her heart ached for both of them.

"Too much hurt," Simone murmured, as she tentatively stepped between them, shaking her head. "It's time to call a halt to all this pain. You two, my dearest children, you must look forward and become strong together. But instead of leaning on each other, you've been splitting apart." Knowing that she could make things worse if what she said was taken in the wrong way, Simone stroked Carrie's arm. "Caryn, *ma chérie,* you must court patience. Give Alex the time he needs to recover from this tragedy. I know it has been difficult for you, but you have the strength to handle this. You always have."

Then she turned to Alex. "And Alex, you must develop your own kind of patience and strength." She reached for his hand and squeezed it. "You must remember your love for your wife. And be optimistic. We must *all* be optimistic."

Simone reached for Carrie and pulled her over to Alex's bed. "Now kiss and make up. From what Dr. Karachi told us, Alex, it seems that whatever the clinic is doing is beginning to help you. I find that reason enough to celebrate, don't you?"

Although Carrie took Alex's cool, unresponsive hand, she didn't smile when she looked into his eyes, and neither did he.

Needing some time to think, Carrie took the long way home, heading south to Kalapana, riding along the edge of moss-green cliffs that fell straight down to black lava beaches. The ocean seemed bluer on this side of the island and the white froth of the waves whiter when washing against jet black sand. The smell of saltwater bit at her nose and pulled against the loose tendrils around her face. She didn't turn on the radio, preferring instead to just watch the road twist and turn in front of her. Fan palms framed the drive, bougainvillea and plumeria grew wild like a South American jungle, and ferns filled the spaces in between. This side of the island, with its rain forest and thick growth, was so different from the more arid Kona Coast. The thick air slowed her down, calmed her.

Without a word to Simone, Carrie found a place to pull off on the side of the road. She could see the tar-colored mounds where the most recent volcanic flow had stopped. She heard the hissing sound of the volcano's runoff spilling hazily into a boiling ocean. Without speaking, she got out and found a well-worn path which led down a steep walkway to a private beach. She and Alex had found this place three or four years ago and the memory of their lovemaking made her stomach quiver.

The waves thundered against the rim of black rocks that formed a tight cove like a protectively curving hand. Carrie strolled down the beach, letting the sound and smell of the ocean pound her, pummel her senses, until all she felt was a weightless emptiness. It always amazed her that this was the same ocean she saw every day in Kona. Its personality seemed different. Perhaps it was the black sand or the rock-protected cove, but whatever it was that made it so, she could feel it with every cell in her being.

She watched several joking fishermen carry their catch of the day up the other side of the cliff. They held the pole on their shoulders, balancing the fish between them. It struck her that Hawaiian fishermen still used the same techniques that their forebears had many centuries ago, and she remembered an old Hawaiian legend about a man named Kewalo.

Matt had told her the story the night of her high school graduation, after they'd shared a six-pack of beer and gotten beyond the giggling stage. She'd asked him why he never admitted going fishing, no matter how many times a day he'd head to the beach with a fishing pole over his shoulder. If she'd say, "Going fishing, Matt?" he'd say, "Nah, I'm just going to sit on the beach for a while." At first, she'd thought he just didn't want anyone to know where his favorite fishing spot was, but after a while, she began to wonder.

"Not rude, Carrie," he'd said seriously. "It's bad luck."

"What do you mean, bad luck?"

"Let me tell you the legend of Kewalo. You know Pélé, right?"

"Yes," Carrie answered, "the volcano goddess, the one your mother calls the Old Woman of the Pit."

"Well, she's got a brother named Kamohoali'i, and he takes the form of a shark. That's why you see a lot of my bruddahs with sharks' teeth around their necks. It's their *'aumakua*. You know, like a rabbit's foot or a guardian angel. Luck."

She'd nodded and urged him on.

"Kewalo was a man who lived near the sea. In his village, all the men went fishing almost every day. Kewalo used to wait for the men to walk past his door, and he'd ask them if they were going fishing. If they said yes, they wouldn't have good luck fishing and a shark would kill all or some of the men. If they said, 'We are going *holo holo'*—you know, just for a good time or a pleasure ride—they'd have great luck, catch lots of fish and no one would even *see* a shark.

"One day the villagers decided to find out if Kewalo had something to do with their bad luck, and they sent some of the guys to spy on him. Sure enough, Kewalo followed some fishermen down to the ocean, dove into the sea, turned into a shark, and ate all the fishermen. Since then, Hawaiians don't admit it if they're going fishing. It's bad luck."

Carrie appreciated the Hawaiians' rich, deep attachment to mythology and mystical powers and understood why Alex was so fascinated by their mystery. As soon as he heard the legend of Kewalo, he claimed he could see a lot of intelligence in the fishermen's reasoning. After that, he became more spontaneous, almost like the Hawaiians themselves. But Alex hadn't completely followed the Hawaiian philosophy or he wouldn't have had the patience to plan a wedding. He probably would have wanted to elope. And that would have ruined one of her fondest memories.

Still, Alex's philosophy had become "don't waste a moment." Most of the time, Carrie admitted, it was fun to be so impetuous, but she'd forgotten how to plan things, to prepare for unexpected tragedies. So had Alex.

Now she didn't know what he wanted to do. The tables had been turned completely. Instead of following Alex's serendipity, she was now left to lead the way, in an organized, methodical fashion. And, to make it worse, Alex didn't want to cooperate. Carrie's mouth squared shut, and she folded her arms over her chest. With both feet firmly sunk in the sand, she watched the horizon turn from crimson to violet, refusing to look anywhere else, or to move, until her anger subsided.

When she reluctantly climbed back to the top of the path, she found Simone pacing anxiously.

"I'm sorry I kept you waiting, *Maman*," Carrie stood on the path below her mother, looking up into Simone's face and seeing a look of such tender understanding that she instinctively reached out toward her mother.

They held each other tightly for a few moments without speaking, then Simone patted Carrie on the shoulder. No words passed between them, yet Carrie knew her mother sensed how she felt. Simone wouldn't push for discussion, Carrie knew. She'd wait for Carrie to come to her.

"We'd best be leaving, *ma chérie,*" Simone said, her voice tight. "I promised Jerry some Mexican food tonight."

On the short walk to the car, Carrie caught herself looking sideways at her mother, her wisdom giving a proud thrust to her chin. "I don't know where you get your energy, *Maman.* I just wish I'd inherited some of it. I could use it right now."

Simone laughed. "I take a lot of naps, *ma petite.* Catnaps. The secret to withstanding old age."

In bed later that night, the moonlight coming in her bedroom window to gently silhouette Jerry's sleeping form beside her, Simone thought back on that comment and summarily rejected the idea that she was becoming old.

No, what she felt was not old age, not with a man as agile and as deeply passionate as Jerry in her life. She sighed and felt contentment creep over her like warm velvet. I've been very lucky, she mused, fingers absentmindedly trailing her thigh, to have not one, but two men in my life. And they are so completely, totally different. *Mon Dieu,* not even one of their traits is like the other's.

Philip would surely have enjoyed a good Texan belly laugh had he discovered Simone's lover was a pale, shy Japanese man who spent more time making leis than discussing world economics, but the joke was on Philip. Jerry Kahala made Simone feel more sexually alive at fifty-one than she had in her mid-twenties, when she'd first met Philip.

She smiled in the dark and reached her hand out to hover half an inch above Jerry's body, close enough to feel his heat but not actually touching his skin. She felt the fine hairs on her arm rise, almost magically, to reach toward him. The tiny muscles in her pelvis vibrated and her breathing quickened.

If Jerry wasn't in a deep sleep, most of the time he could sense Simone's hand and would reach up to touch her. The touch would be shy at first, but Jerry's fingers had a language which grew more eloquent every time he stroked her skin. His caress was magnetic, all he had to do was point toward her and her body would automatically lean into his.

She held herself stiff and silent, sure that, this time, she'd be able to fool him.

But she couldn't.

And when he turned over, pressing his body firmly against hers and moving in slow, erotically circular motions, she didn't care that he'd won again.

She didn't care at all.

As they pressed their bodies together, Simone sighed and wrapped her legs around his strong, slim ones. She knew that she was a Rubens to him. He celebrated her compact voluptuousness, feasting on her body as if each move she made served only to heighten his desire.

Jerry traced the line of her spine, passing over the ticklish spot on her buttocks gently, knowing of her tenderness there. He'd get back to that later, she knew. With his tongue.

Simone sighed and laid back against the pillows, opening herself to him, inviting him into her arms. He nestled his head against her breasts and stretched out his tongue to flick gently at her distended nipples. She caught her breath and felt a ripple go through her body. Cradling his head in her hands, she let him love her until pulsations rippled through her body.

Blissfully, she began to drift off to sleep, one of her last thoughts in that haze between wakefulness and deep sleep a mother's worry for her only child. She cuddled into Jerry's back, winding her arm around his stomach.

No, she thought drowsily, the secret to withstanding old age is not the catnaps, it's what you do before the catnaps.

Ten

When Carrie arrived at the office, the phone was ringing and an inch-high stack of pink phone messages was thrust into her hand by a harried Matt. He told her Isaac was down with the flu and nothing was going right. He asked if she could take out the afternoon cruise. She agreed. The way Matt looked, he'd most likely feed the thirty tourists from Kyoto to the sharks.

She gulped down a cup of coffee and a candy bar before running to the boat. But she needn't have rushed for the Japanese passengers. None of them paid any attention to her rehearsed spiel, probably because they didn't understand a word she was saying, so she soon gave up, concentrating instead on sounding for whales and pointing the tourists in the right direction when she spotted the gentle giants.

By the time she got *The Big One* back into dock, she had lost her voice. Heading straight for the office and a hot shower, she was stopped three times—once by Mark Hyman, the harbormaster, who wanted his rent; then by Jimmy Alakua, who wanted to know if she could give his son a summer job; and the third time, she practically ran over an insipid reporter for the local paper who'd been bugging her to let him do a human interest story on Alex. By that time, she'd lost her patience.

"I don't think Alex wants anyone to pity him," she snapped as she continued walking toward the office where she could see her mother frantically waving at her to come to the phone.

"But, Ms. Madison, think of what it would do for business."

"If that's the way to get business, I'll close down tomorrow." She paused a moment and looked down at him. She wanted more than anything to forget about life for a little while, but people like this reporter kept her aware of how close to the razor's edge she had come. Sometimes the smallest decision, like whether to buy a Coke or an iced tea, had her in a panic. She could handle the big problems, the fact that Alex might never walk again or deciding whether to claim bankruptcy, but the insignificant things were blowing her mind.

"So, can you at least answer that question for me, Ms. Madison?" The reporter looked up at her expectantly.

"I'm sorry. What did you say?"

The man's expression turned cold. Although he kept a smile on his lips, his eyes narrowed. "Never mind," he said, flipping his notebook closed and walking away. "I'll catch you some other time."

"Good riddance." Carrie didn't bother to lower her voice. Still muttering when she reached the office, she waved to her mother sitting at the desk and to Matt, who was on the phone, then headed directly to the back room to take a shower.

"Who was on the phone for me?" she asked her mother as she flew by.

"Just another bill collector. I saw you out there looking disgusted with that reporter and thought you might like some diversion."

Her mother handled the office well. The desk was now so organized Carrie could instantly put her hands on anything she needed. Simone's impeccable phone personality, as well as her calm and efficient manner, had actually boosted *The Big One*'s business. None of the other whale-watching cruises could boast a French-speaking reservationist. The Canadian tourists loved being able to speak to someone who understood their language. Carrie had to laugh when she realized one of the reasons she was getting more calls from the hotels was simply because their people liked talking to Simone. One of them had reportedly said, "She's like talking to royalty. A real class act."

"You had someone here looking for you this morning," her mother called through the open door to the back room where Carrie was peeling off her sweaty T-shirt.

"Another bill collector?"

"No, but he didn't know your name, so he wasn't a friend either. He said he was looking for the owner of *The Winsome Blonde.*"

"Probably someone who'd seen the ad. Did you tell him it was sold?"

"No, *chérie,* I did not. I do not think he wanted to buy the boat. He just wanted to see you."

Carrie paused, her leg in mid-air, her shorts hanging from her toes. "What did he look like?"

"Oh, let me see if I can remember. . . . Ah, oui,

he had dark hair, very dark and . . . yes . . . bright green eyes. Very attractive man, as a matter of fact."

"He's one of those Greenpeace guys I told you about. Matt, remember the last time I took out the—"

"Yeah, you told me," Matt answered, hanging up the phone. "If he had mentioned Greenpeace, I would've put two and two together, but the dude kept asking questions, so your mother and I just sort of played it safe."

"What do you mean?" Carrie came to the doorway wrapped in a white terrycloth robe that was up to her calves, about five inches too short for her, as was just about everything else she owned. She pulled at its hem and watched the silent interchange between Matt and her mother. "Okay, what's going on, you two? What aren't we saying here?"

Matt grinned sheepishly. "We told him we didn't know where you were or how long you'd be."

Carrie considered what he said for a moment, then shrugged her shoulders. "Doesn't matter. He probably just wanted to thank me again or something." She ducked into the back room and headed for the shower.

Although she tried to get her mind back on what she had scheduled for the rest of the day, she found herself wondering whether Jack Briskin would ever pay her another visit.

Matt caught Simone's eye after Carrie disappeared. They raised their eyebrows in a silent, simultaneous look of surprise.

What do I know? Matt thought. Carrie's been weird about everything lately.

Thankfully, he didn't have to say anything. After Simone had briefed Carrie on her schedule for the rest of the day, as well as the rest of the calls, she left Matt and Carrie alone so they could take out the last cruise.

Carrie and Matt were so busy the rest of the day, they barely spoke to each other. The afternoon cruise was even larger than the morning one, and Matt scrambled to keep several very active children from falling overboard. After they docked, he stayed behind to put the boat to bed while Carrie headed back to the office.

It was getting late, and he still had plenty to do before heading home. He had promised himself to relax and watch the baseball exhibition game on cable that night, had already bought his beer in fact, and since Isaac professed to feeling better the last time Matt called, he promised to bring home a pizza. With everyone else in the house down with the flu, they'd be able to commandeer the remote control to the television, and maybe they would get back some of the camaraderie that had been missing from their relationship.

He held one hand flat over his belly button and groaned as another wave of nausea crept over him. He hoped the rumbling in his stomach meant he was just hungry and not coming down with the same bug as the rest of the family.

God, just let me get through tonight, he prayed, and make Isaac better enough so he can take my place tomorrow.

By the time Carrie was ready to leave the office, dinnertime had come and gone, the sun had set, and

the harbor lay silent except for the distant clanging
of a bell buoy. Turning to lock the door, she mentally
ran over her list of things she had to do at her
mother's, where she was headed for a cold late dinner
before returning to the office to collapse on the cot
she had set up in the back room.

She carried her keys in her left hand, jingling them
absentmindedly as she walked to the truck in a daze.
Lately it seemed her mind refused to work after 9
P.M., almost a protective mechanism. She was fighting
a yawn when a dark, tall figure stepped out of the
shadows beside the truck. She jumped, dropping both
her keys and the pile of work she was holding.

"You're really in another place," the man said as
he stepped closer. "What's the daydream about? Must
be a good one. You didn't even hear me say hello."

Something about the deep, gravelly voice made
Carrie pause in recognition. He came into the light,
the skipper of the Greenpeace boat.

"Well, we meet again, Captain Briskin." Carrie
bent to pick up her belongings, a perfect excuse to
hide the unexpected grin on her face. "I hear you
came to my office this afternoon. Having trouble with
the Ocean Fresh boat again? Need Wonder Woman's
help?"

His rumbling chuckle matched the appreciative
glint in his eye. "It's Jack, and no, I really just wanted
to thank you, but I never got your name. And when
I found your boat, it didn't belong to a long-legged
blonde anymore but to a rather dowdy insurance bro-
ker from Cincinnati. I began to doubt we'd actually
met."

Now it was Carrie's turn to chuckle. "I suppose

you're going to say something now about mermaid myths."

"As a matter of fact, the thought did cross my mind." Jack passed her the notepad he'd picked up and smiled. He had the brightest eyes. Even in the dim harbor light, they seemed to sparkle with some barely contained excitement, like a pirate's or a devil-may-care explorer's.

"I'd be satisfied just to know your name so when I tell my story about the mysterious woman single-handedly saving an ocean full of dolphins, at least my grandchildren will know Wonder Woman really exists."

Carrie opened the truck's door and threw her stuff on the seat, stalling a little so she could decide whether or not to tell him her name. In a way, she felt uneasy, sure he'd find out that one of the reasons she'd joined his battle so readily was that he'd been fighting her father's company. Would Jack understand?

She'd written to her father about the incident, haranguing him once again about his responsibility to make sure his boats obeyed the laws. But she hadn't sent the letter. In fact, the fourth draft was in her purse, stuck in the notepad Jack had just picked up and handed to her.

"My name is Carrie," she finally replied. "Carrie Madison. I own *The Big One* whale-watching cruises, as you know, and I no longer own *The Winsome Blonde,* which you also know."

Jack held out his hand and they shook formally, almost soberly, like two business acquaintances.

"Nice to meet you, Carrie Madison."

She pulled her hand away and nervously glanced

at her watch. "Listen, I'm sorry, but I'm late. I promised my mother I'd come over for dinner." She climbed into the truck and swung the door closed.

"Maybe we can have coffee someday, and you can tell me about your whale watches. And I'll tell you how I feel about them."

Starting up the engine, Carrie leaned out the window. "I can imagine how you feel, Mr. Briskin, but before you say anything, let me assure you, my husband has always made sure our cruises educate the public and that they don't upset the whales or the environment . . ."

"Husband?"

Carrie could swear Jack sounded disappointed. "Yes, Alex Madison. You might know him. He's done a lot of research on whales and dolphins and—"

"No, I don't. And it's Jack, remember?" He stepped back as she put the truck into gear. "But maybe I'll meet him someday."

"Maybe . . . when he gets out of the hospital," Carrie called as she drove out of the parking lot with a flippant wave.

All the way to her mother's house, she berated herself for being so short with him. He was just trying to be friendly. What made her think he was coming on to her?

Horniness, she decided. I haven't been to bed with a man for a couple of months and I miss it. Lord, what was it like for women during the war years? They had to go without a husband for a lot longer than a couple of months.

"Yeah," she said aloud as she turned up the hill toward Simone's. Alex wasn't thousands of miles away, but he might as well have been for the gulf between them seemed nearly that wide.

The door slammed, waking Matt from a dream about surfing in Australia. "This better be good," he muttered, lifting himself to a sitting position on the couch.

"Hey, *Br'a,* what you still doing up?" Isaac strutted into the room, the smell of beer wafting in before him.

"Waiting for you." Matt leaned back against the couch, rubbing his stomach. The pizza he'd eaten all by himself three hours ago lay heavily on his stomach. The flu must have settled in while he was asleep. "Thought you were sick. Did you go out?"

"Yeah, I did. Why? You my mother now or something? I ain't your *keiki.* Don't treat me like one."

"I don't want to be your mother, little brother, I want you to take responsibility for yourself. Like, if you have a job, you have to show up for it. Don't get me to do it for you because you're sick, then go out and party all night."

"Hey, man, what am I supposed to do? I'm almost eighteen. Grown. A *kahuna.*" Isaac swayed a little and put his hand out to steady himself.

"Some *kahuna.* You can't even stand up straight. You've been drinking, haven't you?"

"And you never did when you were in school?"

"That doesn't have anything to do with it. I asked you a question."

"Well, I ain't going to answer it."

Matt took a deep breath and waited a moment for the rumbling in his stomach to subside before he answered. "I think you'd better," he said, his voice low and ominous.

"Fuck you!" Isaac brushed past and headed for his bedroom. "And you can tell your blond boss I ain't coming to work no more."

Matt lurched to his feet, anger propelling him. He reached Isaac just as he was about to close the door to his room. For a moment, they struggled. Isaac seemed amazed that Matt had come after him, and terrified. Although Matt usually was the calm, sensible one in the family, when he had had enough, anyone in the way better watch out.

"Open the door, Isaac, or I'll tear it off its hinges," Matt growled.

Immediately, the door flew open. Matt reached out with one arm and pulled Isaac off the floor by his shirt.

"I'm done running around trying to take care of you," he said, his face less than half an inch from Isaac's. "You've been Mama's baby long enough. Now it's my turn. And I agree, you ain't no baby, *Bruddah*. Now you either straighten up, go to work, quit partying, and get back into your studies again or you'll have to answer to me. Get it?"

He let go of Isaac's shirt and the boy thudded to the floor. He appeared suddenly sober. A look of resignation passed over his eyes and, with it, a curtain, which seemed designed to keep Matt at a distance.

"So, do we have a deal?" Matt asked. "Are you going to clean up your act?"

Isaac nodded, and Matt felt his resentment. So be it, he thought. I'm sick of babysitting this boy.

He turned to walk away, with the uneasy feeling that his problems with Isaac had only just begun.

Eleven

It's surprising sometimes how in tune mothers can be with their daughters, Simone thought, but then again, Caryn tends to be so transparent that it really isn't difficult to figure her out.

Rounding the driveway into the Waimea Gallery parking lot, Simone found herself relieved she didn't have to work with her daughter today. It would have been hard to conceal that she knew Caryn was attracted to that Greenpeace activist. Despite Simone's French Catholic upbringing and her intense distaste for infidelity, she was not surprised that something like this was happening. But she also knew instinctively that Caryn would fight the attraction and suffer from overwhelming guilt. Simone felt sure her daughter's sensibilities would keep her on the right track.

The gallery's holdings had changed since the week before, Simone noticed immediately after walking in the door. One of the dolphin sculpture tables was missing—that must have been a nice commission for Monique, she thought—and Warren Maitland had brought in some new work: a light-filled landscape of a Kauai valley and another in his series of surfer portraits. When Maitland had first approached the gallery about selling the portraits, Simone had predicted they'd be the laughingstock among Hawaii's art galleries, but she'd been delighted when proven wrong. Three of his paintings of sun-bleached and tanned gods of the beach had sold during the first two weeks, and every time Maitland brought in new ones, they left the shop equally as quickly. It was almost as though the paintings never hung on the gallery's walls for more than a couple of days before disappearing.

As she walked to the office to store her handbag, the phone rang.

"Aloha! This is the Waimea Bay Art Gallery. How can I help you?"

Although the letter had been in Carrie's hands for the past fifteen minutes, she still hadn't done anything except stare at it. Outside her office she heard indistinct grumbling rising above the blaring rap music Isaac habitually played whenever he was working. That could only mean one thing, once again Isaac wasn't happy with the work Matt had assigned him.

"If you two knuckleheads don't cut it out, I'm going to take both of you up to Kilauea and dump you in." As she spoke, she walked outside and shook her finger at the two brothers. "Pele will deal with listening to you both bitching and moaning. Honestly, if I didn't know better, I'd swear you were married."

Isaac tittered. Matt shot him a dirty look, then turned back to Carrie and said, "I *never* heard you and Alex argue and you're married. Arguing's got nothing to do with being married and vice vers—"

"Come to the center. You'll hear us arguing!"

She'd tried to become immune to her husband's constant complaints, but she dreaded each visit. A week or two before, she'd still clung to a thread of hope that, sooner or later, Alex would come out of it, make some effort to be human again. But even McElroy was beginning to lose hope. Alex had no interest in physical therapy, thought the center's water therapy breakthroughs were a joke, and made sure he broke every nutrition rule his team of doctors set up.

"He's impossible," Dr. Karachi said the last time Carrie had seen him. "He's resigned himself to the fact that he's going to be an invalid for the rest of his life. I'm afraid even McElroy's Center hasn't found a cure for a broken spirit."

Unfortunately, thought Carrie, Alexander William Madison was not the only person whose spirit had been broken in the past couple of months. She saw dispirited people all around her, including the one who looked back from her mirror every morning. She felt incredibly guilty for hating Alex for giving up, for putting so much stress on her mother and Matt— and on herself—but she couldn't help herself. If anyone had put this situation in front of her in a hypothetical fashion several months ago, she would've guessed Alex would beat all the odds. The thought that he'd given up disappointed her incredibly.

With a sigh, she winked at Matt. "Don't worry, *Bruddah,* something's got to go right." She gave him the *shakah* salute, the surfer's thumbs up that meant all was well, then disappeared back into her office.

The letter to her father lay on the desk where she'd left it.

"What better place to send my anger," she muttered

as she raised her pen and edited the last line for the tenth time.

Half an hour before her afternoon whale watch, Carrie finished the letter, now a whopping seven pages, and balanced its hefty weight in her palm, fighting a last-minute urge to rip it up and toss it in the bucket. She'd pulled out all the stops this time, withholding nothing, making sure her father knew just how illegal, improper, and utterly unconscionable his actions were. She planned to mail the letter to him at his office address rather than at home. Gives it more weight, more importance, she thought. Besides, this way, she'd be sure he'd read it. His secretary would make sure of that.

If the letter went to his house, his new wife, whose name she couldn't remember, would probably suffer a curiosity attack and open it. Once she'd read the scathing names Carrie had called her father, once she'd read the in-depth description of what had happened the day Carrie had helped the Greenpeace boat, once she'd realized that the politics of the whole miserable situation went far beyond familial ties, well, what would the poor beauty queen do? Would she show Philip the letter? Would she hide it, hoping it would cause an even bigger rift between her husband and his daughter? Or would she burn it and deny it had ever existed?

Whatever the options, Carrie had to be sure that this time Philip DeBary would be thoroughly and violently chastised for destroying thousands of the world's most intelligent and peaceful mammals for absolutely no reason. Except money. The Almighty Buck.

Carrie slammed her palm down on the stamp one more time, then stalked to the mailbox and didn't hesitate a millisecond before dropping the letter in.

"Let's see you explain away this one, Mr. DeBary," she said to the mailbox, giving it a cocky little salute.

"Boy, first I catch you in Never-Never Land, now you're talking to mailboxes. I think you've been working too hard, Carrie Madison."

Carrie whirled to face Jack Briskin. God, had he heard her mention the DeBary name?

"You do seem to catch me at funny times, don't you?" She backed off a bit and looked down at her bare feet. For some strange reason, she was suddenly aware that her T-shirt had a hole in it and her cutoff jeans weren't fit to be worn in the shower, never mind in public.

Jack's left eyebrow lifted quizzically. He looked as though her reaction had made him forget what he was going to say. In an open-collared white polo shirt and khaki shorts, he looked more the wealthy tourist than the passionate activist. Behind the radical exterior she could sense someone comfortable with money. That revelation completely surprised her, but she stored it for later. "I'm signed up for your cruise," he said.

"The four o'clock?"

"Yeah. That okay?"

"Sure. We take anyone. I mean, we give—"

"There you go again." Walking toward her as naturally as if they'd been best buddies since kindergarten, Jack patted her shoulder and smiled into her eyes. "Now don't get nervous. I promise I won't point your skipper in the wrong direction or anything. I just had the day off and . . . well, figured it wouldn't hurt to be a tourist. Just for one day. See what it's like, y'know."

Why were her knees like Jell-O? She heard Matt yell for her and bolted toward the sound. Great timing, Matt, ol' boy, she thought. I could kiss you.

"What is it?" she asked as soon as she reached the office. Matt paced in front of the building, his square face ominously red.

"You tell her, Isaac," Matt spat.

The teenager bobbed his head from side to side and shuffled his feet. "It's your fault, too," he whined.

"C'mon guys, I've got a cruise boarding in fifteen minutes and no one's at the boat," Carrie said.

"I didn't get the ads in for the evening cruises," Isaac spoke quickly, like a little boy.

"I gave those ads to you three days ago! I told you to take them directly to the newspaper office."

Matt's arms fell to his sides. "Oh, now I get it. That was the night of the big date. You lost the envelope, didn't you?"

"Okay, guys, that's enough." Carrie stepped between the two of them. "Now, do you think we can take a group of people on a nice cruise?"

"I'm not going anywhere with him," Isaac began to walk away, watching Matt warily over his shoulder. "I ain't going anywhere with you, *Bruddah!*" His voice grew louder, more confident, with each step he took. "No more pushin' me around, man. You think you're the big *kahuna,* but you ain't nothin', man."

Carrie expected Matt to go after his brother one more time, but behind her, Matt snorted and said wearily, "Let him go. He just makes more work for me anyway."

"Are you sure we'll be able to do the cruise alone?" she asked. "We've got forty-two people signed up. That's almost our maximum."

"We've done it before."

"And if you need any help, I've been around a few boats in my time," Jack chimed in. He stepped forward and offered Matt his hand. "We met the other day. I'm Jack Briskin."

"Yeah, the Greenpeace guy." Matt eyed Jack, then his glance flickered over to Carrie as if waiting for her to make the decision.

"Thanks, Jack," she said as nonchalantly as she could manage. "An extra hand is always welcome, but Matt and I have a system. I think we can manage the boat itself, but if you want to entertain the passengers, feel free . . ."

"To pass out Greenpeace literature and tell them how backward the United States is when it comes to taking care of the environment?" Jack's eyes twinkled.

"You know how I feel about the whales," she responded. "Just don't go rustling the cattle so much that they stampede."

She headed for *The Big One* and motioned for both of them to follow.

"Yeah, we need all the business we can get," Matt added.

"Has it been slow?"

"Not exactly," Carrie said over her shoulder without breaking pace. "We've just had a pretty bad year."

"With your husband in the hospital?"

"Umm-hmmm." She boarded the boat and headed straight for the cabin. Jack followed her in and gave a low whistle.

"You've got more sonar in here than we do on the *Warrior.*"

"I have to know where the whales are. No whales equals no business."

"What did you do, hit a sale at the sonar factory?" He touched one view screen, then followed the blip on another, as fascinated as an adolescent with a new Nintendo game.

One by one, Carrie turned on each piece of her equipment, testing the computers quickly, though the boat had just gone out that morning.

"Alex, my husband, was a bit of an electronics freak. Most of this he built himself, but some of it came when we bought the business."

"Whatever made you get into this?"

"Love," Carrie answered. "We love the ocean, the dolphins and sea turtles, the whales, and Hawaii itself. We love the reverence everyone has for the sea. When we heard this boat was for sale, it seemed the best way to put it all together."

The boat rocked gently as the passengers began to board. Through the side porthole, Carrie saw Matt watching her curiously. She flashed him a confident you're-too-suspicious smile. He grinned back and shook his head.

Jack stayed beside her, asking questions and listening intently to her answers until all of the passengers were aboard and *The Big One* was heading slowly out of Honokohau Harbor. When he left the cabin to mingle with the tourists on deck, Carrie felt her shoulder muscles relax. Until then she hadn't realized she'd been holding herself so rigidly. Once again she reminded herself that Jack Briskin had committed no improprieties, had not come on to her in any way, and that her imagination, not Jack's, was going to be what got her into trouble.

Before they even left the harbor, a humpback cow and her calf circled the boat several times, passing underneath it and blowing when they were close by, giving the passengers a show. Carrie smiled. It was good luck to see the humpbacks so close to shore. The whales, as always, seemed to respond to the yelling, laughing, and clapping as freely as curious puppies.

Matt had his hands full, Carrie could see. Several of the passengers were leaning precariously over the side railings trying to touch the giant mammals. They didn't seem to understand that if they fell into the ocean, the whales could easily crush them against the boat, or worse.

Carrie signaled to Jack, got his attention, then pointed to Matt, pantomiming that he should help Matt restrain the more rambunctious members of the group. Jack gave her the high sign and moved over to them, talking and smiling as he went. Within moments, the group clustered around him, listening.

Carrie spent the next hour doing her own job, sounding for whales, then navigating the boat within viewing distance. Every so often, she found herself checking the decks for Jack's dark curly head, and every time she spotted him, he was deep in conversation with one of the passengers. Well, she thought, at least none of them have jumped ship. For the first time in weeks she found she was enjoying the cruise instead of simply waiting to get back to dock so that she could catch up on the pile of paperwork awaiting her in the office.

When the trip was over and the boat heading back to harbor, a peaceful pause settled over their group of passengers, as often was the case.

Matt glanced into the cabin and caught Carrie looking at him. He waved in her direction and she waved back.

With Jack beside him he moved on, getting into place to help the passengers disembark. It was noisier now, people were sharing memories of what they'd seen and were ready to get on to the next part of their vacations. For the next fifteen minutes, Matt, Carrie, and Jack were kept too busy to speak to each other, but Matt surreptitiously watched Jack, impressed by the fact that he pitched in even when he wasn't asked to. The job was a lot easier when three people worked together.

When Carrie stepped onto the dock, clipboard in hand, the two men were making plans to go out for a beer like old friends.

"How about a cold one, Carrie?" Matt asked as the three of them walked back to the office. "You've put in a long day. Time to relax. What you think, *Sistah?*"

"No, I really can't. I have some reports to do, then the schedule for next week and—"

"Isn't Simone coming in tomorrow?"

"Well, yes, but . . ."

Matt firmly took the clipboard out of her hand and

threw it on the desk, then he grabbed one arm and motioned to Jack to grab her other one. "Consider yourself shanghaied, Boss Lady. You need a Bud."

"Okay, okay," she squealed, her feet barely touching the ground. "But I don't want a Bud."

"Then what?"

"A Mich Lite."

Jack groaned and Matt roared with laughter. "Watch out, man. She'll drink us under the table. I've never seen anyone guzzle beer the way she does."

"Ha! No one outdrinks an old sailor like me."

Carrie stood in front of them, hands on her hips. "You don't think I can do it because I'm a woman, right?"

"No, no, no," Jack answered, shaking his head. "That's not it at all."

"Ho, Ho!" Matt teased. "How you gettin' out of this one?"

Jack's green eyes took on that special spark as he turned back to Carrie. "Guess we're just going to have to make an old-fashioned bet, aren't we?"

"What's the bet?" Carrie asked with a grin.

"You drink us under the table, and I'll donate my services for . . . well, let's say the weekend."

Carrie and Matt exchanged conspiratorial glances. "You're on," they said in unison.

Twelve

The morning light seemed to inflate the blue and white skies above her. Simone was glad she'd chosen to walk to the harbor. She enjoyed feeling the strength in her legs and the crisp morning air flowing through her lungs. Her years of t'ai chi had taught her how to breathe deeply and fully, and the ebb and flow of that concentrated energy to her muscles always made her feel refreshed and relaxed.

When she reached Carrie's office, she felt like continuing, savoring the brilliant morning sunshine, walking until she had no more strength in her legs. It was with a deep, heartfelt sense of regret that she put her key in the door.

Usually, Simone opened the office in the morning, put a pot of coffee on, complete with her special dab of cinnamon, then went into the back room to wake Caryn.

It was 8:30 now, and none of the office lights were lit.

"Caryn! It's late! Our first passengers will be here in less than an hour!" Simone flicked on all of the lights. It took only a few seconds for her to assess the condition of the office and pronounce sentence upon the two men sprawled in the desk chairs. A stale smell of liquor made her wrinkle her nose.

"Mon Dieu! What in the world has happened here?" She grabbed the smallest telephone book and smacked Matt's bare feet off the desk. "Matthew Kamehea! What would your mother say if she saw you like this? I'm ashamed of you! Caryn! *CARYN!* Come out here *tout de suite!"*

Carrie poked her head through the doorway and peered sleepily at her mother. "What's up? What's all the noise about?"

Simone pointed wordlessly at Matt, who sat slumped in the chair, groggily rubbing his feet. On the other side of the desk, Jack lounged, his feet propped on the desk, too, one arm draped over his face, the other over the side of his chair. A loud snore escaped his half-open mouth.

Carrie giggled, then stifled it, looking guiltily at her astonished mother. Suddenly, Simone caught on. She looked from Matt to Jack to Carrie, then back again and shook her head.

"You've done it again, haven't you, Caryn?"

Carrie grinned sheepishly. "You know I can't turn down a challenge."

"But, *ma chérie,* can't you have a little pride?" Simone groaned almost simultaneously with Jack, who lifted a hand to his forehead and opened one bloodshot eye.

Without moving his head, he looked around the room. "Where am I? No, never mind, don't answer. Don't think I could stand the noise."

Clucking all the while, Simone bustled over to the coffeepot. When she placed the first cup in front of

Matt, he sniffed, then stumbled out the front door. Jack simply disappeared into the bathroom after receiving his cup, but Carrie accepted hers with her eyes still only half open.

Simone watched her daughter drain the whole cup, then reach for a refill. As she poured it, Simone shook her head, then her shoulders began to shake with silent laughter that finally found its way up and out of her mouth. Carrie paused, her coffee cup still halfway to her lips.

"What's so funny?" she asked.

"Never in all my years would I have imagined I'd have a strong, foul-mouthed sailor of a daughter who could swim with the dolphins and drink like a fish. But, I must admit, it certainly has been more fun than raising the debutante your father expected you to be."

"Why, Mother," Carrie said indignantly, raising herself to her full, haughty, Amazonian height. "I have no idea what you're talking about."

From the back room, the toilet flushed, then a door slammed, and the two women looked at each other in mock surprise before joining in raucous guffaws.

Lunch had been simple, a milkshake and a well-done hamburger. Anything else would have made him sick, Matt thought. Any more and he definitely would have been of no use on this afternoon's trip. Slowly and carefully, he scanned the dock, then turned his head to the side until Jack came into view. Both men had already assured each other they would not soon repeat last night. And both had agreed that Carrie Madison must have some magical blood in her veins.

Not only had she outdrunk them almost two drinks to one, but the witch had had the gall to wake up this morning with scarcely a trace of a hangover. It just wasn't fair.

Matt took a deep breath of sea air and leaned his head back against the wall. He sat against the harbor's main office building, his thick legs stretched out in front of him, his eyes closed against the midday sun. If no one bothered him, within a few moments, he'd be sound asleep.

Beside him, Jack Briskin imitated Matt's pose, even to the point of softly snoring through a partially open mouth. The guy was all right, Matt had conceded. At least from what he could remember of the previous evening. He hadn't tried anything on Carrie, he knew that much. And it didn't look like he was going to either.

At least not today.

Carrie carefully navigated *The Big One* out of the harbor, consciously keeping one eye on her crew, Matt and Jack. Isaac hadn't shown up that morning and she'd found herself worried about him. But she didn't say anything to Matt. He probably wouldn't have the energy to deal with it anyway. She had, however, called Matt's mother to check on Isaac. Auntie Pudding had seemed nonplussed by the fact that neither of the boys had made it home the night before.

"Nice and quiet here last night," she had said. "Both my *keikis* got so *huhu*. Too angry, my children. Good for them to cool down a while. They'll come home when they're ready. Maybe it's better they don't see each other for a while."

Carrie had to admit Auntie Pudding was probably right. She knew her sons well and dealt with them in the traditionally relaxed way most Hawaiian women dealt with their men. And, maybe, as Simone had pointed out, Pudding was just a little tired of the constant bickering that had filled her tiny house. Carrie couldn't blame her for wanting some peace and quiet. With eight kids, silence was a rare commodity.

This morning's trip was a light one, only eighteen passengers on board. Thank God, Carrie thought. Jack and Matt don't look like they could handle any more than this.

She had wondered why Jack had come back today, after a quick trip to the house he shared with several other Greenpeace workers. He had showered, shaved, changed, and showed up at her office less than an hour later, explaining that he knew Isaac wasn't going to be around and hoped he could help. She didn't argue with him. Actually, she enjoyed Jack's company more than she wanted to admit, hangover or not.

Last night, before they'd had so many beers that conversation didn't make sense, he had shared his life story with her and Matt, and it was an interesting one. She thought about him now as she watched him joke with Matt on deck.

Although she had seen no evidence of it yet, Jack constantly made reference to his dark temper, inherited from his mother and honed to perfection on the streets of Los Angeles. He'd grown up there, on a hill overlooking Sunset Boulevard, part of a close family with one older sister, a younger brother, and a father who worked as a bus driver. He told her stories about finding foxes in his backyard and an owl who nested in one of the trees on the street. Later, he began to wonder how they managed to exist in such a well-developed area. When he realized that humans had pushed the animals out of their natural habitat and that the animals had simply adapted, he was amazed.

Memories like that had triggered his interest in the environment. Although he'd started UCLA with the goal of getting a degree in philosophy, he said, "I was more interested in going to the Greenpeace meetings which were held in the basement of one of the older dorms on campus."

By their third beer, Jack had waxed eloquent as he described devoting more and more of his time to fighting what he called "the good clean fight."

Carrie had agreed with him. Perhaps that was part of the reason she wanted to know more about him. In a lot of ways, his passions were Alex's passions, and Alex's passions were hers. But Jack Briskin— John Andrew Briskin—was deeper than Alex, more multifaceted. His way of dealing with people had an edge to it which Alex's did not. He got into the thick of things, travelling to Alaska to stand in the way of fur exporters who clubbed baby harp seals to death, to Japan when talks about international fishing rights began, to France to stop a freighter carrying irradiated fuel elements from Japan's nuclear reactors. Jack's was a dangerous life, an existence totally devoted to righting the wrongs of the world.

Alex's concerns were more localized. He cared about the ocean's inhabitants but wanted to take care of them one-on-one, to learn about them by living with them, by trying to teach them. Yes, the seine nets infuriated him, and he'd often jumped into the ocean to save the mammals caught in them, but angry as he was, he wouldn't pit himself against the giant corporations Greenpeace took on. And he didn't always agree with the radical approaches Greenpeace sometimes took.

Forcing herself to pay attention to what she was doing, Carrie let the wheel slip through her fingers and listened to the bleep-bleep-bleep of her instruments.

In the distance, she saw several adult humpbacks breaching, then slapping their huge tails against the ocean's surface. She reached for her binoculars and focused on them, recognizing one of them as a regular by the distinctive white splotches on his flukes. Then she checked her watch and realized there was not enough time left to head out further to check the whales out. The cruise was almost over, and if she took one more loop around the general area, it'd be time to head back in. Picking up the microphone, she called Matt to the bridge.

"Let's get ready to head back to dock," she said when he poked his head into the cabin. "We've got a lot to do before this afternoon's cruise."

"Aren't you going to see Alex today?"

Carrie raised her eyebrows. She'd completely forgotten today was Wednesday. "Do you think you and Jack can take over?"

Matt grunted sarcastically. "What do you think?"

"I don't think you'll have any problem at all," she answered. "But you'd better ask Jack if he wants to do it."

Matt headed back out on deck.

"Tell him I can't pay him," Carrie called after his retreating back.

By the time they reached harbor, Jack had agreed to the afternoon's work. "I've got a few days off and this is fun," he'd assured her. "Just don't plan on me being here next week. I've got to go to Peru for a conference."

Perhaps it's just as well he's going away, Carrie thought. I could get used to this.

Simone had spent the morning cleaning the office, leaving all the doors and windows open to air out the stale beer smell which had permeated the small room. Between sweeping the floor and cleaning the windows, she was kept busy enough that she hardly realized two hours had gone by until she glanced at the clock on the wall. Again, the phone rang, as it had so many times already.

"Can I speak to Carrie Madison?" Philip asked.

"She's not here right now, Philip," Simone answered.

"Simone?"

"Oui, I am caring for the office for a while."

"Oh." Philip sounded disappointed and frustrated. "When will she be back?"

"She's out on a trip right now . . ." she looked at the clock, then at the schedule, "but she should be back in about half an hour."

Silence.

"Philip? Can I have her call you?"

"Did she tell you about the letter she wrote me?"

Simone gripped the phone a little tighter. "What letter?"

"The one about Ocean Fresh and the boat she stopped from laying seine nets off the Kona Coast."

Although Simone knew she shouldn't get involved, she heard the brittle tone in Philip's voice and felt she should make some sort of comment. "I knew about the boat. I didn't know she had written to you."

He sighed. "Why is she always so angry, Simone? Why can't she understand I'm not an ogre? Doesn't she know I love her?"

"Ah, Philip, you are asking me questions I cannot answer."

"I guess I am."

Simone heard rustling and realized Philip must be in his penthouse office in the DeBary Building, which housed most of his Houston corporations. Although she had rarely visited him there, she vividly remembered the pathetically amateurish modern art and sculptures the interior decorator had chosen for the room. If not for the spectacular view, the office would have been one of the starkest she'd ever been in.

"I really want to talk to her, Simone," Philip continued. "But I'm headed out right now and I won't be back for a couple of days. Do you think you could tell her I called and have her call me on Thursday?"

"Perhaps you should just call back when you're available," Simone offered. "I can no longer act as your intermediary."

"I guess you're right. I just don't understand her. I mean, she's my daughter and all, but we're about as different as a chicken and a swan." Philip gave a short laugh. Simone imagined him nodding his head and running his manicured fingers through his gray-tinged copper hair.

"Not quite," she answered. "After all, you both have the habit of sticking with your beliefs."

And so many other similarities, she thought. He'd had a wildcat reputation through school, just as Caryn had had, and could also hold his liquor better than anyone else, just like Caryn. And both of them could be extremely stubborn. Yet neither wanted to admit how much alike they were. Perhaps staring at a mirror image was the most unacceptable of reflections.

"I just wish she'd talk to me rather than writing me these damned long letters," Philip was saying. His voice sounded farther away, as if he was getting ready to leave.

"At least she's talking to you again, no matter how she does it," Simone replied.

"You got a point." Again, there was a pause and more paper rustling. "Listen, don't tell her I called, okay? I'll call when I get home from the Orient. Maybe we can iron out our differences once and for all."

He asked for Carrie's schedule and seemed to be writing it down, then cut the conversation short. After Simone hung up, she reflected on the call. Philip still didn't realize all the problems he'd created between Carrie and himself, no matter how much he admitted the fault was his. It'd take a lot more than one phone call. Quite a lot more.

Moments before she pulled *The Big One* into its berth, Carrie spotted Auntie Pudding pacing the dock and immediately knew there was something wrong.

Matt had seen her, too, and stood on the bow, ready to jump off the instant the boat touched the pilings. Something must have happened to Isaac.

It took Carrie almost fifteen minutes to shut everything down. By that time, Matt and his mother were long gone. She found Jack outside the office and hailed him.

"Do you know why Matt's mother was here?" she asked, sliding her sunglasses on.

"Something about Isaac being thrown in jail," he answered. "I didn't catch why though."

Carrie's heart dropped. "Did you catch where they were going?"

"The police station, I guess."

Carrie was about to run to the truck when Simone came around the corner. She herded her mother into the office for a moment.

"Did Auntie Pudding come by your house?" she asked, throwing her log on the desk and grabbing her pocketbook.

"Well, no, but—Where are you going?"

"If Isaac's in jail, then that's where Matt is. I'm going to help. You can handle things here, can't you?"

Without waiting for her mother to answer, she sprinted out the door and headed for the parking lot.

The truck was stifling hot from being closed up all day, so Carrie left the doors open while she cranked the engine. It gave one stubborn grunt after another, but nothing caught.

"Oh, shit, not now," she muttered, pumping the gas pedal furiously. "C'mon, baby, c'mon."

Five tries later, the engine still wouldn't turn over.

She leaned her forehead against the steering wheel and swore under her breath.

"What's the matter? Won't start?" Jack stood next to the truck, his jacket slung over his shoulder, a motorcycle helmet in his hand. He looked tired but concerned.

"No, dammit, and I want to get to the police station to see what's going on with Isaac. Do you have a vehicle? Could you give me a ride?"

Jack juggled the helmet in his hand. "If you're willing to sit on the back of a Honda 450, I can. I'll even let you wear the helmet."

In her haste to get to the station, she didn't think about what it would be like to be on the back of a motorcycle, her arms around Jack's waist. She tried to concentrate on the road ahead, even started thinking about the next day's trips to occupy her mind, but nothing stopped the furious pounding of her heart. There was no way she could deny the urge to lean her head against his shoulder. She sat stiffly, trying not to lean into him, but when he took a corner, she had no choice but to let her body bend in the same direction as his.

"You've got to hold on tighter," he yelled back at her. "We'll tip if you don't."

Biting her lip, she did as she was told and felt his hips move against her thighs, his calves flex as he shifted to balance the bike.

When they reached the station, she found herself wishing the ride had been longer. And with a thought like that coursing through her mind, she couldn't meet Jack's eyes. She bounded into the office without so much as a thank you.

Thirteen

"Can you repeat that please?"

The waiting room fell as silent as a morgue. Matt's face turned gray and all color drained from his full lips. Beside him, Auntie Pudding, dwarfed by her second oldest son, stared at the officer in disbelief. Jack stood behind them, though he'd resisted coming into the station.

"Ten thousand dollars," the officer repeated. "Vehicular homicide is a pretty heavy charge, and if bail isn't posted within twenty-four hours, we'll hold him until his arraignment Friday morning."

"Friday . . ." Auntie Pudding breathed shakily. She clutched Matt's arm and looked up into his face. "Ten thousand dollars. Oh my God, Matt, what are we going to do?"

Standing behind them, Carrie wanted to reach out to them, to offer a hug or a word of encouragement, but she was just as stunned by the officer's announcement as Matt and Auntie Pudding. Although Isaac had been causing problems for a while, Carrie was shocked it had gone this far. To kill someone, even by accident. . . . She wished she could say something reassuring, but the words stuck in her throat. Nothing seemed appropriate.

The crowd Isaac hung around with had been skirting the fringes of Hawaiian law for years. At first it was only drunk driving, joyriding, speeding. Then they'd graduated to small-time drug deals, gang fights, anything that would give them a thrill. Originally, the group had congregated in Honolulu, irritating local businesses and hotels with small-time burglaries. Pranksters, the newspaper had called them. But the game got to be too much fun and some of the kids took it with them when they moved to other islands. Their latest foray into small crime had landed six of them in jail, and Isaac was one of them, the youngest one.

Matt put his arm around his mother's shoulders and held her close as she sobbed freely.

"I'm sorry, ma'am," the cop said, though only Carrie seemed to hear him.

Isaac has really gotten himself into one hell of a scrape this time, she thought. And Matt wouldn't be able to get his brother out of this one, no matter how hard he tried.

The officer told them the evening had started with some innocent drinking, but as the boys had consumed more and more beer, bravado had taken over. Four of them had decided to race over the Saddle Road to Hilo, two guys in each car. Carrie gasped. She avoided that route at all costs, even if she had to go all the way around the island. Its hairpin turns and deeply elevated curves gave her vertigo under the best of conditions. How the boys had ever raced that road, and at night, without throwing themselves into flight was beyond her comprehension.

But they had miraculously made the ride to Hilo

in one piece, the cop reported, and several of the boys had decided to celebrate with another round of beers. Their fatal mistake was in believing they could make the trip back. One of the boys had also picked up an ounce of grass in Hilo, and the plastic baggie it had come in was still there when the police arrived on the accident scene.

The two cars involved in the race were damaged beyond repair, but the one they hit was totalled beyond recognition. Isaac's friend Jimmy was dead and his two other friends lay in critical condition in Kailua-Kona General Hospital. Isaac was the only one intact.

"Can we see him now?" Auntie Pudding asked, dabbing at her eyes with a soggy Kleenex.

"Just family members. No one else," the officer replied.

Carrie looked at Jack as Matt and Pudding followed the sergeant from the room. Jack stood slouched in the corner, his hands in his pockets.

"Welcome to Hawaii," she said. "Nothing like baptism by fire. Sure doesn't seem like paradise when stuff like this happens, does it?"

Jack straightened a little and tried to smile, but he seemed extremely uncomfortable. "You really love this family, don't you?" Jack took his hands out of his pockets and looked directly into Carrie's eyes. She felt, at that moment, that he understood her completely.

Averting her eyes, she answered, "They're great people."

"So are you," Jack replied. "I've never seen anyone

work as hard as you do. Your commitment must be the reason Matt stays. That and your friendship."

"Matt stays because he loves the ocean. This is his home. Besides, there aren't any jobs for philosophy majors around here, except teaching and that's out."

"Philosophy?"

"He's got a degree in Asian Philosophy from U.H. That's where he met Alex."

Silence. She stole a sidelong glance at him and caught him moodily gazing into the distance.

"Philosophy, huh? Why doesn't he teach?"

She laughed. "They'd make him wear shoes. Plus he hates to talk."

"I feel like an idiot. Here I was going on about my philosophy degree and there he is with one of his own."

"Matt's like that. He doesn't brag. Doesn't even share much of his life. He'd rather keep to himself." Carrie shifted her weight to the other foot. "To tell you the truth, I'm kind of surprised he's taken to you. He usually doesn't let people get very close."

"But you're friends with him."

"I lived next door. I'm family. You've only been around a week or so, and here you are, taking part in a personal tragedy."

Jack raised his black eyebrows, as if apologizing. "Seemed like the thing to do. You don't mind, do you?"

"No . . . no, of course not. It's kind of nice . . ." She'd almost said "having a man around."

Pushing herself away from the wall, she headed for the water fountain. What was it about Jack that kept making her smile even when there was nothing to smile about? She knew she shouldn't be enjoying the feeling, but there was so little in her life these days that made her happy. Was it so wrong to get some pleasure out of her friendship with him?

And that's all it is, she reminded herself as she sauntered back toward him, her hands in her pockets, her eyes on the floor. Friendship.

"I didn't do it, Matt. Honest! Please believe me. Mom, talk to him."

Isaac paced on the other side of the table from where Matt and his mother sat. It was obvious Isaac had been crying, but try as the kid might to drum up sympathy, he came up empty where Matt was concerned. The boy had been asking for it, pure and simple.

"How many times are you going to lie to us, Isaac?" Matt asked.

"I'm not lying, Matt. I didn't do it." Isaac's voice deepened, taking on a serious adult tone. "I can't explain why, right now, but I'm telling the truth. You've got to believe me."

For a moment, Matt almost did. Then he glanced at his mother's hopeful face, and a surge of anger ripped through him. He couldn't stand to see her hurt anymore.

"Prove it," he demanded.

"I can't. Not right now."

"You can't or you won't?"

"Matt, please," Pudding put her hand on his arm. "It's not important right now. We've got to get him out of here *wikiwiki*. That's all that counts."

"How?"

Matt reached up and gently brushed his mother's graying hair away from her face. "This isn't fair to you, Mom. We've given all we got. What more can we do?"

"We've got to try, Matthew," she replied. "This is our family. We have to keep trying for each other. There has to be a way."

He sighed and turned back to his brother, determined, for his mother's sake, not to let his disappointment show.

"Okay," he said. "We'll try, but I don't know what good it'll do."

"You won't be sorry, *Bruddah,*" Isaac said. "I promise."

Rising abruptly, Matt knocked over his chair. It clattered to the floor and he let it remain there, even after two officers rushed in, demanding to know what was going on.

"Don't promise me nothing," he said, pointing his finger at his brother. "Just don't fuck me over, Isaac. I'm warning you. This is the last time."

"Do not be so upset with yourself, Simone," Jerry pleaded. "Sometimes the time is just not right for disturbing news. The wise person is the one who knows when to wait."

For two hours, Simone had waited for Caryn to return from the police station with news of Isaac. And for every moment of that two hours, she'd berated herself for not telling Caryn about her father's phone call, even though Philip had asked her not to.

"Could I be unconsciously trying to keep them

apart, Jerry? You know how much I want my daughter to be happy and how much her father upsets her. Perhaps making excuses not to tell her what Philip said is just my way of keeping them separated."

Jerry sat silently at the kitchen table, his gaze questioning but patient.

"Perhaps I am just trying to protect her, to be the mother goose."

"Hen, darling."

"Comment?"

"I believe you meant mother hen."

"Oh." She picked up the ceramic teapot and poured hot water in their still steaming cups. "Am I wrong, Jerry?"

"About what?" He crossed his arms and looked at her thoughtfully, his half glasses on the middle of his nose like a professor's.

"About protecting her. Is that the wrong thing to do?"

Jerry leaned forward and reached for her, but she passed by too quickly. "I believe you are really getting yourself much too agitated. Come here. Stop wringing your hands and sit down."

Simone did as she was told, but still couldn't stop her mind from racing. It was a little after three A.M. Soon the sun would be rising.

"Where do you think they could be?"

"Still at the police station, probably. Now, calm down. There will be plenty of time to talk to her when she gets here. That is, if you are going to tell her."

"What other alternative do I have?"

"Wait. See what has happened with Isaac. Then try to determine, logically and rationally, if it might be best to simply keep your news until a more appropriate time"

Simone stirred her tea with quick, jerky strokes. "He will never be out of my life, Jerry. I will always be caught in the middle."

"Only if you let yourself be, my dear." Jerry's slim, elegant hand covered her fidgeting one. "Only if you allow it to happen."

She let that piece of advice seep in, considering it carefully.

"You are right, *mon chou,* as you always are. What would I do without you to teach me patience?"

"You do not need a teacher to master patience, Simone. You have always had that talent within you. You just allow yourself to embrace frustration far too easily. Now it is time to let your problems unravel themselves. Slow down. Breathe deeply. Meditate. Concentrate on the strength deep within you."

Simone felt her body automatically relax and knew he was right. She hoped Caryn would arrive before she changed her mind.

"I can't let you give your bike's title for collateral, Jack," Matt said. "You've done enough already."

Matt, Pudding, Jack, and Carrie sat at the coffee counter at Hattie's Diner. They were the only ones in the ramshackle restaurant. They had gone there directly from the police station, determined to put their heads together to discover a way to raise Isaac's bail. The bondsman had told them the court would accept car titles or property titles in lieu of cash. When Matt had decided to put up the Camaro, Jack offered his motorcycle.

"Why not, man?" Jack asked. "Besides, it's only temporary. I know I'll get it back."

Matt looked at his mother, then to Carrie. Both women nodded their heads. "That'll satisfy the court," Carrie said. "God, Matt, I wish I could help you out, but I don't think they'd take title to anything I own . . . or should I say what the banks own."

"Yeah, you don't have much of a choice, Matt. So just take the piece of paper. I know I'll get it back. I'm not worried." Jack clapped Matt on the shoulder and winked at Auntie Pudding.

"What do you think, Mom?" Matt asked his mother.

"Jack's right. We don't have any choice."

"Well, if we're going to do it, we'd better get going or it'll be morning and Isaac will've already stayed the night." Jack got out of his chair and threw a ten-dollar bill on the counter to cover the check. "I've got to go to the harbor and get the bike's papers. They're in the jacket I left in the audience," he said over his shoulder as he headed for the door. "Want a ride, Carrie?"

Although Carrie had definite misgivings about getting back on the bike with him, she nodded, not wanting to ask Matt or Pudding to take her back. They made plans to meet at the police station an hour later, giving them time to run to the harbor and back again.

While they walked to the bike, Carrie said, "I can't believe you. What you're doing is really nice."

"They're nice people," Jack answered.

It took less time to get to the harbor than they thought. While Jack retrieved his papers, Carrie tried starting the truck again. This time it turned over.

"Let's take the truck," she yelled, spotting Jack going back to the bike. "I want to keep it running, get the battery recharged."

He nodded and gestured for her to wait a moment while he secured the bike. The truck still sounded like it would stall at any moment, so she gunned the engine.

"Needs a tune-up," Jack said, looking through her pile of cassette tapes. "Mind if I put this on?" He held up Ziggy Marley.

She nodded, glad she wouldn't have to make conversation. For a few minutes, they simply listened to the music, then she reached over and turned it down. "I have to go by my mother's for a minute. Do you want to come in?"

"Sure. Speaking of your mother, I've got to tell you, I've never seen a mother and daughter that look less alike than you two. You must've gotten your blond hair and your height from your dad."

"Uh-huh, Dad was tall." Carrie desperately tried to think of something else to talk about.

"What does he do?"

"Daddy? Well, he's a. . . . He's a businessman."

Jack tapped his fingers against his knee and looked out the window, totally unaware of her discomfort. "What kind of business?"

"Banking . . . and stuff. Well, here's my mother's street. Looks like she's waiting up for me." She pulled the truck into her mother's driveway and switched the conversation back to Isaac.

Simone met them outside, Jerry right behind her. She glanced at Jack curiously, but her unspoken question was answered the instant Carrie explained that they were headed back to the station to give Matt the motorcycle's title.

"We can't stay, *Maman*," Carrie said, bussing her mother's cheek. "I just wanted to let you know what's going on with Isaac."

Simone and Jerry listened intently and expressed their shock about the death of Isaac's friend. "Is there anything we can do?"

"I'm afraid he's going to have to figure things out one day at a time," Jack offered. "First, we get him out of jail, then tomorrow, he's going to have to start looking for a good lawyer. Vehicular homicide's going to be pretty easy to prove, especially since they pulled Isaac out of the driver's seat. He's going to need a lot of help."

Before they left, Simone gave Carrie another hug and told her to have Pudding call. "Maybe I will visit her tomorrow. Yes, tell her that."

Carrie nodded and began to back up, but her mother clung to her arm as if she wanted to say something else. "Listen, we have to go," Carrie said. "I'll call you later, okay?"

Biting her lip, Simone nodded and stood next to Jerry. When Carrie's truck pulled out of the driveway, Simone lifted her hand to wave goodbye and Carrie could see her duck her head into Jerry's shoulder as though she were crying. In the rearview mirror, she watched them walk slowly back into the house. For the first time, Carrie noticed the streaks of silver in her mother's hair and her slightly stooped way of walking.

The stress is starting to show on her, Carrie thought, and she promised herself to give her mother the rest of the week off.

Fourteen

The rain fell in silvery sheets, surrounding Honokohau Harbor with a gloomy melancholy which affected everyone. Carrie sat in her office, trying to concentrate on making phone calls in order to adjust her schedule. Several trips had already been cancelled because of the inclement weather, and each represented money lost to her. If this rain lasted any longer, the whole weekend would be shot, and that meant six trips, the equivalent of a week's pay. She was already behind at least two months with all the bills.

At least she'd be able to visit Alex. It had been almost two weeks since she'd had a chance to go to Hilo, what with Isaac's arrest and Matt being out of work. At first, she'd handled the office and the trips alone, simply locking the door and putting on the answering machine when she couldn't be there to answer the phone and greet clients. When Jack came by, after he got back from Peru, and saw how close she was to pulling out her hair by the roots, he volunteered to help and refused to take any money for his efforts.

He'd been incredible. In more ways than one.

Right now, he was outside in the rain, untangling some of the lines they'd taken off the boat to be replaced. His yellow slicker shielded his face, which she appreciated. She didn't want him to see her watching him, though he'd caught her doing just that many times during the past week.

And she'd caught him watching her as well.

They were playing a cat and mouse game, she knew. Both of them felt comfortable with each other, that was obvious, but they knew there were limits to their relationship, bounds within which they had to stay in order to keep it at a friendship level. So far, there hadn't been any problem doing that, but when they accidentally brushed against each other or smiled at each other for a fraction of a second longer than they should, both became flustered, pulling away as if burned.

Carrie sighed again. When had life become so complicated? If this was what maturing was all about, she wanted nothing of it. Give her the early years, the days when Hawaii was new to her, when everything was an adventure, and falling in love with Alex the only thing occupying her mind.

Pulling her chair back up to her desk, she reluctantly settled in again and reached for the phone, but it rang before she could pick it up. Her mother's voice greeted her.

"Maman, aren't you working today?"

"Oui, but I wanted to see whether you are."

"Not really. Nothing's happening in the harbor, and from the look of the weather reports, this is going to continue all weekend. Bummer."

Simone laughed. "What a distinct way of putting it. Do not feel badly. The gallery's been quiet as well. Perhaps we can get together for lunch? A bowl of chicken soup? Jerry made a delicious *potage* last night. You could meet me at the house—"

"Sounds good, but I don't think so." Carrie looked out the window and spotted Jack coming toward the office. She tucked her hair behind her ears and checked her reflection in the stainless-steel coffeepot next to the desk. "I've decided to go to the Center this afternoon. I haven't been able to get there in awhile, and Matt told me Alex is asking where I've been."

"Matt has seen him?"

"He went a couple of days ago when he brought Isaac to the lawyer's. He said Alex is starting to learn how to use a wheelchair and they're thinking of trying to get him up on a walker."

"What? But how? He cannot use his legs."

"I don't know. That's why I'm going over. I'd like to see if I can catch McElroy and ask him what's up."

The door opened. Jack slipped off his raincoat and shook the water off it, then hung it on the hook near the door. When he disappeared into the bathroom, Carrie continued, her voice subdued.

"Besides, I think it's time I told Alex what's been going on. You know, about *The Blonde* and all."

"Caryn," Simone's tone changed to an admonishing mother's, "you have not told him yet?"

"Well, I was going to, but then everything else came up . . ." Carrie wriggled in her seat, knowing full well she should have discussed everything with Alex, but she never knew how he was going to react. And the truth was, he had become increasingly difficult to talk to. She really didn't even want to try anymore.

"Whether he is in the hospital or a therapy center

or right next to you, he deserves to know what is going on," Simone scolded. "What you are doing with the business and your finances affects him as much as it does you. You probably have not even told him you have given up the apartment, have you?"

Again, Carrie wriggled. "I didn't want to worry him—"

"That is no excuse. You are partners, in your marriage, in your business, and in your finances. His body was injured, not his mind. Perhaps if you shared what was going on in your life, he would take an interest. It might even help him make a faster recovery if you let him participate. He was always good at keeping the books, why not take your bookkeeping to him, make him feel useful, give him something to do."

She was right. Maybe it would help. Carrie agreed and said goodbye, promising to go to Simone's for dinner that night. It would be the first time they'd seen each other since the night Isaac was arrested.

"So, what's up for the rest of the day?" Jack settled into the green leather chair across the room from her and looped his leg over its arm.

"No sense in us keeping the office open, unless there's a chance the weather is going to clear up." She stood and walked over to the window, leaning against it. "Pretty depressing, huh?"

"Yeah, just about the only sun I've seen in the past three days is what you've got in your hair. Come to think of it, this is the first time I've seen you in jeans." He closed the magazine and checked her out from head to toe. "I didn't know they made the legs that long."

"This is the only pair I own and the only time I wear them is when I'm cold." She looked at him and smiled, then gave an involuntary shiver, not sure whether it came from the chilly weather or from being alone with him. His own legs were encased in form-fitting jeans, and an L.A. Rams sweatshirt efficiently hid what she knew to be a well-developed chest. His dark hair glistened, damp and curling over his forehead even more than usual.

"Y'know, in weather like this," he said, "you got to get out, move around a bit, get some blood circulating in those veins, ol' girl." He jumped out of the chair and came up behind her, rubbing his hands briskly over her shoulders and arms. "If you went outside and worked a while," he continued, his voice husky and very near to her ear, "you'd warm up in no time."

As much as she enjoyed the feeling of his hands on her body, as much as she wanted to lean into him, let him keep her warm, she pulled away. "I've got to go to Hilo this afternoon, so you can have the rest of the day off."

"Gee, thanks, Boss Lady." He paused for a moment, still so close to her she could smell the rain in his hair. "Going to see Alex?" he asked, before turning away.

"Yes, it's been almost two weeks." She tried to make her voice cheery, but it sounded strained. "He's got to be wondering where I am."

"Don't blame him. I would be, too, if I were your husband."

Something in that comment sounded dangerously close to jealousy. By now she knew Jack well enough to realize he'd wanted very little in his life and was happy with anything he had, but he admittedly had never been able to fulfill one of his dreams—to maintain a long-term relationship with a woman who shared his interests. She suspected one of the reasons for that was he'd never stayed in one place long enough to find someone.

"Well, he won't be my husband too much longer if I don't get my butt over there," she replied, a little too flippantly.

Jack offered to stay in the office for the afternoon to field phone calls and any walk-in customers and told her he'd come by first thing in the morning, just in case.

"I wish you wouldn't do so much for me. You make me feel guilty," Carrie said. "Look, we can't do much of anything here anyway. I feel like you're wasting your time."

He considered her, his eyes serious, almost stern. "Jack Briskin never wastes his time. Don't you worry about me. I'm here because I want to be. No regrets, no guilty feelings, just want to see you up and running again. Whatever it takes."

She believed him. She just wished she knew his motivation. Although she suspected he was as attracted to her as she was to him, she didn't want to deal with the possibility that he was hanging around for that reason. She preferred thinking that he was simply repaying her the favor she had done him with Ocean Fresh. It was safer that way.

Ocean Fresh. The thought of her father's company made her realize just how little Jack Briskin knew about her. He hadn't made any comment when learning Simone's last name, probably didn't make the connection—there were lots of DeBarys in the world—but what would he do when he did find out that Carrie was Philip DeBary's daughter? And how much would she have to explain before he'd understand why she'd hidden that fact from him?

Again, she was forced to realize that Jack was a temporary fixture in her life. He had commitments and a career with Greenpeace into which she didn't fit, even as a friend. She was just a stopping point on his way through the area. When he left, he probably wouldn't even remember her name a month later. The thought depressed her.

Grabbing her jacket, she shoved a sheaf of receipts and bills into the accounting journal on her desk, picked up the pile, and headed for the door.

"See you tomorrow morning," she called, her hand on the knob.

"Wait a minute. Aren't you forgetting something?"

"What?" Her heart pounded as he came within inches of her face.

"The key. How am I supposed to lock up?"

Idiot, she chided herself as she fumbled through her pockets and took the key off her chain. What makes you think he feels the way you do? Better cut it out, girl. You're getting yourself all upset about nothing.

She handed him the key, feeling the warmth of his slender fingers against hers, and for a spine-tingling moment, their eyes caught and held.

"See you tomorrow," he said softly.

Once out of the office, she forgot completely to

put on her jacket, not caring that she was soaked by
the time she reached her truck.

It took her longer than usual to get to the Center,
which, in a way, was a godsend. By the time she got
there, she'd been able to clear Jack from her mind.

When she walked into Alex's room, she saw him
in his wheelchair, sitting before the window, idly
watching the rain. The sight tore at Carrie's heart-
strings. She paused in the doorway, balancing a box
of honey-dipped doughnuts on the pads of her fingers.
The doughnuts were a guilt gift, bought at the last
moment in a supermarket around the corner. Alex had
always loved getting warm doughnuts from the bakery
on Sunday mornings. He'd drink a gallon of coffee
and eat a half-dozen honey-dips while reading the paper, then groan for the rest of the day that he was so
bloated there was no possible way he could move
from the couch. The only antidote, he'd swear, was
watching a football game. After some half-hearted
tousling, Carrie would protest meekly, then retreat
into a book.

Now she reluctantly went over to him. How easy
it would have been to preserve her memory of what
they used to have, of the people they used to be. All
she had to do was turn around and walk back down
the corridor. She wouldn't have to look at Alex's lifeless eyes or hear his brittle voice or admit to herself
that those idyllic days were over.

She thrust the box at him, not bothering to say hello
or to wait until he'd acknowledged her presence. He
was dressed in the same blue-striped cotton pajamas

he always wore, despite the fact that the Center's staff encouraged everyone to dress for the day as soon as they got up in the morning. He obviously hadn't shaved in a couple of days and a stale body odor permeated the room.

"Doughnuts," he said, surprised. "Is it Sunday?"

She slid her jacket off and threw it over the tan vinyl chair in the corner. Leaning against the windowsill in front of him, she forced a smile.

"Doesn't have to be Sunday to have doughnuts, does it?"

For the first time in weeks, Alex actually looked like he was enjoying himself as he tore into the box. He ate two full doughnuts before pausing to look up at her again.

"Thanks, babe. They don't have this kind of stuff here, just that awful granola shit. I haven't tasted anything this good in months." Despite his haggard appearance, for a moment he looked like the old Alex. Even his smile seemed as bright.

She felt a surge of optimism and made a mental note to bring more the next time she came.

"Great. Glad you like them. So, tell me, what's new? What've you been up to? Hope you're behaving yourself."

Alex shoved another honey-dip in his mouth and shrugged. With his mouth full, he managed, "I'm learning how to drive this contraption. They didn't want to let me at first, but," he licked the glaze off his fingers, "I convinced them I wouldn't run anyone over. Of course, I can still do wheelies." He demonstrated, spinning the chair's front tires off the floor as he circled around the room. Certain he'd fall, Carrie reached out for him. His doughnut box tilted, but she caught it and, in the motion, their heads bumped.

"God, Carrie, your noggin's still hard as a rock." Alex rubbed the top of his head and gave her a dirty look.

"You're no softie yourself." She reached over without thinking and touched his hand. Their eyes met and she saw the man she'd fallen in love with. Impetuously, she leaned over and kissed his stubbly cheek. To her surprise, Alex backed away as if embarrassed.

I was wrong, she thought. He hasn't changed. Her hand came up to her mouth, and she fought the urge to turn away. He needs me, she reminded herself.

"Seen Dr. Karachi or McElroy lately?" she asked brightly as she plumped his pillows. When he didn't answer, she peeked over her shoulder at him and was surprised to see tears running down his face.

"Oh, Alex. Oh, honey, what's the matter? Did the doctor say something? Tell me, baby, please." She knelt in front of him, her hands on his knees, looking up into his face, now twisted in pain.

"I'm sorry, Carrie. I'm really sorry," he sobbed. "I've been such a shit. I know how hard it's been for you. I've just been thinking of myself and that's so selfish." He caressed her cheek, stroking one long strand of damp hair over her shoulder. "You're so beautiful and you've been so good to me. This just isn't fair! It's just not fair." His shoulders shook and he bit his lower lip, trying, as always, to control his emotions.

Carrie leaned her head against his knee and wound

her arms around his waist. "It's okay, babe. I'm here. We can talk about it."

He sniffled and she could feel him swallow hard. "You know the day the doctor first told me I'd probably never walk again, I knew my life was over. I never, in all my worst nightmares, thought this could happen. And I guess I haven't dealt with it very well, have I, babe?"

She patted him, unable to speak.

"I hated myself," he continued. "I've hated being alive. I've hated everyone who's tried to help me." With his forefinger, he lifted her face to look at his.

Carrie tried to cover her shock. At this close distance and in the room's artificial light, he'd aged twenty years.

"Can you try to understand how frustrating it is for me?" he asked.

"Of course, I understand."

"Help me, Carrie. I need to become human again and I can't do it alone."

"I'm here," she answered. "I'm always here."

They held each other close until the light coming in his window started to wane. Then they began to talk as they hadn't been able to since the accident. Carrie told him about the trouble between Matt and Isaac, about the new cruises she had scheduled, and the efficient way Simone was running the office. It felt good to share what she'd been doing and to see he was impressed with the changes she'd made.

Confident, Carrie took a deep breath and started telling him everything she'd promised Simone she would—their ever-deepening financial problems, giving up the apartment, and selling *The Winsome Blonde*. She didn't hold anything back, except Jack.

When she finished, she waited for what she thought would be inevitable—the anger. But Alex sat motionless in the wheelchair, except for one hand, which stroked her hair.

"I'm sorry, honey. This is all my fault," he finally said.

"No, no, not your fault. Don't ever think that way." She sat straight up, her eyes flashing. "It was an accident. It wasn't your fault. It wasn't my fault. It was just an accident."

"I should have had insurance."

"We couldn't afford it."

"I should have handled this . . . paralysis better."

"Don't beat on yourself, Alex. I'm not into martyrs these days."

He laughed tentatively, as though he'd forgotten how, and when he stopped, he asked, "Is this how a martyr feels? No wonder there aren't too many saints these days. This isn't fun at all." He reached for the doughnut box again but offered her one this time before taking one for himself.

"You know what my dad used to tell me when we had a lousy summer crop on the farm?"

"No, what?" she asked.

"He'd say that it was nature's way of telling us we never get what we expect, no matter how hard we work for it. You just got to take one day at a time, he'd say. Live all you got for that hour, 'cause there may not be any more. Pretty smart, huh?"

"You're a pretty smart guy, too, Alex Madison,"

she replied, pulling his face to hers for a long, searching kiss.

When they broke apart, Alex ran his hand over his chin. "I've got to shave," he commented, a twinkle in his blue eyes. "Golden Mermaids don't like men with beards."

"And where did you hear that?"

"A little birdie told me." He pulled away and rolled over to the chair where she had thrown her jacket and the accounting books. "Now are you going to tell me why you've brought all this stuff with you?"

Carrie rose and stood beside him. "Since I've got my hands full with everything else and you just lay around here and do nothing all day . . ."

"Nothing!" he said in mock indignation, a twinkle in his sky blue eyes. "Nothing? Let me tell you, baby-cakes, there's not a minute in the day when they don't have something scheduled for me. At eight A.M., it's breakfast, then at eight-thirty-five, it's off to water therapy for an hour and a half. The wrinkles have barely disappeared from my little toes and they have me off to physical therapy where they push and prod my poor body for another hour. Then it's lunch, and after lunch, I have to play ball and after that—"

"Does that mean I should take all this home?" Carrie played his game, enjoying herself, and him.

"Well. . . . Let me see if I can fit in some time during the evening to help you out. But I'll only do it if you pay my fee. And I'm pretty expensive, you know."

"What kind of fee?"

He looked thoughtful for a moment. "Two visits a week instead of one."

She opened her mouth to protest, to remind him that she was handling the business alone, to complain about the long ride to Hilo, that what he was asking was literally impossible. How could she get away? But, on the other hand, how could she deny him? Especially since he'd begun acting like his old self. Surely this was a sign of recovery.

"Okay," she finally said.

"It's a done deal, then. Now let's see what we have here." Alex began flipping through the bills, pulling a few out to look at them more closely. He grew ominously quiet and his face took on a darkness so unlike him. When he started studying the accounting journals, he shook his head, and she suddenly knew she'd done the wrong thing by bringing the bookkeeping to him.

"What the hell is going on here? You've got more expenses than you can possibly afford! What's this mooring fee? We've never paid one before. And trash collection? Since when can't you make a simple once-a-week trip to the dump? And where's all the extra money these nighttime trips are supposedly bringing in? You're not making more, you're spending more!"

"Alex, hon, please don't shout!"

"Don't 'Alex, hon' me. You're running my goddamn business into the ground. What am I going to have when I get out of here? No place to live, no sailboat, an almost out-of-business business—" He threw the files at her. Sheets of paper flew in every direction. "Get someone else to do this. I can't figure the damn thing out."

She scrambled on the floor to collect everything. Her hands shook. For a moment, she considered reasoning with him, but she couldn't think of the right words. Behind her, he rammed the wheelchair back and forth across the room, knocking things over, swearing loudly, and acting like he'd suddenly gone insane. She ran out the door and down the hall, forgetting her raincoat.

Once she was in the truck, the dry sobs stopped and she gained control of her breathing. That's it, she thought. McElroy better have one damn good reason why this miracle treatment isn't working or I'll have Dr. Karachi yank Alex out of here once and for all!

With the truck's windshield wipers slapping angrily, she drove back to Kona, determined to keep herself even busier than usual from now on. She'd show Alex who was capable of taking care of the business. She'd run it her way or she'd run it into the ground. It was a win or lose proposition now, nothing in between.

Fifteen

Still steaming mad, Carrie stalked into her mother's kitchen, letting the door bang behind her. Jerry, at the stove, brought his head up sharply at the noise.

"What is wrong? Is Alex all right?" Simone asked, immediately wiping her hands on a dishtowel and crossing the kitchen to Carrie.

"Alex is a goddamn bastard!" Carrie slammed into a chair, pushing away her mother's offer of a hug. "I don't care if I ever see him again. He can die for all I care!"

"Now, Caryn, you do not mean that. Anger has a way of clouding our emotions—"

"Well, maybe I don't. But I'm seeing things more clearly than I ever did before. What the hell does he think—that no one else has any feelings? No one else hurts? I thought I had him back tonight, *Maman*. We talked. I told him everything, and at first, he really seemed to understand. Then I gave him the bookkeeping like you suggested and wham! He blew sky high! Jekyll and Hyde, that's what he is. You were wrong, he *didn't* just damage his back in the accident, he knocked his brain loose, too."

She drummed her fingers against the kitchen table. It was the only sound in the room. She looked sharply at Jerry, standing in the middle of the floor, a pan in one hand, a spoon in the other.

"What the hell are you doing, Jerry—posing for Animal Crackers?"

"Now, Caryn—"

"Leave me alone, *Maman*. Just leave me alone."

Simone slid into a chair and folded her hands in her lap, then looked down at them. "I was wondering when this was going to happen," she said.

"What?"

"I was wondering how long it would be before your patience left completely."

Carrie snorted. "Well, now you know." She shot another look at Jerry, who immediately concentrated on his cooking. Then she turned back to her mother. "I'm tired, *Maman*. I'm so goddamn tired."

Without warning, her throat closed up, and suddenly the warmth of her mother's arms surrounded her. All the grief and heartache she'd been holding back welled up in her eyes, and she let it out in the safety of her mother's embrace. When she finally finished, she felt completely drained and totally unable to do anything, even eat.

In silence, the three of them sat at the table for dinner. They pushed their food around, made some perfunctory comments and some plans for the next week, but their plates were just as full when Carrie dragged herself out the door half an hour later as they'd been when Jerry placed them on the table.

When she got back to the office, Carrie could see the answering machine's red light flashing even before she got inside. Soaked to the skin from the walk from the parking lot and still aggravated, she debated whether to listen to her messages. Habit took over, and she crossed the office in the dark to wearily rewind the tape. She pressed the play button.

"Carrie? Carrie, are you there?" Alex's voice filled the small room.

She immediately regretted turning the machine on, but curiosity won out. Still dripping, she stood in the middle of the floor to listen to what he had to say.

"I need to talk to you, Carrie. There's a few things you should know about running the business. Maybe I didn't take the time to explain them to you when you were at the Center today. First of all, you shouldn't—" The machine cut off Alex's voice after thirty seconds.

Carrie reached for the light switch and snapped it on, wincing as the bright light filled the room with garish shadows. Twelve-fifteen, the clock on the wall said. Too late to call him back.

The tape continued. Again, it was Alex. This time he talked more quickly, giving her instructions on how to schedule trips, who to contact at the different hotels, how much to charge them.

"Tell me something I don't know, Alex." She tapped her foot and muttered, "Isn't it simply amazing how I've gotten anything done without your company secrets. You must really believe I'm stupid!"

Again, he was cut off. Again, he called back. And again. And again. After the fifth call, his voice became strained and harsh, as it had been when she'd left his room earlier. He had no patience anymore, she thought. At one time, patience had been his greatest virtue.

This time he screamed, "Where the hell are you?"

"Oh, Alex, I don't even know you anymore," she whispered, as she reached for the switch and turned the machine off. She paused, then pulled the cord out of the wall before retreating to her cell-like room and the hard cot.

Alex could wait until tomorrow.

Simone's bedside light cast a small bright circle on the paperback in her hand. Beside her, Jerry slept on his side, snoring softly, his back to her. She had read the last paragraph five times, yet still couldn't comprehend its meaning. It wasn't that the book was especially complicated; she just couldn't concentrate.

She'd been prepared to tell Caryn about Philip's call at dinner tonight, but the fight with Alex was enough for one night. She couldn't see the sense in adding to her daughter's anguish. One major problem at a time was plenty.

Simone glanced at Jerry and reached out idly to touch his hair. During the past two months, they'd become incredibly close. His quiet wisdom suited her. She needed his steadfast seriousness more than she ever thought she'd admit. They spent all their nights together now. Jerry hadn't gone home in weeks, except during the daytime when Simone was at work, and then he'd simply tend to his gardens, grab another change of clothes, and come straight back.

At first, it had been disconcerting for her to walk into the house where she'd spent so many years alone and find Jerry in her kitchen fixing supper. Now she could barely remember what it was like when he wasn't there.

With a sigh, which was a mixture of the contentment she felt with Jerry and the frustration she felt with Caryn, she reached for the bedside light and turned it off. She had barely crawled under the covers when the phone rang.

"Simone DeBary, please."

"This is she."

"Simone, I don't know if you remember me. I am Philip's attorney, Harry Sanford."

"Yes, of course I do," she said politely, though her body stiffened with anticipation.

"I'm afraid I have some bad news."

"Yes?"

"Philip is dead, Simone. He died this afternoon, in Tokyo of a massive heart attack."

The knock on the office door interrupted Carrie's dream of riding a wild Apaloosa across the bluebell-painted meadows of Miss Kiki's Ranch for Girls. She had just come to a fence and was anticipating a jump. She awoke angry, the dream stolen from her.

"Just a minute! Just a goddamn minute!" she yelled as she struggled into the jeans and T-shirt she'd left crumpled on the floor the night before. Still bleary-eyed, she tried to focus on the alarm clock's neon numbers. Six-o-five. She groaned as she stumbled toward the door.

"Carrie, let me in!" Jack demanded, brushing past her, seeming not to notice she was half-dressed.

"Didn't you see the note I left on the door?" He plunked the two plastic coffee cups he carried on the desk.

"What note?" Carrie yawned and rubbed her eyes with her fists.

"Ha, you *did* have the phone off the hook!" Jack turned the machine back on and put the phone back into its cradle. "Y'know, you can drive a sane person nuts doing something like that."

Carrie plopped into the chair and put her feet up on the table. "Well, someone was trying to drive *me* nuts so . . ."

Jack glanced up, his dark brows arched questioningly. Then, his question forgotten, he leaned forward on the desk, and said, "We got problems, Boss Lady. The boat's taken on a bit more water than she needs, and if we're going to take her out today, we'd better get busy."

Carrie cradled her head in her hands and massaged her fingernails against her scalp. A pounding headache monopolized her attention.

"You okay?" Jack asked.

"Not really."

"I'll go out and start if you want to wake up for a couple of minutes."

She shook her head, drew herself up, and walked over to the desk. "Let's see what we have on the schedule," she said, as she slipped into her desk chair. She lifted her head to look out the window and was amazed to see her mother and Jerry approaching the door.

Simone clutched her keys in her hand until they left imprints on her palm. It had been a shock to see the light on in the office, Caryn already at her desk, and Jack intimately leaning over her. Could they have spent the night together? The possibility stunned her so completely she almost forgot why she'd come. Jerry put his hand lightly on the small of her back, whether to steady her or to push her forward, she didn't know.

For a few long seconds, Simone stood in the doorway, noticing the slim columns of light the early morning sun cast on the office floor. Dust motes circled in the silent air, and she felt almost as though if she shut the door on this scene, it would remain the same forever, as if it had been caught in a snow globe.

Jack pulled away from the desk in slow motion when he spotted them, as if realizing the full impact of what was about to happen. It seemed he was experiencing a sense of déjà vu. When he glanced back at Caryn, Simone tried to ignore the affection in his gaze.

"*Maman,* what are you doing here so early?" Caryn rose.

Simone noted the dark circles in the near transparent skin under her daughter's eyes, the tangles in the beautiful long platinum hair, the wrinkles in Caryn's dirty T-shirt, her bare feet, her pale cheeks.

How could she add any more anguish to what the poor girl was already going through?

Simone felt as if she floated toward her. The sensation unsettled her. She took her daughter's hands, wanting to feel something solid, warm. Caryn was cold.

"Sit down," Simone said. "I have something to tell you, *ma chérie.*"

With a puzzled look, Caryn returned to her chair, removing her hand from within her mother's two firmly clasped ones.

"What is it?" she whispered. "It's not Alex. He didn't do something . . . nuts, did he?"

Stroking Caryn's tangled hair away from her face, Simone wished she could smooth away the pain she was about to inflict.

"I've been trying to call you for hours," she began. "Jerry convinced me to wait until morning to come here. I hope I've done the right thing."

"What is it, *Maman?*" Caryn's grip tightened.

Simone took a deep breath. "It's your father."

For a fleeting instant, a look of relief crossed Caryn's face, only to be quickly replaced by one of dismay.

"What about him?"

"He has died, *chérie.* His lawyer called around two this morning. Philip was in Tokyo negotiating a business deal when he had a fatal coronary. They are bringing his body back to Hous—"

"Dead? Dad's dead?"

"Yes, Caryn. He is gone."

Caryn's eyes flickered to the answering machine, then to Jack and Jerry, who stood near the door. Finally, she looked back at Simone. "It's over, then," she said, a note of finality in her voice. "We'll never talk now."

Simone waited for Caryn's tears, but they didn't come as hers had. Pulling Caryn close, she caressed her daughter's stiff body. Caryn's reaction scared her.

Perhaps this was the last straw, the last trauma her daughter would be able to take.

Finally, Caryn pulled away and fiddled with the answering machine's buttons. "Alex kept calling last night," she said. "He kept calling and calling and calling. I didn't want to talk to him, so I shut the machine off."

Simone stroked Caryn's shoulder, grateful when, finally, she leaned into Simone's arm with a whimper.

"I'm here, *chérie*. I'm right here," she said, as the whimper turned into sobs. "It's all right. *Maman's* here."

Behind them, the office door quietly opened and closed. Without looking, Simone knew Jack and Jerry had left them alone, and she was grateful.

Sixteen

By the time the men returned to the office, Carrie's sobs had subsided and she was deep in discussion with her mother.

"Harry Sanford said he wants you to come for the reading of the will," Simone was saying.

Carrie dabbed at her eyes. "Oh God, *Maman,* why should I have to be there? Dad's probably leaving everything to Pamela and the baby anyway." Although she had never met her father's new wife, she instinctively knew that she and her mother had been replaced by Pamela and her new son. Otherwise, wouldn't he have made some kind of effort to let her know how much he cared long before his trip to visit her in the hospital?

"You are his daughter, Caryn Marie, *that* is why you should be there," Simone replied indignantly. "He was your father."

"I don't want anything that belonged to Philip De-Bary. He was never there for me. He didn't even bother to answer the letter I sent him last month."

Out of the corner of her eye, Carrie noticed Jack had stopped moving and was staring straight at her as if he'd just had a revelation. Now he knows, she thought. Well, it was inevitable. I wouldn't have been able to hide who I am forever. I shouldn't have been so secretive about it to begin with. Serves me right if he's totally pissed.

Simone sighed loud and long, drawing Carrie's attention back to her. "There is something I have been trying to tell you for the past week or so, but every time I tried, it seemed something else always got in the way."

Simone stopped and squared her shoulders. Her eyes wavered and Carrie could tell she wanted to apologize. She never had an easy time admitting she'd made a mistake.

"Your father did call." Simone took a deep breath, then continued. "He called me at the gallery the day he received your letter. He wanted to talk to you but could not reach you since your apartment phone had been shut off, and he didn't have the office number. The letter upset him, Caryn. Greatly. He never was one to reveal his emotions, but I know he loved you very much. He was not so hard as you believed. There's nothing more devastating than knowing your child doesn't love you in return, and you made that quite obvious." She cleared her throat.

"He said he was leaving on a business trip that afternoon but would call when he returned. He wanted to speak to you directly, get things settled between you once and for all—"

"But he didn't come back, did he?" Carrie finished the story for her mother.

"No, *chérie*. And I blame myself that the two of you never had the chance to make peace."

"It's not your fault, *Maman*. How could you have known?" Carrie returned her mother's embrace and looked toward the window at Jack and Jerry. Jerry sat with both feet flat on the floor, arms crossed over his chest, looking like a proper Japanese gentleman. To his right, Jack, his elbows propped on his knees, balanced his chin in his hands. Sympathy was written on every feature of his face.

"Guess I won't be doing too much today," she said to him with an apologetic smile.

"I'll take the trips out," he offered.

"You can't do it alone."

"I will help him," Jerry piped up.

Simone whipped her head around and broke the hug.

Despite herself, Carrie giggled. "You haven't been on a boat in your whole life, Jerry Kahala."

"Why not call Matt?" Simone asked quickly, almost as if protecting Jerry. "Pudding told me he's ready to return any time you are ready. I think he is bored being home alone with Isaac. Perhaps it would even benefit Isaac if Matt brought him along."

"Simone's got a point," Jack added. "It doesn't make sense for *The Big One* to shut down, especially since this is the first day all week the weather's been any good."

Carrie glanced out the window, surprised to see the harbor awash with sunlight. It struck her that her father would have loved such a day, the trees shiny and dark with rain, the air smelling fresh and clean. She stopped, amazed at herself. It was the first time in ages she'd thought affectionately about Philip. Fresh tears came to her eyes. She blinked fiercely.

"Okay," she said to Jack. "If Matt can come, he'll help you clean the boat up, then the two of you can take her out. I'm going to my mother's for the rest of the day. You can reach me there if you need me." She grabbed her bag, turned on her heel, and left the office without a goodbye.

Once she and her mother were settled, after they'd talked for hours and there were no more tears left, Carrie wandered into the yard, needing to be alone.

Lifting her chin, she inhaled the heady mix of fragrances—plumerias, gardenias, roses, and orchids—which made her mother's garden a haven. This island, her home, differed from Texas in so many ways: the rich greens and blues of the ocean, the lush, tropical vegetation, the endlessly perfect weather—just the opposite of the browns and corals of most of Texas's landscape, its miles of open ranchland, barren save for a few scraggly trees, the horrendously hot, dry summers and windy, frigid winters. Yet, as much as she wanted to forget it, Texas had been home, too.

The thought of going back to Houston made her shiver. Besides, how would she get there? She'd run out of money long ago and had already plumbed every prospect of getting more. The plane ticket would cost almost a thousand dollars, and that didn't take into consideration the spending money she'd need while there. She didn't even have a place to stay, though she knew if she called Lorilene, her old friend would find her a room. She wondered if she even had Lorilene's number, it had been so long since they'd spoken.

Although she had friends besides Lorilene in Houston, none of them had kept in touch after the first year of sporadic letter writing. She simply wasn't part of their lives anymore.

All of the girls at Miss Kiki's school had powerful, wealthy parents; they had all been raised in a fast-paced, image-conscious society—debutante balls, holiday parties in the Cayman Islands, birthdays celebrated with royalty, shopping sprees in Paris, and, of course, the hunt.

That was what Carrie missed most—the horses. Although she had been invited to ride at the Parker Ranch on the northern coast of the island, she had gone only once a long time ago. After that first visit, school and her mother's work schedule had interfered with any hopes of riding on a regular basis. Besides, being at the ranch had reminded her too much of Spencer, the Morgan gelding her father had given her on her tenth birthday, the horse she had had to leave behind when she and her mother had headed for Hawaii. Carrie had chosen to soothe the emptiness she'd felt by filling her days with sailing. The freedom of being on an open sea almost matched the thrill of flying over an open field with a strong horse beneath her. But she couldn't be friends with a sailboat, so she'd shoved her loneliness aside and learned to forget everything associated with the life she'd known in Texas.

Now, she was forced to remember.

She bent her face to a delicate white orchid and let its scent fill her nostrils. Her mother was right, flowers did have magical healing power. Already she felt a sense of calm creep through her body. Sitting on the stone bench Simone and Jerry had placed near the rare orchids Simone cherished, Carrie brought herself back to the present to face the decision she had to make.

Perhaps Simone had been right when she'd reminded her that going back to Houston would allow her to grieve for her father. Perhaps she would even be able finally to close the door on the past.

"You are a stubborn, willful girl," her mother had said. "Sometimes you do not want to admit that you might be partly to blame for the trouble between you and your father." When Carrie tried to protest, she had simply lifted a finger to silence her. "Unsolved conflicts will only act like loose threads in the material of your life, *chérie*. Better to weave them in with the rest. Do not let the past leave a hole in your soul."

Carrie, surprised at her mother's philosophy, had sarcastically commented that her mother sounded as Japanese as Jerry. But here, in the peaceful garden, she could admit her mother's words held a sort of wisdom. Perhaps she was right.

Rising from the bench, Carrie realized she'd made up her mind. Somehow, she would find a way to go to Houston.

It was almost dark when she reached the harbor. She breathed a sigh of relief when she turned the corner and noticed the office light still on.

Matt must be here, she thought, and felt a surge of gratitude. When she drew closer, she realized the dark head bent over the schedule calendar was not Matt's but Jack's. For a moment, she considered making an about-face and going back to the truck, then she found herself standing in the cool nighttime air, watching Jack's glossy head, feeling a strange flutter in her stomach.

When she opened the office door, Jack looked up, startled, then smiled when he saw who it was.

"Hi. Didn't expect to see you tonight," he said, getting up from the desk. He wore a pair of khaki shorts and a loose shirt unbuttoned to reveal his curly black chest hair. She found herself noticing the indentations of the muscles in his thighs and the bulges in his forearms and mentally admonished herself.

"How you doin'?" he asked, pulling a chair out for her. "Y'know, you didn't have to come back to check up on us. We're managing okay."

"We? All I see is you. Where's Matt?" She looked around the office, purposefully keeping her eyes away from his face.

"Matt, Isaac, and Jerry went home after the last trip. I told them I'd close up."

"Did the trips go okay? Did you get the water out of the bilge? Did any of the hotels call? How many—"

"Whoa! Whoa, whoa, whoa. I can only handle one question at a time. First of all, yes, the boat's okay. Got her all pumped out this morning. Wasn't as bad as I thought it'd be. And the trips were fine. Jerry was funny. Had to put him in a life jacket. Beyond a little seasickness, I think he was okay. His legs looked a little rubbery when he got off the boat, but he'll live. He and Isaac got along great. They know each other?"

Carrie nodded and leaned her head back against the chair. Exhaustion suddenly took over, and she yawned, stretching her long body from head to toes.

"Don't do that," Jack said, his voice husky.

"Don't do what?"

"Move like that. You don't know what it can do to a person to see a body like yours go through those motions . . ."

Carrie sat up, pulling herself into what she thought was a proper and prudent sitting position. "This better?" she asked.

He groaned. "I think I'd better go. It's been a long day." He stood once again, now towering over her, and reached past her for his jacket. For one tantalizing moment, his musky scent tempted her. She felt like touching his arm, asking him to hold her, just for a moment. God, did she need a hug. But, once again, she caught herself and reminded herself she was not single.

"Can I ask you one thing before I go?"

"Sure, go ahead," she answered.

"How come you didn't tell me Philip DeBary was your father?"

"I'm sorry," she began. "I know I should've told you, but I guess I was . . . well, I was embarrassed. You know how I feel about Ocean Fresh. The fact that my father owned the company makes it worse. I really didn't want to admit I was related to the man who ran a business with such unscrupulous practices. Just because I'm his daughter doesn't mean I have the same beliefs he had."

"I gathered that," Jack said. "But I still don't understand why it needed to be such a big secret."

"That's my hang-up," she said. "Ever since *Maman* and I left Texas, I've been trying to rid myself of his influence. I guess I just go too far sometimes."

Jack leaned against the edge of the desk. "There's a lot more to it, isn't there?"

She nodded, studying her broken fingernails.

"Tell me about it," he said in a hushed, understanding voice.

"It's a long story."

"I have plenty of time."

Carrie glanced up and licked her lips once again. "I can't talk about it tonight. There's been too much going on, Jack. Maybe another time. Right now, I have to figure how I'm going to get to Houston for my father's funeral."

"What do you mean?"

"I don't know how I'm going to get a ticket."

"Money problems?"

She laughed sardonically. "That's putting it mildly."

"Listen," he said, taking one of her hands in his. "I know we haven't been friends very long, but I want to help. Here, I'll let you use the only piece of plastic I own." He placed a well-worn MasterCard in her hand. "Get yourself to Texas and back. No woman should miss her father's funeral."

Carrie turned the card over and over in her right hand, leaving her left in Jack's grasp.

"I can't do this," she whispered.

"You got a better idea?"

"No."

"Then, looks to me like you should make yourself a reservation. And don't you worry about the business while you're gone. You have an able-bodied crew of four to keep *The Big One* afloat while you're away."

He hadn't finished his sentence before she was crying. She let him hold her close against his chest while she sobbed. When she pulled away, he seemed to understand.

"I'll pay you back," she sniffled. "Somehow I'll pay you back."

A few moments later, he left. She stood in the office, watching him ride off on his motorcycle, and found herself wishing he'd stayed, to hold her again, to give her the comfort she'd missed for so long.

With a sigh, she turned back to the desk, intending to pick up some work to take back to her mother's. It was then she saw the answering machine's red light blinking. Her breath caught and she realized, for the first time that day, that she'd never returned Alex's calls.

Seventeen

Carrie stopped at a light less than half a mile from the Center and slipped her feet out of her pumps to wriggle her toes. It had been years since she'd worn heels, and they were as uncomfortable as she remembered. She whistled tunelessly, her stomach in knots, her head spinning with the possibilities of what lay ahead in Houston.

Her flight from Hilo to Honolulu would leave at nine, but she'd risen early so that she'd be able to squeeze in a visit with Alex before leaving. He still didn't know about her father's death.

The light changed and the truck lurched forward. She still didn't have her foot properly back into the shoe and struggled briefly with the clutch, swearing under her breath. Her skirt rose up with her squirmings, and she yanked at it. Why didn't I just wear jeans? she thought.

The black linen skirt was the mate to a jacket thrown over the back of the seat, a suit she'd bought to attend a friend's wedding three years before. Surely it was out of style by now, she thought, but it was the most up-to-date piece of clothing in her closet. Surprisingly, one of her mother's silk blouses, a soft pink with a rolled collar and pearl buttons, had fit, so she borrowed it. Put your best foot forward, her mother had said. Do not let them think you have failed.

Drumming her fingers against the steering wheel, she pursed her lips, remembering the closets full of finely tailored designer clothes she'd left behind in Houston. The only problem in those days was deciding what to wear rather than worrying about whether she had something appropriate. She wondered what her father had done with all her suits and dresses, the one-of-a-kind gowns and hand-woven sweaters, her specially made jodhpurs and Italian leather shoes.

Brushing the question from her mind, she pulled into the Center's parking lot and instantly spotted Terry McElroy walking briskly toward the entrance, a stack of file folders under his arm.

"Terry!" she called. "Wait up!"

"Hey, Carrie, long time no see. Where've you been?"

Carrie returned his smile. "Trying to run the business and holding off the wolves. The usual."

"Alex has missed you," McElroy said pleasantly as they fell into step. "I hate to say this, but it might be easier for us, and him, if you visited more often."

"Yeah, I know. Unfortunately, things just keep happening. In fact, that's why I'm here now. I wanted to say goodbye to Alex before I leave for my father's funeral."

McElroy stopped. "Oh, Carrie, I'm so sorry. I didn't know . . ."

She nodded and raised her hand. "Neither does Alex. I don't know how he's going to take it. We had a fight the other night."

"We know."

"You do?"

"Everyone does. Your husband turned into a crazy man that night. We almost had to put him in restraints, and you know how much I oppose that type of treatment." He held the door open for her.

"Now it's my turn to say I'm sorry."

"Don't," McElroy smiled. "It's a normal reaction to what he's been through. We can deal with it."

"Is there anything I can do to help?"

They walked into the quiet lobby, its floor covered with a muted rose carpet and the walls with vibrant Hawaiian paintings. Carrie knew the entrance had been designed to give visitors a distinctly optimistic first impression of McElroy's Center. It worked.

"As a matter of fact, you can do a lot," he replied. "Alex has gone past the point of requiring sympathy. Now it's time for tough love. You know what that's going to take?"

"More visits?"

"Not necessarily, although it wouldn't hurt if you could find the time to come more often, and tell his friends to drop by occasionally, too. We see the big guy every once in a while. What's his name?"

"Matt Kamehea."

"Yeah, him. But surely Alex has some other friends he'd like to see."

Carrie shook her head. "He's pretty much a loner. There's only Matt, me, my mother, and her friend, Jerry."

"Well, then, see if you and Matt and your mother can take turns coming over. Give Alex someone to talk to at least twice a week, other than us. And you've really got to urge him to start taking an active part in life again. He just sits in his room day after day watching television."

"I know what he's been like," she said, stopping at the door to McElroy's office. "In fact, that's what the fight was about the other night. I was trying to get Alex to do some bookkeeping for the business, but he just. . . . He just doesn't like the way I'm handling things, I guess."

"That's too bad." McElroy shifted his files to the other arm and opened his office door but didn't go inside. "He certainly could use something to divert his attention, something to keep him from feeling sorry for himself. We need to find a way to jolt him out of the depression he's fallen into. It's the only way we're going to be able to work with him. You know, Carrie, the mind is incredibly powerful. It can cure a body or it can damage it beyond repair. If we don't get to Alex soon, nothing we do is going to help him physically."

Carrie pushed her hair behind her ears and looked down at the carpet. "I guess my news isn't exactly going to help the situation, is it?"

"Who knows?" McElroy answered. "It might be like shock therapy. I hate to say it, but maybe it'll finally show him there's something worse than what he's going through right now. Maybe he'll see that he needs to support *you* rather than vice versa."

McElroy's words echoed through Carrie's mind as she continued down the corridor toward Alex's room. Little did McElroy realize that Alex had never really

cared for Philip DeBary and probably would have little sympathy for Carrie and Simone. Before the accident, he would have offered her his hugs and an
understanding ear, but now she didn't know what to
expect.

She knocked softly at Alex's door, knowing he was
inside. McElroy had made sure of that before letting
Carrie go, calling the therapist with instructions to
delay Alex's treatment.

"Come in," Alex called. "Where the hell have you
been? I've been wait—Carrie! What are you doing
here?" Alex sat in his wheelchair, wearing only his
pajama bottoms. As usual, he hadn't shaved or showered yet.

"I came to talk to you." She put her purse on the
chair and stood beside it, unable to bring herself to
go over and kiss his stubbly cheek. For the first time,
the thought of being close to him turned her off. Mentally, she chided herself for being so shallow.

"About the other night, right? Well, I tried to call
you a million times. Where were you? You never
called me back."

"I wanted to come in person," she said. "I thought
it'd be easier this way—"

Again, he interrupted her, "I suppose you want to
apologize. Well, apology accepted. Now, tell me what
you're going to do about *The Big One*. Are you going
to let me do the bookkeeping or did I totally blow
that?" He smiled at her and reached out his hand.
"They're going to start new therapy on me, you know.
They told me yesterday. More work. Like I don't have
enough to do."

Remembering what McElroy had said, Carrie went

to Alex and took his hand. "You have to cooperate with them, babe. You know they're just trying to help, and you haven't exactly been easy . . ."

Alex's face hardened. He dropped her hand. "Why is it that every time you come to see me, you end up telling me what a bad boy I've been? You don't like coming here, do you? You just can't deal with having a husband in a wheelchair."

"No, that's not it—"

"Why do you bother?" he snapped, his eyes narrowed. "If you wanted to be here, if you wanted to see me, you'd pick up the phone or come over more often. Where are you going anyway? Why are you all dressed up? Got a date? A business meeting?"

She swallowed hard. He wasn't making this very easy for her.

"I've got something to tell—"

"That's it, isn't it?" Alex wheeled backward a few feet. His mouth turned into a snarl. "Caryn Marie DeBary Madison has a boyfriend. I should have known. How could I expect you to stay faithful? Look at you—short skirt, long tanned legs, makeup, lipstick, your hair down. Of course! I'm not blind. I may be crippled, but I'm not blind!"

"Alex, you're totally wrong. How could you think—"

"No answer the night you left here. All night I called. No answer the next morning. No apartment anymore. Why? Have you moved in with *him?*"

Carrie found herself getting angry. How dare he accuse her of cheating on him? How could he not understand all the hours she spent on the dock, all the nights tossing and turning on the two inch cot mattress, the days she went without lunch because she had no money, the hours she spent repairing *The Big One* by herself so that she'd be able to pay the hospital bills, the phone calls from the bill collectors, and now her father's death. And absolutely no support from this selfish person she used to love.

Used to love. The thought shocked her. Was Alex right? Had she stopped caring simply because he was no longer the vibrant, active man she'd married? Had she forgotten the phrase "in sickness and in health"?

Alex was still ranting and raving when the door behind Carrie opened and a therapist poked his head in. "I don't mean to interrupt, but Mr. Madison has a 9 A.M. water therapy treatment."

Startled, Carrie checked her watch. She had fifteen minutes to get to the airport and get checked in.

"Take him. I was just leaving anyway." She crossed the few feet to Alex's side, leaned over and pecked him on the cheek. "You're wrong, you know," she said. "Dead wrong."

She left, tears stinging her eyelids, without saying another word.

When she reached the ticket counter at Hilo International, her hands were shaking. Ten minutes to boarding time. She had no idea how she'd gotten there so quickly. In a daze, she handed over her one suitcase and headed for the gate. She was so involved with thoughts of Alex that if Jack hadn't walked directly in front of her, she wouldn't have seen him.

"What are you doing here?" she asked.

"Jeez, Boss Lady, I thought you weren't going to

make it," he replied with a teasing smile. One hand on her elbow, he guided her out of the way of other travellers and sat her in one of the waiting areas. He slipped in beside her and handed her an envelope. "I know you only have a couple of minutes, but I wanted to catch you and give you this."

Inside the envelope were a bunch of twenty dollar bills.

"What—oh, Jack, I can't let you do this." Carrie tried to give the money back to him, but he wouldn't take it.

"You can't go to Houston without some pocket change. Consider it a loan. You can pay me back some-day when you have it."

He smiled again and Carrie found herself drawn in by his green eyes. Suddenly, she didn't want to go to Houston, she wanted to sit and talk with him as they had so many afternoons in the office. She wanted to hear about South America and Tahiti and Indonesia. She wanted to watch his face light up when he spoke about his family, his sister and her kids. She wanted to hear him laugh and to have him tease her, to make her feel alive, like a woman again. She wanted him to take her away from the reality of her life, to make her feel that adventures were still possible, that being in debt was a problem that affected only other people. She wanted to feel that the future was still something to look forward to.

Impulsively, she reached over and gave him a hug.

"What would I do without friends like you?" she said, as she inhaled the fresh scent of his soft hair and felt the hardness of his shoulder muscles beneath his shirt. Unconsciously, she dug her fingers in one

second longer than she should have, then reluctantly
pulled away.

"Don't give me so much credit. I've always believed you get back what you give. Just remember
that," he said, his voice low, his eyes intent on hers.
"They're calling your flight."

They rose together, still looking into each other's
eyes, both pairs of hands still grasping the envelope,
fingers touching fingers. Carrie didn't breathe, but her
mind forced her legs to move in the direction of the
gate. Silently, Jack walked with her.

When they reached the line of passengers boarding
the plane, Jack drew her aside and, without a word,
took her into his arms for another hug. She clung to
him, every part of her desperately wanting nothing
more than his arms around her. Bending her head
back, she searched his face questioningly, and the answer in his eyes was all she needed to know. Their
lips met as if they had kissed many times before, as
if this was the way it should be, and when Carrie
broke away, she knew, finally, what she had suspected
all along.

Eighteen

Although it had been seven years since she'd last seen Lorilene Weirback, Carrie had no trouble spotting her friend's tousled head of sienna curls towering over the others waiting for disembarking passengers. Lorilene had always been the only woman Carrie knew who was as tall as she. Their height was not the only thing they had in common, but it was one of the first reasons they'd become friends.

"Lookit you, Carrie DeBary!" Lorilene squealed as she held both of Carrie's hands and spun her in a circle. "Still drop dead gorgeous and skinny as a rail while ol' Lorilene's packin' it on in the saddlebags." She chuckled in her high-strung, squeaky voice, throwing her head back delightedly, a trait which had always made Carrie smile.

Born into the prestigious cattle-ranching Weirback family, Lorilene had been primed for the social circuit as soon as she could ride a horse, but she had never acted as uppity or distant as some of the other Houston socialites. Perhaps that's why she and Carrie had gotten along so well. Neither of them had ever considered money as important as the rest of the factors which made up a person's character.

Lorilene threw her arm around Carrie's shoulders,

hugging her tightly as they walked the concourse to the baggage pick-up.

"I hate to say this, but why is it that only a funeral would bring you back to visit your best friend?"

"I never really wanted to come back before. No offense," Carrie replied. "Besides, why didn't you come to Hawaii? Lord knows, you've got a hell of a lot more money than I do these days."

"That bad, huh?"

Carrie nodded, then added, "But what better place to be broke? Perfect weather, I can sail anytime I want, *Maman's* got a permanent garden, and Alex loves being two minutes away from his work."

"Sounds like heaven. Plenty of room for horses?"

"The Parker Ranch has almost as many as you do."

Lorilene laughed again, but all chances of further conversation were squashed as they hunted for Carrie's luggage. Although she wanted to talk, the noise level in the baggage area was simply too high to hear anything, so she looked around instead. Every man she saw seemed too tall. All wore Stetsons and expensive cowboy boots. Almost everyone seemed as well dressed as Lorilene in her soft suede pantsuit. Nowhere did Carrie see the friendly round Hawaiian faces she'd grown so accustomed to. Although no one around her was speaking anything except English, she felt as though she'd landed in a foreign country.

"This all you have?" Lorilene asked when Carrie pulled her battered gray Tourister off the baggage carousel.

"Uh-huh."

"Hoo-eee, girl, looks like I'm going to have to take you shopping. You can't very well go to the funeral and the lawyer's and to meet your stepmother in that suit. Unless you've got something absolutely stunning in that suitcase, you're going to need some goin'-to-meetin' clothes."

"But—"

"No ifs, ands, or buts about it. No friend of mine is going to have these hoity-toity Houstonites looking down their noses at her. Especially that woman who married your father. You just let ol' Lorilene take care of you, darlin'. We'll get you back in shape in no time. Besides, you know how much better you'll feel if you've got the right clothes. You know what they say—you are what you wear."

"I think that's you are what you eat."

"Same diff." Lorilene brushed a bit of dust off Carrie's shoulder. "Now let's get you all spiffied up before you have to meet everyone."

Carrie tried to protest again, not really wanting to be forced into performing like a trick pony for the crowd of socialites she remembered as gossipy and self-centered, but Lorilene had disappeared into the crowd.

It took all her effort to catch up.

They went shopping first, before heading to the Weirback Ranch or letting Philip's lawyer know she was in town. Lorilene drove her silver Mercedes the same way she spoke, jerky and fast. She told Carrie she insisted on driving herself rather than have the family chauffeur take over, despite the fact that her driving record, as she said with a snicker, was "so awful they're afraid to let me pull my oldest's little red wagon on the road."

Lorilene was no longer a Weirback, at least legally. She'd married Jimmy Allen Baker, of the Dallas Bakers, three years before and had already had two children. According to her, they were deliriously happy, living in a specially designed fieldstone house on her mother's ranch, raising thoroughbreds and following the show circuit around the world. Jimmy was perfect for her, Lorilene insisted. He stayed around home enough to keep her happy, but he travelled enough for her to maintain her independence.

"Mama gave us a hundred acres," she said, as she drove Carrie through heavy downtown traffic, "so we built us a little place with a fifteen-stall stable, and we have a couple of fish ponds stocked with bass for Jimmy and his football buddies—he was a tight end for the Steelers, you know—and a tennis court—got that when I got it into my little pea brain that I was going to lose these few extra pounds I've packed on, but the only time we use it is when we have people over for a summer barbecue weekend. People tell me it's a great court. I wouldn't know the difference."

Lorilene stopped in front of a parking space in front of The Yellow Rose, an exclusive boutique, and prepared to back in, talking all the while about her kids and how she was preparing to teach the two-year-old how to ride. She tapped the Jaguar in front of her, giggled, then did the same thing to the Cadillac behind. Through it all, she kept talking.

Carrie listened intently, laughing in all the right places and asking all the right questions, but she was a million miles away, back in Hawaii, with Jack.

* * *

Two hours later, they climbed back into the Mercedes. Carrie's legs were killing her, her arms full of packages from I. Magnin and Neiman-Marcus. No matter how much she insisted that Lorilene didn't have to buy her anything, her friend ignored her, reminding her how much fun they used to have as teenagers making each other over. The bags were filled with everything Carrie could possibly need, from a new lingerie wardrobe to a simple black dress designed by Robocco to a whole line of new Chanel cosmetics. Lorilene had even had Carrie measured for jodhpurs and a riding jacket, "just so that you'll remember to come back and visit during hunt season."

As Lorilene headed out of town into the country, Carrie found herself checking her watch. It was barely two and the funeral started at four. She sunk into the butter-soft leather seat and stared mindlessly out the window, only half-listening to Lorilene's constant patter.

"Hey, Carrie DeBary, penny for your thoughts."

Carrie roused herself and shook her head. "Nothing. I'm not thinking of anything."

"From the wrinkles in your brow, I'd tend to say you were thinking of something pretty heavy. Y'know, I haven't said it yet, but I want you to know I'm real sorry about your dad. I know you two had a falling out, but—"

"I know, he was still my father."

"Right." Lorilene fell silent for the first time.

They drove past acres of rolling meadows and impeccably landscaped grounds that Carrie knew provided privacy for some of the finest homes in Houston. The area looked vaguely familiar to her, and she knew they were nearing the Weirback Ranch, where she'd spent most of her adolescent years. She sat up a little straighter.

"Are you all right, hon?" Lorilene asked softly.

Carrie reached over and patted Lorilene's hand with a close smile. "I'll be okay. I've already done most of my crying. I guess I. . . . I just never planned on coming back. This trip's got me confused. There's just been too much happening in my life the past four months. I don't know how much more I can handle."

"It all happens for a reason. You know what they say about building character and all. I have no doubt you can handle whatever that man upstairs happens to throw at you. Carrie DeBary is the strongest person I know."

"I don't know, Lori. I don't know. It sure would be a hell of a lot easier if I could pay the bills. With Alex in therapy still and the business not doing as well as it should be . . ."

She heard the negativity in her voice and instantly clamped her mouth shut, determined not to sound as though she was indulging in self-pity. Even though Lorilene was her best friend, it wouldn't take long for rumors to spread about how poorly Carrie and her mother had been doing since leaving Houston. More for her mother than herself, Carrie thought it wise to keep as much of her life private as possible.

They cut down a side dirt road, which meandered for about a mile before stopping in front of a rambling fieldstone and aged cedar house designed in levels to fit in naturally with the surrounding land. Lavish beds of azaleas followed the loose-stone walkway leading to the double-wide oak front door.

"I got rid of everyone for the day," Lorilene said, as she helped Carrie with her packages. She fit her key in the front door and swung it open, then continued in. "I figured you wouldn't want to meet the two babies and my handsome husband until after the funeral. Jimmy's going to meet us there. I hope you don't mind."

"No, of course not," Carrie said as she paused to take in her first view of the house. "This looks like you," she commented, peering around.

The foyer led to a comfortably furnished great room, graced by a large fieldstone fireplace which filled one entire wall. Soaring ceilings opened to magnificent skylights, letting in the blue of the afternoon sky and casting golden sunspots on the floor below.

"The bedrooms are upstairs. The kids are at one end of the house, so I put you at the other, overlooking one of the ponds. I figured you'd want the peace and quiet."

Carrie followed Lorilene through the house, past an atelier with soaring fig trees and a bubbling goldfish pond, through a family-style kitchen with fieldstone floors and the latest in appliances, up one set of stairs to a cozy loft area filled with books, a many-pillowed couch and a state-of-the art stereo system, then up a second flight to a bedroom decorated simply but beautifully in antique Lone Star quilts and rustic Texan longhorn furniture. Lorilene was right, the ceiling to floor windows looked out on a tranquil pond, beside which two mahogany-colored geldings stood passively, as if someone had painted them there for effect.

"It's lovely, Lorilene. If you'd taken me here blind-folded, somehow I would have known this was your house, even without the horses outside." Carrie gave her friend a warm hug. "Thank you for being here. It's so much nicer than going to a hotel."

"Ah, girl, how could I do that to you? I just wish this visit could've been made under different circumstances."

They pulled apart, tears in their eyes, but Carrie punched Lorilene in the arm to lighten the moment. "So, show me how to work all this new-fangled stuff," she said, turning her back. Control, she reminded herself. Stay in control.

Lorilene showed her where to hang her clothes, instructed her how to use the whirlpool in the huge bathroom, as well as how to adjust the stereo and television system hidden behind in a large pine cupboard. In spite of her admonition to stay in control, Carrie felt an unexpected pang of jealousy. Although Lorilene did well to hide her wealth, she obviously lacked for nothing. Money made her life much easier and more pleasant than it would have been otherwise. Without asking, Carrie knew Lorilene didn't even have to touch a checkbook to pay her bills. She'd have an accountant do them, never worrying about what would happen if one of the family became ill and had to go to a hospital.

Carrie Madison, you stop that right now, she chided herself silently. There are some things far more important than money.

But, for the life of her, she couldn't think of very many.

After Lorilene left her alone to dress for the funeral, Carrie had a bout of loneliness like none she'd ever felt in her entire life. She felt out of her element, like an impostor. She longed for her mother's patient wisdom, for Matt's strong silence, for Jack's understanding smile, even for Alex's nastiness. If only one of them had been able to come with her, just to be there, to talk to her, hold her hand, give her some support.

No, Carrie, she reminded herself, this was your decision. Now it's time to take some responsibility for it. No one's going to help you through this one. You've got to work it out for yourself.

She sighed and opened her suitcase, then hung her meager wardrobe in the closet next to the clothes Lorilene had just bought for her. It struck her that she was living two different lives—one as Carrie Madison, wife of Alex Madison, owner of *The Big One,* resident of Hawaii, barefoot and sun-coddled and broke; the other as Caryn DeBary, daughter of corporate giant Philip DeBary, horsewoman, masquerading as a wealthy Texan socialite. For the first time in her life, she didn't know which Carrie she'd rather be, a disconcerting feeling, to say the least. She'd always known who she was, or who she wanted to be.

She wandered into the bathroom and ran her fingers along the thick plush towels, thinking of the thin small ones she had owned at the apartment. It was the little things that made the difference, she decided. The little things only money could buy.

With another sigh, she turned away and retrieved the new black dress from the closet. It was time to face the music, time to admit her DeBary heritage, time to say goodbye to her father and all he represented.

Nineteen

"No, I don't want it! How could he leave me that goddamn company? He knows how much I hated it!"

Carrie's outcry froze the small crowd gathered in Harry Sanborn's penthouse office. Although she knew she'd probably just made a fool of herself, she didn't care. The past three days had been horrible. She'd gone through the funeral woodenly, greeting people in a mechanical fashion, shaking the hands of her father's business associates, offering her cheek to family friends, distant cousins and long-forgotten schoolmates. She'd even endured the uncomfortable meeting with her stepmother Pamela and her half-brother, ten-month-old Andrew, named after her grandfather. All of it had been extremely trying and so nerve-wracking, that she'd taken advantage of Lorilene's offer to use the phone anytime she wanted and called her mother three times. Simone had offered a long-distance shoulder to cry on, but, more importantly, she had given Carrie the strength to continue.

But *Maman* hadn't expected Dad to will me Ocean Fresh, Carrie thought.

Now, she trembled from head to toe, facing her father's white-haired and silver-tongued attorney as he read the will to a roomful of people, which included

Pamela and her attorney, the heads of all of Philip's major corporations, several of Philip's oldest friends, three of his cousins, and of course, herself.

Pamela sat to the right of the desk, her dark blonde head bowed in grief. Barely thirty, five years older than Carrie, she seemed stymied by everything going on around her. Occasionally, her lawyer bent his head to hers and whispered something in her ear, but she never responded.

In spite of how she'd prepared herself to feel, Carrie believed Pamela really loved Philip. At the funeral, she'd spoken of him with respect, almost reverence. Carrie had wondered then whether Pamela really knew enough about what Philip did to realize that at least one of his companies was nothing to be proud of. Listening to Pamela talk to the hundreds of people at the funeral, Carrie received a skewed picture of Philip DeBary, entrepreneur. It seemed as if Philip DeBary, the father, was a totally different person. But Pamela spoke of him with affection, and so did many of the other people who had stopped to pay their respects. Perhaps Pamela had been the only one of his women to understand Philip as he wanted to be understood.

When they first met, Pamela instinctively reached out for Carrie, pulling her close in a desperate hug, as though holding Philip's daughter would be like holding him and that would ease the pain she felt. Bending over to reach the much shorter woman, Carrie felt strange. It was difficult not to compare her stepmother to her mother. Pamela was almost the same height as Simone, and as Carrie reluctantly returned the embrace, she realized it was her mother's hug she wanted.

However, that's where the similarity ended. In looks, the two women were as different as they were in background. Where Simone's features were dainty, Pamela's were lush, almost to the point of being too large for her face. Pamela's widely spaced, cordial blue eyes were flecked with gold and appeared guileless, unlike Simone's sharply intelligent gray eyes. While Pamela's body was thin, hard and lean, Simone's had taken on the roundness common to most women her age. Even their ways of dressing was nothing alike. Simone's style, soft and feminine, was in direct contrast to Pamela's high-fashion elegance.

It amazed Carrie that her father could have loved both of these women. What happened to the old idea, she wondered, that everyone was attracted to one certain type of person? It certainly hadn't held true for Philip DeBary.

Although they exchanged only the briefest of commiserations, Carrie noted that Pamela seemed far better suited to her father than her mother had been. A born-and-bred Texan, Pamela was a blue-blooded socialite, a warm-voiced horsewoman who apparently understood Philip and his world as well, if not better, than he did himself. Simone had never fit in, with her French accent and subdued ways, her need for privacy, and her cool, almost regal, manner. Pamela not only fit in, she seemed to lead the Houston social scene.

Philip and Pamela's son, little Andrew, had Carrie's white-blond hair and his mother's golden blue eyes, a disarming combination which Carrie couldn't help but love. An enchanting child, always smiling and chortling, he charmed everyone he met. If Carrie had been visiting under other circumstances, she would have wanted to spend all her time with him, get to know her half-brother better.

Perhaps, if circumstances had been different, she could have become friends with Pamela, too. They had many things in common—their love for horses, their similar childhoods—but they were divided by the same thing which united them, Philip DeBary. And his final wishes seemed designed to cut the schism between the two women even deeper.

"I can't take Ocean Fresh," Carrie repeated, talking directly to her father's lawyer, ignoring the other people in the room, "and I certainly don't want his house."

"But, Carrie, darlin'," Harry Sanford began soothingly, "your father wanted you to have the house you grew up in. He's always had that bequest in his will. He may have changed everything else—in fact, he changed it just before leaving for Japan—but you've always been the one to get the house."

"It's not mine anymore." She felt Pamela's eyes on her. "Besides, I'm not here just to see what my father left me. I certainly didn't want or expect anything from him."

"And why not?" Pamela's voice rang clear. "You're his daughter. He's always loved you."

It was Carrie's turn to be shocked. Somehow she'd expected, even wanted, Pamela to be distant, to fulfill her image of the wicked stepmother. She'd wanted to hate her, but Pamela had side-stepped all of Carrie's anger as if she'd expected it, as if she'd understood it.

"You have a right to that house far more than Andrew and I have," Pamela continued. "That was where you grew up. Besides, Philip left us the house in St. John and the apartment in Paris, and more money than I could ever possibly need—"

"I don't want the house, Pamela."

In the ensuing moments, the two women studied each other as if telepathically. Pamela seemed to comprehend that there was no way Carrie would ever live in the DeBary mansion. Perhaps she appreciated the fact that all of Carrie's childhood memories were tied into that twenty-two room house—the good ones as well as the bad. But there was no way she could know Houston had never been home to Carrie the way Hawaii was. And never would be.

When Pamela spoke again, it seemed to be with some relief that she wouldn't have to leave the home she'd shared with her husband for the past five years.

"Your father kept your room just the way it was when you left," she said to Carrie. "I would like for you to see it before you go home, and I think you should feel free to take with you whatever family heirlooms you want from the house."

Speechless once more, Carrie sat back down in her chair with a hard thud. This woman was too nice, not the type of gold-digging young stepmother Carrie had expected. Totally off-guard, she decided not to say another word.

Harry cleared his throat. "If that's settled, I suggest your lawyers arrange for some kind of monetary settlement, then. Now, may I continue?"

"N-n-no." Carrie gripped the sides of the oak chair. "I don't want Ocean Fresh, either."

How could she feel comfortable being associated with a company whose policies destroyed the animals she loved? What would Alex say? And Jack? Besides, she was no businessperson. Alex had caustically pointed that out only last week.

"It's not going to be as easy to get rid of the company as it is the house, Carrie." Sanford looked over his wire-rimmed glasses at her and she immediately felt his disdain.

My lack of business sense must be blinking like neon, she thought. I'm way out of my league.

"Your father made sure his affairs were totally in order before he went to Japan, so the estate will be settled quite soon," the lawyer continued. "Why don't we talk, Carrie? Perhaps we can work out something agreeable for all involved."

Although she felt like stalking out of the room and not looking back, something held Carrie in her chair. She folded her hands tightly in her lap and listened silently to the rest of her father's bequests—over a hundred thousand dollars to cousin Larry, Uncle Paul's only son; the bank and all its assets to Pamela; the radio and television stations to Philip's elderly second cousin R.C. and his wife Lillian, who had become instrumental members of the board during the past decade. Most of the rest of Philip's holdings also went to Pamela, with a large portion held in trust for Andrew. Nothing was set aside for Simone. Philip had known long ago that she wanted nothing from him. She had made that clear when she left. And she had never asked for anything for herself or Carrie. She had far too much pride to accept charity or to beg for help.

But I don't, Carrie thought. Suddenly, she realized that spending the last couple of days among people who had no financial problems had made her sick and tired of being broke. The thought of selling the house to Pamela and using the proceeds to pay off all the bills, to bring her head above water again, was a tantalizing option. If her father wanted to leave her something, why not money? Why did he always have to make everything so damn difficult?

But, first, the curiosity to see her old room had to be satisfied. Pamela was right. Carrie did want to collect some of the cherished treasures she'd had to leave behind seven years before.

Lorilene placed the hot earthenware pot on the table and automatically pushed the baby's hands away from it. "Doesn't sound to me like you're getting the kind of legal advice you need from Sanford. Why don't you let me call Mother's attorney? You remember him, don't you? Geoff Presley?"

Carrie came around the other side of the table with the salad she'd made and pursed her lips, wondering where to put it so that little Janel wouldn't be able to get her fingers into it. "I'm not sure. He's not that kid we always used to tease at the school dances, is he? The one who was all feet and wore his belt up under his armpits?"

"One and the same."

"I can't believe he's a lawyer now."

"And a damned good one. Mother wouldn't trust

anyone else with all her holdings. You know how picky she is about money."

Carrie smiled, remembering the evenings she'd slept over with Lorilene in the big house at the Weirback Ranch. It struck her that Kiki, Lorilene's mother, was always in her office, spending hours poring over her accounting books, because she believed that if she allowed someone else to do it, she'd lose control of her finances. Now that Carrie looked back, she had to admit it was kind of strange for a woman of Kiki Weirback's monetary stature to do her own bookkeeping. But Kiki wasn't the normal Texas socialite, content simply to do her nails and attend parties. She was a cowgirl par excellence, able to handle a wild horse better than any ranch hand she had, and she had some of the best. Perhaps that was where Lorilene got her independent streak.

"Where is your mother? I don't remember seeing her at the funeral."

"I knew there was something I had to tell you. Darn! She'd kill me if she knew I'd forgotten to give you her condolences. She's in Europe right now. Sold some duke over there some of her stallions, and he invited her to check out his stables. I think she's going to be bringing some new brood mares back, but she won't be home until sometime next week."

"I'll be gone by then," Carrie said, her mind already back in Hawaii, wondering how Jack was doing and whether Matt and Isaac had solved their differences.

"I wish you would stay a little longer."

"I've got too much to do, and *Maman* told me yesterday that Alex is starting to raise hell at the Center again. I've got to go back and talk to him. I never even got a chance to tell him Dad died before I left."

"Does he know now?"

"Yes, *Maman* told him." Carrie absentmindedly wiped some spittle off Janel's chin. "Besides, I can't leave the guys alone to run the whale-watching business forever."

"Must be fun," Lorilene mused as she settled in on the other side of the table. Since her husband had a late meeting at the office, Lorilene had given the cook the night off so the two women could eat dinner alone with the children. They had made a traditional Mexican meal, having as much fun in the kitchen together now as they used to as teenagers.

"Lots of work. And I don't even have a nice jacuzzi to slip into at night."

Lorilene looked up, her eyes twinkling. "You can't take it home with you. You'll have to come back every time you want to use it."

"Maybe I will."

"You'd better, honey. You don't know how much I've missed having you around."

After the meal, as they cleaned the table, Lorilene gave Carrie Geoff Presley's number and hung around the kitchen while Carrie spoke to him briefly. When Carrie got off the phone, she leaned against the wide tile counter and looked toward the ceiling.

"So, what's up? What did he say?" Lorilene asked, balancing the baby on her hip.

"Looks like I've really walked into a hornet's nest this time. I can't get rid of the company until I meet with the board. Geoff says he's got to check the corporation papers to see if there's anything else I can do, but he's pretty sure I have to convince the other stockholders that selling the company's the best move. Otherwise, I'm up the proverbial shit creek."

"Did he have any suggestions on how to do that? Sell the company, I mean."

"Only one. There's a party tomorrow night that most of the board is attending. It's Ocean Fresh's tenth anniversary. He suggested I go and meet the company's officers and boardmembers on a social level, so that I can get a feel for what they think. He's going to be there and it'll give me a chance to talk to him, so—"

"Why the glum face? Go! Maybe it'll get you feeling a little better. Besides, if it's the only way to get out of this, what choice do you have?"

"It's not really the party I'm worried about," Carrie said, pressing her fingertips to her forehead.

"Then what's the problem?"

"I don't know. I just got the feeling from the tone of Geoff's voice that there's something else I should be concerned about." Without knowing why, a sense of dread filled her.

"Stop worrying about stuff before it happens. You always did tend to put the cart before the horse. Now, come on, let's dig out that gown we picked up and see if I've got some jewelry to match that'll be impressive enough to wear to this shindig."

Before Carrie could protest, Lorilene had her by the elbow and was propelling her upstairs to the master bedroom.

The gold satin dress perfectly accented Carrie's tanned arms and set off the natural white sheen of her hair. It even brought out the highlights in her eyes more effectively than if she'd held a gold nugget up next to them. The gown's material shimmered as she moved, clinging to her slim hips and long legs as though it was made for her instead of bought off the rack.

"God, I hate you," Lorilene said as she stood back. "That looks ten times better on you than it did on that store mannequin. I could *never* wear something that slinky. And I've got just the thing to accent it."

She reached into her jewelry vault and pulled out a pair of topaz earrings with a matching long drop necklace. "Perfect," she commented again after helping Carrie put them on. "You're going to kill 'em. No one's going to be able to take their eyes off you. They'd sell you the Suez Canal for a dime and thank you for buying it."

"You think so?" Carrie looked into the mirror, amazed to see a mature woman looking back at her. With her hair up in a French knot and makeup accenting the unusual color of her eyes, she'd become a totally different person from the shorts-and-halter wearing captain of *The Big One*. She pulled her shoulders back and practiced walking in the heels Lorilene had lent her. "I feel as nervous as I did the night we were presented."

"You certainly don't look it. And if you remember correctly, we both had zits that night! There's one good thing to be said about growing up—the pimples go away!"

Still laughing, the two women headed for the stairs. Geoff had called that morning and suggested he pick Carrie up so that they could talk in the car before the party. It was the perfect solution to Carrie's nervousness.

When the doorbell rang, Lorilene moved quickly to answer it, and over her friend's shoulder, Carrie spotted a man taller than she, wearing a black Stetson, black lizard cowboy boots, and a finely tailored black tuxedo, complete with a string tie. But she didn't recognize the face until he crossed the foyer to take her hand in his.

"I wouldn't have known you in a million years, Geoff. No glasses, no braces, and—"

"No acne," he finished for her with a deep laugh. "But you, Carrie DeBary, I would've recognized anywhere. Except you've gotten even more beautiful than I remembered." He offered her his arm with a friendly smile and she took it, feeling quite comfortable with this new, mature version of the boy she remembered from the school dances.

Before they left, Lorilene adjusted Carrie's necklace one last time and leaned forward to whisper in her ear, "Don't let the big boys get you down, honey. Just remember you could always see through people. Trust your instincts, darlin'. They're never wrong."

Twenty

The Van Eckren house was nestled deep on a thousand acres beside the Brazos River. To get to it, visitors drove through miles of horse pasture and rolling fields spotted with cottonwood, oak, and pecan trees before reaching the sprawling antebellum mansion. The family held some of the most impressive land in the state, yet they were not oil people or horse people but businesspeople who had come into power on the coattails of Philip DeBary and others like him.

Tonight the road leading to the magnificent estate was lined with hundreds of luminarias. Their candlelit interiors cast dancing snowflake patterns on the tree-draped road and the house beyond. The sight brought back a long-forgotten memory of a birthday when her father had brought home luminarias and a piñata—a day too late. She shook the thought, then covered her discomfort with the comment that this was what the Van Eckren home must have looked like to the escaping slaves it had sheltered more than a hundred years ago.

Geoff laughed heartily. "I'm afraid you're wrong, missy. This place is scarcely ten years old if it's a day. The original building burnt to the ground during the Civil War, then the family rebuilt and that, too, fell to flames around 1941. The Van Eckrens were devastated and took to living in one of those cabins we passed about a mile ago until ol' James accumulated enough gambling money to rebuild. But it wasn't till your father came on the scene and offered James Junior a job that the family actually came into prominence again, and then James had the money to build another, much larger replica of the original family home, with lots of additions and modern conveniences. I guess you don't remember him, do you?"

She shook her head, her eyes taking in the cars pulling up to the house's regal front entrance to discharge their passengers—Rollses, Mercedes, Lincolns, BMWs, limousines—and people dressed to the hilt, talking and laughing as if having a good time had been mandated. Carrie felt guilty coming to a party like this so soon after her father's death, but another familiar feeling, that of being an outsider, took precedence as they drew closer to the front door.

"I'm not sure I should be here, Geoff," she said as he stopped his Lexus before the brightly lit entrance. She could hear faint strains of music coming from inside.

"Now, Carrie, we already talked about this." His voice, though quiet, had the deep profundo of a bass in a gospel choir. He put his heavy hand atop hers and patted it like a big brother. "Raise that pretty little head of yours and think of this as a business engagement. If you're even *half* the diplomat your daddy was, it'll be a piece of cake."

"I'm not like him at all," she protested, feeling a ball of anger well up in her chest at the comparison, but Geoff was already out of the car and circling around to her side.

Relying on all she'd learned from her debutante days, she rose smoothly from the car and glided into the party, a smile belying the swift beating of her heart. The Van Eckrens greeted them at the door with instant recognition and expressions of sympathy. Although she didn't recognize either of them, Carrie reminded herself they were valuable contacts and made it a point to linger a little longer than the other guests, sharing a few memories of her father and promising to be in touch before heading home.

Carrie followed Geoff from the formal foyer into a larger room, where a uniformed Mexican maid took their wraps. When Geoff spotted someone he knew, Carrie took the opportunity to wander to the entrance to the ballroom, milling with party-goers. The mansion, simply decorated with bouquets of white camellias, lilies, and roses throughout, glittered with the lights from crystal chandeliers hanging in each room. The effect was one of purity, simplicity and elegance, a quiet statement that the people who lived here had class. And money, lots of money.

For the first hour, Geoff escorted her around the room, introducing her as Philip DeBary's daughter, which raised enough eyebrows that Carrie finally drummed up the confidence to remind him that her last name was Madison, not DeBary.

"You want these people to know you're the new owner of Ocean Fresh," Geoff reminded her *sotto voce,* simultaneously offering a smile and a nod to James and Susan Hudson of Hudson Oil as they waltzed by. "That's why you're here, remember?"

"I really don't think it's necessary to jump right into it," Carrie replied, taking a glass of champagne a liveried butler offered her. "I just want to know who *they* are."

As they drifted from group to group, Carrie tried to ignore the sidelong glances from men who openly appraised her long slim body. She lifted her head and looked away, her curiosity caught by a small crowd gathered around a newcomer in the foyer.

"Who's that?" she asked, sipping her champagne.

"That," Geoff informed her solemnly, "is the man who wants to fill your shoes. Ishiru Makomoto, Japanese entrepreneur extraordinaire. One of the wealthiest men on his side of the world and your father's greatest competition."

"He wants Ocean Fresh?"

"So bad he can taste it."

Carrie smiled naturally for the first time since walking in the door. "How bad is that?" she asked. Maybe selling the company wouldn't be as difficult as she thought.

"The last offer, so far as I can remember, was several hundred million."

"Whoa—" She reached for Geoff's arm, feeling all color drain from her face.

"Don't faint on me now, missy," he said, barely moving his lips. "Looks like Mr. Makomoto's going to pay us a visit."

Makomoto meandered toward them, keeping one eye on Carrie while greeting those he passed by. He seemed barely five and a half feet tall, much shorter than she, a slim man with pasty white skin and slicked-back black hair, who carried himself as though he were the tallest, most important man in the room. She was instantly reminded of Emperor Hirohito. Behind Makomoto, a much larger man Carrie recognized as being Samoan shadowed him.

The Samoan's eyes were hidden behind dark glasses, his long black hair tied back in a ponytail. A bodyguard, she thought, and, unexpectedly, her knees began to quiver. Her boarding school education had not prepared her for this. She felt an impulse to flee, to catch the first flight back to Hawaii and leave the business details to Geoff.

"Steady," Geoff whispered.

When Makomoto was within five feet, another person stepped in front of him, blocking her view.

"Carrie! Caryn DeBary, my love. How are you? And your mother? Is Simone here?" The familiar voice belonged to Joyce Kincaid, Bruce Kincaid's British wife and her mother's only friend in Houston. They exchanged warm hugs, and over Joyce's shoulder, Carrie could see Makomoto had disappeared. She breathed a sigh of relief.

"Are you sure you don't want me to go with you?" Lorilene asked.

They were riding two of Lorilene's Arabian mares down a path lined with cottonwood trees which whispered as a breeze passed through them. The cool morning air lifted Carrie's hair off her shoulders. By noon, the temperature was expected to be in the mid-90s. By noon, she'd be visiting her old home, at Pamela's invitation.

"No, it's okay," she answered. "I think Pamela will

pretty much leave me alone so I can wander around by myself. It's going to be strange, but I think I'll be all right. I just hope she doesn't expect me to sit and have tea with her or something. I don't think I could handle small talk."

"After last night, you should be able to handle anything. Geoff told me you juggled those biz-whiz kids like you were one of them yourself. What was it you said to Thema Holden about the dolphins that shut her down so completely?"

Carrie chuckled and reached forward to run her hand along her horse's sleek neck. She loved riding again and knew that she'd continue once she got home, perhaps taking advantage of the open invitation to the Parker Ranch. The horse shifted impatiently beneath her, ready to get moving again.

"When did you talk to Geoff?"

"This morning, before you got up."

Shooting her friend a look of mock indignation, Carrie said, "You sneak. You always did manage to find out all the gossip before everyone else. I always wondered how you did it."

"Well, now you know. So tell me what you said."

"Thema started talking about how great Ocean Fresh's business has been lately, then she made a sarcastic comment about the other companies using dolphin-safe stickers on their cans. Something to the effect that it was a good way to build business because, in her words, 'those environmental nuts will think more highly of the product.' She kind of laughed like that was some great marketing ploy instead of the truth," Carrie said, her voice growing tight with anger. "I just couldn't let that pass by, so I told her how frightening it is for the dolphins when they get caught in the seine nets, how they drown if caught underwater for too long. I'm afraid I was a bit graphic describing the time I helped free the ones caught by Ocean Fresh's nets—that was the day I met Jack. I don't think anyone in that room had ever been on a commercial tuna boat or had a thought about what goes on outside the office because the whole crowd just fell silent, almost like they all felt guilty."

"They should," Lorilene retorted. "Why hurt a beautiful animal if you don't have to? Especially one as intelligent as a dolphin."

They rode on for a few more moments, contentedly watching the sun cast dappled patterns on the path and their powerful white horses. Then Lorilene turned around to face Carrie, who had fallen into line behind her.

"By the way, I've been meaning to ask, who's Jack?"

Carrie tried to hide her surprise, hoping the changing patterns of light cast by the trees and sun overhead covered her flushed face. "Just a friend. He works for Greenpeace and he's been helping out on *The Big One* since Alex has been in the hospital."

"Oh, one of those radicals," Lorilene commented as she swiveled around to face front.

"Not really," Carrie answered, a bit defensively. "He's just committed to making the earth a better place, and this is his way of doing it. Some people want to fight fire with fire, like Jack. Others just work quietly, like Alex. One way or the other, they're both fighting for the same thing. It's just that they have different ways."

"And is he very different from Alex, this Jack Greenpeace person?"

Carrie thought about that for a moment, listening to the muted clop-clop of the horses' hooves. "In a lot of ways, yes, but they have a lot of similarities, too."

"Do I hear some affection in your voice, Carrie DeBary? Are you having an affair with the man?"

Pulling on the reins, Carrie brought her horse to a complete stop. She would have preferred not to answer, but she knew that, in doing so, she would have admitted to what Lorilene already seemed to suspect. "I don't believe you, Lorilene. What kind of a question is that?"

"The kind a best friend would ask. Listen, Carrie," Lorilene wheeled her horse around to face her friend, "I know you better than you think. It's understandable that you've been feeling a bit depressed by Alex being crippled and all that's going on in your life. It's only normal. You're a healthy, vibrant woman who's been caught in a bad situation. I just don't think you realize how transparent you are. I've been watching you and listening to you. Jack's name has entered your conversation far more often than Alex's, and every time you talk about him, your face lights up. What's going on?"

"Nothing," Carrie answered, trying to be honest, trying to convince Lorilene—and herself—that her relationship with Jack was nothing more than a very deep friendship. "He's a friend. He's helped me a lot. I'm very grateful to him."

"Hmmmm. . . . Seems to me that gratitude is a dangerous thing."

As they continued to ride, Carrie had to admit Lorilene had a point. But she didn't want to lose the feelings Jack had aroused within her. Since Jack Briskin had come into her life, she'd found herself watching her reflection in mirrors and windows, as well as in his eyes. Her eyes were brighter, her step snappier, and she felt more alive, more womanly, than she had since the accident. It had been a long time since a man had held her and told her, with his eyes or merely his actions, that she was attractive. And she guessed she needed that. But she also needed much more—to be reassured of her intelligence, her worth as a human being. Alex used to do that, but these days he spent most of his time shooting her down. Jack had stepped in to fill that need, and she had come to rely on him.

"You know something, Lorilene," she said brightly. "I do believe you're getting too big for your britches."

"Excuse me?" Lorilene twisted around to face Carrie. Surprise was written on her face.

Carrie didn't answer. They had ridden into an open meadow within sight of the barn. Some of Lorilene's stable hands milled around near the open paddock like worker ants.

"Yes, I do believe I'm right, and the only way to prove it is to challenge you to a race." Carrie brought her mare abreast of Lorilene's and shot her friend a determined stare.

Lorilene grinned. "You're on," she said, nudging her horse to a gallop.

The two women raced, their hair streaming straight out, Lorilene whooping like a cowboy, Carrie giggling, until they reached the barn door. She won easily and Lorilene acceded with a comical bow as they handed their reins over to the stable hands. The women linked arms and headed to the house for breakfast, but before they entered the back door, Lorilene turned to Carrie one final time and said seriously, "You know you can talk to me about Alex, or Jack, any time, don't you?"

"I know," Carrie answered with a squeeze and a wink, "but right now I have to worry about what I'm going to say to my stepmother."

Twenty-one

When her childhood home came into view, Carrie was unprepared for her reaction. Her eyes misted over, and she pulled Lorilene's Mercedes off to the side of the road for a moment to compose herself. With the motor still running, she pressed the button to roll down the window and sat for a moment, listening to the mourning doves coo and the cicadas' low hum. The familiar sounds, the smell of the day's humidity, and the heat of the Texan summer quickly filling the car's interior all worked to bring back memories she'd thought long forgotten.

The house hadn't changed at all. The graceful white pillars lining the veranda still seemed to reach for the sky, as they had when she was five. The massive oaks framing the road that led to the house were still hung with silver mantles of Spanish moss waving lazily in the faint breeze. Wildflowers still colored the edges of the cultivated lawn, which stretched in cool, green strips in every direction. The only thing missing was the horses.

No horses? Had her father sold them or were they just stabled during the afternoon heat? What about Spencer—had he stayed? Would she even be able to find out what had happened to him if he had been sold?

Carrie put the car back into drive, but left the window open to listen to the crackle and crunch the tires made on the gravel. She needed something to break the bucolic, dreamlike state her memories had lulled her into.

When the carved mahogany front door opened and Pamela stepped out onto the veranda, Carrie was jolted back to reality. Parking the car, she grabbed her purse and forced a smile to her lips, not knowing what to expect next.

Pamela, dressed in a mid-calf white eyelet dress, appeared every inch the wealthy young matron graciously greeting a welcome guest. Carrie tried not to feel gawky in the gauze skirt and peasant blouse she'd chosen from Lorilene's closet after dismissing all other choices. She hadn't wanted to be overdressed, but she hadn't felt she could make this visit in jeans either, though that would have been her preference.

Walking toward her stepmother, Carrie wondered if she was truly welcome or if Pamela was just well-schooled in the art of manners. With a half-smile, Pamela reached out both hands. Her tawny hair hung in soft waves to her shoulders, making her appear much younger than she had when they'd first met at the funeral.

"I'm so glad you came," she said, her Texan drawl coming through strongly. "Please do come in out of this awful heat. Lord, I can't remember a summer starting as early as this one, can you?" Without waiting for Carrie's reply, she led the way up the front steps. "I've heard it never gets this warm in Hawaii.

Is that right? I've always wanted to go there, just never had the chance. Seems we always headed for the Caribbean instead of the Pacific."

They entered the cool, dark entranceway, and Carrie paused for a moment to give her eyes a chance to adjust. The center staircase loomed in front of her, its polished cherry steps disappearing up into the afternoon sunlight filtering in through the round stained-glass window her father had bought specifically for that purpose. The rich blues and reds of the pastoral scene it captured drew the eye of everyone who entered. Carrie took a deep breath upon seeing it again. She'd forgotten just how spectacular the window was. It graced the staircase landing where the stairs forked, one side leading to a hallway of bedrooms, the other to her father's office, what used to be the playroom, and the upper floor of the three-story library.

She took a couple of steps farther into the vestibule, her heels clicking against the polished floor, and let her eyes drink in the objects which were familiar old friends. The English grandfather clock whose face changed from sun to moon with the passing of day into night—she'd always begged her mother to let her wind it, but Simone never had until Carrie was old enough not to be interested anymore. And the ten-foot-long mammy's bench which lined one wall—she used to throw her muddy riding boots beneath it before vaulting the stairs to her room. And, finally, her eyes lit on a new addition to the pieces of art hanging in the foyer, a portrait of a man she remembered all too vividly.

"Grandpa," she whispered, walking over to the

painting and running her fingers along the elegantly simple gold frame. The artist had captured Andrew DeBary the way he'd want to be remembered—his well-worn Stetson hanging from his finger, a full laugh on his lips, his eyes crinkled in mirth, and his favorite Appaloosa mare, Applesauce, in the background.

"That portrait was the only thing Philip took from Andrew's home when your grandfather died. He said it made him feel his father had forgiven him every time he looked at it," Pamela said. She stood near the door, her arms crossed over her chest.

"They weren't speaking to each other when Grandpa died," Carrie replied, unable to take her eyes off the painting.

"I know. It killed your father. He disappeared with one of his horses for days . . ." Pamela's voice trailed off and each woman was left alone with her thoughts.

What neither of them commented on was that Carrie and Philip hadn't been speaking either.

"Do you want it?" Pamela asked softly.

"Excuse me?"

"Do you want the painting? Because if you don't . . ." Pamela walked quickly to Carrie's side. "He's *your* grandfather. It's only right you have it. My Andrew never even met him."

For a moment, the spell was broken, and Carrie wiped her sweaty palms against her skirt. Pamela seemed to sense her discomfort, and her eyes shifted to the floor.

"Mercy, where *are* my manners?" she said with a nervous laugh. "I've had Mickey make some iced tea. Would you like some?"

"Mickey? He's still here?" Carrie remembered the short, crotchety cook who'd been a fixture in the house long before she was born. "He's got to be eighty or ninety by now."

"No one seems to know exactly how old he is, including Mickey himself, but he keeps on going." Pamela headed for the kitchen in the rear of the house, calling over her shoulder, "You just make yourself at home. Look around. I'll be back in a few minutes."

With Pamela gone, Carrie relaxed and felt free to open the doors leading to the solarium, which stretched along the right side of the front of the house. Although the wicker furniture her mother had bought still filled the nooks and crannies of the room, along with huge potted palms and seven-foot-tall Victorian brass birdcages, there were new additions as well. An exquisite harp, its frame embellished with gold leaf roses, stood in one corner and a white baby grand piano now took up the space where Simone had stored her weaving loom.

Carrie idly ran her fingers over the piano keys and tried to still the memories rushing through her mind. Perhaps she shouldn't have come. This was the room where she'd first overheard her parents arguing about another woman. She'd been nine years old and had come downstairs unable to fall asleep. Hearing angry voices, she'd hidden behind one of the giant Boston ferns, which had sat on marble pedestals near the door, and listened surreptitiously. The argument had gone on for hours and had ended with Simone in tears. Afraid to move, Carrie had fallen asleep behind the fern. Mickey had carried her up to her room the next morning.

"Here it is," Pamela said brightly, breaking into Carrie's daydream. She placed a silver tray with two glasses on a nearby table, then handed one to Carrie, hesitating upon seeing the far-away expression on Carrie's face. "Should I leave you alone? I thought we might sit for a moment and get to know each other a little better, perhaps discuss the house before the lawyers take over, but if you'd rather I wait . . ."

Carrie shook her head. "No, I'm all right. Just kind of caught up in the past. I guess I didn't expect everything to look the same."

"Oh, there are a few rooms that are totally new, filled with my furniture, but everything fit so well in this old house, I just couldn't see any point in changing it. And Philip was always so comfortable here."

Carrie nodded, though she couldn't remember too many times when her father had actually been home long enough to enjoy the house. "Where are the horses?" she asked.

Carrie had been right: the four Tennessee walking horses, the only ones left out of the dozen she remembered, were in the stables, enjoying the cool shade. From what Pamela said, she rode only occasionally now that the baby took up most of her time, but she was reluctant to give up the horse Philip had presented her on their wedding day. The others served more as company for her favorite since no one had come to the ranch to ride for such a long time. Carrie thought how different it had been when she was younger. All of the horses had been ridden regularly, by either her or her father. Although Simone didn't ride, she'd liked to see them about and when they'd had parties, people had inevitably stayed over to ride the next day.

Although she asked a few more questions and they spoke amiably for quite a while, Carrie purposely diverted the conversation away from the sale of the house as Geoff had instructed her to do. She really didn't want to talk about money anyway; that was the lawyers' territory. And if asked how much she thought her father's house and land were worth, she would have had no idea. Geoff had mentioned a million dollars or more, but who knew what the lawyers would decide? And she really didn't care. Then the conversation came around to Ocean Fresh.

"You know, Carrie, I was just as surprised as you when Harry announced Philip had left you that company," Pamela said, stirring some sugar into her second glass of tea. "He had mentioned you two had a disagreement after he visited you in Hawaii, and before he left for Japan, it was obvious he was upset about something. But I didn't pay it any mind because I was so busy myself."

"So Dad didn't say anything to you about changing his will?"

"I knew he'd met with Harry, but your father was always meeting with his lawyer, always adding codicils to his will. Every time he bought a new piece of property or a business, he had to change the will."

"It almost seems like he wanted to make me angry," Carrie said, instantly regretting her petulant tone.

"No, I'm sure that's not it," Pamela assured her. "I think your father wanted to make sure Ocean Fresh went in the right direction. Who best to take it there than you, someone who cares about what's going to happen to the ocean's population in the future? I'm sure your father decided you were well qualified to meet the challenge."

"Well, he was wrong. I don't want to run that damn company. All I want is to sell it."

"You may do whatever you like with it. It's yours now."

Eager to change the subject, Carrie looked into her tea and asked, "Was Dad sick? Had he been having heart trouble before he left for his trip?"

Pamela's eyes filled and she dabbed at them with a hanky she retrieved from her pocket. "Your father was one of the healthiest people I know. He certainly dealt with more stress than the ordinary person, but he always managed to exercise and the doctor gave him an excellent report after his last physical. I just don't understand it . . ."

She sobbed quietly, unnerving Carrie, who didn't know whether to reach over to comfort her or to pretend she didn't notice. Finally, she awkwardly patted Pamela's hand.

Later, when Pamela had left to check on little Andrew, Carrie headed toward her old bedroom after passing through the library to pick up some of her mother's favorite books. Opening the door to the room, she set the books on the half table beside the vanity and looked around for a moment. Nothing had changed. The bed was still made with her favorite Laura Ashley spread and canopy. The sterling silver

brush set her parents had given her for her sixteenth
birthday still lay in its place on the marble-topped
dresser. Her collection of Steiff teddy bears still occupied their shelf next to the window.

She caught a glimpse of herself in the mirror and
stopped. She'd half expected to see the teenager she'd
been when she'd last entered the room, but the woman
she saw in the reflection looked much more sophisticated than she felt.

Out of curiosity, she pulled the closet doors open
and was amazed to find her wardrobe completely intact, as it had been almost eight years before. Why
had he saved all of this when some other young
woman could have used the clothes? she wondered.
She had never thought of him as sentimental, but
looking at her room, her closet, the drawers still full
of lingerie and bedclothes, she knew now she'd been
wrong.

The boxes Pamela had told her would be there were
stacked on the floor of the closet. Carrie sat down
beside them, trying to decide what to take back to
Hawaii.

An hour later, all of the boxes were full, stacked
to the brim with photos of her in her riding clothes,
at the debutante ball, with Simone on Christmas day
in Jamaica, standing beside Lorilene during one of
the horse shows where both had won blue ribbons.
Her diaries, which had been stuck in the bottom of
one drawer, sat on top of the pictures, and her silver
bureau set was carefully wrapped in another box.
She'd packed a few special outfits, for sentimental
value only. The others wouldn't fit her now, anyway,
and there was no sense in taking clothes that were

almost eight years old. She'd tell Pamela to give them to a charity.

Standing, she surveyed the room once more, then walked out the door, knowing she'd probably never see the house again.

When she called Geoff less than an hour later from Lorilene's house, it was to list the items she'd decided to take from her father's house, including the portrait of her grandfather and one of a younger, happier Simone, standing on the bow of *The Winsome Blonde*, her hair tossed by the Gulf wind. Carrie had almost forgotten that portrait, but she was sure her mother hadn't.

Geoff promised to get a shipping company to the house by the end of the day, then told her he'd call Pamela's lawyer so they could finalize the sale quickly. Carrie sighed. It was better that way; then neither she nor Pamela could ruminate on the idea. And perhaps she'd even go back to Hawaii with enough money to pay Alex's therapy bills.

"Before I let you go," Geoff continued, "I've set up an appointment for you tomorrow morning to see Clark Quincel."

Quincel was president of Ocean Fresh. Carrie had briefly met him the night of the party and had liked the Harvard Business School grad who tugged at his tie the whole time they talked. He'd seemed really concerned about what was going to happen to the company. Of course, any decision would effect his life-style, but Carrie sensed that he was genuinely interested in what she had to say about the dolphins and Ocean Fresh's fishing practices. She figured Geoff was wise to let her meet with Quincel alone before throwing her into the lion's den of Ocean Fresh's board of directors.

"Mr. Quincel will see you now, Mrs. Madison." The secretary motioned Carrie through the open oak office door without taking the phone from her ear or her eyes off the fax machine.

Rising from the waiting room chair, Carrie anxiously pulled at her skirt, then smoothed her hair before venturing into Quincel's office. Inside, she was treated to a bird's-eye view of Houston's bevy of glass skyscrapers. She'd always seen the skyline from the bottom up; never had she imagined the opposite view would be twice as breathtaking. She suppressed the urge to walk the perimeter of the room gazing through the ceiling to floor windows.

Quincel, a headset in his ear, paced behind the desk, talking rapidly, as he gestured her toward a chair. The wall behind her, the only one not made completely of windows, served as home to a large screen television, which appeared to be transmitting live action from the floor of the New York stock exchange. Beside it, a mini-bar held bottles of top-shelf liquor and a small refrigerator.

How appropriate, she thought, remembering how her father had liked his glass of Jack Daniels as soon as he walked in the door after work.

"Go with it, Les," Quincel said before pulling the telephone headset off his head and settling in the large leather chair. He peered at her from behind his half-moon-shaped lucite desk.

"I'm sorry, Mrs. Madison," he began.

"Carrie."

"Carrie, then. Seems like everything always happens at the last minute. Our Japanese stocks are on the dip and the European market isn't even awake yet. If they gave me sixty hours a day, it still wouldn't be enough."

Carrie guessed him to be about forty-five, though she'd heard he was younger. He seemed exhausted, burnt out, like so many other young executives she knew.

"You'll see what it's like," he continued, "when you take over."

"I'm not going to take over," she stated. "I've come to talk to you about selling Ocean Fresh."

Quincel's chin dropped and his light blue eyes flickered briefly. She supposed this was about as close as this CEO would come to being shocked.

"Say what? But aren't you taking over for your dad? I thought . . . from what you said the other night . . ."

"Nope. Morally, I can't support a company like this. Besides, I would have no idea where to start—"

"What do you mean?" Quincel rose and bent forward.

"I want to sell Ocean Fresh," she repeated.

Time slowed. She heard distant echoes of far-away traffic, city sounds, planes, ringing telephones.

"But you can't do that . . ."

"Why?"

"Because the board has to approve any sale," he

said, seeming to pluck the answer out of the air. He stood back from the desk and folded one thin hand into the other. "Your father wouldn't have wanted you to. You know, for the past several years, he's been fighting takeovers. He was the last holdout, the last in the privately held tuna industry. No one could compete with our prices anymore."

"No wonder," Carrie commented, a wry grin on her face, "seeing as he didn't bother to abide by any government regulations, he never had the expenses the other companies had in replacing driftnets."

Quincel walked to the windows, keeping his back to her, but she could tell he had something to hide. And knowing that made her pay attention to him all the more. The great Carrie DeBary intuition, as Lorilene would call it, was at work.

"What is it, Mr. Quincel?" Carrie asked, rising out of her chair and moving to where she could see his face. "Why did my father avoid doing the things he should have? What is it Ocean Fresh is trying to hide?"

"There's nothing to hide, Mrs. Madison—"

"Carrie. Please, as owner of the company, I have a right to know."

Quincel swiveled for an instant, almost as if he wanted to take her into his confidence, then thought better of it.

"You don't know anything about this business, do you?" he asked.

"Only what my father hasn't done." She touched the window, absentmindedly tracing a skyscraper's profile before continuing. "Like I said the other night, I've spent too many years on the ocean to be ignorant of what the seine nets Ocean Fresh uses have done to innocent animals. There's no way I can be part of this company with a clear conscience."

"You're a good person, Carrie." Quincel returned to his desk chair, his shoulders hunched forward as though he was in pain. "Unfortunately, good people don't get very far in the corporate world. Perhaps you're right not getting caught up in this company, but I feel I must tell you something." He stared straight ahead past the collection of Baccarat paperweights on his desk to the television, flashing stock market trading figures.

"What is it, Mr. Quincel?"

He looked up at her almost as if seeing her for the first time.

"If you sell Ocean Fresh, things will get even worse than they already are. The animals, your beloved dolphins and whales and sea turtles, will be in even deeper danger. That's not what your father wanted, and from what you've told me, it's not what you want either."

Carrie knew the look on Quincel's face to be one of complete honesty. She felt she could trust him.

"Why?" she demanded. "What's going on?"

"Ishiru Makomoto."

Twenty-two

The steam rose from Lorilene's hot tub located in the horseshoe-shaped garden area behind the kitchen. A completely private spot, Carrie thought. The garden's pecan trees and hydrangea bushes were shaped so that the inhabitants of the hot tub could see a wide open sky above them. Tonight, as Carrie put one foot tentatively into the hot, swirling water, the sky shivered with thousands of stars. She was reminded of the vast black velvet Hawaiian sky and felt a pang of loneliness.

"You're ready to go home, aren't you?" Lorilene asked. She was already immersed in the tub, her head back, lazing against its pillowed sides.

"Yes, I think I am," Carrie agreed, finally lowering herself into the steam. "Too much has happened in the past couple of days. I feel like a planet spinning off its axis and I'm heading for the black hole."

Lorilene's shrill guffaw filled the night. *"That's* the Carrie I remember, not the melancholy, quiet woman you brought with you. Listen, hon, I know you've gone through a lot in the past couple of months. Lord knows I wouldn't find it easy to manage if Jimmy was crippled like Alex, nor could I take over his business. But I know you're going to make it through all this horse crap, and all these business tycoons will sit up and take notice by the time you're through. Hell, you have a lot more common sense and integrity than most of the Harvard and Yale group."

Carrie laughed with her friend, buoyed by Lorilene's irreverent views on the corporate world and life itself.

When Lorilene became serious again, she looked over at Carrie, her eyes thoughtful.

"It's been a long time since I've had adult company. You don't know how nice it's been for me to have you around. Jimmy's not home much these days . . ." She flicked both hands out of the water, comically throwing them up in the air. "As you can *obviously* see. But, seriously, Carrie DeBary, I wish you could hang around a little longer. I've missed you."

That heartfelt comment stopped her. She watched a shooting star leave a diamond-like streak behind it and heard the low nicker of one of the horses in the stables. Thoughts of Alex and how it used to be with him invaded her peace.

"I feel guilty," she said, turning to Lorilene.

"Why? You can't help it if you can't come to Texas very often."

"I'm not talking about that. I'm talking about Alex." She watched Lorilene's eyes closely, searching for understanding.

"Why do you feel guilty about Alex?" Lorilene asked, sitting up straighter, her breasts rising above the steamy water.

"I can't cope with him anymore," Carrie confessed. "And sometimes I really can't stand being around him. That makes me feel horrible." She pounded the sides of the tub with her closed fist. "When I married him, I promised to be with him 'in sickness and in health.' I *never* thought I'd have a problem taking care of Alex if anything happened. Never. Now look at me."

"You're only human—"

"That's not the point. If it was me, if *I'd* been the one to have the accident, Alex would've been there for me."

Lorilene listened silently, reaching over to pat Carrie on the arm.

"I'm not the wife I promised to be," Carrie said, biting her lip. "I can't believe I'm doing this. I can't believe my husband's in the hospital and I'm falling for someone else."

"I knew something was going on," Lorilene whispered. "Why couldn't you talk to me about it?"

"I'm not very proud of myself."

"Good Lord, girl, how many female saints do you know in your neighborhood?"

"Huh?" Carrie's head swung around and her forehead wrinkled.

"You're twenty-five, almost twenty-six, right?"

Carrie nodded.

"Your whole life's ahead of you—a career, babies, maybe some traveling, your own home. Then, *boom,* everything, every one of your dreams, disappears. Who wouldn't be miserable?"

Carrie gasped inadvertently.

Lorilene reached over and patted her arm again, then leaned forward until they were almost nose to nose. "It's true, girlfriend, admit it. He can't move his legs. Can't function sexually. Can't go to the bathroom without help. And, on top of all that, he's got a rotten attitude. Takes a superhuman to overcome all those obstacles, if you ask me." She tapped Carrie on the nose, then settled back against the hot tub, her face turned to the sky. "On top of everything that's wrong with Alex, you're financially destitute. Then your daddy dies. I'll tell you what, if that don't make you run for some handsome stranger's arms, I don't know what will!"

Lorilene's arguments made sense. Carrie felt as absolved of her guilt as if she'd gone to church, but in the back of her mind, she knew other women had gone through worse and still didn't cheat on their husbands.

"God, Lori, how can you make it all seem so sensible?"

"Well, I look at it this way. You're on the inside looking out. I'm on the outside looking in. Maybe it's easier for me to give the advice. Y'know, if you lived here, you could have the value of my golden advice all the time."

"I promise I'll be back." Now it was Carrie's turn to reach over and squeeze her friend's hand.

"Next time you come, it'll be a happier visit."

Carrie nodded. "It better be."

Two days later, when Carrie boarded the flight for Hawaii, she looked back at the disappearing Houston skyline with mixed emotions. The trip home had done many things for her, from reassuring her that she could come back to her childhood home with her head held high to reinforcing the questions she'd always had about her father. She supposed she'd always have to live with the regret that their differences were never reconciled. From what she'd been able to piece together from speaking with her father's friends, Pamela, Geoff, and Clark Quincel, her father was more of an enigma than ever. She found it hard to believe he'd shared some of her opinions. If he had believed, as she did, that protecting the sea's creatures was his responsibility, why hadn't he changed the driftnets to something less dangerous, less damaging to those fish and mammals who swam above the tuna? And what about Ishiru Makomoto? Why did she get the shivers whenever she thought about him?

Those questions, combined with her need to get home, should have kept her awake on the flight home, but they had the opposite effect. Moments after the plane was airborne, Carrie fell asleep, her hand in her pocket guarding the $100,000 house deposit check Quincel had given her that morning.

"Whoa, *Sistah!* Look at you! You're a bird of Paradise." Matt took Carrie's bags with a flourish and a large smile. His eyes glowed as he looked her over once more and nodded, obviously approving of her new image.

Behind him, Simone stood quietly, holding a paperback mystery in one hand, her purse in the other. For a moment, she didn't move, then she started forward uncertainly, a tentative smile on her lips.

"Maman!" Carrie threw her arms around her mother, holding her hard, then drew back. Something

was different, yet she couldn't put her finger on it. "I didn't expect you to be here, but I'm so happy you came. I've missed you."

"And we have missed you, *chérie*. Welcome home."

Carrie followed them to the car, chattering inanely about how good it felt to be back and how much she was looking forward to going to work. She could sense Matt and her mother judging her new clothes—the bone-colored linen suit and peach silk blouse—but neither said anything. Her newfound confidence dissipated quickly in front of these people who knew her so completely.

On the way out of the airport, Matt took a side street rather than heading for the Saddle Road.

"Where are you going?" Carrie asked.

Matt exchanged a puzzled glance with Simone. "Thought you'd want to see Alex before we head home. The big *kahuna's* been asking for you."

Carrie smiled, as she suspected Matt thought she should, and settled back into her seat. After the long plane ride and the tumultuous events of the past two weeks, she just wanted to get back to the harbor. Deep in the back of her mind, she knew she'd rather see Jack right now than Alex. She wasn't ready for another of Alex's confrontations, and she knew there'd be one when he found out what her father had left her. Yet she knew if she admitted that out loud, she'd have a lot of explaining to do to Matt and her mother.

"How is Lorilene?" Simone asked cheerfully, her question slyly covering for what she really wanted to ask.

"Fine. Hasn't changed at all. Two kids and she still

acts like a kid herself. Even tried to teach me the Electric Slide the night before I left."

"The electric what?"

"It's a new country dance, *Maman*. Everyone's doing it, I guess."

"Oh." Simone made a pretense of finding space in her purse for her paperback.

"I saw Joyce," Carrie offered. "She wanted to be remembered to you."

"Oh?" Simone brightened. This is what she really wanted—some gossip, news about old friends and acquaintances—but she had always figured asking questions would be considered prying. And her strict French Catholic upbringing demeaned that kind of nosiness as rude and uncouth.

"She looks well," Carrie continued. "They still have the ranch, plus their Galveston house, and she still goes sailing twice a week. She asked if you were still sailing and was disappointed to hear we'd sold *The Blonde*. But she was really pleased to hear you're well and happy. Said you should send her the new gallery brochure when you get a chance and she'd love a long, newsy letter."

"Yes, I must write to her soon."

Carrie continued telling her mother about the people she'd seen and kept Simone diverted until they pulled into the Center's parking lot. Although she knew where they were, Carrie kept talking, half hoping Matt would take the hint and keep on driving. Finally, Simone opened the car door and got out, motioning for Carrie to do the same. Reluctantly, Carrie slid across the seat and joined her.

Immediately, Simone returned to the car, got in, and closed the door.

"Aren't you coming with me, *Maman?*"

"Mon Dieu, Caryn, you haven't seen your husband for almost three weeks! Why would I want to come in with you? Besides, Matt and I just visited Alex a few days ago. He's tired of seeing us. It's your turn now." She settled back into the seat, pulled her paperback from her purse and opened it, summarily dismissing Carrie.

With a feeling of impending defeat, Carrie turned and entered the Center.

It took her almost fifteen minutes to locate Alex. After not finding him in his room, she wandered down to the nurses' station. Since no one at the Center wore uniforms, it always threw Carrie off when she had to ask questions. If not for their name tags, she wouldn't have been able to identify members of the Center's staff, and when she did, they sent her on a wild goose chase. One woman directed Carrie to the whirlpool room, where, so she stated with an air of superiority, Alex was scheduled for treatment. When Carrie found the room empty, it was another couple of minutes before she could summon someone else for information. This time she was sent all the way to the ultraviolet tanning room. Still no Alex.

On her third try, she found him in physical therapy, hanging from a sling attached around his waist like a diaper. Two attendants worked on his legs and back as he sat, suspended in the air. He seemed shocked to see her.

"Well, look who's here. George, Jamison, this is my wife, the almost-invisible Carrie Madison," Alex said.

George nodded and Jamison said, "Ah, the Golden Mermaid. He's told us all about you."

"I hope it was good," she said, believing it probably wasn't.

"Look at me, honey. I'm flying!" Alex said, holding both arms out straight.

The two attendants laughed condescendingly, as they would at an inebriated person. Carrie felt incredibly uncomfortable, yet went along with the feeble attempt at a joke.

"Looks like they've got you pretty busy," she said to Alex, her hands tightly clasping her pocketbook straps. "Maybe I should come back some other time."

"Don't you dare," Alex growled as George and Jamison undid the straps holding him up. "I haven't talked to you in weeks and I want you to tell me all about Houston."

George and Jamison lowered him into a nearby wheelchair, glancing curiously at Carrie once more before leaving the room.

Alex wheeled toward her, then circled around her, giving a long, low whistle, the kind he used to give her when they'd dressed up for a night out. "What the hell did you *do* in Houston, rob a bank?"

"No," she replied, flustered. "I went to my father's funeral. I tried to tell you before I left—"

"I know, I know. I didn't listen. Haven't been much of a conversationalist lately, have I? I'm sorry I didn't act very nice to you before you left, babe." He reached for her hand. "I wish I could've been there with you. The funeral wasn't too bad, was it?"

She chose to remain silent. If she spoke, everything would come tumbling out like marbles out of an open bag.

Alex stared at her as if puzzled, then wheeled away with a quick flick of his wrists. "Don't you want to ask me what's new?" he said.

She walked over to the other side of the room, determined to put as much distance between them as possible.

"No answer, huh? Well, I'll tell you anyway. I've been working my ass off every day, eating my green beans and my soybean burgers, and doing everything good ol' Terry McElroy and Dr. Karachi tell me to do, and look where it gets me. Look!"

She still didn't glance his way. Why hadn't she taken Lorilene up on her offer to stay in Houston? Why had she allowed Matt and her mother to bring her here? She was too stressed out to deal with Alex logically. And too tired.

"Carrie, look at me," Alex pleaded and, for the first time, she met his eyes. The familiar, cherished features were twisted into an obstinate grimace.

"You sold out, didn't you?" he hissed. "You got back into that whole phony social scene even though you always said you wouldn't. Look at you, all dressed up like an executive in your new suit. Bill Blass, isn't it?" He wrinkled his nose and pushed the wheels of his chair.

Inadvertently, her eyes were drawn to his shoulder muscles. He looked as though he'd been lifting weights. She'd heard paraplegics' arms built up after awhile, but she couldn't believe the difference in just the past couple of weeks.

"You're getting better, aren't you?" she asked. Again, she ignored his sarcasm. "Even your razor-sharp insults have more slice."

He chuckled. "More slice. Yeah. I've got plenty of time to think up fast quips seeing as I'm alone most of the time."

This isn't fair, she thought. My father just died, dammit. Am I to be punished, Alex? Please, not now.

She pulled on her pocketbook strap until it made an indentation in her shoulder. "Well," she said, keeping her voice cool and edging toward the door, "I just wanted to see if you were okay. Matt and *Maman* are waiting for me in the car."

Alex wheeled around and blocked her exit. "They can wait a little longer. What's the matter? Don't you want to visit with your husband?"

"No, that's not it—"

"You know what you remind me of?" Alex challenged.

"No, what?"

"You remind me of my little brother when our shepherd's foot got mangled in a tractor accident. Bryan couldn't stand the way the dog looked with a cast on its leg afterwards. I guess at five years old it's kind of hard to understand how animals can adapt. And that dog was damn good at running on three legs." Alex stopped to snicker and shake his head. "Bryan screamed the first time he saw Rinny in the cast. He was the one who named the dog Rin-Tin-Tin after that TV character. I guess he thought it was his dog, until the dog wasn't normal anymore. Then

Bryan didn't want anything to do with him. He was terrified of the animal. Used to get a look on his face just like the one you have on yours right now."

Nothing could have surprised Carrie more than this story.

"Sometimes you *do* scare me, Alex," she admitted. "I don't know you anymore. I've tried to understand how you feel, I've tried to be patient. Can't you find it within yourself to even tell me you're sorry my father died?"

Chagrin etched itself on Alex's face and softened the hardness of his mouth. "It's kind of easy to get selfish when everyone's concentrating on you twenty-four hours a day. I feel like if I don't perform adequately, everyone's going to be disappointed. This must be what it feels like to be in a zoo."

Carrie reached over to tentatively stroke Alex's cheek. "I'm sorry you feel that way, honey, but I think you'd better start looking toward the future. They're going to kick you out of here one day, whether you behave or not."

Silenced, Alex sat mournfully staring at his hands. Then, as if remembering something he'd meant to say, his head snapped back, and his eyes drank in her new clothes once again.

"What happened while you were there? In Houston?" he asked.

"I went to the funeral and the reading of the will and I stayed with Lorilene a while and visited with Pamela—"

"How much did he leave you?"

"What?"

"You're not deaf. I asked how much it took for him to buy you out."

Carrie's mouth fell open. She glared at her husband. "I don't believe you! The money I brought home is going to get us out of the hole. You should be thank—"

"Why should I be thankful? The only favor the old man ever did for us was to die."

Before she could stop herself, Carrie swung her right arm and delivered a stinging slap to Alex's cheek. He winced, an instant red splotch rising where she'd hit him, but he blinked back the tears gathering in his eyes before they dropped to his cheeks.

"You sold out, Carrie. I never thought I'd see the day, but you've sold out."

"Well, I never thought I'd see the day when I'd say this, Alex. I never want to see you again!"

With a strength she wouldn't have thought possible, she shoved his wheelchair out of the way, not caring if it fell over, and bolted through the door, slamming it behind her. She flew down the corridor, pushing past attendants and visitors, angry tears burning her eyelids.

In her rush to get as far from Alex as possible, she never noticed Terry McElroy and Dr. Karachi heading for her, tentative smiles on their faces.

Twenty-three

"Here, this one's for you."

Carrie ripped out the check from her ledger and handed it, with a flourish and a smile, to Jack. He'd been sitting in the office all morning, patiently reading some new Greenpeace bulletins while she sorted the mail and paid some bills. He'd been quiet, as he'd promised he would be, not even arching an eyebrow when she whooped and hollered her joy about being able to pay off all her bills.

They'd spent most of their days together since she came back from Houston, and Carrie readily admitted to enjoying his company. She'd gotten used to seeing his dark head bob around the corner every morning and had come to love the meticulous way he helped her lock up every night. Sometimes they had supper together if they had a late whale watch, but the season was practically over and Jack usually had Greenpeace business to attend to at night. They were putting together some information about Hawaii's endangered endemic bird species, and since he knew the island better than just about anyone else on staff, his presence was required. It was okay, Carrie figured. If they spent any more time together than they already had, people would start to talk.

Carrie watched his face as he read the check she'd given him, delighting in the moment to covertly study him. She loved the way his hair curled around his face like a cherub's cap, the way he smelled of oatmeal soap and herbal shampoo, and how his dark shadowy beard mysteriously appeared on his face at the same time late every afternoon. She had a hard time keeping her distance, holding her hands close to her sides, clenching the fingers that wanted to caress every millimeter of every curve of his face, but thus far, she'd controlled her urges. He, too, appeared to be mentally reining himself in.

Although the sexual tension in the office grew thicker every day, Carrie found herself becoming more and more relaxed with him. They'd shared jokes, talked about her father, fallen into familiar patterns. She didn't ask him to bring the coffee, but he did, so she automatically got into the habit of supplying the morning doughnuts. Jack's way of working meshed completely with hers, and if she hadn't been friends with Matt for so long, she would have been tempted to hire Jack full-time. But, for now, he was part-time. Temporary.

Yes, her intuition had already told her Jack Briskin was a temporary fixture in her life. She fully expected to find him gone one day.

"This check's for a hell of a lot more than what I paid for the plane ticket," Jack said, waving the check in the air with a frown.

"What do you think, I'd let you work here for *free?* No way, my friend," she answered. "No one's going to say Caryn Marie DeBary Madison uses her friends. Nosirree!"

"Listen, Carrie, I don't want this. Now don't fool around. You know I was doing you a favor, just say thank you." Jack reached for her hand, shoved the check into it, then folded her fist around it. He was so close she could feel his breath muss her hair. She sat very still, realizing he wasn't going to back off this time. Then, suddenly, he pulled her up out of the chair, both of his hands still surrounding hers and held her so close to him she could feel his heart beating against her chest. She stood in front of him, eye to eye, and it was the first time in her life she was glad to be tall.

"I don't want you to do this," she said meekly, though she didn't know whether she was talking about taking back the check or about his body now so dangerously near hers.

"What if I want to?" he whispered huskily.

"I have to want it, too."

"Do you?"

She didn't answer with words, just surrendered herself to his arms and let the check flutter to the floor.

Their mouths found each other, exploring slowly at first, then more hungrily, sucking and nipping, until she found herself moaning aloud. She drove her fingernails into his shoulders, felt his warm skin beneath his shirt. Slipping her hands underneath the material, she spread her fingers wide to memorize the angles of his shoulders, the back muscles which she remembered had rippled like rope as he worked on the boat. She pressed him against her breasts and held him there tightly.

"Oh, God, Jack," she moaned. "We can't do this. Not here." Reluctantly, she pushed him away. His lips parted, rosy and full, and she longed to kiss him again. But now her eyes were open and she was acutely aware of the people walking by just outside her office windows.

"Everyone can see us," she said, trying to calm her trembling.

"Back here, then." He was trembling, too. Looking at her from beneath lowered lids, he took her by the hand, drawing her into the back room.

"You're driving me nuts," he groaned as he once again brought her into his arms.

His hands cradled her head, tunneling beneath her long, heavy hair, then deftly moving her so he could devour her mouth once again, driving his tongue deep within her with the uncontrollable urge of a schoolboy. She responded just as eagerly. She'd waited a long time for his touch, and although she knew what she was doing was forbidden, it felt wonderful.

Jack rolled her head back and brought his lips to her neck, exploring every inch of her throat, even finding the tiny, sensitive hollow which made her cry out with pleasure. He spent what seemed to be hours kissing her, ignoring her plaintive urges to explore other parts of her body aching for his touch.

Finally, breathless and unable to wait any longer, she tore at her own T-shirt, yanking it up out of her shorts and over her head to reveal taut, round breasts. Then she took his hands and placed them upon her.

Now it was his turn to groan.

Her nipples grew hard and full beneath his fingers. Still, he continued, trailing his lips slowly down her bare shoulder, until his tongue reached her perfectly aroused peaks, and she heard him murmur, "Oh Carrie, I couldn't have waited any longer."

Within seconds, they both realized any attempt at slow lovemaking was out of the question. Their clothes flew to the floor and the thin cot protested beneath them.

Jack's body, hard and heavy atop hers, moved with purposefulness and grace. He positioned himself so that he could please her in three separate places, simultaneously. She burrowed her face in his soft chest hair and thought she'd go out of her mind, felt herself reeling as though falling into unconsciousness, as though she would drown in the waves of tiny orgasms crashing over her body. She rode the storm with him, calling out his name, her voice sounding like the wind. Her whole body rocked with his as they came together, quickly and tumultuously. They melded then, as though their two bodies had passed into and through each other.

She kept her eyes closed, purposefully perpetuating the dreamlike state, and almost drifted off to sleep, but she soon felt a cool breeze lick at her erect nipples, reminding her that someone could walk into the office at any moment. Reluctantly, she opened her eyes to find Jack's face less than an inch away, his emerald eyes watching her. He gave her a contented smile.

"I'm afraid to move," he said. "If I do, I'll either break the spell or this old cot will split in half beneath us."

She chuckled. Although the cot wheezed, she couldn't resist dropping little butterfly kisses on Jack's love-bruised lips. Then she settled back to study his face, the cute way his eyebrow hairs curled indiscriminately, the light in his eyes which shone specifically for her, the sensuous curl his lips made when he smiled.

"Next time," he said, brushing her hair away from her face, "it'll be a lot more romantic. You deserve it." Although his tone was joking, his eyes were serious. "I think I'm in love with you, Carrie."

She stiffened inadvertently.

"You can't be . . . we can't . . ."

"Why not? We work together well, we like the same music, read the same books, care about what's important, and you've already told me you don't think you have much of a marriage left . . ."

Alex!

Shaking her head, she pushed Jack away, then rose from the cot herself.

"It's too complicated," she said, hurriedly pulling on her clothes. "You know that."

She went back out into the front office, fervently hoping her mother wouldn't come by unexpectedly as she had been doing during the past week. Carrie suspected her mother was trying to find the right time to corner her for a long talk about Alex. Although she had never told her mother what had happened when she'd visited Alex that first day home, she knew Simone suspected something was wrong when Carrie stopped making her weekly visits to the Center.

She didn't want to see Alex. She didn't want even to think of him. Especially now.

Jack came out of the back room and leaned against the doorjamb. "I care about you, Carrie," he said softly, juggling the T-shirt he held from one hand to the other. "I wouldn't do anything to hurt you."

"I know that," she replied with a deep sigh. "There's just too much going on right now. I'm not ready to add any more stress to my life, even though I want to be with you . . ." She stopped herself from going any further and stepped behind the desk as if putting something solid between them would protect her from her own traitorous emotions.

"I won't forget what you've just told me," he said. "But I'm going to warn you, I'll wait, for as long as it takes, and meanwhile, I'll be here as your friend."

She nodded, a lump in her throat. "That'd be best, I think. I need every friend I can get right now. Maybe you can even help me figure out what I'm going to do about Ocean Fresh."

Jack pulled his T-shirt over his head and walked to the window. Ocean Fresh had been a subject she hadn't wanted to discuss with anyone, especially Jack, since she knew what he would advise. Although she didn't want anything to do with the company, except to get rid of it, Jack had already intimated that he thought she could make a difference if she took it over.

"You know what I think, Carrie," he said now. "I don't want to be pushy, but have you ever considered the fact that your father might have done this on purpose?"

"How could he? He didn't know he was going to die. He was more fit than most men twenty years younger than he. There was no real reason for him to even write a will."

"Then why didn't he leave you one of the banks or the radio station?"

Carrie's brow wrinkled. "Boy, do you know how to blow a high or what? Here I was, tickled to death to finally get all my bills paid, I even started thinking about looking at houses so that I'd have someplace decent to live once the rest of the money for the Houston house comes in, then I thought I'd sell the company to that Makomoto guy and I wouldn't have to worry about a damn thing for the rest of my life. And now you've got to bring up these weird possibilities. Who do you think you are, Perry Mason? Just drop it, Jack. You're wrong. Dad just left me the business to bust balls with me. It's like reaching out from the grave to tweak my nose. The last laugh's on me, I guess."

"I don't know, Carrie. I think you'd better really consider this plan of yours inside and out before you make a move." He strode to the other side of the desk and rested his foot against the open bottom drawer. "You could make a big difference, y'know. Get the company to stop using driftnets. If the Japanese companies keep it up, they're going to disrupt the whole North Pacific ecosystem. Hell, only a couple of weeks ago, one Greenpeace crew counted eighty blue sharks, sixty-six dolphins, and God knows how many seabirds and other creatures caught in a Japanese net in the Pacific. The damn net covered one hundred and thirty-five miles, Carrie! A hundred and thirty-five fucking miles!"

She held up both hands. "I know what you're saying. Believe me, I do, and you can't imagine how it feels to be responsible for a company that does something as ugly as that. I just can't take over Ocean Fresh. I know absolutely nothing about how to manage a big industry. I even have trouble balancing the books for *The Big One.*" She tried for a laugh, but it came out as a croak. Taking over the company terrified her, even though she knew Jack was absolutely right. If she sold it to someone else, Ocean Fresh's abominable fishing practices might become even worse.

"And Makomoto, of all people!" Jack continued, his voice rising indignantly. "He's made his money breaking every rule in the book! His company was responsible for more sea life deaths last year than all the American companies combined."

Carrie leaned her head on the desk and pressed her fingers to her throbbing temples. "What the hell do you expect me to do? I don't even know where to begin."

Jack sat down and lifted her face so that she'd look at him. His full lips were stretched into a determined straight line. His nostrils flared and sharp creases stretched across his wide forehead. "You begin by doing a hell of a lot of research, then you go in fully loaded with the big guns, and take on the assholes who make the decisions," he said, drawing his words out with a steely precision. "You don't want to see the dolphins die, do you?"

"That's hitting below the belt."

"No, that's facing reality."

She thought hard but still couldn't come up with an easy solution. "You're right, Captain Jack," she finally admitted. "But I can't do it alone."

"I'll help you."

"I need more than you. No offense, but you're a loose cannon. What I really need is some damned good legal advice."

"What about your lawyer in Houston? Elvis Presley."

"It's Geoff Presley," she replied with a surprised giggle.

Carrie thought about Geoff and how responsive he had been when she was speaking about the dolphins at the Van Eckrens' party. She nodded. "Yes, maybe he'll help. I'll have to call him."

"Well, then do it. And I'll start getting together some info on Makomoto so you can see what he's all about." Jack got up and made for the door.

Carrie watched him, feeling more unsure than she had in her entire life. As she got up from the chair, intending to walk him to his motorcycle, she caught sight of the piece of paper on the floor. His check, forgotten in the heat of their passion. Remembering their lovemaking made her blush. She covered it by bending over to pick up the check, then handed it to him.

"Take this," she said, "and put it in the bank. No arguments, just do it. You're probably going to need it."

He took the check from her, his hand closing over hers, and their eyes met for a long moment. "I meant what I said," he murmured, "I love you, Carrie Madison. And nothing's going to change that."

Twenty-four

Matt closed the Camaro's door and waited for Isaac to get out of the passenger side before continuing.

"And I really don't think you've gotten the message yet. I meant it when I said there's got to be some rules followed, *Br'a.*" He shook the keys he held in his hand, feeling as he always did when he talked to Isaac that his little brother had tuned him out.

"Do you have your ears open?" he asked, exasperated.

"Yeah, I'm listening," Isaac muttered, though his attention seemed focused on a long white limo pulling into the harbor's small parking lot, jockeying for a space.

"You may have gotten away with the all-nighters and the beer parties and the dope smoking for the past couple of years," Matt continued, "but that was before you had to face going to jail. Now it's gonna be different."

He strode toward the office, Isaac keeping in step beside him. The teenager wore a Houston Oilers baseball cap backward on his head. Carrie had bought it for him in Houston and he had yet to take it off. Jet black curls sprouted out from the hat's edges, making him look like a clown. Matt knew enough not to comment on it. Besides, Isaac could look a lot worse. He could've shaved his head completely, as some of his friends had already done.

A car door slammed and Isaac snapped his head around to look. "Shit, those guys sure ain't goin' fishin'." He gave a low whistle. "That rig's somethin' else."

Matt followed Isaac's gaze and noticed two men, one resembling a sumo wrestler. They were walking away from the limo, headed in Matt's direction. The smaller guy's head swiveled as though he was looking for something, then he spoke sharply to the big guy. Both men wore suits that, even from a distance, Matt could tell were expensive.

"Y'know, I understand how fascinating the rest of the world is," he said, his eyes still on the strangers, "but I'd really appreciate it if you'd pay attention to me for a change, little brother."

Isaac sighed. "You've said the same damn thing over and over again, Matt. I think I get the picture."

"Well, then, why don't you tell me what happened the night of the accident instead of keeping me in the dark? This bullshit story about not being responsible—"

"I wasn't, Matt, okay? And I'll tell you why when the time is right."

Matt stopped and put his hands on his hips. "The time's *never* going to be right. Weren't you listening to the lawyer, man? You could end up in jail for *life!*"

"I know, I know."

"Well, you'd better start doing something about it, 'cause no one can help you unless you open your mouth."

The men from the limo brushed past Matt and

Isaac. The big guy wasn't Japanese after all, Matt realized. He guessed Samoan, but whatever the man
was, he was huge. Matt figured he had to be at least
six foot four and weigh in close to two hundred seventy-five pounds. All of it muscle.

Impressive, he thought. Not someone I want to
meet in a dark alley.

Something about the purposeful way the pair
walked made Matt watch them more closely. They
were headed straight for Carrie's office.

"What the hell . . ." Matt shot Isaac a puzzled look
and without a word, the brothers followed them. By the
time they reached *The Big One's* office, the strangers
were already inside, and from where he stood outside
the door, Matt could hear Carrie's voice, clear and
strong, saying, "Mr. Makomoto! What a surprise! I
never expected to see you here in Hawaii."

The Samoan's back was to the door, effectively
blocking the entrance. Matt could hear the other man
answer but couldn't see past the Samoan. He tapped
on the large man's shoulder and with a timid smile,
asked him to move. The man grunted and slid about
six inches to the side.

Matt squeezed by the Samoan to stand next to Jack,
lounging near the window. With a surprised glance,
Matt took in Jack's and Carrie's disheveled appear-
ances, their overly red mouths and Carrie's whisker-
bruised cheeks, and knew in an instant that what he'd
suspected for the past couple of weeks was true.

Oh, shit, Carrie, he groaned inwardly. How could
you?

"Perhaps I should come back another time," the

man Carrie had called Makomoto was saying. "It appears you're busy."

Matt watched Carrie draw herself to her full height. Her eyebrows knitted together and her lips pursed slightly. She made that face when she was confused. And Carrie didn't like being confused.

"These are my employees." Carrie flung her hand to the side in a sweeping gesture, then settled into the desk chair, never taking her eyes off Makomoto. Her fingers made a temple in front of her face and she looked over her oval nails, smiling as if someone had whispered a private joke in her ear. "So, what is it that brought you all the way to Hawaii, Mr. Makomoto?"

"Ocean Fresh, Mrs. Madison." Makomoto slipped his lithe body into the chair opposite Carrie's desk and mimicked her relaxed stance.

"What about it?"

"I'd like to buy your company." The man had very little trace of a Japanese accent. His voice was as smooth and cultured as some of the aristocrats' she'd known in Texas.

"Really?" Carrie's overly gracious tone mocked Makomoto's. Her eyes grew dark and her lip curled up. Matt had never seen her this defensive. If he didn't know her better, he'd swear she was ready to do battle. He wondered how much of it was an act for Makomoto's benefit.

Carrie hoped she didn't look as nervous as she felt. Although she'd known she would eventually have to deal with Makomoto, she'd never expected him to come directly to her office.

Thank God Jack and Matt are with me, she thought.

"I'm prepared to make an offer. Right here. Right now," Makomoto continued.

Out of the corner of her eye, she could see Jack looking at her. He was dying to say something, to dive into the conversation, perhaps even to take it over, but she ignored him.

This one's mine, Jack. I'll take care of it.

"That's something you'll have to discuss with my lawyer," she said to Makomoto.

"Two hundred and seven million dollars."

"Excuse me?"

Outside the door, she heard a cough and caught a glimpse of a Houston Oilers baseball cap. The Samoan still stood in front of the door, legs spread, arms crossed over his massive chest. He hadn't taken his eyes off her since they'd come in. She shot him an irritated glance, trying to match the burn in his stare.

"I'm prepared to offer two hundred and seven million dollars," Makomoto repeated.

Carrie tapped a pencil against the desk, mostly to cover for her right knee which had suddenly started twitching. "As I said, you'll have to speak with my attorney."

Makomoto crossed one slim leg over the other, adjusting the seam of his tailored pants. He smiled at Carrie, a smile which said, Come on, we both know you don't need your attorney to make a decision.

"Why don't we discuss it between the two of us?" he suggested with the same cold smile. "Then you can take my offer to your attorney and have him finalize the deal. That's the way your father and I did business."

"I'm not my father." Carrie's comment slipped out before she realized it was probably not the wisest thing to say. She wanted to follow it with a statement that she knew Makomoto had threatened her father and that, like her father, she didn't appreciate being pushed around, but she wisely kept quiet.

"Three hundred."

Matt exhaled, the sound like a wheezing balloon. The Samoan stepped toward him threateningly. Without turning around, Makomoto said sharply, "Toto, stand still!"

Jack looked at Carrie. *Toto?* he mouthed. She put her hand over her mouth to cover a grin.

"Let's face it, Mrs. Madison," Makomoto said. "You don't have the background or the education to run a business like Ocean Fresh. I do. Your father realized long ago that I was the most qualified buyer to take over his company. When he came to Tokyo, we were about to make a deal, but, unfortunately, he died before we were able to finalize the agreement. I'm sure he'd want you to take up where he left off. So why not let me take Ocean Fresh off your hands and make you a wealthy woman."

"Why? So you can drain the oceans even more than you already have?" Jack's angry voice ripped through the room. "We know what you're all about, so why don't you take your hundred million dollar offers and—"

"Jack!" Carrie rose and stood behind the desk. "I

think you need to remember this is between me and Mr. Makomoto."

"But I—"

"Please. I can take care of it myself."

He shrugged and went back to leaning against the wall, though his hands turned into fists and his mouth tightened into a sneer. The change in him since they'd made love only half an hour ago was incredible. When Carrie felt certain he'd remain quiet for a while, she turned back to Makomoto without bothering to sit down.

"I think it's best for you to leave. This is not the time or place to be discussing Ocean Fresh. I'll have my lawyer get in touch with you."

Makomoto rose, brushing his hands together lightly as if repulsed by the slightly shabby office with its very shabby furniture. "Toto will give you my business card," he said. With a slight bow, he turned on his heel and left the office.

Toto lumbered over to Carrie's desk and retrieved a card from a sterling silver case, dropped it in her hand, then wheeled around and brushed past a startled Isaac.

When both men were gone, the room erupted with excited comments.

"Wow, that man could take Hulk Hogan apart with one hand and brush his teeth with the other!" Isaac blurted.

"You're not going to take him up on it, are you?" Jack demanded, putting himself between Carrie and Matt.

"Carrie, are you all right?" Matt pushed Jack aside and forced Carrie to look at him. When she saw the concern on his face, she felt suddenly drained, all her make-believe bravado instantly leaving her body. She sank into her chair and put her hands up to silence the men surrounding her.

"Let me think. You guys are chattering like magpies, for God's sake. Shut up!"

Makomoto had definitely stepped way out of line. Now she understood why Geoff Presley and Clark Quincel had spoken so disdainfully of the Japanese businessman. If only she knew more about what had gone on in Tokyo. Three hundred million dollars. That was more money than she'd ever dreamed. God, if she only knew how her father had dealt with this man, then, maybe, she'd be able to handle herself more professionally.

Wait, what am I thinking of? I'm never going to see him again. I'll just call Geoff and let him handle all the details. All I want to do is get rid of this damn company, not run it!

"Three hundred million dollars," Isaac breathed. "That could buy a lot of shit."

"You got that right," she agreed. "But if he's offering me that much now, what's it going to be later? And why is he doing this?"

"He wants control of the oceans," Jack said. "The man is known as the 'Sea Rapist' and now he wants to add Ocean Fresh to his list of companies. Pretty soon, he'll be able to go anywhere in the world and do anything he wants. Y'know, there are stories about him that would raise the hair on your head. And now that I've met him, I believe every one."

"And what do you think I should do about it, Mr.

Briskin?" Carrie asked, though she really didn't want to hear his answer.

"Keep Ocean Fresh. Make the changes that should be made. Lead the way so that others will see you don't have to use seine nets to fish and make a profit. Eventually, you might come head to head with Makomoto, but he can't force you to do business with him. Let me tell you, Carrie, I've heard stories about Makomoto having people killed just to get what he wants. He's obsessed with being king of the sea and Ocean Fresh is just another step toward his goal. You can't let him do this!"

"I don't want to run the damn company," she said sharply.

"Well, then, find someone else who will run it right. Just don't let Makomoto take over."

"He's making a damn good offer."

"Is money all that matters?"

Carrie thought of how it had felt to pay off all her bills, the euphoria which had rushed through her body when she realized there'd be no more phone calls, no more waking up in the middle of the night wondering where she was going to get the money to stay in business, no more worrying about how she'd pay for Alex's therapy.

No, money was not all that mattered. But it sure as hell helped.

"You've got the chance to make a difference, Carrie." Jack leaned over her desk, his eyes pleading with her. "Your father handed that opportunity to you, laid it right in your lap. Don't you think that by giving you Ocean Fresh, he was saying something about your abilities? Maybe even saying he agreed with your politics? I'd say that was a pretty big compliment coming from someone like your old man. Aren't you going to do something with it?"

She averted her eyes and caught Matt's knowing glance. In a flash she realized Matt had figured out the relationship she and Jack had fallen into. Just as quickly, she shoved that epiphany aside and brought herself back to unravelling the mess her father had bequeathed her.

"I'm going to call Geoff," she said. "So I'd appreciate it if you'd all just leave me alone for a while."

Jack slapped the desk and stormed out of the room. Matt's eyes followed him, then he motioned to Isaac that he should leave. When he was alone with Carrie, Matt went to her and put his arm awkwardly around her shoulders. "You know I'm with you whatever you do," he said. She nodded. "But I think you know in your heart Makomoto's not exactly a nice guy. Anyone who'd hire a Samoan bodyguard has a reason for doing so."

"I know. I think I knew that the first night I saw him."

"I don't envy you, *Sistah*. But I know you'll do the right thing."

"I hope so, Matt. I hope so."

He left. Carrie pulled out her address book, thumbed to Geoff's number, and picked up the phone. For the first time, she realized her hands were shaking uncontrollably.

Twenty-five

After leaving a message for Geoff to call her back as soon as he got in, Carrie surveyed the office. It wasn't as bad as she thought it would be. Her desk, littered with schedules and half-written brochure material, occupied the central space in the office and, for the first time in months, no bills joined the various piles of paper scattered across its top. Matt had left a half-empty coffee cup on the table in front of the two green leather chairs Carrie kept for customers. Picking up the cup, she made a mental note to replace the chairs with something more aesthetically pleasing. In fact, as soon as she had enough money, she'd redecorate the whole office, put in a new bathroom, buy a rolltop desk to replace the battleship gray metal one she had now, maybe even get her mother to pick out some nice prints for the walls. Currently, the only art on her office walls was the calendar over her desk, a freebie from the local sail shop. Yes, she thought, I'll paint the walls and put in a screen door so that we'll be able to have some air in the office without the bugs.

She dumped the cup into the barrel absentmindedly and caught a glimpse of herself in the window of the half-open front door. The reflection stunned her. She ran her fingertips over her full, bruised lips, the small, pointed nose people accused of being snubbed, and her wide, tanned forehead. The movement naturally led her hands into her tangled hair, and as she combed her fingers lazily through it, she shivered a little, remembering how intimately Jack had touched her less than an hour before.

Is it wrong to feel so good when everything around me is falling apart? she wondered.

Her hands lightly examined her body, passing over her breasts and her tight waist, ending at her muscled thighs. Although she had often wished for a more voluptuous figure, Alex had never complained. In fact, he'd always said he liked her long, lean body because it fit so nicely into his.

She flushed, thinking that Jack's larger frame had made her feel small, vulnerable. But perhaps that was only because she'd been so aware of her runaway emotions and so afraid of the consequences.

What does he see in me? she asked her reflection. How do I look to him?

She touched her lips again and both corners turned up in a contented smile. Closing her eyes, she leaned back against the desk, trying to quiet the turbulent quivers which had taken over her body. The warm, liquid sensation between her legs caused her daydreaming to abruptly stop. She chided herself for her instant animal reaction. How could she have? She was married!

As quickly as if a faucet had been shut off, the fantasy about Jack stopped and her thoughts took a hairpin turn.

She remembered Ishiru Makomoto sitting cockily

in her office chair. Something about him bothered her. Something more than what Jack had already told her. Something about Makomoto's overbearing attitude, his certainty that he'd own Ocean Fresh. Yet, she couldn't quite put her finger on exactly what bothered her most.

But she would, she promised herself. Her intuition would kick into gear when she least expected it and she'd figure him out. Hopefully, that would happen before she made any decisions about selling the company to him.

What do you do when you're trying to sell a company? Research the competition? Investigate the buyers?

Was Jack right that Makomoto might have had something to do with her father's death?

Why did Makomoto want Ocean Fresh so badly?

How could she deal with him on his level when she'd never worked in an office other than her own, had never had one day of experience in the corporate world, had never dealt with more than fifty dollars at a time?

The sight of him and his gargantuan bodyguard had been enough to make her knees buckle. Yet she had no concrete reason to be so nervous, just a bunch of nebulous comments from people who also had no solid proof that the man was the Hitleresque character they made him out to be.

What would Dad do? she found herself thinking. Surprised at herself, she shook her head violently, sending sprays of white-blond hair over her shoulders.

Maybe Jack was right. She'd been given a chance

to right things. Maybe she should take that chance. Maybe Jack could help.

Jack.

His face loomed in front of her, his green eyes warm and teasing, his nostrils flaring with passion. She grabbed the edge of the chair for support, then began to pace back and forth in the small office, back and forth, back and forth. The fifteen-foot width seemed to shrink by six inches each time she walked it.

Three hundred million dollars.

The amount was unfathomable.

Of course, not all of it would be profit, she was sure. There'd be accounting matters to settle, lawyer's fees to be paid, taxes. Snippets of her parents' conversations at the dinner table came back to her. Nothing came easily in the corporate world, she remembered. Talk of mergers and takeovers and buyouts had always peppered her father's speech. Unfortunately, she had absolutely no idea what all of it meant. And she really didn't want to know.

She stopped pacing and dropped into her desk chair, her head spinning, her thoughts now totally fragmented.

There was something about Makomoto . . .

"What's wrong, Matt? God, man, you haven't opened your mouth since we left the office." Jack stood on *The Big One*'s deck, helping Matt stock the soda coolers for the morning trip.

The warm sun had already melted some of the ice in the cooler, and each time he dropped a can in, the water splashed against his arm. He wiped it off before answering Jack.

"Nothing's wrong, *Br'a*." He ducked his head. He'd never been good at lying. Even a complete stranger could tell by the look on his face. How could he tell this man, who'd become his friend, that what he and Carrie were doing was wrong, that he'd be hurting someone who'd been a friend much longer than Jack had? Did he have any right to say anything in the first place? Would Carrie be angry if he did?

Somehow he felt all of that mattered little when he took into consideration the marriage at stake. It wasn't just any marriage. Alex and Carrie's marriage had been almost perfect, until the accident. They'd been the couple he wanted to emulate when he finally found someone to love, someone he wanted to spend the rest of his life with. Even though Carrie and Alex had spent almost every moment of the day together, Matt had rarely seen them argue. They'd shared the same passions, they'd worked well together, they'd looked toward the future together—partners, friends, lovers. Matt couldn't forget the special way they'd had of looking at each other. And it tore him apart to see Jack and Carrie exchanging similar glances.

Carrie had been lonely. He knew that without being told. And vulnerable was too light a word to describe the state she'd been in lately. It was almost as though she'd been swimming with her belly exposed, the perfect target for a shark. But was "shark" the right term to use for Jack?

Matt shoved his fist into the ice to make room for more cans and wished he didn't like Jack so much. In that instant, he understood exactly how Carrie must feel. Sometimes people came into your life when you least expected it and turned it completely around. He pulled his hand out of the cooler and shook it, enjoying the frigid feeling for a moment before wiping his palm against his shorts.

This *haole,* this Jack Briskin, just came along at the right time.

Jack's strong hands reached past Matt to close the cooler case. He studied the short black hairs on Jack's knuckles, concentrating on them so that he wouldn't have to look up, to face Jack's questioning eyes.

"It's Carrie, isn't it?" Jack asked, his voice right above Matt's head.

Startled, Matt forgot himself and looked at Jack, knowing his surprise showed, but there was no way to hide it. "What d'you mean? What about Carrie?"

"You're worried about her."

"You mean with Makomoto?"

"Of course, what else?" Jack cut himself off and stood up, stretching his back. "Aaaah," he said, realization dawning in his eyes, "so that's it."

"What's it?"

"You know."

"Know what?"

"Let's not play games, Matt. You're not stupid and neither am I. You've put two and two together. You've figured out how I feel about Carrie."

Matt stood and juggled a can of soda from one hand to the other. "Yeah, I guess you could say I figured it out, but it sure doesn't take an astrophysicist to see how you two look at each other."

"And you don't approve . . ."

For the first time, Matt felt he should explain. "No,

I really don't, *Br'a*. Don't get me wrong," he was quick to add, "I really like you and I'm really happy you've been around to help Carrie out, but—"

"There's always a but."

"Not always. If Carrie was single, you'd be the best thing to happen to her in a long time."

"But she's not."

"You've got that one right, *Bruddah*. She's one married *wahine*. And the other half of the Madison team happens to be just as special as she is."

Jack swung the cooler into the corner and shoved it with his foot. "Maybe you're making a little more of this marriage than you should," he said seriously. "I certainly wouldn't even consider getting into any kind of relationship if I thought Carrie was happy, but she's not."

Matt pulled on a line, then leaned against the mast and popped the soda can open. "I don't think you get it, Jack. She's married to a guy who's crippled. Man, you know that's not easy, but it sure as hell don't help when you're hanging around offering her something normal. If you were half the friend you say you are, you'd be giving her advice about how to keep the marriage together."

Jack wrapped his arms tightly around his chest and rocked up and down on his toes, a defiant stare on his face. "What if she doesn't want to keep it together?"

"I find that very hard to believe."

"She told him she was never going to see him again the last time she visited him. Did you know that?"

Shocked, Matt let go of the line. "No," he said. "I didn't."

"Well, that's what happened. They had a fight and she hasn't been back there since." Jack unwrapped his arms and swayed awkwardly for a moment before sticking his hands deep into his pockets. "I don't know how much difference it makes to you, Matt, but I love her. I've been looking for someone like her all my life. And I didn't come this far to give up so easily." Again, his eyes became defiant. "I think I'll wait for her to tell me to go away, thank you very much."

The sun beating on Matt's shoulders suddenly seemed exceptionally strong. He felt the burn creep over the rest of his body and up into his face. "Suit yourself," he said, spinning around and heading for the bridge.

"I will," Jack answered quietly.

Simone walked Wana'ao to the door and handed her the painting she'd just purchased. *"Mahalo,"* Simone said with a smile as she held open the door for the young woman. "I am sure Lopaka will love this one as much as the others."

"I hope so," Wana'ao replied. "It's our fifteenth anniversary."

Reaching past the package, Simone hugged her favorite customer warmly and gave her a kiss on the cheek. "You tell that man he owes me a visit. I have not seen him since he won the surfing championship."

"I'll tell him."

Behind them, the phone rang. "Go ahead," Wana'ao said. "I'll see you some time next month. *Aloha!*"

Simone was still smiling when she picked up the receiver, but her grin soon turned into a frown after listening to Caryn's story of what had happened that morning.

Philip must have known what this Makomoto was like. How could he put Caryn into such an awkward position?

Oh, la vache! she thought.

If Philip wasn't already dead, she'd be tempted to put him in a grave and toss the dirt in after him.

"What are you going to do?" she asked Caryn.

"I have to wait here for Geoff to call me back, then I think I'm going to have to go back to Houston. The sale of the house is Wednesday anyway. I can take care of that and see Geoff while I'm there. Maybe I'll even arrange a meeting with Clark Quincel. Maybe he can give me some insight into what's going on at Ocean Fresh. I just know I don't want to deal with Makomoto any more than I have to. The man gives me the shivers."

Caryn paused and Simone immediately sensed there was something else she wanted to say. She waited, knowing that Caryn would talk if she wanted to but not if she was forced.

"Maman?"

"I am here, *chérie.*"

"Have you seen Alex lately?"

So, that was it. Caryn was feeling guilty.

"No, I have not. The last time I visited was about a week after you returned. Why?"

"Just wondering how he was." Caryn's voice trailed

off, almost as though she was thinking of something else. "Well, I'd better go. I've got to keep the phone open for Geoff to call back."

"Let me know what he says," Simone answered, her curiosity piqued. What else was it that Caryn wanted to say?

Twenty-six

Houston's skyscrapers wavered like pieces of silver cellophane in the late afternoon light. It was a brutally hot day. The city shimmered as the mirrorlike windows of dozens of buildings caught the heat and threw it back so that it beat relentlessly against the cars below.

While she sat in rush hour traffic, Carrie listened to the news on the radio for a few more minutes, distractedly drumming her fingers against the rental car's steering wheel. Then she couldn't stand it any longer. She reached over and switched off the announcer's nasal twang and concentrated on what had been bugging her for hours: the day's events still ricocheting through her brain like lost bullets.

On the seat beside her, her new ivory-colored leather handbag bulged with copies of the closing papers, which officially handed ownership of her father's house to Pamela. Somewhere in that package was a treasurer's check for one million seventy-five thousand dollars and thirty-two cents—Carrie's share of the closing proceeds after lawyer's fees, taxes, and recording costs. Enough to keep her, her mother, Matt and his family, Jack, Alex, and half of the residents on the Kona Coast happy for the next ten years. But

Carrie's thoughts didn't center on her newfound prosperity. Although she'd walked out of Pamela's attorney's office floating about three feet off the ground, she had come down with a solid thump a couple of hours later.

On a whim, she'd asked Pamela to have lunch with her after the closing procedures were finished, intending to grill her stepmother about her father's business dealings with Makomoto. Although she had no idea what she might discover, nothing could have prepared her for the Pandora's box of questions the luncheon unleashed.

At first, Carrie found herself regretting having made the invitation. Pamela knew little, if anything, about Philip's business dealings, which didn't surprise Carrie. Her mother had never been privy to her father's corporate life either. But, as his wife, Pamela did know what upset Philip. After living with him for the past five years, watching his every move, loving each emotion that passed over his face, she had come to know his moods. And one of Philip DeBary's major stress inducers in the months before his death had been a Japanese businessman named Ishiru Makomoto.

"Philip never said much about what went on within his corporations. I guess he thought it'd bore me," Pamela told Carrie, as Guenevere's dining room swirled with elegantly dressed Houstonites, all seemingly anxious to impress clients or friends. A nouveau restaurant whose specialties included Gulf shrimp in a lemon and wine base and specially prepared pasta and vegetable dishes which changed every day, Guenevere's was run by an attractive young blonde woman who'd made quite a splash in the culinary world since graduating with honors from the Culinary Institute of America. Carrie had heard all about Chef Jennifer's creations while she was in Hawaii, and Lorilene had raved about the chef's luncheons to all her friends. Guenevere's had become the spot to be seen in Houston, and Chef Jennifer's clientele particularly appreciated the gentle harp music she provided during what would normally be a hectic lunch hour.

Carrie heard the strains of "Greensleeves" begin as Pamela held her wine glass a couple of inches above the table and studied it as though seeing some blemish in the pinkish liquid.

"Philip did spend a lot of time in Tokyo last year," Pamela said dreamily. "When he came home, I could always tell he was upset. He'd be distant, really reluctant to talk. Almost like he didn't know where he was sometimes." She looked up at Carrie with innocent, childlike eyes, eyes that said I don't understand what went wrong, please help me understand, he was your father. "You know what I mean?" she asked.

Carrie nodded knowingly. Even though she wanted to add a comment, she held her tongue, realizing her childhood memories of her father would add nothing to Pamela's more recent, and painfully accurate, observations.

"Did Daddy ever talk about Ishiru Makomoto?" she asked. "Did he tell you what the deal was? How much Makomoto was offering for Ocean Fresh?"

"Not to me, darlin', but I know he spoke to Clark Quincel an awful lot. That man was your daddy's right hand. He ran Ocean Fresh when Philip was busy with his other obligations." She clucked her tongue, then her eyes wavered, and Carrie could see her stepmother's attention was diverted. Pamela smiled graciously at a classically-coiffed redhead in a brown double-breasted crepe suit. "How *are* you Lillian? And Gregory? Is he well?"

The two women spoke of families and parties, soirées to which Carrie had not been invited, nor would she care to be. For the moment, she was forgotten.

She didn't mind. It gave her a chance to mull over what Pamela had just said, to flesh out the little pieces of information she'd been handed and to put the puzzle together. She took a few thoughtful bites of her Caesar salad and tuned out the inane conversation between her stepmother and the redhead.

Perhaps she'd find out more from Quincel when they were able to meet alone, away from the other board members. How much would he reveal; how much could he tell her? He'd been so close-lipped during their last meeting.

As for Makomoto, he was wily and devious. Carrie knew that just from her brief encounters with the man, but she could hardly believe he had as much power over her father as Pamela implied. No one could push Philip to a point of nervousness. He was far too self-assured, far too much the insouciant businessman, the sly, on-top-of-everything executive known for undercutting everyone else's deals. How else could he have remained in business for so long and have been so successful? And although Carrie knew nothing about corporate politics, it didn't take a Harvard Business School degree to tell her how powerful her father had been.

For some inexplicable reason, an undeniable belief

that her father had known his life was in danger and that there had been no one he could turn to for protection crossed her mind. But why?

Something more dangerous than corporate politics was going on, she had realized.

She and Pamela had talked for a bit longer, then Pamela had stopped mid-sentence, as if suddenly remembering something.

"You know what's come back to haunt me, what I thought was really strange, is that Philip went to see his lawyer right before this last trip to Tokyo. I believe that's when he added the codicil to the will, the one which gave you control over Ocean Fresh. And I know there were an awful lot of meetings during that last week, almost as though he were tying everything up. If I didn't know better, I'd swear your father knew he was going to die."

Carrie had held her fork motionless over her salad. By the innocently puzzled look on Pamela's face, it was obvious her stepmother hadn't realized exactly how shattering her revelation was or how important it might become, considering Makomoto's visit and the dangerous position her father might have knowingly thrust upon Carrie.

Pamela had continued, adding little details she had recalled, remembering bits of conversations she and Philip had had during the last couple of weeks before his death, but she had never pointed a finger, never suggested that her husband's death was anything but a heart attack. Sitting opposite her stepmother, Carrie's mind had reeled with the possibilities, and she had suddenly realized that no matter what, she had to know why her father had made sure all his business and personal affairs were taken care of. She had to know why he had changed his will so that she would take over Ocean Fresh. She had to know the truth, even if finding out turned her life completely upside down.

A horn blared, bringing her attention back to the present. Carrie concentrated on negotiating Route 45, heading north out of Houston. She'd forgotten what rush hour was like. In front of her a red Volkswagen cut through traffic, then slammed on its brakes. She reacted instantly, then flicked her blinker to indicate she was taking the next right. Daydreaming while driving in rush hour traffic was not exactly brilliant, she decided, but she couldn't stop thinking about Ocean Fresh.

She pulled the rented Grand Prix into line behind a beaten-up beige station wagon chockful of dark-haired kids. Her thoughts turned to Jack.

He'd taken her to the airport when she left, though he couldn't understand why she had to go back to Texas or why she didn't give Geoff power of attorney so that she wouldn't have to attend the closing. Jack had groused about Makomoto, telling her he was sure the Japanese businessman would be back, that they hadn't heard the end of him. Through it all, she had listened to Jack's worryings and warnings silently, embroiled in her own inner conflict, a conflict which had nothing to do with business yet everything to do with the dark-haired man sitting beside her, the man who was not her husband, the man about whom she had very strong and conflicting feelings, the man whose very presence terrified, yet comforted, her.

When Jack had reached to hug her in the airport,

she'd clung to him for a few moments, almost as though he were her husband, as though he were Alex, then she had pushed him away and run for the gate, determined to forget what had happened between them only a few days before, no matter what it took.

But she soon discovered she didn't want to forget. A re-run of their frantic lovemaking played over and over in her mind until she saw it from all different angles. It was as though she were outside her body, watching herself and Jack writhing on the tiny army cot in her back room, seeing her enraptured face, hearing the words he whispered in her ear over and over again.

She wanted his love. She wanted his support. She wanted him to worry about her, as Alex had, and she knew deep within her reasonable self that what she felt was both very wrong and very exciting. She also knew that, sooner or later, she'd have to make a decision. Sneaking around didn't appeal to her. She wanted everything honest, aboveboard.

She'd refused to listen to her mother's admonitions that she should see Alex before going back to Houston. She simply wasn't ready yet to see him, perhaps because she was sure he'd be able to read her face. He'd be able to tell what she'd been doing without her uttering a single word.

And he must have felt the same way since he hadn't called her, hadn't made the slightest attempt to apologize for his actions or to ask her to visit, or to tell her he still loved her, despite their arguments. Maybe he, like her, had begun to wonder if the marriage was over.

Beeping her horn, Carrie swung around to pass the

car in front of her. City traffic. She'd much rather deal with the nauseating twists and turns of the Saddle Road on the Big Island than with the stop-and-go of Houston's highway traffic. All she wanted was to reach Lorilene's and sink into the hot tub, drown the irritations and tensions of the past couple of months.

She felt as though the very essence of her character had undergone a major change in the past month or so. She'd become strident, stronger than she'd ever been, and the thought depressed her. No longer did she feel relaxed, able to smile at Matt's silly jokes or marvel at the miraculous surrender of Kona's sunsets. She felt stifled, unable to enjoy the quiet life she'd come to know in Hawaii. She wanted that Pacific paralysis back. It numbed her, let her ignore the demands life made on her. But life had been different then, back when Alex was with her. She'd had little to worry about besides making the rent payment. Even though the check she now held in her pocketbook would ease all the financial worries she'd inherited, with Alex's accident had also come other urgent necessities, like extra salaries and higher phone bills. She knew nothing would ever be the same.

If only she could drown those feelings in the warmth of Lorilene's hot tub, if she could wash them down the drain with the steam and the bubbles, let the water cleanse her soul, her mind, her heart.

If only it was that easy.

"Do you think you're being just a tad paranoid?" Lorilene stood beside the bar in her great room, mixing what she called "killer Margaritavilles." They had spent over an hour in the hot tub, during which Carrie had simply laid her head back against the tub's pillowed sides and let the pores in her body open up and accept the warmth and solace the bubbling water offered. She hadn't said a word until Lorilene had handed her a thick terrycloth robe, urging her to get out before she shriveled up and slithered down the drain. Now Carrie was talking as she never had before, telling Lorilene all about her conversation with Pamela. She needed to see whether Lorilene would believe her suspicions about Makomoto.

"I don't think I'm being paranoid. Paranoid is when you're afraid of something that might happen," Carrie answered, reaching for the frothy lime-green margarita Lorilene handed her. "My father's already dead. Makomoto sure as hell wants Ocean Fresh, and he's made no bones about the fact that he's a threat. And now that Pamela's told me about Daddy rewriting his will. . . . I think the sum of all these facts is what Perry Mason would call pretty decisive evidence, don't you?" She took a sip of the drink. "God, girl, this is one potent cocktail."

Lorilene winked and took a sip herself before answering. "Maybe you ought to talk to Quincel and your father's lawyer before you go jumping off the deep end. You don't know whether Pamela's got her dates mixed up. Let's face it, she's still a fresh widow and she might be feeding you information she thinks you want to hear. Who knows where that little Miss Innocent is coming from? I hear tell she's been known to stir things up a bit on occasion."

Carrie thought about that comment for a moment.

Maybe Lorilene was right. Maybe she ought to hold off on making unfounded speculations until she'd done a little more investigating.

"Perhaps I'm in over my head," she conceded, "but I can't help feeling something else is going on. It's nagging at me."

Leaning against the fieldstone fireplace, Lorilene reached for a poker and stirred up the embers. Although the day had been hot in the city, the country evening wind had lowered the temperature quickly to a chilly forty-eight degrees. Lorilene's auburn hair took on the fire's glow and for a moment she looked like she had a halo. When she turned back to Carrie, her cheeks were flushed and her eyes glittering.

"If it's nagging at you, Carrie DeBary, then you'd better pay attention to it. I've yet to see you strike out intuitively. Just be careful. I don't want to see you getting yourself in so deep we have to hire a tractor to pull you out."

Carrie laughed and settled back into the comfortable leather club chair, feeling the fire's warmth against her face. After spending so much time in the hot tub, she needed to continue the day's warmth. With both hands wrapped around her margarita glass, she sipped her drink with the calming knowledge that Lorilene sat companionably in the next chair, doing the same.

When Lorilene finally broke the silence and asked when Carrie was going to tell her what was going on at home, Carrie cringed as though her friend had reached over and pinched her hard.

"Sometimes I think you're a witch," she said.

"How did you know I wanted to talk about Jack and Alex?"

Lorilene grinned, her white teeth gleaming in the firelight. "We haven't been friends forever for nothing. So, what gives? You leaving Alex? Don't tell me you are or I'll be pissed at you forever."

"No, I don't think so. At least not now. I just don't know what to do about all of it."

"All of what? Spill the beans, girl. Give me the gory details."

So Carrie did. They talked by the fire for hours, continuing their conversation even after Jimmy came in from work and interrupted them for a while. She told her old friend everything: about how frustrating it was to deal with the new Alex, about how demanding and obnoxious he'd become, about how guilty she felt that she was the one responsible for the accident and how angry at herself she'd become, how understanding Jack was, and how much she needed him right now.

"I know my mother suspects something," Carrie said as the grandfather clock in the hall struck twelve, "but she won't say anything. You know how prim and proper she is."

Lorilene nodded knowingly.

"She keeps telling me I should go see Alex and she won't listen when I tell her how we've been fighting and how mean he's become. He's her son-in-law and she wants him to stay that way. I think she also doesn't want to see me follow in her footsteps. She's never really approved of divorce, you know. And she certainly wouldn't understand that her daughter's having an affair. You know how she felt about Daddy."

"I can see her point," Lorilene interjected.

Carrie shot her friend a surprised look. Lorilene had never taken any adult's side. Must be a sign of aging, Carrie thought.

"I think your guilt has made you more angry with Alex than you ought to be," Lorilene said. "If the accident had happened when you weren't there, maybe you'd be better able to deal with his mood swings. I think that when Alex gets mad, you've been countering his anger with anger of your own instead of turning the other cheek, so to speak. Obviously that isn't working, so instead of dealing with him and understanding what's making him like this, you've cut him off and turned to someone else for solace. Have you ever thought that what you feel for Jack is just a band-aid covering a much bigger wound?"

"This isn't what I want to hear. I want you to tell me I deserve to feel good and that what I'm feeling for Jack is not wrong."

"Well, I'm your friend, Carrie, and friends are supposed to tell you the truth. Even when it hurts."

A log sputtered and broke in half, sending showers of sparks throughout the fireplace. Carrie stared at it, tears teasing her eyelids. Lorilene's comments had hit too close to home, but she didn't seem to understand how difficult it had been for Carrie.

"Alex just isn't the same anymore," she muttered.

"Neither are you, my friend," Lorilene answered wearily. "Neither are you."

The next morning, Carrie left for Houston before Lorilene got up. Once on the highway, she realized one of her reasons for making her appointment with Clark Quincel so early in the morning was so that she wouldn't have to face Lorilene's bright morning cheeriness. Carrie had slept poorly, going over her conversation with Lorilene and trying to rationalize her feelings for Jack. There were no black and white solutions, only vague gray areas. Nothing was clear anymore and that irritated her. She needed to find answers about everything—her father, Jack, Alex, life.

Quincel met her at Ocean Fresh's private, executives-only elevator. His eyes swept over her appraisingly, and she could see him mentally calculating the cost of her ecru silk suit, one of the extravagances she'd allowed herself when she'd landed in Houston. His gaze fell to her Italian leather pumps, ran up her ivory-stockinged legs, over the slim skirt, finally resting on her face. She'd pulled her hair back in a barrette, her old Texas style, and had even applied makeup and lipstick, which felt foreign every time she licked her lips. Lorilene had been right about dressing for the occasion. Carrie felt more confident with him this time. She had a goal. She'd come to find something out and she wasn't leaving until she got some answers.

"So, have you decided to keep Ocean Fresh?" he asked, leading the way into his office. He wore no jacket and the sleeves of his starched white shirt were rolled up to his bony elbows. Banker's suspenders held up his cuffed black pants. His body seemed strange to her after years of seeing tanned men with well-muscled chests and strong legs. He obviously needed the suspenders, she thought. He had no hips whatsoever.

"I haven't decided," she answered, taking the seat

he offered and once again enjoying his impressive skyline view. "I have a lot of questions which I hoped you might answer."

As he adjusted his glasses, she detected a nervous tremor in his hands and wondered if he knew what she was going to ask, if he had perhaps talked to Pamela, or even suspected that Carrie might, at some point, wonder what business decisions her father had made before he died. The ball was hers, she assumed, and it was time for her to make the touchdown run, or at least feint a pass.

Ah, hell, she thought, might as well go for the jugular.

"I've been told my father rewrote his will before he left for Japan, and since that's kind of strange, I'm wondering why he would do that and whether that move had anything to do with the way my father felt about Ishiru Makomoto. I figured you'd be the best person to ask."

"I did know what was going on between your father and Makomoto . . ."

"Then why don't you fill me in?"

"What do you need to know?"

In other words, you want to know what I know, she thought. Well, I'm not going to play your game until I know which team you're on. "Tell me everything," she answered.

"Like what?"

"Whatever happened with Makomoto, what types of dealings my father had with him, where negotiations stood when Daddy died. Everything."

Quincel folded his fists under his chin and studied her over the top of them as a banker would study a prospective loan applicant. She gave him back her most relaxed smile, a smile which promised she could stall with the best of them.

"So, you want to know everything."

"That's right."

"Where shall I start?"

"The beginning might be a good place."

Quincel smiled and rolled his eyes toward the ceiling. "Your old man knew what he was doing when he gave this company to you. You even talk the way he did. Cut right to the quick. No screwing around."

"I don't have time to play games, Mr. Quincel. I suggest you remember that my father's dead and I now own this company. Whether I decide to keep it or not is a moot point. Right now, I need information. I'd appreciate it if you would just tell me the story. Or do I have to get the files and find out myself?"

"You won't find your answer in our files." Quincel leaned back in the chair. It screeched, a scratchy, high-pitched sound that sent a shiver up Carrie's spine. She fought her instinctive recoiling reaction and sat very still in her chair, matching Quincel's glare.

After a moment of consideration, he seemed to realize it was futile to keep up the pretense any longer. Perhaps he appreciated the fact that her father would have wanted him to divulge all of his information, or perhaps he finally acquiesced to the knowledge that Carrie was his boss, for he started to tell her the story, from the beginning, as she'd asked. It was a long tale, full of corporate terms she didn't understand and more twists and turns than one of her mother's mystery novels. More than an hour passed before Quincel finally stated, "That's it in a nutshell."

Carrie sat back for a moment, stunned. If every-thing Quincel said was true—and it made sense that, as president of Ocean Fresh, he'd be privy to most of what he'd revealed—then her father had had major problems with Makomoto, more than she'd suspected.

"Let's see if I've got this right," she said, lowering her eyes and concentrating on her fingernails. "Mak-omoto did a private eye thing on Daddy when Daddy wouldn't sell Ocean Fresh and Makomoto caught Daddy switching money from one account to the other, right?"

From across the desk, Clark Quincel grunted.

"So Makomoto's got the upper hand and starts put-ting on the pressure big time, hoping Daddy will sell instead of risking a major scandal. In the meantime, Daddy's trying to put through new environmental standards at Ocean Fresh, but Makomoto's blocking him every step of the way."

"Right again. Your father started seeing losses about a year ago, and I think he was actually happy about it because he thought Makomoto would lose interest. But that wasn't the case. Word is Makomoto never lost a bid to take over a company, and he swore your father wasn't going to be the first to slip away. He was pretty obsessed with making your father kneel in abeyance." Here, Quincel laughed ruefully. "And you know *no one* made Philip DeBary kneel."

"But you said Daddy told you he was about to make a deal with Makomoto when he headed for Tokyo."

Quincel nodded. "Your father was Makomoto's key to Ocean Fresh. Without Philip's shares, Makomoto had nothing. Philip told me before he left that he thought he'd be able to talk Makomoto into switching from seine nets to a more environmentally safe way of fishing. But he thought it would take all the strength he had to write that into the deal."

Added together, the facts pointed to a volatile situation, one which even Philip DeBary would have been hard-pressed to handle.

"Sounds like blackmail to me," she said thoughtfully.

"That's Makomoto's style. I heard once that he slaughtered a whole herd of dolphins just to feed guests at a party he was hosting." Quincel loosened his tie and took off his glasses. "I also heard he has syphillis and is going insane because he refuses to go for treatment." He wiped the glasses with the tail of his tie. "You never can tell what's fact and what's fiction."

She barely heard his last comment. Her mind was filled with an ugly image—a blood-red sea filled with hundreds of dead dolphins.

To cover her shock, she commented on the politically correct way to handle the situation, the way *she* would've saved the dolphins, and was surprised to see Quincel glowering at her.

"Although I understand what you're trying to say, I'm getting pretty tired of the holier-than-thou activist tone," he said, his voice cutting and gruff. "Seems to me that a lot of you do-gooders don't ever think of the corporation's side, though you expect us to consider yours. A business has to make money and sometimes the only way to do that is to put aside environmental standards, or what some people would consider environmental standards. I'm not saying that it's right or wrong, just that it happens and you have to look at both sides. If a company expends x amount of dollars to revamp its production standards, then the money it spends to do so must be doubled, or tripled, by profits for the company to come out in the black. Do you understand what I'm saying?"

"Yes, but—"

"Let me finish. Ocean Fresh had been teetering on the edge for a good ten years before your father bought it out. He, with his acute business sense, helped the company show a profit within the first two years. That profit kept a lot of people from being homeless. You know the saying that most Americans are only a paycheck away from poverty? Well, think about it, your father was responsible for approximately seven thousand five hundred American families and, believe it or not, when he walked through one of Ocean Fresh's canneries, he knew a lot of the people who worked on the line *by name*. His employees liked him. They trusted him to take care of them. If you had to choose between feeding your children and endangering the life of an oceanic creature, which would you choose?"

"But if we endanger lives in the animal kingdom, we also endanger our own."

"Yes, I agree, but when all the cards are on the table and Joe Smith is down on his luck, he's not going to worry about Flipper. He's going to worry about James and Linda, his kids. That's what your father worried about. And that is, basically, what got him into trouble. In order to keep Ocean Fresh's employees gainfully employed, he hocked his life, almost got himself thrown into jail. In other words, by stealing from his own bank, he robbed Peter to pay Paul."

She considered this for a moment, wondering how

a person could make a decision like that without long hours of thought. Besides, she knew instinctively her father would not have been stupid enough to make that kind of transaction if he'd had any fear whatsoever of getting caught. And transferring money from one place to another definitely left a trail.

"And that's what brought Makomoto in?" she asked, still not sure. "Knowing my father was in trouble and that his Achilles heel was his need to keep his people working?"

Quincel nodded, and she suddenly noticed the dark circles under his eyes, like the circles her father had had under his when he'd visited her in the hospital.

They went around the subject for a little longer, exploring all the details and attempting to illuminate the corporate intricacies Carrie didn't understand.

"I really think your father's life had been threatened," Quincel said in a somber voice when he'd finally run out of steam. "But I have no proof. He never said anything, yet I could tell he was scared. I could see that more and more. Every time Makomoto came by the company, it seemed as if your father shrunk into the corner, like there was something more terrifying than losing some of his business or getting bad publicity. That, in itself, was unusual because Philip didn't pay attention to threats. He got them all the time. But with Makomoto, there was an undercurrent of evil. You've met him. You know what I mean."

Carrie knew all too well, but she also knew Makomoto was something elusive like a lightning bug that flickers and disappears into the night, something no one would probably ever be able to pinpoint. Now, more than ever, she had to know exactly how Makomoto had manipulated her father and whether Jack was right, whether her father's death had not been accidental, as they'd all been led to believe. Perhaps Quincel was right about Makomoto's bout with syphillis. Maybe the man was insane.

Certainly her father wouldn't have sunk to Makomoto's level. Or would he?

There was only one way to find out. She needed to retrace her father's steps in Tokyo.

Twenty-seven

"What did she say?" Simone asked Jerry as he hung up the phone. For a moment the only sound was the patter of rain against the banana trees outside.

"She wants me to go to Tokyo with her. I cannot go back to Japan," he answered, the phone still in his hand. He shook his head sadly.

Simone watched him intently, feeling jealous of the memories which must be spinning through his head. She wanted him to share them with her, though she knew he would not. He was a very private man. In a lot of ways she respected that because she was also one who kept to herself. Yet she knew that her daughter needed him, and perhaps that was good. Caryn had not needed an older man, a father figure, in a long time. It struck her as strange that, at this precipitous moment in her life, Caryn had turned to Jerry. Could she finally be accepting him?

"I cannot go," he said again, standing at the kitchen door with his back toward her, his hands clasped behind him.

She went and stood next to him, listening to the soft, moist sound of the rain falling in her garden, onto the hibiscus bush and the leaves of her precious flowers. Looking outward past the meticulously designed pathways, she reminded herself to stake the vanda orchids tomorrow. They were delicate, demanding extraordinary amounts of her time, almost as much as her relationship with Jerry. Now that she thought of it, there were a lot of commonalities between the garden and Jerry. She loved them both and felt replenished when she spent time nurturing either of them. Both were well organized, yet occasionally, they would surprise her—a flower popping up unexpectedly, a spontaneous, loving remark or hug from Jerry. Both the garden and her relationship were well worth her efforts. And both had given her many hours of an almost mystical kind of pleasure.

Simone felt Jerry's warmth next to her and longed to reach out and hold him, though she knew that was not what he needed right now. If only he could tell her about Japan, share the memories of his past with her. She knew only slivers of the story, yet she never asked for more, respecting his privacy as much as he respected hers.

So she stood beside him and became lost in her own memories. The wet garden smell brought back memories of the meadows of her childhood and the times when she had begged her mother to let her cross those meadows to her friend Cécile's house, over a mile away. Her parents had always objected, telling her it was not polite to visit unannounced. To this day, she adhered to the same policy—she never even visited her own daughter without calling first.

In a lot of ways, she had been brought up with similar rules of manners and protocol as Jerry had: respect others' privacy, listen to the words between the lines, remember that the family is the most integral unit in the whole universe.

She looked over at him, again longing to reach out and touch his arm softly, reassure him that fear was the only thing he had to conquer. Nothing else mattered.

Finally, she took the step and touched Jerry's arm. "You need to go back to Japan," she whispered. "You need to return to your homeland. Put your past behind you. And take care of my daughter for me."

He looked at her, surprised. She found herself envying his smooth face, the lack of silver in his black hair, the strength in his arms. Jerry would never look old.

"I need to think about it," he replied. "I need to be alone to think about it."

She longed to beg him to talk to her about his memories of his wife and his family in Tokyo, to share with her all his frustrations and fears, but she knew that to do so would be invasive. Instead, she nodded knowingly and said, "Go. Do what you need to do. I will be here when you return."

When he left her kitchen, she stood near the door for more than fifteen minutes, listening to the rain, her arms wrapped around her, and knew without a doubt that both her daughter and her lover would be leaving her soon. As much as she loved them, she knew deep down that they had to face their individual fears alone. All she could do was pray that they find the courage they needed.

* * *

Jerry's niece, Takako Owada, met them at the airport.

"Welcome, honored Uncle," Takako said softly, bowing to Jerry. Then she turned and offered her hand to Carrie, shaking it tightly and strongly. "And you must be Mrs. Madison. Welcome to Tokyo."

Carrie smiled and said, "Please call me Carrie."

"Is this your first time in Japan?" Takako asked as the three of them walked toward the baggage area. She had to raise her voice to compete with the thousands of people around them.

Carrie nodded, feeling like Gulliver among the Liliputians. She found herself slumping. "Use your height," her mother had always admonished her, but Carrie had never been able to keep that in mind. Using it to her advantage was too much like calling attention to herself.

Takako helped retrieve their baggage and guided them to the car she had hired for them.

"I also employed a driver," she said, her English as perfect as if she'd spent years in London. "I wanted to be able to sit with you and talk. I hope you don't mind."

"Of course not," Carrie reassured her, with a tentative glance at Jerry who had remained ominously silent since getting off the plane. It was obvious he had nothing to say to his niece, a woman he really didn't know, who he had never met because she'd been born after he'd left, and who he knew only as his brother's daughter. Carrie hooked her arm into his, giving him a smile she hoped would soothe his nervousness. The gesture was one she'd never attempted before with him, but it felt right. He actually seemed to relax a little.

After packing all the suitcases into the Mercedes waiting for them at the curb, Takako said, "I have booked you at the Hilton near the Imperial Palace. Will that suit your needs?" When Carrie and Jerry nodded, she continued. "Mr. Makomoto's main office is less than three blocks away. You shouldn't have any trouble finding it, though I will show you the way."

Their car began the forty-mile ride into the city, and even though Carrie longed to hang her head out the window to better see the manicured trees whizzing by and the crowded suburbs they passed through, she controlled herself. Everything was surprisingly clean, and she realized why after they passed women with buckets who kneeled on sidewalks to scrub them with wide, sweeping movements. Cherry trees rose above the pagoda-style roofs of houses, and everywhere she looked, the signs were written in those lines and squiggles that were the Japanese language. It was all so new, so different, that she felt a bit overwhelmed and concentrated on absorbing the information Takako presented to them in a clipped, organized fashion.

"I know you only have a short time here," Takako was saying. "Therefore, I've done as much of the research as I could for you." On her lap, she held a leather portfolio bulging with papers. "Luckily, in my business, I have complete access to the computer which holds the city's business records, and it wasn't difficult to obtain a type of prospectus on Mr. Makomoto's companies. Currently, he's searching for investors, so the information is readily available. However," she opened the portfolio and turned to Carrie with a wry smile, "your Mr. Makomoto does not always tell the truth, and that's where things get interesting."

She flipped through a couple of pages and pulled out a list of numbers, handing them to Carrie, who held them uncertainly in her hand and studied the page of what appeared to be ancient Mayan pictographs. How the hell am I supposed to decipher this? she wondered.

"Let me explain what all of this means," Takako said. She pointed out the Japanese names for each of Makomoto's company divisions, described the products each produced, what its base capital was, and its yearly profit for the past five years. "This may seem like extraneous information, but by looking at this analysis, I can tell there's been an inordinate number of financial changes among the companies, something like what Jerry explained to me your father had been accused of, shifting money from one company to the other. It seems Mr. Makomoto is a professional at misappropriating funds, but the difference between your father and him is that Makomoto's gotten away with it for well over a decade."

It bothered Carrie that Takako was comparing her father to Makomoto, but she didn't say anything. After all, what if he was misappropriating funds? She still didn't feel totally comfortable talking about him. After years of hating him, it was hard to put all her resentment aside after he died. And now that she had to handle all his problems, she felt even more resentful, in one respect. Yet, she also felt closer to him.

Takako produced another sheet of paper, this one a magazine article illustrated with photographs. Although it was written in Japanese, Carrie recognized a photo of Makomoto, a blurry shot taken in what appeared to be a darkened alley.

"What's this about?" she asked, studying the other photographs illustrating the article, all of rather seedy-looking characters, most with cigarettes hanging out of their mouths and narrowed, mean eyes.

"Have you heard of Yakuza?"

Jerry sucked his breath in sharply while reading over Carrie's shoulder.

Carrie shot him a puzzled look, then turned back to Takako. "No, what is it?"

"Not what, who. They're the Japanese underworld, something like what you Americans call the Mafia."

"And what does Makomoto have to do with them?"

"Everything. He's suspected of being one of their leaders." Takako looked up from her papers. "A very dangerous man," she said. "You should know he could make big trouble for you."

"Holy shit," Carrie whispered. "What the hell have I gotten myself into?"

"Something bad," Jerry muttered. "Something very bad."

Almost an hour later, traffic slowed to a crawl as the car crossed a small river, which Takako told her was the Sumida. Its brown water flowed beneath them. Apparently it was once a wider river, from the look of its banks, but now merely a trickle.

"The walls around the bay were built to protect Tokyo against possible tidal waves. You see," Takako said, "this city is in a quite active earthquake zone, much like your San Francisco."

Jerry took up the story, his voice sonorous and slow as if recalling many centuries of family history. "At one time, a fishing village named Edo, the name meaning 'rivergate,' stood at the mouth of this river. It was a small village, easy for the shoguns to over-turn when they moved in during the early seven-teenth-century. Ieyasu Tokugawa, the first of the Edo shoguns, used this area as a military headquarters for the whole country. This is where the Kabuki theater came from, and sumo wrestling, and the elegant art of the geisha."

Jerry continued, his comments quietly interspersed by Takako's. Together they told Carrie of the sophis-ticated, artistic culture which arose around the warring shoguns. So many of the arts Westerners had come to think of as distinctly Japanese had been part of these people's everyday lives. Carrie listened, fasci-nated by the exotic country whose history stretched back more than four hundred years before the first European had set foot in North America. Long before Paris began its reign as the romantic center of the universe, Tokyo's inhabitants had been creating sen-sual myths of star-crossed lovers, lovers whose esca-pades would put Romeo's and Juliet's to shame.

She sank back against the seat, watching intently as they came into downtown Tokyo, from ancient his-tory into the present. The Ginza strip, with its neon-lit skyscrapers and wall-to-wall traffic, was one of the most expensive areas to shop, Takako said. "But you can buy just about anything here, from all over the world."

The noise level rose to an almost ear-splitting pitch, as business-suited men and women scurried along the sidewalks in much the same way as Wall Streeters did in New York, glancing at their watches, their foreheads knit in concentration. Signs for Coca-Cola and McDonald's were balanced with Japanese ads for cameras and the latest computers. The mirrored windows of some of the buildings reflected the brightly lit signs on others until the area became a kaleidoscope of neon colors and insistent advertising.

Jerry shook his head, amazed. "So much has changed," he murmured.

"Now, dear Uncle," Takako added, "we are very prosperous. One of the largest urban areas in the world. So big that our Shinjuku moves two million people a day."

"Shinjuku?" Carrie asked.

"Our subway system. You have probably seen photographs of the 'pushers-in.' They wear white gloves and literally push riders onto the trains and pull them off, so that the trains can run as efficiently as possible."

"Remind me to walk or take a cab," Carrie chuckled.

What impressed Carrie most was that this city with its millions of people was one of the cleanest she'd ever seen, and she was sure that once she met more of its inhabitants, she'd discover that the city's pride reflected its inhabitants'. She mentioned that to Takako, who laughed politely behind her hand.

"We are very rude," she said with a giggle. "English people are always surprised how much we Japanese push and shove each other."

Beside her, Jerry nodded knowingly. "When I first

came to Hawaii, I was surprised people excused themselves. It took me a long time to learn how to do so."

The comment finally sparked some conversation between uncle and niece, and Carrie was happy to see Jerry finally talking in Japanese, probably catching up on his family. It had been a good idea to bring him along, and she smiled in spite of the fact that she could not tear her mind away from what Takako had already revealed about Ishiru Makomoto.

When they came around the east edge of the Imperial Palace's impeccably maintained grounds, Carrie strained to catch a glimpse of the fabled buildings, once home to shoguns, now to the Emperor. All she could see were golden-brown stained brick walls and elegantly shaped yews. It was quieter here after the hustle and bustle of the Ginza. Even the air had changed. No heavy traffic smell, even though they still barely crawled, bumper to bumper.

"This whole area is called the *yamanote* or the high town." Takako gestured to where Carrie could see some of the shrinelike buildings Takako called "bachelor residences," pagodas where Japan's noblemen lived with their samurai while their wives stayed on the family estates. A moat surrounded the area and graceful willows swayed in the warm afternoon breeze. Carrie wondered whether she'd have time to take a tour of some kind, then sharply reminded herself of the reason for visiting this exotic city, business, not pleasure. Maybe another time.

The Hilton, only a short distance away, felt like every other Hilton Carrie had ever visited, and she found herself a little disappointed, but maybe it was just as well. She'd be able to concentrate on the task at hand, rather than wandering around fascinated by the new, strange world within which she found herself.

Takako left them once they were settled in their rooms, promising to come back the next day after they'd had a chance to adjust to the time change.

After she unpacked, Carrie stood at the window for a few moments, then a wave of exhaustion suddenly overtook her. I'll just lie down for a moment, she thought, but the bed felt wonderful after the uncomfortable airline seat, and once her eyes closed, they didn't open again until the first splinters of sunrise were beginning to find their way into her room.

The energetic Takako led them down yet another side street along the Ginza strip. Carrie paused momentarily to let an old woman with shopping bags in both hands pass by. The woman looked up, seemingly amazed at Carrie's height, and said something in Japanese, nodding and bowing as she continued on her way. Not knowing what else to do, Carrie smiled and bowed back. Ahead of her, Jerry caught her eye and nodded, as if she had done exactly what she was supposed to do, as if he was proud of her, like a father.

They had been walking for what seemed like hours. Every once in a while, Takako would stop someone and ask a question. Carrie still had no idea what was going on or whether Takako was getting anywhere with her investigation. Perhaps she and Jerry would have been more useful back in the hotel room, doing some kind of research, yet she wouldn't have given up the experience of discovering Tokyo's streets for anything.

She'd been tempted to stop several times and explore the city's celebrated department stores, where she'd heard hostesses welcomed their customers and even dusted escalator rails before the customer put their "honorable fingers" on them. She wanted to investigate each new smell, taste each unfamiliar dish, talk to Tokyo's people, feel the city's pulsing energy. Tokyo buzzed with activity and productivity. It was no surprise to her that this country led the world with its work ethic. The Japanese seemed proud of their jobs and anxious to do their best. Her mind slipped back to Hawaii, and she thought of Isaac and how he complained every time he worked on *The Big One*. It was the first time she'd thought of home in days.

"Are you hungry?" Takako asked Carrie. Jerry walked ahead of them, apparently as caught up in sightseeing as Carrie was.

Carrie nodded gratefully, called to Jerry, then followed the smaller woman into a tiny restaurant tucked into the first floor corner of a high-rise near Mitsubishi's round tower. Only moments later, a shy waitress dressed in a colorful kimono served them a vegetable soup Takako called *miso*. Carrie ate it hungrily, surprised at its tastiness. While the plates in front of them were replaced with new dishes, Takako verbally pieced together what she'd discovered that morning with what she'd researched on the computer before they'd arrived.

"To say the Makomoto name is to strike fear in people's hearts," she said. "Did you notice that man this morning who ran away when I asked him a question?"

Jerry nodded. "Did I hear him say he worked for Makomoto Seafoods?"

"Yes, but that's all he would tell me," Takako answered. "I have a strange feeling we will not find out much more today. Word travels quite quickly on these streets. Before too long, everyone will know that we are asking questions."

After Jerry had shown Carrie how to eat the new dish, a simmering vegetable and pastry combination he called *oden,* he asked Takako, "Perhaps it would be better if we split up. Can I ask some of the questions while you do some research?"

Takako's prominent lower lip stuck out even more as she considered the prospect. Finally, she shook her head and, apologizing to Carrie, switched to rapid Japanese to make arrangements with her uncle. When they finished, Jerry turned to Carrie and suggested it might be best if Takako went on alone, while he and Carrie visited the Mainichi building, one of Japan's leading newspapers, to further research Makomoto's past business dealings.

"What are we looking for specifically?" Carrie asked.

"Anything that will link Makomoto with your father. Perhaps some business article about how Makomoto wanted to buy your father's corporation or some indication that Makomoto Seafoods is going through some changes. I think we shall also look for articles which might associate the honorable Ishiru Makomoto with the not-so-honorable Yakuza." Jerry's voice turned sarcastic.

For the first time, Carrie realized how he must feel to be investigating his lover's ex-husband's death. With all that had been going on in her own life, Carrie had selfishly ignored Jerry, and she admonished herself. Now she appreciated Jerry's anguish upon returning home after such a long absence for such a strange reason. She reminded herself to tell him how grateful she was for his help.

Hours later, Carrie reached her arms above her head and stretched her stiff back. They'd been reading microfiche and copying articles since early afternoon and now it was dark outside. She glanced at her watch.

"Wasn't Takako supposed to come back and pick us up at five o'clock?" she whispered to Jerry who sat next to her, his half glasses perched crookedly on his nose, all his attention focused on the reading screen in front of him.

"What time is it now?" he whispered back.

"Almost seven."

"It is not like Japanese to be late," he said, his eyebrows knitted together. He thought for a moment, then said, "Maybe she discovered something. I am confident she will return. Let us continue looking. We will not get another chance to do so."

Stiff as she was, Carrie agreed and lowered her head to the tiny type once again. She had the English version of the big city newspaper in front of her. So far, they had checked back at least five years, day after day, month after month. The stack of articles on Makomoto was impressive. And she hadn't had the chance to read them thoroughly yet, nor to put the larger picture together. Tired, she decided to do just that and settled back to begin to read.

When Jerry looked toward the door worriedly, she checked her watch again, it was almost eight. Time to start worrying.

"What should we do now?" she whispered to Jerry, feeling like a child in the town library.

"Perhaps I should call my brother, though I really do not want to worry him."

"Maybe we *ought* to be worried," Carrie answered, shuffling the pile of articles she'd just finished reading. "It doesn't seem like Makomoto plays by the rules. From what they say in here," she patted the pile, "he's been suspected of killing quite a few people. But nothing's ever been proven."

She hadn't meant to upset Jerry, but a look of terror passed over his normally calm features, as if he'd forgotten what a dangerous position they had put themselves in.

Rushing out of the building a few moments later, they practically ran into Takako. Her usually silky hair flopped wetly over her forehead and a sheen of sweat glazed her upper lip. "We need to talk," she said breathlessly, "someplace where no one else can hear us." She glanced furtively over her shoulder. "I think someone's following me, so let's split up and meet at your hotel."

With that, she sprinted across the street and disappeared into the evening's crowd of diners and partygoers. For a moment, Carrie stood completely still, stunned. She glanced at Jerry who appeared as shocked as she. "Do you think you can find your way back to the hotel?" he asked. She nodded, then, without another word, they scurried in opposite directions.

Carrie's heart pounded and she hoped she was headed the right way. It wouldn't do any good to get lost in a city where she couldn't even read the street signs.

She walked quickly around the block and, spotting the hotel down the street, hurried toward it, her chin tucked into her chest, as if that would disguise her Americanness. With each person who bumped against her, she had to remind herself not to say "excuse me," for it would only bring her to their attention and she wanted to remain as anonymous as possible. God, why couldn't she have been born small and dark like her mother instead of gawky and blonde.

In the hotel's lobby, she stopped for a moment, scanning the area for anyone who looked like they might be watching for her. Everyone seemed preoccupied with their own business, so she headed for the elevator and hoped Takako and Jerry would make it back safe and sound as well.

Less than fifteen minutes later, Jerry and Takako knocked on the door to Carrie's room.

"If anyone was followed, it was me," Carrie stated, throwing her jacket on the bed. "God, how could they miss this geeky American? I stick out like a sore thumb."

"Excuse me: Geeky? Like a sore thumb?" Takako giggled.

"Just a stupid saying," Carrie replied, waving a hand as if to dismiss her comment. "What have you found out?"

Takako cleared her throat and closed the drapes over the room's windows before settling into the straight-backed chair to Carrie's right. She folded her hands demurely in her lap, but Takako's demeanor was just a cover for the woman's incredible energy.

"From what I can tell," Takako began, "Mr. Philip De-Bary and Mr. Ishiru Makomoto were engaged in a corporate war over their tuna companies. Surprisingly enough, your father had initially tried to buy out Makomoto Seafoods. He almost succeeded, but after Makomoto discovered that your father had had him investigated and, as a result, had discovered some of Mr. Makomoto's less reputable business, and social, practices, he became quite angry."

"The shit hit the fan, in other words," Carrie interjected, feeling unreasonably proud of her father.

"Excuse me?"

"Another stupid American saying. In other words, all hell broke loose."

That one Takako understood. She nodded enthusiastically. "*Hai,* that is correct. Over a period of five years, they battled back and forth. DeBary wanted to buy out Makomoto. Makomoto wanted to buy out DeBary. Finally, the fight turned bloody. DeBary—excuse me, your father—revealed some of the information he'd discovered about Makomoto to some stockbrokers."

"Like what?" Carrie sat on the edge of the bed, her hands between her knees.

"It's not clear, however, it must have been very traumatic, because from that point on Makomoto's pursuit of your father's company became ruthless. It seemed your father never was quite able to gain another foothold."

"Corporate politics," Jerry murmured, shaking his head. "It sounds like all of this has very little to do with tuna fishing."

"Absolutely nothing," Takako agreed. "I don't believe either man considered anything more important than his battle with the other. It became a contest of strength. It probably didn't even matter to either of them what the ultimate prize was. Both of them had all they could ever need, but the thirst for power—"

"What do you think my father found out that drove Makomoto so nutty?"

"I couldn't get specifics, but it seemed he uncovered Makomoto's link to the Yakuza, and, I suppose, a connection like that would endear Makomoto to American business. Besides, without your father's consent, Makomoto could never maintain control over Ocean Fresh. Your father held the majority of the stocks."

Carrie harrumphed. "American businessmen are not much better than your Yakuza. From what I know of them, corporate executives think the jugular is the tastiest part of the body."

"The point is," Takako said, "none of us will ever know exactly what happened. However, I came across another piece of information that might enlighten us about your father's death."

Leaning forward a little more, Carrie twisted her hands together. Suddenly, she wasn't so sure she wanted to know. Beside her, Jerry shifted in his seat, as if he wasn't so certain either. She kept very still and waited anxiously for Takako to speak. The Japanese woman stared at the wall, apparently trying to put her words together. The room became stifling and quiet.

"It has been said that the Yakuza are very clever," Takako said, smiling ruefully at her uncle. "They have discovered more ways to kill than any other group in history. We Japanese are very good at dying. One of the forms of execution Makomoto has perfected is to sprinkle digitalis powder in his victims' food. Death occurs from an apparent heart attack and the digitalis is not easily detected unless someone is looking for it specifically."

Carrie drove her fingernails into her palms and a tight fist squeezed her chest. But Takako wasn't finished.

"I was lucky enough to talk to someone who knows a woman who used to be one of Makomoto's secretaries. He took me to her and we had an interesting conversation. That was what took me so long to get back to you." She took a deep breath and looked directly into Carrie's eyes. "The night he died, your father had a dinner engagement with Makomoto."

Twenty-eight

Carrie was in that vague state between sleeping and wakefulness when a knock at her door forced her to roll out of bed.

"Who is it?" she said, still unsure of her bearings.

"Pardon me? Miss Madison?" The voice was decidedly Japanese and quite meek. She wondered what time it was.

She moved closer to the door, trying to focus, trying to decide whether it was still nighttime or whether she'd just overslept. It had not been a relaxing night. Every fear imaginable had crept under the sheets with her, invading her dreams. She knew by the grittiness of her eyelids that she must look like she'd been through Dante's inferno.

"Yes?" she said, through the closed door.

"I have your breakfast, Miss Madison."

Automatically, she reached for the knob and before the door was wide open, she turned to grope her way to the bath on the other side of the room.

"I'll tip you later," she said, closing the bathroom door behind her. The harsh light insulted her eyes, and she yawned, promising herself to crawl right back into bed for at least a couple more hours before facing reality. She'd planned to head over to Makomoto's office, to confront him with what she knew about her father, even though both Takako and Jerry had urged her not to. The plan had kept her awake until the late hours of the morning, so she figured right about now she'd be running on only about three hours of sleep out of the past thirty-six hours. Her normal would be eight or nine.

She heard the door close again and assumed it was room-service leaving. She splashed a little lukewarm water on her face and returned to the bedroom.

Makomoto sat on a chair in the middle of the room. A tray of breakfast food sat on a silver luggage stand in front of him. He lifted his head when she emerged and glanced at her through half-closed lids.

"Ah, Mrs. Madison. I see we woke you up. Please accept our deepest apologies."

Her heart beat madly against her chest and all her senses were at full alert. She walked slowly into the room, thinking that this was what it was like to snap out of an almost catatonic state with lightning speed. She experienced an intense sense of invasion, like someone waking to find his home burglarized, his personal items rifled through.

On the other side of the bed, filling up all the free space in the small room, stood Makomoto's bodyguard, Toto. She thought of Dorothy's dog.

"What are you doing here?" she breathed.

"I came to join you for breakfast," Makomoto answered pleasantly. "I understand you are very diligently looking into my business affairs, so I thought I would make it easier for you. What would you like to ask?"

She felt exposed in her flannel nightgown, barefoot, eyes still full of sleep, mouth still pasty and dry. Why couldn't he have given her the decency of calling to make an appointment? Well, she reasoned, why should he? She hadn't planned to make one with him, she was just going to barge in and demand an explanation.

"Why don't we discuss this another time?" she said with a failed attempt at a smile. "I'm really not prepared to talk this early in the morning. Shall we meet around, say, one o'clock, at your office?"

He shook his head slowly from side to side, as if it was not acceptable for her to make the rules. Then he gestured with one long finger to Toto. "Mrs. Madison seems hungry, doesn't she? Don't you think we ought to introduce her to our illustrious cuisine?"

She knew, without a lot of analysis, that she had been brought this tray of food for a reason. Just as Makomoto had invited her father to dinner for a reason. Was what she had discovered so threatening that he needed to kill her? Perhaps this was just his way of getting at Ocean Fresh. After all, with her out of the way, there'd be no more impediments. He could take over easily.

Glancing quickly at Toto, Carrie wondered just how much of all of this he understood. Sometimes he seemed to have the IQ of a pit bull. He lumbered over to her, leering like a deranged ax murderer and pulled a chair in front of the tray with the dishes topped with silver domes. One by one he uncovered the plates, then fishing in one of his side pockets, pulled out a small brown vial of white powder which he liberally dusted over each dish. She watched, paralyzed by the knowledge that the white powder was digitalis and that she'd be shipped back to Hawaii in a coffin, her mother getting the story that poor Caryn had died of a heart attack, just like her father, it must run in the family, isn't that sad. In a flash, she imagined everyone's reactions to her death—Jack's anger, his determination to find the culprit, his guilt at not having insisted he accompany her to Tokyo; Alex's sadness upon realizing he had never apologized after their last fight; her mother's devastation; Matt's confusion and loneliness upon losing both his friend and his job; Jerry's guilt for not having been in the same room with her.

Or would he be killed, too? Was there a way she could alert him? Should she scream? Knock something over? No, she couldn't let this happen. She couldn't give in to the fear which rooted her feet to the floor.

"I'm not a breakfast person," she insisted, her voice still higher than usual, her vocal chords pulsating like taut elastics. "I normally don't eat until lunchtime. You know, no one in my family ever liked breakfast. Probably comes from my mother. The French just drink lots of café au lait and eat croissants. Quite civilized, not eating in the morning, don't you think? I'd much rather take a shower and get myself situated before subjecting myself to a big meal. Helps the digestive system."

With each nervous word, she edged herself back into the bathroom, hoping fervently that the door had a strong lock and that it would hold Toto back for at least as long as it took for her to scream her bloody lungs out. Jerry might hear her next door. She'd fight, she decided, to the end, if necessary. Wasn't that what the police told you to do, to keep yourself from becoming a victim?

No sooner had the thought entered her mind than she caught a glimpse of the door connecting the two suites edging open. Had Jerry overheard the whole conversation?

She continued babbling, covering for Jerry, praying that she'd be able to distract Makomoto and Toto. She spoke more quickly, talking about what her mother served for breakfast, what her husband liked best, asking Makomoto, who stared at her with a puzzled expression, what he liked to eat first thing in the morning and if he ate before seven o'clock or after. She described the difference between Rice Krispies and Corn Flakes, between oatmeal and porridge, completely confusing the two men, who kept looking at each other as though trying to figure out whether she had suddenly gone insane or whether they should try to answer her questions. All she wanted to do was keep their attention riveted on her.

Jerry crept into the room like a ghost, moving as slowly as he did when practicing t'ai chi. Carrie swallowed hard and breathed in shallow, short gasps, everything in slow motion. She searched her thoughts for some more inane comments to make and chattered about how slow the mornings started in Hawaii, all the time realizing that she might never see those mornings again. Each word became precious, another second of life, another microcosm of time she so desperately needed to encase within longer moments.

When Jerry was within an arm's length of Toto, something made Makomoto turn. What happened next passed so quickly that if Carrie were to have to repeat it in a police interrogation later, she couldn't have said who moved first or how, but at the end of a few blurred movements and utterances of surprise, Toto had tumbled loudly to the floor, Jerry had knocked over the food tray with a quick kick, and Makomoto had ended up on his back, still in the chair.

If she hadn't been so scared, she would have laughed to see Jerry, a small, elegant, aging Japanese man, still standing, his arms raised in the dragon position, while two-ton Toto and menacing Makomoto were on the ground looking up. By the way they lifted themselves off the floor, dusted themselves off, and acted as though the incident had never occurred, she knew they were just as surprised as she, and angry with themselves for getting caught off guard. In that small moment, she felt incredibly proud of Jerry. No matter what else happened, Jerry was a hero.

Makomoto and Toto left quickly, chattering angrily in Japanese. Carrie stood in the bathroom doorway, unsure how to react. At first, she wanted to pick the yellow and white breakfast mess up off the floor, but her hands shook too badly. Then she realized how strange it was that the two men, reputed to be terrifying members of the Yakuza, had left as meekly as dogs with their tails between their legs.

Jerry was the first to speak. "We have had our warning. We were lucky I could catch them off guard. We will not get that chance again. We need to leave, immediately."

She agreed, uninterested in going any further with her investigation. Within an hour, their bags were packed and they were on the way to the airport. Jerry made a quick phone call to Takako, who promised to get out of the country. Not out of the city, Carrie noted, not out of the area, but out of the country.

It wasn't until she boarded the plane five hours later that Carrie took a full breath. They had been incredibly lucky to get a flight. If not for a cancellation at the last minute, they'd still be in Tokyo. A perfect target for Makomoto.

"We were almost killed," she said to Jerry, as if he hadn't noticed.

"They would not have killed you in an obvious manner," he said. His pale face accentuated the blackness of his eyes. He had held her arm protectively, but without a word, since leaving the hotel. "It had to be done with the poison. Apparently, Makomoto wants you to die the same way your father did. Once we made some noise in the room, they knew there would be witnesses who would report what happened to the authorities. I think you must learn a lesson from this, Caryn. I think you must learn what your father did not."

She knew he was right, but as she looked at Jerry's intense features, she also knew that now, more than ever, she had to find out why her father had left the company to her.

Why had he put her in such a dangerous position?

Their flight from Tokyo to Honolulu was an easier one than the trip from Houston to Japan, taking a lot less time and hitting less turbulence. When she saw the familiar curve of Waikiki and the recognizable jut of Diamond Head, she relaxed, finally allowing her tense neck muscles to loosen. Home. She was safe now.

A group of Oriental tourists got out of their seats and crammed into the left side of the plane to take pictures and jabber excitedly. She wondered if the sudden shift in weight was one the pilot would feel and found herself chuckling. It was the first normal thought she'd had since leaving Tokyo.

Neither she nor Jerry had slept during the long flight. Instead, they'd whispered among themselves, while everyone else around them had snored. Diligently, Jerry tried to convince her that Makomoto was not about to give up, that he'd probably never stop trying to gain control of Ocean Fresh.

"The Yakuza has long arms," he said. "If Makomoto wants to find you, there is not much you can do about it. Please, Caryn, think about your mother. If you should be killed, she would find her life worthless. Just sell the company to him. Rid yourself of this fear."

"Makomoto's not going to kill me," she scoffed, though in her heart, she was sure Jerry was right. "He's just trying to scare me."

"You read the articles, Caryn. You heard what Takako said. Do you think I would have asked her to leave the country if I had thought Makomoto would just forget about everything?"

"He has no real reason to kill any of us. We were just snooping around."

"You have done more than 'snoop.' You have discovered very damaging information about him, information I am sure he does not want anyone to know, especially in America where he is trying to gain a foothold. You could destroy him very easily."

"If I was involved with that crap. I'm not. I just wanted to find out what happened to my father."

"You have done that."

"Yes, and now I know he didn't die of a heart attack. He was murdered!"

"You are just suspecting that. You are not sure."

"What do I need to do, exhume the body?"

She exhaled, frustrated.

Jerry leaned toward her, his face in the shadows cast by the tiny light above his head. "Even if you were able to do that, exhume your father's body, have an autopsy performed, I am not sure how easy it would be to have Makomoto prosecuted. Think about it. Your father was a well-known American businessman; Makomoto is a leading Tokyo citizen. The likelihood of an American being believed in the Japanese court system seems slim. Besides, who would you get for a lawyer? Your man in Houston? Would he be able to practice in Japan? Would you have to travel over there for the trial?"

"You've been watching too much 'Perry Mason,' " Carrie said, not wanting to admit Jerry was probably right, again.

"I do not watch television, you know that."

She patted his arm. "I know. I just don't want him to get away with it. There's got to be a way we can stop him."

"Perhaps there is," Jerry said slowly.

"What?"

"Find another buyer for the company."

"Sure, that'd get him off my back and maybe set someone else up. And it still doesn't change the fact that he was responsible for my father's death."

"Again, Caryn, you are not sure of that." Jerry enunciated his words clearly, as if by doing so Carrie would finally understand she was helpless.

But that was one thing she did understand. And she hated the feeling with a passion.

She called her mother from the first phone booth she found in the airport's lobby, feeling slightly disoriented and out of place in the suit she had worn on the plane. She longed for the comfort of her shorts and T-shirt. Everyone around her smiled and joked, on vacation, colorful leis around their necks, away from the problems and conflicts of their daily lives. She envied them their nonchalance.

Her mother sounded surprised to hear from her but instantly seemed to sense the urgency in Carrie's voice and wasted no time asking questions, other than the arrival time of their flight to Kona. "I will meet you at the airport," she said. Her matter-of-fact voice and the way she took over without thinking, always the mother, the caretaker, soothed Carrie and she fought the urge to weep.

She called Pamela next and told her what she had discovered. The silence on Pamela's end of the line told Carrie how shocked she was.

"He tried to kill me, too, Pamela," Carrie said. "He's got to be stopped, but the only way we can do it is to prove he killed Daddy." She paused, hoping she wouldn't have to tell Pamela exactly what needed to be done to prove Philip had not died of a heart attack.

"I can't do it," Pamela said, her voice thick with emotion. "You're going to have to find another way, Carrie."

Another moment of silence, then Pamela continued.

"My husband, your father, is dead. Nothing is going to change that. And I will not have his body exhumed. I can't bear the thought."

That was it, Carrie realized. In order to have an autopsy done, she needed Pamela's permission, and she could tell that Pamela definitely was not going to give in. In a way, she couldn't blame her. The thought of disturbing her father was not one Carrie liked either. Still, she felt she had to give it one more try.

"The man's insane, Pamela. He's not going to stop. I don't want to end up the same way Daddy did."

"Then get protection," were Pamela's last words before she hung up in tears.

Carrie sat in the phone booth for a few minutes, hands shaking, on the verge of tears herself, before she picked up the phone again and called her office. She expected Jack to answer, but it was Matt whose deep voice greeted her, with apprehension she thought.

"Are you okay?" he asked. "What's going on?"

"Nothing. We came home early, that's all."

"Aw, c'mon, Carrie, you ain't gettin' away with that with me. You know I can tell when you're lying. Spit it out. What happened?"

"I'll tell you all about it when I get home."

"Give me a synopsis."

She sighed and leaned heavily against the side of the telephone booth. "I'll make it really quick if you promise not to ask any questions, okay?"

"Okay."

"Makomoto is a vicious thug. He's involved in something called the Yakuza, which is like the Mafia, and he probably murdered my father and he tried to kill me, too. That's why we came home."

"That son-of-a-bitch! Let him come here again. We'll show him what for. Man, I can't believe it. Are you sure you're all right?"

"Yeah, I'm okay."

"And Jerry?"

She laughed a little. "Jerry's better than having Chuck Norris around. The man's an absolute hero, a karate expert par excellence. You wouldn't have believed him! If it wasn't for him, you wouldn't be talking to me right now."

"Well, listen, *Sistah,* don't waste any time getting home. I want to hear about everything in detail. Besides, we need you here. Lots of shit coming down." He paused a moment and said something unintelligible to someone in the office. When he came back on the phone, his voice was hushed, secretive. "Alex has been asking where you are, y'know."

Jack must be the person Matt was speaking to, she thought.

"Oh."

"Yeah, I saw him last week. You need to talk to him, Carrie. He's changed a lot. I think he's pretty sorry about what he's done."

"That's something I can't really deal with right now. Not with everything else . . ."

"You used to be able to talk about things. He used to be able to help you settle your mind. Maybe he can help now."

She shook her head and muttered a defiant, "No," then looked away into the crowd, searching for Jerry among the colorfully dressed tourists.

"Give him a chance, Carrie."

She didn't want to talk about this. "Where's Jack?"

"He went out on *The Rainbow Warrior* a couple of days ago. He's supposed to be back tomorrow." Matt's voice turned frosty.

She decided to ignore the judgment in his tone. "Has Isaac been working with you?" Out of the corner of her eye, she saw Jerry waving at her and pointing to his watch.

"Yeah, he's doing okay. Actually, I think he's kind of smartened up in the past couple of weeks. Maybe he's growing up."

"Listen, Matt, I have to go. Our plane's leaving. I'll call you later tonight from my mother's house."

They said their goodbyes and Carrie walked on rubbery legs to wait with Jerry, who was already standing in the line for the flight to Kona.

Twenty-nine

After much deliberation, Carrie decided not to tell her mother about Makomoto's threats, his attempt on her life, or her suspicions that her father had been murdered. Since Pamela wouldn't agree to exhuming Philip's body, perhaps it was just as well Simone didn't know. Although Carrie was frustrated, she understood. She just wished things were different so that she could prove Makomoto had murdered her father. But, like Pamela had said, it wouldn't bring him back.

Deep down, she knew her mother would be furious with her for withholding information. She could even imagine the discussion about it: her mother would ask who was the adult in this situation, who was the mother? It had become one of Simone's favorite questions during Carrie's teenage years.

But, for many reasons, Carrie figured her decision was the right one and she stuck to it, making Matt, Jack, and Jerry swear to keep the secret as well.

Jerry supported her decision to keep Simone in the dark, perhaps because he knew she worried too much already. He told Carrie a few days after their return that Simone had questioned him at length about what happened in Tokyo, but she had accepted his laconic way of answering her and had let the matter drop.

"Somehow I satisfied her curiosity," he commented with a conspiratorial smile.

The friendship between Carrie and Jerry deepened as a result of the terrifying experience they had shared. She felt a kinship with him which bordered on the love she might feel for a favored uncle, the same type of feeling Takako might have for him.

Takako. From what Jerry could find out, his niece had taken refuge with another branch of the family, a cousin who lived in Shanghai. He couldn't find out if she was all right, but Jerry's brother commented that Takako's life would be enriched by her "trip abroad." Jerry's telephone calls to Tokyo were careful ones, always conducted with the knowledge that someone else might be listening. He told Carrie that he felt his brother seemed angry with him for coming back into the family's lives and causing such a disruption. That saddened him and Carrie felt somewhat responsible for bringing him home only to take him away again from everything he loved, from the only family he had.

A few days later, Simone shared the news with Carrie that Jerry wanted to make another trip to Tokyo in the future, with Simone at his side. That made Carrie feel a little better, but both she and Jerry knew he couldn't return to Tokyo until something was done about Makomoto. And neither could Takako. Or Carrie herself.

The day after she returned to work, Jack burst into the office and swept her into his arms.

"You look so good," he whispered into her hair. "I've never been so worried about anyone in my entire life. All I thought about was how you were. Couldn't even concentrate on anything else, and boy,

we've had a lot going on lately." He held her away
for a moment, his green eyes glittering. "You *are*
here, aren't you? You *are* real?"

She nodded and pulled him back to her, reveling in
the solid feel of his body, the peaceful way he made
her feel. But that peaceful feeling didn't last long.
Within moments, it was replaced by a free-wheeling
passion that took over her whole body as Jack's hands
found their way up her back. His fingers massaged her
as they travelled to her shoulder blades, past the tender
valley of her spine. He nuzzled her neck, pressing his
face against hers, kissing each of her features with great
tenderness, moving with aching slowness down her
cheek until he found her waiting mouth.

Once their tongues reached each other, the volcano
erupted. Carrie lost all control over her emotions.
Thoughts of what should be and what should happen
flew out of her mind as quickly as spiderwebs in a
tornado. She was truly swept away. And she welcomed the escape from reality.

They attacked each other as if hiding in each others' bodies would make sense of the world, as if nothing mattered but each other and the solace they found
in their embrace.

Brazenly, Carrie slipped her hands beneath the
waistband of Jack's shorts, wiggling her fingers impatiently until the snap popped. Without bothering
with any more formalities, she had them down with
one quick pull and sunk to her knees in front of him.
He smelled like salt and Ivory soap.

Jack groaned in submission, then reached down to
catch Carrie by the elbows and pull her up to him.

Both his eyes and voice were smoky when he said,

"Some day I'm going to let you finish that. But not right now. Right now I want you."

"Is that a threat or a promise?" she murmured, pulling her shirt up and pressing her hard nipples against his chest.

Without a thought for who might see them, she wound one leg around Jack's hips and writhed against him. They both moaned this time.

"If I don't make love to you right now," Jack growled, "I'm going to burst."

"The back room," she whispered.

Immediately they retreated into the back room, where their lovemaking mirrored the first time they'd explored each others' bodies. The only difference this time was that afterward they lay side-by-side and talked quietly, their fingers entwined, their noses almost touching, their breath intermingling in the air between them. Carrie wanted to stay in that position forever, to deny that the rest of her life existed, to forget her problems with Alex, to simply feel the silkiness of Jack's leg hairs against her calves, to hear him tell her over and over and over again that she was the most important person in his life, that he never again wanted to be separated from her, that he needed to be beside her, to watch the changes in her face as she grew older, to hear her laugh with delight at his stupid jokes, to learn her body as well as he knew his own.

All of it was incredibly corny, she knew, and extremely risky, but she needed the fantasy, that Cinderella-type love affair where the man said all the right things and the woman felt as adored and revered as the madonna.

With each day that passed after that, the moments

they shared became more and more addicting. They grew closer, more dependent on each other, and Carrie found she could not make a decision without watching Jack's eyes for his affirmation or opinion. Although that feeling was not one she was familiar with, she had no urge to get out of the relationship. It was the only thing in her life which was stable, and although she knew she would have to come up for air sooner or later, she enjoyed the languid days and nights of loving Jack too much to analyze what might happen tomorrow.

Matt maneuvered the Camaro into a parking space between a blue Honda and a white LeMans. He observed the cars in the Center's parking lot more closely than he would have any other day, perhaps because his level of concentration was so high that everything seemed extremely lucid, almost as if someone had held a giant magnifying glass to the world around him, pointing out the faults and incongruities as well as the beauties and perfections. He supposed the reason he felt so attuned with the world around him was because he'd planned this visit right down to the smallest detail. He thought of Percy Bysshe Shelley's comment about fate:

> *Fate, Time, Occasion, Chance, and Change? To these*
> *All things are subject but eternal Love.*

And wasn't that what he was fighting for here? The chance to challenge fate, to change time, occasion, and chance, and to give Alex's and Carrie's eternal love a chance to last? He had to believe it was possible that two people could love each other forever. If the Madisons couldn't, then he couldn't believe in everlasting love for himself.

So this trip to visit Alex was for three reasons: no one else seemed to be coming anymore; Alex needed to pay attention to the way his life had gone on without him; and Matt felt that simply watching Carrie and Jack's relationship would be, in a sense, giving his approval, and he didn't want to approve of their marriage ending.

He felt guilty about all of the above, yet he had to admit his motivation sprung from a need to protect his friends and, in this particular case, keep their marriage intact, for his own selfish reasons.

Leaning into the car, Matt grabbed the magazines Isaac had asked him to take to Alex and the casserole his mother had pressed upon him before leaving the house, and, once again, he rehearsed what he planned to say to his old friend. He had done quite a bit of soul-searching before deciding to tell Alex. On a couple of previous visits he'd come close, but today, he promised himself, he was definitely going to say something. He was going to actually come right out and put it all on the table. Let the cards fall where they may. Something had to be done. It seemed appropriate that he do it.

He gave his shorts a tug and started walking toward the building, remembering, for some strange reason, something Aristotle had said: "Plato is dear to me, but dearer still is truth." The phrase kept ringing through his head, convincing him, once again, that he needed to step in, to be the catalyst to get Alex to notice that the world continued to revolve even without his participation.

When Matt entered the room, he saw Alex slumped in the chair next to the window, sound asleep, a book about baseball on his lap. Someone had thrown a light blanket over his legs, and from where Matt stood in the doorway Alex looked old enough to be his own grandfather. Matt's heart twisted with the irony of it all. Alex's grandfather was still alive, living somewhere in Minnesota, and his family, his large midwest farming family, didn't even call, never mind visit. Matt understood they were poor and he didn't put any blame on them, but couldn't they afford a long-distance telephone visit every once in a while? Didn't they know exactly how disabled Alex had become? Were the family members so disconnected from each other that they didn't care what had become of him?

Alex had never really talked about his family, except for a few terse sentences one day when he and Matt had gone fishing. Matt didn't feel he had the right to dig, especially when the few questions he did ask seemed to make Alex uncomfortable. Family was so important to Carrie, so much a part of her life even though her mother was the only family she had, that it seemed odd for Alex to be just the opposite. The nice part was that Simone had extended her familial arm to hook Alex, bringing him into their small circle. Matt shared her feeling for family and knew he was very lucky to be part of a large, loving clan, even if some of them, like Isaac, were slightly weird.

As he crossed the room to his old friend, he thought of his younger brother and his mother with affection, keeping the things they had sent for Alex close to his body.

"Hey, *Br'a,* wake up you old *kahuna,* you!" Matt called, raising his voice to a cheerful pitch.

Alex's eyes opened and as soon as he saw Matt, he smiled like a child presented with a gift. "This isn't your day to visit," he said groggily.

"So, you want me to leave? You can't stand me coming here more than once a week?"

"No, no, no. Sit. What's that you got in your hands? Do I smell food?"

"Yeah, Ma wouldn't let me leave without giving you some of her chicken and pineapple casserole. You know, the one you like so much?"

"Give me that," Alex demanded, his hands out, opening and closing greedily.

Matt gave him the casserole and hunted for a fork in the mess on Alex's table. "Isaac sent these magazines, too," he said while he looked. "He thought you might like to take a look at them." Alex had taken to reading and writing lately and the table was full of ongoing work. Finding anything in the mess he'd created was literally impossible. Finally, Matt spotted a spoon and wiped it on his shirt before handing it over.

For a few moments, the only sound in the room was Alex's murmured compliments as he shoveled the casserole into his smiling mouth. Matt sat and watched him, again rehearsing what he had come to say.

"Oh, man, my mother never cooked like that," Alex said as he took the last bite and wiped his mouth. "And anything's better than the tofu shit they serve here."

"Well, hey, when you get out of here, you can hire my mother to take care of you and tell her exactly what you want her to make every day. She'll love having someone around who appreciates her cooking."

"Yeah, one of these days. God knows when they're going to let me out of this prison."

"Maybe when you get a little more capable of taking care of yourself," Matt said. "Who the hell wants to wipe a grown man's ass?" Instantly, he knew that was the wrong thing to say. Alex's face darkened. Then Matt thought, too bad. You need something to shock you out of this, *Bruddah.*

"So, what's happening down at *The Big One?*" Alex asked, leaning forward a little. Matt knew Alex wouldn't admit it, but what he wanted was news about Carrie.

"Well, it's pretty slow right now, but we're doing okay. Carrie has been spending money left and right, fixing up the office, buying new equipment for the boat. I think she even went out looking at houses the other day. And Isaac's been a little better than usual. He's getting good at deciding when it's time to quit though."

Alex laughed. "Did you tell Carrie I want to see her?"

This was the opening Matt had been waiting for. "Yeah, man, I did, but I'm not sure you're going to see her unless you make a phone call or something. She's been pretty busy showing the new guy around."

Alex's eyes widened. "The one who works for Greenpeace?"

"Uh-huh. They're spending an awful lot of time

together. You'd better watch that, man." Matt remembered to keep his tone light, joking.

Alex's forehead crinkled. "What do you mean?"

"Just that they're spending a lot of time together."

"Are you trying to tell me something?"

"Yeah, actually, I am. I'm trying to tell you it's time to get off your ass. You ain't going to get nowhere feeling sorry for yourself. That's over, man. Carrie isn't even interested in coming here after that last time you reamed her out. If you want to put things back together, you'd better start thinking about how to do it."

Alex's face fell and his eyes moistened.

"Is she cheating on me, Matt?"

"I don't know, *Br'a*," Matt softened his voice. There was a time when the whole, brutal truth was just not necessary. "But if you want to keep Carrie, you've got to wake up and smell the coffee. Can't you start doing what these guys here are telling you? They know what they're talking about. Hell, they're specialists. Just try for a change. Stop giving up! Maybe if you do something, Carrie might start wanting to come here again, even if it's just out of curiosity to see how you're doing."

Alex's eyes wandered as he considered that possibility. "I didn't realize she was losing interest . . ."

"Oh, right. That's why you haven't seen her since she came back from Houston. Shit, man, the woman's been back and forth to Japan, she's sold her daddy's house, gotten rich, practically changed her whole life, and she hasn't been around to see you and you didn't realize she was losing interest? Get real!"

Looking down at the remainder of the casserole in

front of him, Alex muttered, "I guess I just never thought she'd be interested in someone else, no matter how bad things got."

"So, you were going to test her to see how much she could take? You're fuckin' nuts! She's a beautiful woman, *Br'a,* you can't let a woman like that out of your sight! I know plenty of guys who'd give up everything for an intelligent, together woman like Carrie."

"Carrie's not like that. She wouldn't cheat on me."

"Hey, man, you may not have a marriage left for her to cheat on. Did you ever think about that?"

"No . . . I guess . . ."

"How long you been out of commission?"

"It's been a while." He sat back in the chair and counted on his fingers. "I'll tell you exactly how long it's been. Six months, two weeks, five days and God knows how many hours."

"Long enough for someone to forget what it was like when things were good."

Silence. Alex ran his fingers through his greasy blond hair, then over his stubbly chin. He glanced down at the useless legs beneath him. When he looked back up, his eyes shined.

"I don't want to lose her, Matt."

"Well, then, do something about it, dammit!"

"What can I do? She needs a whole man, not a cripple like me . . ."

"That's bullshit and you know it! Carrie doesn't care whether you can walk, she just wants someone who's going to be there for her. Someone who can love her. Someone who's not afraid to *try.* Shit, man, you're no quitter, never have been. Why start now?"

Alex blinked quickly then wiped his face, trying to hide his tears. "I never had to face failure before," he muttered into his hand.

"What?"

"I said I haven't tried because I didn't want to fail. If I didn't make it, if I couldn't move my legs, if I couldn't walk again, then I know I'd lose Carrie forever. I couldn't face that, Matt."

The look in Alex's eyes was forlorn, so broken-hearted that Matt did something he'd never done before with a friend. He gave Alex a hug and a shoulder to cry on, all the while telling him he shouldn't give up, everything was going to be all right.

Carrie walked around the sailboat one more time. It was a brand new, sixty-foot yacht with four cabins and a full gourmet galley. A real beauty, the boat had been designed by Bruce King and featured the teak decks she loved, as well as over thirty-five hundred square feet of working sail. Her heart beat with excitement. It wasn't *The Winsome Blonde*, it didn't have her spare elegance, but that was all right. This one was a sight more modern and she had gorgeous, clean lines. A true sailing yacht. It would go farther and faster than *The Blonde* ever had. Besides, she didn't want another *Blonde*. Those days were over. She needed something with no memories attached to it, something new and different.

"How much did you say again?" She asked the salesman, a short, gray-haired man whose sun-baked face looked much older than his body.

"One hundred thirty thousand."

He hadn't budged one dollar since starting to usher her around the boatyard that morning. She had taken a special trip to Oahu to look at sailboats, not wanting to deal with the same people she saw every day. She figured it would be better if she went to the best ship-builders, the ones who didn't know her, who wouldn't realize she had come into money all of a sudden. Besides, this boat was special, worth the trip. This boat was a dream come true.

"Will you take one twenty-five? Cash?"

He paused a moment and leaned against the hull of another equally beautiful sailboat. "One twenty-eight."

"One twenty-seven and a half."

"Sold."

They worked out the figures, put together the paperwork, and agreed on a delivery date.

"Do you want us to paint her name on before you pick her up? I've got a guy who specializes in gold lettering, looks like calligraphy," the salesman asked.

She nodded.

"What's her name?"

"The Silver Dolphin."

"Nice name."

"Thanks. It means a lot to me."

She left the shipyard with a grin that stretched ear to ear.

Earlier that week, she'd shopped for houses. She'd tried to talk her mother into going with her, but Simone had begged off to cover for one of the other workers at the gallery who had been out all week with the flu. She'd also informed Carrie briskly that she was perfectly happy with her little cottage and, no offense, didn't want the gift of a home that Carrie had offered a few days before.

"You should buy yourself a house," Simone had said. "I have mine. You need a place where you can go after work, a place Alex can come home to when he leaves the Center. I am comfortable here. Besides, how could I ever leave my garden? It would take me years to cultivate another one like this."

Carrie hadn't responded to her mother's remark about Alex, though she had had a hard time holding her tongue, not telling her mother she'd been flirting with the idea of divorcing him. The idea was still a fledgling, perhaps because she associated it with so much guilt, or perhaps because she simply wasn't ready to make the decision. But Jack had been putting a little pressure on her, asking her to promise to take a vacation to Australia with him in September, and even hinting he might want to move in with her afterward. He never mentioned Alex, never acknowledged the fact that she was still married.

At first, she'd let Jack go with her to look at houses, but after a while, she noticed herself deferring to him so much that she became irritated and simply "forgot" to tell him when she had another real estate appointment. She wanted this place to be hers. Her first house, the first time she'd actually own a house.

Yet living with Jack was a tempting thought. She knew they'd probably get along well. They always did. They talked constantly, made love every chance they could, went scuba diving and sailing, on long drives at night when everything was quiet, walks early in the morning. She'd come to appreciate his opinion and his intelligence, but they still couldn't go anywhere in public together. Even worse, she was afraid Matt suspected what was going on between them.

She wasn't ready to make the step of committing herself to Jack. Especially since her relationship with Alex wasn't exactly finished nor was she ready to close the door on that part of her life.

On Friday, she had found a perfect house, a modern, three-bedroom, open floorplan design overlooking a quiet cove. Surrounded by imperial palms, it even had several ancient, immense banyons lining the driveway leading in from the road. They leaned their magnificence in toward the house, almost as if offering a frame for the architect's conception of what the building should look like. She'd always loved banyon trees and thought they signified all that was proud and strong about the Hawaiian islands, the history, the mystery.

The area was private, secluded, the perfect escape. She could imagine laying in bed listening to the waves crash against the beach below and, the most beautiful part of all, she knew she could track whales from both the upper and lower decks gracing the ocean side of the house. A sliding wall of glass covered the back of the house, overlooking the cliffs below. The view made her gasp when she'd first entered the foyer.

That, she suspected, was what had sold her, the feeling of openness, of being part of the world outside.

So far, she was the only person, besides the real estate agent, to see the house. The owners, Californians, had been victims of the latest surge in the recession and, though Carrie sympathized with their plight, she made an offer in the low two hundred thousand dollar range. To her amazement and delight, they snapped it up and made immediate plans to close. She was ecstatic and decided to invite everyone over for a surprise dinner after she signed the papers next week. It pleased her to be able to plan that kind of a party in a place of her own, especially after being homeless for so long.

It was such a thrill to have the freedom to buy whatever she wanted, whenever she wanted. And what a kick to pay with cash! She liked having money, she decided. It gave her control, power, independence— things she never believed she'd have, never even knew she wanted.

Yet with all her purchases, she still had enough money left over to live on for quite some time—years, in fact. A million dollars went a long way, bought a lot of things, but what was best was not having to worry about bill collectors. She didn't have to be afraid to answer the phone anymore.

The only worries she had now were whether Mako-moto would show up again before she'd made her decision about Ocean Fresh and whether her visit with Alex that afternoon would turn out to be a disaster.

He'd called her four days before, begging her to visit. At first, she'd simply said no, but her guilty conscience had kept her awake at night. She knew she wasn't being fair. She was not normally a mean human being, yet it felt like that was what she was turning into.

Over the following three days, Alex had bombarded her with phone calls. He had also called Matt and

Terry McElroy, who, in turn, called Carrie and relayed the message: Alex wanted to see her, needed to see her.

Her resistance wore down. Finally, she agreed to visit him.

"You won't be sorry," Matt promised. "Alex looked a lot better when I saw him a couple of weeks ago."

"He's doing really well in therapy," McElroy reported. "I think he wants to share his success with you."

"I promise I won't argue with you," Alex had said when they'd spoken the day before. "Really, babe, I've changed. Just come and see."

At the end of the conversation, his voice had lowered when he'd told her how much he loved and missed her. She'd held tightly to the phone, amazed that his words could still make her stomach flip. And she found herself telling him she'd missed him, too.

When she hung up, her hand hovered over the phone for a couple of seconds and she realized she'd never had the same reaction when Jack had told her he loved her.

Her palms sweated and her stomach tied itself into knots when she got out of the truck and walked into the Center the next day. Her morning had been so filled with other activities, she hadn't really thought about visiting Alex until getting into the truck and heading over to Hilo. It had hit her like a bullet.

What would she say to him? How would she say it? Whatever she said, the words would not come easily. But before she went any further in her life, she had to know where she stood with Alex. He had been her first love, her husband. It was only fair to both of them. She owed him that much.

The door to his room was partially ajar. She had phoned beforehand and knew he was expecting her. Tentatively, she pushed the door with her fingertips and called his name. From somewhere inside the room, he answered and asked her to come in.

She took a few steps into the room and saw a dark figure silhouetted against the window in the afternoon sun. She was about to nod and say hello, assuming the person was a doctor or a therapist, when she noticed the figure was leaning against a steel walker placed in front of him.

"What do you think?" Alex asked.

Dumbfounded, she stood and stared at him. His blond hair was slicked into a ponytail at the back of his neck, his face clean-shaven and scrubbed. He was dressed in a T-shirt and loose jogging pants and he was standing. Standing!

"Well, tell me what you think before I fall down."

His voice sounded shaky and she could see his legs start to quiver. Still, she couldn't speak. A large ball had lodged itself in her throat and she could get neither words nor swallows past it. Her eyes filled and she dropped her pocketbook to go to him.

He let her hold him, seemingly afraid to take his weight off the walker and they laughed and cried, then laughed again. Finally, he said, "You have to help me sit down. I'm not good at this yet."

While she helped him to a chair, her mind reeled. How? When? Why not before? What was she going to do now? She had come into the room prepared to tell Alex she wanted a divorce, but now she wasn't so sure. The exhilaration she felt was genuine. It flooded every inch of her body. How could she not respond to his hug? How could she not return his jubilant smile?

They settled into chairs opposite each other and she stared at him, unbelievingly. He was the old Alex, the handsome husband she had lost overboard, the boy with the warm blue eyes and bright smile who had promised her forever. All of the animosity she'd felt during the past couple of months disappeared instantly.

"When did this happen?" she finally asked him, realizing that they still held tightly to each other's hands as if when they let go time would throw them back several weeks to when Alex had still been chained to his wheelchair.

"I've been practicing," he answered with a sly grin. "I figured I had to get out of that chair sooner or later and finally, I just did. Of course, I fall on my face on a regular basis, which seems to crack everyone up, but I'm on my feet. They say it's kind of a miracle." He looked sheepish, but smiled proudly.

"I knew you could do it," she whispered, lifting her hand to touch his cheek and smooth back his clean hair.

Never taking his eyes off hers, he turned his head to kiss the palm of her hand. She could see him swallow, the moistness in his eyes, but he didn't stop smiling.

She still loved him. She wondered how she could ever have believed she would stop.

"We have to talk," he said seriously. "I've been

doing a lot of heavy-duty thinking, and I want you to listen to what I've got to say."

She took a deep breath. "Yes, I have a lot to tell you, too."

"Well, I'm going first. All the assholes go first."

"You're not an asshole."

"Yes, I have been. I've been a royal, number one dick, and I want to talk about it." He cleared his throat and settled back in the chair, seemingly exhausted. "You know, I never thought I'd ever get out of this chair again. It just seemed impossible. I couldn't move my toes, never mind my legs. And maybe I'll never be able to walk, I'll just be able to stand, but at least I'll try now."

"That's the important thing, trying."

"But it took me far too long, Carrie. I should have started trying a long time ago. I've wasted months of our lives, almost totalled our marriage. I'm sorry." Suddenly, his face crumbled and he gasped like he'd lose his breath if his sobs caught hold of him.

She sprang to her feet and folded him within her arms, holding him tightly while he let the tears flow. Then Alex pulled her into his lap, talking into her breasts.

"I've been so damn miserable without you," he said thickly. "I can't imagine spending the rest of my life without you there by my side. When we got married, I knew I'd made the best choice, the right choice. We were meant to be together. But after the accident, I was so sure it'd be wrong for you to waste your life with me—"

"Oh no," she protested into his hair. "Please don't say that."

"It's true. Let's be honest. Neither one of us wanted to live out the rest of our marriage that way, me a cripple and all. It took Matt yelling at me to get me to realize that's why I'd been acting like such a jerk."

He pulled his head away from her breasts and looked into her eyes. "I've never been good at expressing how I feel and maybe I'll never be able to convince you how deep my love for you is, but dammit, I'm going to spend the rest of my life trying. God, I'll try until I die."

She kissed his long, fair lashes, tasting the sweaty drops beneath them, and held his head in both of her hands.

"And, I'll never stop trying to walk," he continued, his words were punctuated with gasping cries.

They tore into her heart until she, too, cried, as she hadn't when her father had died, as she hadn't since she'd brought Alex to the hospital. All the tension and stress she'd been holding in came out as they wept together, holding onto each other, cleaving to each other like two precision-fit pieces of a puzzle. And she knew then that she could never have divorced him, because she'd never stopped loving him. She'd simply been incredibly angry with him and guilty for not dealing with the part she had played in all of this.

He kept on talking while simultaneously sliding her down further into his lap so that he could reach her face. He pushed back the mess of hair that had fallen over her shoulder and for long seconds they stared, mesmerized, into each other's reddened eyes. Their sobs subsided and something different began building, a passion Carrie hadn't seen in Alex for such a long time that she'd thought it had disappeared, never to return.

"I love you, my Golden Mermaid," he whispered hoarsely before surrounding her mouth with his.

She responded, a new bout of sobs lifting its way through her throat. When was the last time he had called her that? On the boat. It had been on *The Blonde*.

They had finally come full circle.

Their movements were slow, not the feverish love-making she'd experienced with Jack, but a touch that went deeper than the surface, a touch that knew what it would arouse, a touch that was almost religious, almost holy, and his caresses made her feel loved, made her lift right out of her skin, floating against the ceiling, looking down on the two of them, en-twined in his chair, his hands in her hair, his mouth on her cheek, her throat, her breast, and watching her shirt slip slowly, fluttering to the floor so that his hands could reverently lift her breasts to his mouth, tracing the indentation beneath them, and feeling her head loll back, her eyes closed, her breath seeping slowly out of her open mouth, while her own hands held his shoulders, found their way down the flat planes of his stomach so that they were pressed be-tween the two of them until her fingers snaked down to caress his hips, until she realized that the act of love would be consummated, that he had come alive, that he'd done more than learn how to walk again, and she touched him with the tips of her fingers and heard her moan mingle with his, then she came back from her lofty place against the ceiling, to feel the warmth of his body, the hot moistness he was creat-ing, the need, the overwhelming need, to be one with him, to be his wife, to be his lover, to feel that joining, and he moved ever so slightly so that they were aligned and held her away so that he could watch her face, all the while whispering, "I love you, Carrie, my beautiful Golden Mermaid, my wife, my life. I love you so much. Please don't give up on us. Let's try to make it. Give me another chance."

Staring back into his sea-blue eyes, Carrie made herself a promise to be totally honest with herself and with Alex. No matter what her decision would finally be.

And as she folded herself back into his arms, she thought of the other man, the raven-haired man, who had held her close not so long ago. And she wondered how she'd gotten herself into such a situation, in love with two men.

Thirty

When Carrie pulled into her parking space at the harbor, she didn't even get a chance to get out of the truck before Jack was beside her, his T-shirt stuck to his back, large circles of sweat underneath each arm.

"Makomoto's fleet is about three miles offshore," he said breathlessly. "They're laying miles and miles of seine net."

"What?" she cried, immediately dismissing the dreamy feeling she'd had during the ride back from Hilo. "What do you mean?"

"He's got his boats out there and they're laying more net than any other company ever has." He took her arm and propelled her toward the office, walking with long, loping strides. "We've got to get out there and stop him. Nothing will be able to make it past that net alive."

She ran with him, remembering the large herd of spinner dolphins they'd passed the other day when they'd taken *The Big One* out to test its new equipment. The dolphins' silver bodies had gleamed in the afternoon sun as they'd leap-frogged over each other, hundreds of them playing and cavorting. They'd been the largest group she had ever seen. If they got caught in the net, it would wipe out half the herd's population. She squeezed her eyes closed a moment, trying to shut out the sounds she knew the dolphins made when they were dying.

Together, Carrie and Jack ran down the dock, passing the office, flying by Isaac, who yelled after them that they should be careful.

"Makomoto and his gang aren't playin' games anymore," he warned. "Don't do anything stupid!"

"Where's Matt?" she asked Jack as they boarded *The Big One.*

"He went home for lunch. Don't worry, Isaac will take care of everything."

"I'm not worried about the office," she replied, throwing her bag into the cabin. "Just thought we could've used an extra hand. Too late now." Quickly, wordlessly, she prepared the boat so they could get out of the harbor as fast as possible.

They didn't speak again until they were in open sea. Carrie opened the throttle completely, letting *The Big One* race as she never had before, all the while listening for any telltale signs that her old reliable boat would not be able to take the strain. The money she had spent on *The Big One* was for new computers and diving equipment; she had yet to get the engine overhauled. But Jack and Matt had taken care of keeping everything in tip-top shape. She was grateful for that. She didn't need the engine to seize, not now.

"Do you see anything yet?" she called out to Jack, though she knew she'd probably be the first to notice anything. With all the equipment she had in the cabin for whale watching, she could pick up the most infinitesimal movement of a hermit crab on the ocean floor.

"Nothing," he called back. He stood on the bow, his dark curly hair whipping in the wind, his eyes focused on the horizon. "I heard they're about two or three miles northwest, so just keep heading in that direction."

He stayed outside, for which she was thankful. It saved her from having to talk. Once underway, memories of her afternoon with Alex kept resurfacing, bringing smiles to her face that she didn't want Jack to see. He wouldn't understand and this was definitely not the right time for an explanation.

At the same time, her heart pounded as she thought of what she would do if Makomoto was actually on one of his tuna fishing vessels. He wouldn't be, she reasoned. He was far too much of a big shot to lower himself to boarding a tuna boat, mingling with the men and the fish and the smell of it all. Unless he thought that, by doing so, he was baiting her, luring her into open sea. To do what? Would he take the chance of killing her out there, in American waters, in front of witnesses? No, he couldn't be that stupid.

Perhaps not that stupid, she thought, but crazy. Yes, he was definitely crazy.

A blip on the screen to her right. She tuned it in a little better and saw the blip again. It could be a whale, she thought, but there were few in these waters at this time of year. No, it was a large school of fish. Or a solid, moving object. The screen to her left started bleeping. Now she was sure of it. They'd found the net. And the net had found a school of large fish. She bit down hard on her lip and hoped they weren't dolphins.

"There they are!" Jack yelled from the bow. "On the starboard side!"

She looked where he was pointing and saw the boat in the distance, a mere pinprick on the horizon. Spinning the wheel, she headed in that direction.

Suddenly, her radio sputtered, her office's call letters and Matt's voice. She debated whether to answer, then decided it would be unwise not to. Matt would think something had happened and would worry.

"K245O, *The Big One* here. What's up Matt? Over."

"Where the hell are you? Over."

"We've got Makomoto's boats in our sights. We're heading in that direction, about . . ." She looked at her instruments and gave him the readings.

"What are you, nuts? Turn around. Come home. Don't get near that boat! Over."

For a moment, she didn't reply. "Cannot do," she finally said. "We've got to go in. Over." She shut the radio off and wiped a sheen of sweat off her forehead. They were going in all right, and she didn't know if they'd get out of it.

"What do you mean she has gone out after that crazy man's boat?" Simone's hand flew to her throat.

She had come to the dock to invite Caryn to dinner, knowing that Caryn had visited Alex in the afternoon. Simone's curiosity had come to a head and she'd finally convinced Jerry to tell her everything he knew— all about Tokyo, Makomoto, what had happened with Caryn. After pacing the floor and ranting in French at Jerry, Simone had decided the only way around the situation was to talk to Caryn directly, never expecting to find Matt in such a state or Caryn going out to sea, half cocked and totally unprepared, against Makomoto's tuna fleet.

"I can't believe it either," Matt said, raking his fingers through his hair, his eyes wild. "I don't know how that woman thinks some time. And Jack! Damn him! Why couldn't he just let things be? Crazy *haole!*"

Simone sat down heavily in the desk chair and cradled her head in her hands. "Try to reach her on the radio again, Matt," she said thickly. "Tell her to come home."

While Matt stated his call letters and tried time and time again to reach Carrie, Isaac stood behind Simone, his hand awkwardly on her shoulder. When she looked up at him with a wan smile, she saw he wasn't looking at her at all but at his brother frantically trying to reach *The Big One.*

"It's no use," Matt finally admitted, sinking back against the chair.

"We've got to go out after them," Isaac said. "We've got to help them."

"How?"

Simone sat up straight in the chair. "*The Silver Dolphin.* We will take her!"

Her instruments told Carrie the net was directly beneath them now and so was a school of large fish. Her worst fears were realized: the net had found the spinner dolphins they'd seen the other day. She cut the engine back to half, then to a quarter, then to a full stop.

Jack came into the cabin behind her. Without turning around, she said, "Okay, what do we do now?"

"Funny, I was just wondering that myself." He edged his way in beside her, joining her at the wheel. His eyes were dark, dangerous, his jaw set, almost as if he were clenching his teeth together. He thought for a moment or two more, then said, "I think we have two choices. There are only two of us and a lot of them. We could confront them and try to get them to pull the net in like we did the day I met you or . . ."

"Or what?"

"Go below and cut the net. Slice it right away so that the dolphins can get through."

"But this net goes on miles and miles and miles! We can't possibly get enough done to make a difference."

Jack nodded determinedly. "Yes, we can. It'll take a lot of work and we'll probably be out here overnight. But we can make a split here, then go a few miles up the net and make another one and keep doing that till the net is ruined."

She whistled softly. "They'll kill us. Those nets are worth thousands and thousands of dollars, not to mention what they're going to lose in tuna."

"Do we have any choice?" His voice was low and cold.

She looked toward the bow and caught a glimpse of silver against the aquamarine ocean, then another and another. The dolphins were dying down there. "No, I guess we don't."

Together they secured the boat and donned their

scuba gear. Carrie's mind worked quickly, her senses taking in everything—the bright blue cloudless sky, the sun's heat on her head and shoulders, the smell of the rubber hoses, the feel of the heavy cold tank leaning against her legs, the sound of Jack's grunts as he adjusted his straps. Fear invaded her every limb, paralyzing her momentarily, but she fought it, reminding herself she needed the adrenaline for more important things.

When finally ready, she cast one more glance in the direction she'd last seen the tuna boat, that ominous dark blot on the horizon, and swore it seemed closer than it had been only moments before. With that thought lingering menacingly in her brain, she balanced backward on the railing, then, with the signal from Jack, flipped into the ocean.

It took a couple of seconds for her to adjust, but when she did the first thing she noticed was that the water was teeming with fish—dolphins, small sharks, triggerfish, even a marlin. All of them swam in tight circles, instinctively terrified. They felt the net's threat, that was obvious, but she couldn't spot the almost invisible wall yet.

Through the bubbles in her mask, she spotted Jack. He waved to her and pointed straight ahead. There it was, and there were so many dolphins already caught that the water pulsated with their thrashing. She wondered how she and Jack would be able to get through to help them.

She touched the knife in her belt, reassuring herself it was still there. The net looked a little different from the others she'd encountered, stronger, more shimmery than the nylon seine nets. She wondered if it was made of a newer material, and if their knives would cut through it.

Following Jack, she brushed past some dolphin calves, who nudged her anxiously, seeming confused as to whether they should play or run away. She wondered if any of them were related to the larger dolphins caught in the net.

Jack motioned to her again. He headed toward a huge male whose left flipper and snout were tangled in the net. She came up on the male's right side while Jack took the left. Making eye contact with the animal, she found herself trying to soothe it, though she realized they were probably scaring it even more. She wrapped her arms around its belly, guiding it gently backward while Jack tried to carefully cut the net above the dolphin's head, working downward, but staying away from its snout. At first it struggled, but Carrie stroked it and eventually the dolphin relaxed.

It took them a good five minutes, she figured, but finally the male swam away with a powerful flip of its tail. By releasing it, they had started a pretty good split in the net. Jack talked to her in sign language, telling her with his hands that she should continue working on this rip and make sure she completed it so the net would fall away, hopefully sinking to the ocean's floor before trapping anything else.

When she was about halfway down the net with her knife, a medium-sized tiger shark swam threateningly close to her. She stopped, watching him, waiting for a sign he was going to attack, but he seemed uninterested in her and swam away. She stayed still for another moment, not trusting the beady-eyed creature, but he didn't turn back and she could finally finish her task.

They worked steadily for what she thought was half an hour, by the feel of her tanks, freeing dolphin after dolphin, a large tortoise, several smaller fish (some of which fell away dead), and the sailfish she'd passed earlier. Her hands stung and she knew they were sliced, bleeding, from the unrelenting nylon and from working with a knife she was unused to using. She hoped that the smell of her blood wouldn't attract the bigger, more dangerous sharks.

Knowing she didn't have much air left, she motioned to Jack that they should go up. He nodded, and they swam side by side to the surface. Clambering aboard *The Big One*, she barely had time to take her tank off her back when Jack nudged her. She raised her head to look at him and immediately saw why he hadn't spoken. The tuna vessel had moved so close they could see the company name on its bow and its fishermen working on deck.

"I wonder if they've figured out what we're doing," Jack said quietly as he laid his own tanks on deck.

"If they haven't, they sure as hell will if they come any closer."

"Start the boat and move south a bit, away from them. I'll get fresh tanks and we can go down again."

She nodded and headed for the cabin, feeling exhausted but excited. It had been ages since she'd been underwater for so long. The strength it took to release the dolphins and other fish had pulled some of the muscles in her back. She stretched and massaged her shoulders with her fists.

It was going to be a long day.

* * *

Matt took the tiller while Simone adjusted the mainsail. Neither of them were familiar with Caryn's new sailboat, but both were excellent sailors. They'd learn quickly, Simone knew. They had no choice.

She reached for Jerry's hand. He'd insisted on going with them, and it was the first time they'd been on a sailboat together. But there was little time to relish the experience.

The boat was wonderful, sleekly designed, fast, responsive. She could see why Caryn had chosen it. Simone wasn't aboard more than fifteen minutes before the sea and the salt and the spray awoke her long-repressed love for sailing. She took over the tiller from Matt, skillfully steering into the wind and trimming the sails more expertly than Matt had. *The Dolphin* skimmed along the water and she revelled in the feel of salt air against her face. It had been a long time. Too long. She only wished the trip were for pleasure.

She hoped Caryn and Jack didn't do anything reckless before they got to them.

Again, she tacked and got a little more speed from the magnificent boat.

Adjusting the scuba tank's mouthpiece, Carrie glanced up at the tuna vessel once more, then dismissing the danger it represented from her mind, followed Jack overboard. There weren't as many fish caught in the net this time. They worked quickly, cutting another escape hole, then freeing a few smaller dolphins. They were about to go up when Carrie suddenly noticed a dark shadow passing overhead. She frantically waved at Jack, trying to get his attention, but he was too busy with a small sea turtle to notice. The creature wriggled impatiently while Jack tried to free it.

Swimming over to him, she caught his arm and gestured upward. His glance followed hers and his eyes widened in surprise. No other boat could cast such a big shadow. It had to be Makomoto's tuna boat, and it was heading right straight for *The Big One.*

Her first inclination was to surface, to wave the tuna boat down, tell them to stay away from her boat, but she knew, with a sinking feeling, it was too late. Still, she felt paralyzed, unable to take her eyes off the boat's hull as it passed above them.

Jack tugged on her, dragging her to deeper waters. At first, she didn't understand why and fought him, but he held on tightly and kept swimming downward. She had no choice but to follow.

A rumbling, like the sound of hundreds of thundering hooves pulsed through the water. Oh God, she thought as she looked upward, tell me I'm not seeing this.

The tuna boat rammed *The Big One,* splitting it in half as easily as if it had been made of sugar. It took a few seconds for the rumbling sound to stop and the shadow to move on. Pieces of *The Big One* fell slowly, almost in slow motion, sinking to the ocean's floor. In a daze, she watched pieces of her boat drift toward her. She wanted desperately to scream.

* * *

Simone screamed. Not a yell or a short burst, but a long, piercing screech that she couldn't stop or control. She held the tiller tightly, unwilling and unable to let go, and continued to scream until Jerry found his way over and hugged her tightly to him.

"You must be strong," he whispered. "Do not give up. Caryn would not."

Less than a hundred feet away from them, large chunks of *The Big One* drifted in the water like pieces from a giant child's game.

"Caryn!" she yelled again. "Caryn!"

In the distance, she spotted a boat heading in a northeasterly direction. She pulled away from Jerry and peered toward her daughter's boat sinking quickly.

Matt dove into the ocean, swimming strongly toward the wreckage. Numbly, she watched him, praying he'd find Caryn clinging to part of the hull or one of the lifeboats, though she couldn't see any signs of life from where she sat.

"Oh, Caryn," she murmured. "Please be there."

Jerry's dark almond-shaped eyes watched her intently. "Caryn is a wonderful swimmer," he reminded her needlessly. "She will be all right."

"But look where we are, miles from land, and the boat is ruined. Oh, Jerry, I pray to God you are right."

Matt finally reached what was left of *The Big One*. In silence, they watched him swim carefully around the larger pieces of the boat, diving under a few of them, then coming back to the surface to shake his dark head like a seal.

"Can you see anything?" she yelled.

Matt shook his head and dove again.

To the right of the scattered mess, a head bobbed

to the surface, then another. Simone caught her breath. Could it be possible? The first person took off a diving mask and Simone caught a glimpse of light blond hair. Then, the other, a dark head.

"Matt!" she called and pointed. "Over there!"

Matt swam to them and Simone watched them talking excitedly for a few moments before the three of them headed back toward *The Silver Dolphin.*

As she and Jerry pulled Caryn aboard, Matt and Jack climbed up the ladder and Simone's pent up anxiety released itself in a flood of disjointed sentences. All Caryn replied was, "My God, I've never been so happy to see anyone in my whole life! I thought we were dead."

Simone hugged her, not putting into words that she had felt the same way, had feared the worst, that her daughter had been taken from her and would never return.

As they tacked, turning *The Silver Dolphin* to head for home, Simone watched Caryn swivel to watch *The Big One* as the last pieces of the boat sank into the dark ocean. When she turned back, her face had hardened to stone.

Thirty-one

Matt looked toward the dock, still not feeling back to normal after what Jack was calling "the rescue at high sea." Everyone laughed nervously, covering their fear and quelling the leftover adrenaline still rushing through their veins by talking about how lucky they were. If the truth were known, Matt thought, all of them had been breathing the same sigh of relief he had. None of them wanted to deal with another tragedy.

Carrie sat at the bow of the boat, staring lethargically toward her office as if she couldn't wait to get on dry land again. Matt reflected that she must be exhausted, in more ways than one. How much more could she stand before she lost it?

It was Carrie who spotted Isaac half running, half stumbling down the pier toward them as *The Silver Dolphin* majestically maneuvered its way into its berth.

"Matt, is he bleeding or is it my imagination?"

Shit, Matt thought, the kid's at it again and here I thought we could leave him with the responsibility of minding the office. Goddammit it, when's he going to grow up?

While everyone disembarked, Isaac danced from one foot to another, ignoring all of their questions until Matt, the last one to disembark, finally stood in front of him. Everyone quieted down, prepared to listen. Four sets of eyes shifted back and forth between Matt and Isaac as if waiting for some kind of explosion.

Isaac's nose was bleeding, his lip split and purple.

Matt bit back the words he really wanted to say and simply asked, "What the hell happened to you, *Br'a?*"

"I didn't know what to do, man," Isaac began. "This big dude came into the office and started tearing apart the files and, well, I just couldn't let him do that, so I tried to stop him, but he pushed me back and I fell against the chair. I'm sorry, Carrie, but I broke it. Then this little guy came in, the same guy who was here about a month ago, and he started asking questions about Carrie and the only reason they left was this French guy and his wife came in and wanted to make reservations. Man, I'm sorry, I just didn't know what to do." He wiped at his nose with the back of his hand and winced with the pain.

Matt's blood raced, his fists clenched, and a throbbing began above his eyebrows. "What the hell is going on?" he said, looking at Carrie. "Doesn't this guy know we have laws? Who the hell does he think he is?"

Isaac jiggled again, looking anxiously into Matt's face. "It wasn't my fault, Matt. Honest."

"I know, *Br'a.* I ain't mad at you. I'm mad at that asshole Makomoto."

"The Japanese guy?"

"Yeah."

"Well, I think he's gonna be back."

With those words, the six of them trooped toward the office, a group Matt thought was about as intimidating as the Over-the-Hill Gang. He quickly assessed the situation, believing that he and Jack might be able to hold their own, Jerry could use some of his t'ai chi, and Simone and Carrie could call the cops. He knew that was what Carrie would call a chauvinistic thought, but dismissed it. When faced with a situation like this, the only way to effectively do battle was to know what your weapons were. If it were a war of words, he'd put Simone and Carrie on the front line but not up against a three-hundred pound Samoan.

Isaac fell into step with his brother. "I called some of my friends," he murmured, keeping his voice low as if he didn't want to alarm the others. "They'll be here in about ten minutes."

"Your friends love this kind of shit, don't they?"

"What do you mean?" Isaac looked hurt.

"Fights and street battles. Their kind of Saturday night out."

"Matt, you don't know what you're talking about."

Matt harrumphed. "No, I just spent the past couple of years getting you out of scrapes, paying bail when you went joyriding and killing people, and I don't know what I'm talking about."

"You know, you got that night all wrong," Isaac stopped walking, forcing Matt to do the same. "If you'd listened to me, I told you I was innocent."

"How can a guy be behind the wheel of a car which just rammed into another car, killing the driver of that other car, and be totally innocent?"

Isaac's face paled, making his purple lip and bloody nose even more prominent. "Let me tell you something. I may have been behind the wheel when they found us, but that doesn't mean I was driving the car."

"What?"

"You heard me."

"Are you trying to tell me someone else was driving?"

Isaac didn't reply, just closed his mouth and stared at his brother hatefully.

"Is that what you're trying to tell me?" Matt asked again.

Isaac nodded.

"Explain. And make it quick." Matt glanced toward the office. Everyone else had already gone inside.

"I can't."

"You'd better or that bloody nose you got will get worse."

After a few seconds of tough decision-making, Isaac started talking. "Jimmy Dee was driving. You know him, his old lady just had a kid."

Matt remembered. The girl was just fourteen and Jimmy was barely sixteen. He nodded.

"When we all realized what had gone down, Jimmy started crying, saying he couldn't go to jail with a new baby and a lady to take care of. He really freaked out. Besides, he's gotten busted a few times before. If he went to court one more time, there'd be no getting out of it."

"So, you pretended you were the one driving to protect him?"

"Yeah."

"Without even thinking about what might happen to you?"

"Yeah, I guess so."

"That was pretty stupid."

Isaac huffed and threw his hands up in the air. "Goddammit, I finally tell you the truth and you tell me I'm stupid. Fuck you! D'you hear that? Fuck you!" He spun around and headed down the pier toward the parking lot.

Matt closed his eyes, realizing he shouldn't have been so hard on the kid. "Wait a minute," he called. "Wait a fuckin' minute!"

Isaac stopped, but he didn't turn around.

Catching up with his brother, Matt did something he hadn't done in years. He pulled Isaac into his arms and roughly kissed the top of his head. "It's a stupid thing you did, but a good thing. Now all we got to do is get you out of it somehow."

"I can't get Jimmy in trouble, man," Isaac muttered against Matt's shirt.

"Don't worry about it right now. We'll figure something out." Matt pulled away, aware he was close to tears. "Right now we got something more immediate to worry about."

Isaac smiled, looking much like he had at twelve, when Matt had been his idol.

They walked back to the office side by side.

Carrie went directly into the bathroom when they reached the office and retched. It felt as though someone had tried to pull her stomach up through her body and out her mouth. Weakly, she slid to the floor and leaned against the cool tile wall, her eyes closed, sweat oozing from every pore of her body. She didn't want to move, had no energy to get up off the floor. Every limb felt heavy and powerless; all of her senses had shut down.

Outside the bathroom door, she heard her mother and Jerry talking with Jack about what had happened, asking Jack the questions Carrie had been unable to answer. She heard him reliving the experience of being helpless underwater, seeing the shadow of Makomoto's tuna boat above, how he'd known immediately that the boat was going to ram *The Big One* and figured the debris would reach down the twenty or thirty feet to hit them, how he'd thought if they went deeper, they'd be safer. He described the sound the boats made on impact, the almost slow-motion sinking of *The Big One,* the overwhelming fear that the tuna boat wouldn't stop, that it had been sent there on one mission—to kill Carrie Madison.

Simone thanked him for saving her daughter's life. It was a formal thank you, Carrie thought. Her mother's voice was pinched and almost squeaky, the way it got when her throat closed up with nervousness or worry. Carrie always knew it was time to get out of the way when her mother sounded like that.

She felt weird being privy to the conversation but not part of it. How long could she get away with sitting in the quiet bathroom, out of everyone's sight?

She still had her eyes closed and her head lolled back, her legs stretched straight out in front of her, her arms hanging loosely at her sides, when she heard Matt call out. Isaac swore and, for a moment, everything was silent. Then all the voices clamored at once, a banging, a shuffling outside the bathroom door. Puzzled, she opened her eyes and listened more closely, but there were so many voices, such a lot of noise, that she couldn't tell what was happening. She heard her mother call Jerry's name, then Jerry's harsh, deeper voice, telling her, "Simone, go into the back room and lock the door. Now!"

With a great effort, Carrie picked herself up off the floor and tried the knob, intending to crack the door just a little and peek out, but she couldn't push it open. Something heavy was leaning against it. She put her ear to the door, nervous now, wondering what the hell could be going on. A crash. A sharp cry, like someone had been hurt. Jack's voice calling to Matt to watch out. Now, more voices. Isaac's yell. Another thud and a bang. She pushed against the door again but couldn't budge it. She banged against it, screaming, "Let me out! Someone let me out!"

The sounds moved away from her, as if everyone had gone outside. She heard breaking glass and wondered if someone had been pushed through the door or the window, then thoughts tumbled over each other like waves—How much would it cost to repair the damage? Who the hell was out there? What were they doing? Who was this Jimmy that Isaac shouted to? Were Makomoto and Toto at the crux of what was happening? *Why couldn't she get out the door?*

Suddenly, all the noise stopped. In the distance, she heard the wail of a police siren or an ambulance. She began screaming frantically and pounding on the door with both fists.

Simone opened her door at the same moment Caryn came through the bathroom door. They looked at each other, white-faced and confused. Then Simone glanced quickly around the office. Pieces of glass covered the floor and all of the furniture was broken into splinters. She gasped and motioned to Caryn to be careful where she walked.

"What the hell is going on?" Caryn muttered.

Simone caught jagged glimpses of the office, taking in pieces of information, trying to understand what had happened after Makomoto and the Samoan had stormed into the room—the door hanging off its hinges; the phone, its receiver disconnected from its body; the files strewn across the desk haphazardly; Jerry outside the office window. He was leaning toward someone she couldn't see, someone lying on the ground, someone dead?

Mon Dieu, tell me it isn't true.

She stepped gingerly over a few shards of glass, hearing a crunch underfoot when she hit a piece she couldn't avoid. The siren came closer, then stopped. The vehicle's flashing lights reflected off the broken window. A small crowd had gathered in front of the office door. She was afraid to go any farther but pushed on, terrified she'd find something, she didn't know what.

Right outside the office door, Jerry knelt over Matt's still body, a pool of dark red blood encircling Matt's shoulders and torso. Isaac leaned over his brother. Behind her, Simone heard Caryn call out, a muffled groan.

Jack rushed over to them, but she didn't know where he'd come from. She could hear him talking softly to Caryn, trying to calm her, and could tell he was trying to speak to her as well but she couldn't answer. She simply stared at Jerry's calm, concerned face as he told the ambulance driver that Matt Kamehea had been stabbed by a large Samoan man named Toto.

"Another man, his name is Ishiru Makomoto, was here as well, trying to get some of the files in the office. He owns a seafood company, Makomoto Seafoods. One of his tuna boats just rammed and destroyed Mrs. Madison's whale-watching boat. We had just returned to the office after rescuing them when—"

"Sorry, mister, but you need to tell the cops all that stuff," the paramedic answered. "All we need to know is how this man was hurt."

"He was stabbed, right here in the lower abdomen, with a knife. I do not know what kind or how big . . ." Jerry's voice trailed off and Simone went to him as he stood aside to let the attendants take care of Matt. She wound her arms around him, amazed to find him trembling, soaking wet, and breathing harshly.

"Are you all right?" she whispered to him.

Jerry nodded, his eyes never leaving Matt's inert body. "I was not fast enough. I could not stop him."

"Matt will be okay," Simone assured him. "He is strong and healthy."

The paramedics tried to get Isaac away from his brother, but he kept wailing, "I'm sorry, Matt. Oh, man, I should've been able to stop that bastard." Then Caryn was at Isaac's side, speaking softly but firmly. She pulled him up by the arms, then enfolded him within hers, patting him on the back and reassuring him his brother would be fine. He'd make it. Isaac had to let the paramedics do their job.

Simone held Jerry's hand tightly, unable to ask

what had happened and knowing that he probably wouldn't be able to tell her anyway. She was just happy he was okay.

And now that she had a hold of him again, she wasn't ever going to let him go.

Carrie watched the ambulance pull away, its lights flashing and siren wailing, and suppressed a shiver. Jack put his arm around her and pulled her close, but she resisted him, turning away to survey the destruction of her office.

Her first thought after seeing Matt was that Alex would be devastated to hear his best friend had been stabbed. She needed to call Alex immediately. He would know how to help her through this. He'd say the right things to get her back on track again. And she felt so far removed from everything now, she wasn't even sure she'd be able to come back. Everything seemed surreal.

Everyone seemed to have drifted away—Isaac with his friends, Jerry and her mother sitting down on one of the benches near Halakale's Hot Dog Stand, Matt away in the ambulance, Jack standing beside her. She could feel him staring into her face. She didn't want to look back at him.

"This has got to stop," she said, shaking her head. "I've had it."

Thirty-two

It took Carrie a couple of days to get the debris around the office cleaned up. Simone and Jerry had begged her to hire someone else to do it, but Carrie knew if she didn't go in herself, she'd stay away from the office longer and longer until she wouldn't be able to face it at all. Besides, she wanted to figure out what, if anything, was missing. She did end up hiring someone to replace the windows and to put a new lock on the door, but other than that, she did the work herself.

After many hours of washing everything in sight with a strong bleach, then painting the walls a clean cream color, and moving out the bits and pieces of her broken office furniture, she was bone tired. Stupidly, she'd also decided she couldn't wait to move her furniture and household goods out of storage and into her new home, so she'd been doing that little by little at night while she worked on the office during the day, anything to keep incredibly busy, unattainable, anything to keep her body moving, her mind occupied.

The overwhelming need to be as solitary as possible had ruled her life for the past several days. She hadn't asked for anyone else's help, especially Jack's.

She needed space to think about their relationship, about what he'd become to her and what he might be in the future. If there was a future.

She'd imagined every moment of what their life together would be like, from the incredibly searing nights of sex to the moments when she'd have to avert her eyes if she saw one of Alex's friends on the street.

She found herself comparing the two men, Alex and Jack—as different from each other physically as they were mentally and spiritually.

Memories of those early days of being Alex's wife, the joy of it, the pride she felt when saying "my husband," the contented feeling of knowing he'd always be there for her—all of it nagged her thoughts during every waking moment.

Maybe she'd never have that sort of security with Jack. He was so committed to the environment, he'd always want to be where the action was. Jack loved her, she was certain of that, but she suspected she'd come second in his life. Alex had always put her first.

Besides, her love for Alex had always been a certainty, unlike what she felt for Jack.

Guilt had risen its ugly head, prickling at her subconscious in the middle of the night as she struggled with insomnia, sleeping on a mattress in the upstairs bedroom of the new house. She watched the sky full of stars outside the window, knowing that Jack had no idea what was going on between her and Alex. As she practiced putting together the words to tell him, she wondered whether he was worrying about her.

She had never told him about the house and knew that he believed she'd begun staying with her mother after the incident at the office. Her need for secrecy was a protective mechanism, like her childhood habit of hiding in a closet when she'd heard her father and mother arguing. If she kept the secret, then she was denying the event had ever happened. Right now, that was a more comfortable feeling than talking it out.

As she swept the office floor once more, she knew she'd probably see Jack today and that they'd have to talk. She dreaded it. She wasn't ready for it, wasn't even sure she'd made a decision yet, even though she'd be forced into it sooner or later. And no one could give her the way out—not her mother, not Matt, not the two men involved. She had to find her own answer.

Matt would approve if she returned to her marriage, she thought, envisioning him in his hospital room, where he was recovering nicely. In fact, the doctor had said he could return home tomorrow, which thrilled Isaac. He had come to the office the day before and talked of Matt as proudly as though he'd been decorated in the war. She liked hearing the bragging tone in his voice, though she wished it had not been brought on by such a horrible incident, an incident for which she felt totally responsible. At least the brothers were speaking again and openly showing their love for each other. That was something.

Matt had taken it upon himself to call Jimmy Dee from the hospital and urge him to confess. The teenager seemed almost relieved and immediately went to the police. The day before, Matt had called Isaac's lawyer and told him how Isaac had covered for his friend the night of the car accident and that Jimmy Dee's confession was now a part of the record. Jimmy would be punished, there was no way to get away from that, but it wouldn't be as bad as they had thought. Hopefully, the lawyer had said, they'd be able to get him on a type of probation which would allow him to see his child. Isaac would need to attend some kind of drunk driving school, but at least he wouldn't have to face going to jail.

Carrie smiled to herself as she dragged the broom over the threshold and stood back, with her left hand on her hip, looking at the office. "You've come a long way, baby," she muttered.

She'd replaced all the furniture with new pieces she'd chosen from the latest office catalog. A large oak desk now dominated the far corner, accompanied by a cushiony office chair that tilted for comfort. Above the desk, Carrie had hung a Hawaiian watercolor her mother had chosen at the gallery. The walls had received a new coat of paint, she'd replaced the green leather chairs with modern slingbacks, and the new glass-topped coffee table had been graced with a stone sculpture of a mother humpback with her calf. Perhaps the office had needed to be destroyed in order to be made better.

Just like her life.

The impact of her revelation rocked her on her heels. She supposed it was best to look at it that way, but she would never have thought that several weeks ago, even several days ago. Yet, she admitted, something good had to come from all this, and it wasn't over yet. Her biggest problem had yet to be solved.

She still had to do something about Makomoto.

Even though they'd given all the information about the fight to the police—how Makomoto and Toto had pushed their way into the office; Jerry's tremendous display of bravery in taking on Toto, as Jack had told the police, with an eye-dazzling array of martial arts techniques; how Toto had finally resorted to knives, stabbing Matt as the two tangled right outside the office door; and about the threats Makomoto had hissed before he and Toto had fled after hearing the sirens coming in their direction. The incident still appeared pretty unbelievable.

"The man looks insane," Jack had insisted. "I don't think any normal corporate executive would do what this man is doing. First, he tries to kill Carrie in Tokyo, then he has the balls to storm the office while his tuna boat is sinking Carrie's whale-watching boat. The guy's a goddamn psycho, I tell you!"

Before Jack's outburst, the cops had blamed the whole battle on Isaac's group of friends, had even arrested some of them in the dock's parking lot. They were still a little dubious that the gang had been there to give Carrie's group some help but had arrived on the scene too late to help Matt.

Simone and Carrie had commiserated with each other, regretting having been behind locked doors when all the commotion had been going on. Simone, sure she could have done something to help, even taught Carrie a few t'ai chi moves that would have protected them had they been caught in the fray.

But it's too late now, Carrie thought. Makomoto wasn't in Hawaii. He'd immediately flown back to Tokyo, out of the jurisdiction of the FBI officials, who, upon finding out about the fight, appeared on Carrie's doorstep. They grilled her for hours. They'd been looking for a way to nab Ishiru Makomoto for a long time.

It was all very confusing, she decided, putting the

broom away in the back closet. And it would be very nice to put it all behind her, restore things to the status quo. Normal? Did she know what the word meant anymore? She sighed, checked her watch, and thought about giving Alex a call. He'd been concerned about what was going on, especially with Matt, but she'd been careful not to tell him everything. Maybe someday she would, but not now.

Patting her chestnut hair one more time, Simone bit her bottom lip and studied the fine lines at the corners of her eyes. She thought her face declared her age, even though she still felt like she had in her twenties. How odd that this dichotomy should exist. Would it be this way until the day she died or would her emotions sooner or later catch up with her physical being?

She fussed with the toothpaste, cleaned the sink, then left the mirror behind. It only served to remind her of the passage of time and how she was wasting it.

For the first time in months, Jerry had spent the evening in his own house. She missed him incredibly. The house was too quiet without him. She had grown used to having him around, comfortable in the knowledge that if she thought of something to say, she could speak to him. To her surprise, she came to the conclusion that she wanted someone there to share the rest of her life. She had never believed she would feel this way again, had probably been fighting it right from the very beginning, thinking that being single, having her own home and her freedoms, was the way she wanted to spend her time. She had always thought having another man around would make her fall into the same obsessive habits she'd had while living with Philip—asking for his opinion about even the most mundane subjects, waiting to make decisions about what they would eat or which play they would see until he was there, giving up friends he disapproved of, neglecting to feed her own interests so that she could serve his.

But she had to admit, she'd never done that with Jerry. Nor would he ever ask. He was not invasive but supportive. It dawned on her that her individuality had never been threatened. Perhaps that was the part of their relationship she cherished most.

She didn't need him, she wanted him.

With that thought still fresh in her mind, she left her little house and headed down the road to Jerry's. It suddenly seemed imperative that she tell him how she felt.

It was almost two in the afternoon when Jack poked his head in the door and called out, "Anyone home?"

Engrossed in rearranging the files, Carrie jumped. "God, you scared me."

"Wow, this place looks great!" He stood in the doorway and surveyed the office with a look of surprise. "You do this all yourself?"

She pointed to her paint-stained clothes. "What do you think?"

"Why didn't you call me? I would've helped."

She shrugged, knowing she couldn't tell him she didn't want anyone to help. It would sound insulting.

He sat in one of her new chairs and ran a hand admiringly over the stone whale sculpture on the table. "So, you're going to stay here, huh?"

She stopped filing and stared at him. "What do you mean?"

"You're going to keep the whale-watching business going."

"Of course. Where else would I go? What else would I do?"

Jack lowered his head, denying her the opportunity to scrutinize the emotions in his eyes. "I don't know. I just thought, you know, since *The Big One* is gone and everything, that you'd just kind of . . . leave."

"I don't know where you got that idea. Hawaii's home. I'm going to get another boat and start over," she smiled. "I can afford to now."

She put the file down and sat behind the desk. In a way, she wanted more than anything to go to him and put her arms around him, but that would only cause complications.

"Start over, huh?"

"Mm-hmm."

"Have you heard anything more from the police?"

"No. They said they'd get in touch with me if they found out anything."

"Right, if something else more important doesn't happen. Want me to call and check for you?"

"No, that's okay." She looked at the top of his head, wanting to thank him for all he'd done for her, but knew that he would immediately pick up on everything else she wanted to say. Just as she could read his eyes, he had learned to listen closely to what she said between the lines.

"I just don't want to see this fall through the cracks," he said.

"I'm sure it won't."

"What're you going to do about Makomoto?"

"I don't know yet."

His eyes came up and met hers. "You don't know? The man takes apart your office, destroys your boat, just about kills you in Tokyo and you don't know? Goddammit, woman, you've got to fight fire with fire—"

"No, I don't. I don't have to do it your way, Jack," she said reasonably, thinking that this show of temper was something she'd been expecting for a long time.

"You've got to go toe-to-toe with the man. Get him to understand you mean business." Jack's green eyes jumped with ire, just as she'd imagined they would.

"Jack, you're not listening to me—"

"The man needs to be put out of business." He slammed a fist into his open palm. "He's trying to take over the whole damn Pacific Ocean, and you can't let him!"

"I'm not Greenpeace. I'm one woman. I'm not prepared to go to war with this man." There was more than one way to fight a man like Makomoto, she knew. Alex had taught her that.

Jack stood up, bumping the glass coffee table. Its top jiggled dangerously. "You're just like your old man. Let it happen. Don't do anything but stand by and let it happen."

Carrie stood, too, pulling herself to her full five feet ten inches, which put her on a pretty equal stance with him. She didn't want to fight, but he wasn't giving her much of a choice, especially after making that comment about her father. He knew how she felt about being compared to him.

"I think you're assuming a bit too much, Jack Briskin. I really don't want to discuss this with you right now." She turned and went back to her files.

"Fine, but you're going to discover that if you don't do something drastic, he's going to keep on interfering in your life and trying to get at Ocean Fresh."

With her back to him, she said, "You are overstepping your bounds. This is my life and my problem. I'll take care of it my way."

"Okay, Frank Sinatra, do it your way. But exactly what is it you're going to do? Are you going to go after him legally or will you just give him more targets to shoot at? Have you even called your lawyer yet?" His voice had turned sarcastic, hard-edged.

Suddenly, she didn't like this at all. "I think you'd better leave."

She heard him walk to her and felt his hand on her shoulder. "I don't want to leave. I want you to turn around and talk to me. What's happening here, Carrie? It's more than just Makomoto and Ocean Fresh, isn't it?"

Turning, she looked him squarely in the eyes and said, "Yes, there's a lot more going on and maybe you're right. Maybe we should talk. Right now. Right here. Before it goes any further."

His hand fell from her shoulder and he took a step backward. "I think I know what you're going to say," he said, his voice no longer angry, a defensive look creeping into his eyes. "I think I've expected it from the very beginning."

"I've thought about this for the past couple of

days," she said, trying to remember exactly how she'd rehearsed it. "You've been so good to me—"

He put his fingers on her lips. "Don't say it, Carrie. I don't want to hear you say it. Let me just leave. That way we'll be able to remember what we had with fondness rather than regret." He moved his fingers to her cheek and stroked it lightly, then pushed his hand into her hair and drew her to him. Their kiss was bittersweet and gentle.

"I'll always love you, Carrie Madison. You just remember that," he whispered.

As he walked out the door, she touched her own lips and fought down the lump in her throat. Even though she had done the right thing, it still hurt.

She also knew, in that flash of an instant, in that moment when time had stopped, frozen in a painful tableau, that the memory of Jack Briskin would haunt her forever.

Thirty-three

"You're getting what?"

Carrie almost dropped her teacup. She stared across the table at her mother and Jerry, sitting hand in hand on the other side. Her mother looked radiant, more beautiful than she ever had before. She beamed at Carrie.

"We are getting married."

Carrie laughed out loud and knocked over her chair in her rush to get to them. Hugging both of them hard, she laughed again, then the three of them began talking at once.

"That's the best news I've heard in ages," Carrie managed to say as she picked her chair up off the floor and settled back into it. She lifted her juice glass. "A toast. To the best couple in Hawaii. My mother and my future stepfather!"

Simone and Jerry exchanged loving glances, then raised their glasses to clink them against hers.

"So, when's the big event?"

"We were thinking of next week."

"Next week?" Her heart plummeted. She had come here to tell them she was planning to go back to Houston next week, to try to settle the situation with Makomoto and Ocean Fresh once and for all.

"Is there something wrong?" Jerry asked.

"Well, I . . . uh . . ."

"We have waited this long," Simone said, reaching across the table to pat Carrie's hand. "If our date interferes with your plans, we will change it. Of all the people in our lives, you are the most important. We want you to be there, to be part of our marriage."

Carrie smiled apologetically. "I have to go to Houston. I've already called and made an appointment with Geoff and asked Clark Quincel to get Ocean Fresh's board together for a meeting. That's what I came here to tell you."

Simone's face fell. "Will this ever be settled? Will this foolish company Philip insisted on giving you haunt us the rest of our lives?"

Carrie was shocked by the anger in her mother's voice, but she realized immediately where it came from. "It'll be over soon, *Maman.* Trust me. It'll be over soon." She raised her glass again and forced a smile to her lips. "Let's go out to dinner tonight and celebrate. Happy engagement, you two wonderful people!"

Fiddling with the pencils lined up neatly on the desk, Matt stared out the office window at Isaac and Jimmy. When he had left the hospital three days before, he'd figured going back to work would be no problem. Little did he know how weak he'd be and how drained he'd feel after a small bit of exercise. Even something as simple as walking across the floor exhausted him.

This sitting and supervising was no fun. He'd rather

be outside with the boys, cleaning up the debris Carrie had left piled up beside the storeroom. Well, at least he didn't have to worry about missing any whale-watching trips. Everything had been cancelled until Carrie's return from Houston. She'd promised to take him with her to choose a new boat—if he was feeling better, she reminded him with those arched eyebrows of hers. Perhaps they'd find a bigger one, maybe something with the capacity to handle the nighttime cruises Matt had suggested. He'd been surprised she wanted to continue in the business, but pleased. Nothing bothered him more than the thought that he'd be losing his friends.

Still stiff, he shifted in the new, comfortable office chair. The wound was healing now, its tightening scar itchy. He reached under the bandages to scratch his stomach and sighed with relief.

Outside the window, Isaac seemed to be doing a good job directing Jimmy, telling him where to coil the ropes and stack the buoys. Matt smiled. Someday his brother would make a great supervisor, but he'd always be a lousy worker.

Matt was about to get up and go outside to watch them more closely when the phone rang.

"Hey, *Bruddah!*" Alex's familiar voice called out. "I didn't expect to find you on the other end. I was trying to catch Simone to find out if she's heard from Carrie."

Matt checked his watch. "I don't think she's landing in Houston until later this afternoon. She couldn't catch a direct flight from Kona, so she went through Honolulu and had a couple hours' layover."

"Oh," Alex answered. A pause, as if he was checking his watch. "So, how the hell are you? You making trouble for everyone?"

"Only Isaac. He still can't stand having anyone tell him what to do."

"Who can? Did he bring his friends along? Carrie told me he was going to."

"Yup, they're outside right now playing janitor." Matt rolled his chair over to keep an eye on the boys. They had slid out of sight and, although he kept reminding himself things had changed, he was still nervous that they were sneaking a joint around the corner. But then he saw them, leaning against the piling watching a bikini-clad beauty strut her way to a sailboat at the end of the pier. He relaxed and leaned back into the chair.

"Hey, listen, Matt," Alex was saying. "I never had the chance to thank you for what you did for me. If it wasn't for you, Carrie would've never come to the Center."

"No problem, man. That's what friends are for. You don't have to thank me. What I did could've boomeranged on me, y'know. I was taking one hell of a chance."

"Well, it didn't. So, thank you. Maybe I can do the same for you some day."

Matt guffawed. "I hope not," he said.

They talked for a moment longer, then hung up after Alex said he had to go to a therapy appointment and would call Carrie later.

As Matt looked out the window again, he realized he hadn't seen Jack Briskin in well over a week. As much as he liked the man, he hoped Carrie had been wise enough to end it. He knew she would never talk about the relationship. It was okay. He understood her need for privacy.

Her heels resounded against the polished marble floor of the long hallway. Carrie strode quickly, her long legs propelling her to her destination—Geoff Presley's office, where he and several FBI agents awaited her arrival. She felt as though she was going into battle.

Although she knew Makomoto was already in trouble in the United States—though she had no idea why—she had arrived completely prepared to prove the Japanese businessman shouldn't be allowed to come back into the country. She'd brought the clippings, accounting sheets, and written testimony Takako had uncovered in Tokyo, as well as a sworn deposition from Takako, which she'd faxed from Shanghai the day before. Jerry had written one, too, and told about Makomoto's threats and about the evidence they had uncovered which pointed to the likelihood that Makomoto had killed Philip DeBary. The file was heavy in the new black leather briefcase Carrie held in her left hand.

Every time she caught a glimpse of herself in a mirror or window, she was amazed at the professionalism she exuded. She wore her hair in a French twist adorned with a pearl clasp and her straight-skirted gray and coral linen suit was specially tailored to skim her long torso and flat hips. She had to admit it felt good to have clothes that fit perfectly.

She stopped in front of a huge mahogany double door, its ivory handles so beautifully crafted she wanted to study them rather than use them. But perhaps that was just an excuse to put off the dreaded moment. Taking a deep breath, she smoothed her hair, adjusted her jacket, then reached for the handle.

Even though she'd gone over the facts a thousand times in her head, Carrie could hardly believe what she was going through and the responsibilities weighing heavily on her shoulders. She had taken the burden unwillingly, would give Ocean Fresh gladly to the first taker, but she discovered she liked the excitement, the challenge of uncovering the labyrinthine underpinnings of big business. She finally understood why her father liked being on the edge and knew that she, too, could get used to it, if not for the fact that she'd made the decision long before on another type of life.

Geoff's plump, soft-spoken secretary ushered Carrie into the office. Her heels sunk into the luxurious carpet beneath her feet. The small group of men and women surrounding Geoff's desk simultaneously lifted their heads.

"Here she is now." Geoff rose and came to her, giving her a wink no one else could see. "Let me introduce you to everyone."

He went around the room and Carrie followed his introductions, nodding at all four men and both women, even though she knew she probably wouldn't remember their names. Each agent wore a charcoal gray suit, a white shirt, and an indiscriminate tie, even the women. Although one of the men was considerably younger than the others and quite handsome, all seemed cut out of the same piece of cloth. She couldn't have picked them out of a lineup if someone paid her. And, she supposed, that was probably the point. Maybe there was a line or two in the handbook: "All agents must not exude brilliance or style in their mode of dress. Strive for an air of conservatism."

For the first few minutes, they exchanged niceties and general information, clarified some details about where Carrie had first met Makomoto, and went over the story of what had happened in Hawaii.

Then the young agent looked at the man next to him, a gray-haired gentleman with half-glasses on his bulbous nose. "Strange that Makomoto should visit Mrs. Madison's office himself instead of sending one of his henchmen," he said.

"Doesn't really matter now," the older man replied.

"What do you mean?" Carrie asked, perturbed that the men were acting as if no one else in the room existed.

Geoff began shuffling papers on his desk. The agents exchanged glances, as if reading each other's minds. Finally, the one standing next to her, who seemed to be their leader and who had introduced himself as Neil Schwartz, sat down and bent his elbows on his knees, leaning toward her.

"We had some news from Tokyo just yesterday. At this point, it's not documented, but we believe our source to be privy to inside information."

She waited for him to continue, her eyes flitting from one closed face to the other, trying to discern what it was they were about to lay on her.

Spit it out, she wanted to say. Don't dance around the subject. I'm getting really tired of playing games.

"Seems the Yakuza has split into several factions," Schwartz continued, "sort of like Mafia families do every once in a while. One person wants more power, another person needs to stop them or to hold on to their own position. We don't quite understand what brought this all to light or what the circumstances were that preceded it."

C'mon, Carrie thought, get to the point. She nodded as if she understood and recrossed her legs.

He looked down at his hands for a moment. "One of these warring factions is related to Ishiru Makomoto. We believe he was in power over there, but he started losing control when he couldn't bring your father's company into his own empire. A lot of the philosophy the Yakuza believes in is that the leaders have to show quiet, all-inclusive strength. Makomoto seemed to believe that his inability to take over Ocean Fresh undermined his standing in the Yakuza, at least that's how it looks to us.

"There have been rumors in the past couple of months that Makomoto was losing his grip on reality. Unfortunately, we had to consider any information like that to be strictly heresay, but you can't deny a fact when you hear it repeated over and over again."

The other agents nodded and murmured assent.

"Then we heard about the dealings between him and your father. Makomoto would never have appeared in person to carry out the threats he made to you. It was completely out of character for him. He always uses his associates to do his dirty work. We suspect the reason he came loose and stopped watching his back was because he thought he'd gotten rid of the competition. Then you came along."

"Me?" Carrie started to protest, but the agent continued.

"Yes, you," Schwartz replied, pushing his glasses up onto his nose. "You dug a little too hard, discovered a bit too much, came too close to uncovering the truth."

"What truth?"

"That he did kill your father and that we already knew about it, as well as that Makomoto had been blackmailing your father for ages."

"How?"

The plump, dark-haired woman on Schwartz's right spoke up. "Makomoto planted one of his people in your father's accounting department long ago. A computer genius. The man fixed the figures so that it looked as though your father was shifting funds from one company to another. Then Makomoto presented those 'adjusted' figures to your father, telling him they'd be published if your father didn't cooperate. Of course, there'd be no way for your father's associates, or anyone else for that matter, to tell that the figures had been falsified."

Schwartz took up the story. "At first, your father didn't cooperate at all and rumors began to circulate in the inner circles of his corporations, rumors that Philip DeBary had been transferring funds etc. Associates who would've normally jumped at the chance to provide venture capital for your father closed ranks against him. Your father's world was about to collapse around him. He'd be completely ruined if Makomoto's accounting sheets became public property, and both he and Makomoto knew it."

"So, my father did exactly as he was told."

"Not exactly," the female agent added, then gave

Carrie a wry smile. "Your father contacted us and we've been inside ever since."

Carrie barely had time to digest this revelation when the thinner, dark-haired man to her right, put his hand on the back of Schwartz's chair and began to speak.

"We got a report several nights ago that there was a battle between the warring factions of the Yakuza down near the Murayama Reservoir," he said.

Carrie vaguely remembered hearing something about the reservoir while she'd been in Tokyo but couldn't place its location.

"Several people were caught in the crossfire and killed," the agent continued. "Of course, the Yakuza takes care of their own and it took a lot of finagling to find out exactly who had died. The bodies were immediately taken away from the scene, and, of course, there were no obituaries in the newspaper."

He paused. Carrie leaned forward, afraid she knew the answer.

"Is he dead?" she asked in a whisper. "Did they kill Makomoto?"

Schwartz nodded and Carrie felt her face drain.

"Thank God," she said, closing her eyes.

Thirty-four

The meeting went on for another couple of hours. The agents had many questions to ask, blanks to fill in about Makomoto's dealings with American businesses. They said they wanted to better understand the Japanese corporate structure, but Carrie knew that what they really wanted was to poke holes into the Yakuza mystique. That was one place she couldn't help them. She knew nothing, except what Takako had discovered while she and Jerry had been in Tokyo. She told them that, but the agents persisted in asking questions. Answering them, she hoped now that Makomoto was dead, Takako could go home to her family.

Jerry, more than anyone else, would understand how relieved she felt about Makomoto's death. It was the first time in her life she had celebrated a person's demise. It almost made her feel guilty. Almost.

Just when she thought she wouldn't be able to answer another question, the agents decided they were finished. Geoff motioned for Carrie to stay as he ushered them out. Then he came back to his desk with a huff and an exhausted roll of his eyes.

"Bet you're glad that's over." He put his cowboy-booted feet up on his desk and leaned back in his chair, linking his hands behind his head.

Following his lead, she slipped her shoes off and
bent down to rub her sore toes. "Here I thought I'd
have all kinds of trouble keeping Makomoto out of
my life and now—"

The phone's buzz interrupted her and she waited
patiently, her eyes closed, while Geoff took messages
from his secretary. He hung up and resumed his pose.
"Your stepmother called about an hour ago," he said.
"She'd like you to go by the house after you finish
here. Something urgent, she said."

Carrie slumped forward. What else could go
wrong? "Did she say what it was?"

"No, but I don't think it's anything for you to be
worried about. If there's one thing I've come to know
about Pamela, it's that her urgencies aren't the same
as everyone else's."

"I hope you're right," Carrie said, slipping her feet
back into her shoes and collecting her things.

"Have you thought about whether you're going to
keep Ocean Fresh?" Geoff asked as he walked with
her to the door.

"I thought I had decided, but what I just found out
kind of changes the way I'm thinking. I'll let you
know soon. Quincel's getting the board together for a
meeting tomorrow, so I've got some hard decisions
to make tonight."

"Well, don't stretch that brain too much," Geoff
smiled, crinkling his acne-scarred cheeks. "You might
need to use it again someday."

She smiled weakly. "I hope I don't have to real
soon. I feel fried."

"I'm not surprised."

He handed her a few files, copies of the recorded

deeds and sale papers for the house. They spoke casually for a few more moments about mutual acquaintances, but Carrie was anxious to leave and cut the conversation short. She wondered, as she once again walked down the marble hallway, what Pamela considered so urgent that it couldn't wait.

As Carrie neared the house, she wished Pamela had suggested meeting on neutral ground.

"I thought I'd seen the last of this place," she muttered to herself, looking up at the tall white pillars of the magnificent structure which had once been home and still evoked powerful memories.

Before she reached the top of the porch stairs, the front door swung open. Pamela stood in the hallway. Her eyes red and her makeup tear streaked.

"I'm so glad you could come," she said. "I didn't know whether you'd be going right home . . ."

Carrie stepped into the foyer. "No, I have a meeting with Clark Quincel and the Ocean Fresh board of directors tomorrow morning."

Pamela nodded numbly and turned away. "I've found something I think you should have," she called over her shoulder, leading the way into the library.

Following her, Carrie wondered why Pamela couldn't have mailed whatever it was.

Pamela led the way through the massive library to the corner where her father had kept his desk and reading chair. He had loved to escape there, near a tall, thin window which let in just enough light for reading, he'd said, and gave him an unobstructed view of the paddocks behind the house. Seeing his worn

leather chair, the desk set Carrie had given him one
Christmas long ago, the framed pictures of Pamela,
Andrew, and—could it be?—herself at sixteen, smiling out at the photographer, wearing her jodhpurs and
hard hat, her arm around Spencer's neck. The picture,
one of her favorites of her cherished horse, gave her
a start. She hadn't expected yet another emotional jolt,
but there it was.

Pamela pointed to a white envelope in the middle
of the desktop. "I was cleaning out your father's desk
today and I found that. It's for you. Please forgive
me, but I've already read it." With that comment, she
drew away and left Carrie alone in the library with
the haunting memories of her father.

She stood where she was and stared at the envelope, not wanting to pick it up, especially if the letter
was responsible for Pamela's distress. Carrie trailed
her fingers along the desk's edge, feeling the slight
oiliness of a recent polishing, the grain of the scal-
loped lip around the desk's inlaid top. Slowly, she
walked around to her father's chair and touched it,
running her nail along the cracks in the leather, wondering why her father had never replaced it with
something more modern. He, too, had been a creature
of habit, needing the comfortable, the familiar.

Feeling like a child, she lowered herself into the seat,
sitting in it gingerly, as if afraid her father would come
through the door at any moment and oust her from it.
The chair had the soothing smell of oil soap. She sunk
into it, letting herself relax, and leaned her head back,
then stretched her fingers out along its arms.

Again, she stared at the envelope.

Moments passed before she could will herself to

reach for it. Once she did, she turned it over and over in her hands. On the front, her name was written in her father's scrawly hand, as if he'd meant to mail the letter, but just hadn't gotten round to it. Or had he intended to give it to her in person? Her throat closed up and she thought of all the things she had imagined saying to him, all the letters she'd written and wanted to mail but hadn't.

Perhaps this letter revealed yet another object he'd willed to her. Maybe it had been written long ago, when she was little. Or it might contain some bit of advice he had longed to give her, or an explanation of his actions so many years ago. Or maybe it would finally clear up the question of why her father had willed Ocean Fresh to her.

I can sit here forever and drive myself nuts, she thought, or I can open the damn thing and get it over with. Open it, she exhorted herself. Solve the mystery.

She flipped up the unglued flap, realizing once again that Pamela had read the letter. Had it been open when Pamela had found it? It looked like it had been, not appearing to have been ripped. At least Pamela didn't go to great lengths to deceive her. She had to admire her stepmother for that.

The letter had some heft to it, four pages worth, and Carrie knew she was in for a long diatribe. She hoped it wasn't one of her father's holier-than-thou pieces of advice. With a sense of dread and an uncontrollable curiosity, she settled back and heard her father's voice speaking to her.

My dearest Carrie,
    If you are reading this letter, I am obviously

no longer around, for one reason or another. I hope that you've been able to come to terms with whatever's happened and that you've also been able to meet with Pamela and with your half-brother, Andrew. They are two very special people to me, Carrie. I hope you can see why.

I've been lucky to be able to pick up my life and carry on. I never thought I'd be able to do that in those early days after you and your mother left. You don't know how heart-wrenching it was for me to realize the mistakes I'd made and the hurt I'd caused. I only wish now that we'd been able to talk about it.

When I came to Hawaii to see you, I had hoped we could mend our bridges, but you were so angry with me, I knew I'd been wrong not to start trying long before that. To have lost my only daughter because of my own stupid mistakes has been one of the hardest come-uppances in my entire life.

Every day of the past eight years you've been in my thoughts, but when we spoke in the hospital, I found out, for the first time, how you felt about dolphins and whales, and about how I, failed you, once again, by not running my company the way it should have been run. You were so right, my dear Carrie. I have not done a good job with Ocean Fresh, and I am ashamed of everything that's happened. Perhaps, with your patience, I can explain some of it.

Years ago, I was a brash young businessman with a lot of guts and very little diplomacy. I thought that to get to the top, you had to cut everyone at the bottom. And that's how I first tried to deal with Ishiru Makomoto. Unfortunately, he and I were very similar, and he met me horn to horn, as your grandfather would say.

In a nutshell, I was brazen enough to investigate Mr. Makomoto's background, his personal history, and to try to use that information as leverage for a buyout. It didn't work. In fact, it backfired directly in my face. I don't know why I so naively believed I had nothing in my past Makomoto could use against me, if he wanted. Perhaps I thought I was invincible. Obviously, I'm not.

Makomoto not only stopped me, he turned me into a frightened dog with my tail between my legs. He also gained control over Ocean Fresh, forcing me to do whatever he wanted, rather than what I thought was right. To put it bluntly, he blackmailed me into a corner, and I had no way of getting out. Now, with the help of the FBI, I'm sure you've discovered the details, the truth. If not, take my word for it that Makomoto set me up—quite nicely, I might add. And it's not something I'm proud of.

I know what Makomoto intends to do with the tuna fleet once he gets his hands on it. He cares nothing about dolphins and whales and sea turtles and everything else you love in the sea. He only cares about how much profit this company will produce for him.

Stop him, Carrie. Use all your strength, your indignation, and your rage to stop him. Only you can do it. Only you can ignore corporate politics, turn your back on the lobbyists and the stock-holders, to make Ocean Fresh respectable again, and keep the dolphins safe.

I've left Ocean Fresh to you because I know you can do it. I know you're not influenced by money and that you've always done the right thing without a thought as to who you might offend. Please understand why I've done this, why I believe you are the one and only person to take over Ocean Fresh, and do your best, Carrie. That's all I ask. Do what I should have done. Do what I couldn't do.

I trust you. And I love you. You're the most precious thing I've ever had in my life. I only wish I had told you that long ago. Please forgive me and accept my deepest apologies. I never meant to hurt you. If you can't accept anything else, believe that.

Through the haze of her tears, Carrie put her finger to her father's scrawled signature and traced the hills and valleys of the one word which bound the two of them irrevocably together—"Dad." And in the staid quiet of the English library her mother had loved so much and her father had found refuge in, she found the words which finally healed the wounds of so long ago.

"I love you, Daddy."

Thirty-five

Carrie hoisted her suitcases from the Hilo airport's baggage trolley and headed down the long hallway toward the parking lot. She hadn't called anyone to meet her; she didn't feel like talking yet. Too many emotions swam close to the surface. One word or gesture could make her fall apart.

Just that morning she'd met with Ocean Fresh's board of directors. She'd had a tough night deciding what to do with the company, jotting down plan after plan until she'd finally come up with something that would free her up to go back to Hawaii, an idea she believed would please her father.

When she had stood in front of the long cherry table, specially designed so that each member of the board could see all the other members, she had felt as natural as if she'd done so on a daily basis for many years. She'd been intimidated, nervous. The only person she knew had been Clark Quincel, and he'd sat back in his chair, his arms folded over his chest. He'd expected her to sell the company. It had been her favored option, and with Makomoto out of the way, the idea had been even more tempting. But that wasn't the reason her father had given her Ocean Fresh and she now knew one of her responsibilities was to make the company better, what her father had wanted it to be, what she wanted it to be.

After introducing herself and asking them to do the same, she'd told the twelve-member board briefly of her meetings with Makomoto, of Makomoto's death (which had shocked a few of them), and her own environmental policies. It had been a truly discomfiting moment for her when a few of them had smirked and started fidgeting. They had expected this. She was an upstart. A young woman with no experience.

She'd understood their impatience, as well as their prejudice. All she'd wanted was for them to listen for a while before making any judgments.

Finally, she had caught their attention. Now, she'd told herself. It's time. She'd cleared her throat and plunged ahead.

"I've done a lot of thinking about Ocean Fresh's future and about the people behind the scenes, all the workers in the fisheries, the canning departments, the fishing crews, and you people. All of you would be out of jobs if I decided to sell Ocean Fresh, so I've decided not to do that."

A sigh of relief had gone around the table.

"At first I thought that the only way to keep the business going was to run it myself. But I don't have the expertise, nor do I want to move back to Texas to be the head of this company. Besides, Mr. Quincel is doing a fine job as president and I believe he'd like to stay on."

Clark nodded, then leaned his chin on his hand, his steady eyes focused directly on her.

"So, what I propose to do is completely unique, as far as I know, and it's an idea which excites me. I've briefly sketched out my plan, but I realize that in order to make this transition we're going to have to have a lot more meetings. This is just the beginning. It'll take a while for all my changes to be made, but I believe they'll work to make Ocean Fresh much better, more efficient, more competitive than it's been in a long time."

She'd paused to take a sip of water, looking around the table at the men and women who had so much invested in Ocean Fresh, wondering briefly how many of them had been her father's true friends and how many would become hers.

"What I propose is that we begin a program which will allow Ocean Fresh's employees the opportunity to invest in the company. I want to give them each some portion of stock as soon as they've been with the company for three months, then to let them increase that amount in whatever increments they wish. I want them to have voting power in major decisions, and I want them educated in the business. With more interested employees, we'll have a firm owned by the people who work for it. It's a philosophy no one will be able to beat."

Everyone around the table had started murmuring and looking at each other in shock. She'd suppressed a smile. It had been exactly the reaction she'd been hoping for.

She raised her voice to compete with them. "I don't want a position of control, as I've already said, so I will be more a figurative chairperson, with voting privileges, but I won't be here to oversee the day-to-day functioning of the company. However, there are a few changes I insist on and I want to see them implemented right away. Number one is the removal of all seine nets. I want our research and development people to immediately begin investigating ways to fish for tuna in an environmentally safe way and we've got to start putting pressure on Japan to do the same. In addition, our marketing, public relations, and advertising departments need to start planning a five-year strategy to bring Ocean Fresh to the forefront of the fish industry. We can do it. It's what my father wanted to see happen. And, with your help, we can make his dream, and mine, come true."

She'd stopped, out of breath, her heart beating wildly, waiting for their reaction. Grateful tears had come to her eyes when, one by one, the members of the board had risen and applauded her till the sound had filled the room and echoed down the hallways.

It had dawned on her, as she'd boarded the plane in Houston, that what she had suggested to Ocean Fresh's board was that the company be run in much the same way as Japanese companies were—people taking care of themselves; putting time, energy, and pride into their work; caring about the business.

Now, with her suitcases heavy in her hands, she reflected that there was still a lot of work to do, but she knew she could rely on Clark Quincel to do the bulk of it, freeing her to help Alex begin his marine lab. He didn't know it yet, but his lifelong dream was about to come true. It was his way of preserving the environment, a way Carrie could support wholeheartedly.

All around her in the usually quiet airport, people jostled for their bags. The beginning of tourist season, she thought. Everyone's coming to Hawaii, to paradise. A family to her right, the husband holding a crying toddler, looked frazzled. Not a good start to their vacation. And in front of her an elderly, over-weight woman slowly made her way through a turn-stile.

Suddenly, the woman stopped, as though stuck. Carrie tried to see beyond her, wondering what would happen if the old woman couldn't make it through. Were there any other exits? She wanted to get home. She wanted to see Alex.

The woman moved slightly to one side and Carrie's eyes widened.

"No," she whispered, not believing what she saw in front of her. "You're dead."

Makomoto stared back at her with flat gray eyes. "Not dead, Caryn Madison. But, soon, you will be!" In his hand, a huge Samurai sword glistened. The fat woman screamed.

Carrie dropped her bags and pushed the old woman out of the way in one fluid motion. The woman crawled away, whimpering like a wounded animal.

The knife sliced past Carrie's face, so close she could feel the air swish.

Then, suddenly, from all directions people fled, knocking each other over in their hurry to get away from the obviously insane Japanese man trying to kill the tall blonde woman.

Makomoto yelled something in Japanese, some-thing Carrie knew instinctively was a curse. Then he screamed, a long, guttural, *"Aaaahhh!"* as he came toward her, the knife in both of his hands, his mouth open, his eyes unfocused and staring.

God, I'm going to die.

The sword has a red and gold handle, she thought

inanely. He's going to kill me with something pretty, something ceremonial.

She looked wildly around for an escape. One heel caught on the mat below her and she felt her knees buckle. She was going down, and no matter how much she flailed her arms, she couldn't regain her balance. Her cheek smashed to the floor and pain shot through her head. She lifted her face quickly. Makomoto's yell split the air once again.

"Alex!" she screamed, as she tried to lift herself up.

Makomoto's weight came down against her. He was light, almost like a child. Once again, she fell to the floor, this time with him on top of her, and in that long moment before her head hit the ground, she realized she'd never had children, she'd never had Alex's baby.

Repulsed, she thought about Makomoto on top of her. The last man who would ever be against her body. She knew she'd made terrible mistakes, and now she'd never be able to make up for them.

Although she felt no pain, she closed her eyes and listened to the wheeze which could only indicate one thing: life leaving a body.

She was still muttering, "I'm sorry, Alex. I'm sorry," when the FBI agents pulled her to a sitting position. Makomoto was gone, but there was blood everywhere. She watched it puddle on the floor in concentric circles. Magenta. Maroon. Brick red. Pink. And wondered whether someone would ever get around to taking her to the hospital.

Looking up, she stared blankly at the group of people surrounding her. She caught her breath and listened to what she supposed were comforting words. Finally, she could speak.

"You've got to take me to the hospital," she said breathlessly to a woman wearing a black baseball cap and a vest, both printed with the letters F.B.I.

The woman laughed and squeezed her arm. "You'll be all right in a moment, Mrs. Madison. It's Makomoto who needs the hospital." She pointed to the stretcher carrying Makomoto's body.

Carrie's eyes focused on Makomoto's lifeless face. She knew without being told that he was dead.

"But, how—"

"We followed you from Texas, Mrs. Madison. We've learned you can't always trust Japanese rumors. Sometimes it's better to be safe than sorry. When we heard Makomoto was dead, we knew we should check into it a little more. The man had obviously lost touch with reality. Never can tell what a person like him is capable of doing. Lucky for you our director is a cautious man. He gave the order for us not to close the case yet and told us to follow you. We wouldn't have been here otherwise."

Carrie took one deep breath, then another, and clinging to the agent's arm, she felt her whole body quiver. Then rippling laughter took over until the quivers and the laughter and the tears were all mingled in one and she was sure they'd end up taking her to the hospital, too—to the psycho ward.

"This is so ironic," she said, looking into the woman's face. The agent, who couldn't be much older than Carrie herself, had luminous brown eyes. "Every time something happens to me, I get rescued by a woman. My mother rescued us from my father, then she did it again when Makomoto split my boat in half, and now . . ." She ran out of air and grasped at the agent's arm. "Men. They need us. You know?"

The woman nodded, then closed her eyes for a second before waving to another agent for help. "You'll be okay, Mrs. Madison," she reassured Carrie again.

All around them, agents rushed back and forth, talking into hand-held radios. Small groups of them held serious, hushed conferences. Sirens. Lights. Orders barked by uniformed Hilo police officers.

How many people knew about this? she wondered. Why didn't they tell me?

Carrie struggled to sit up and gathered her suitcases to her. A few spots of blood stained her new suit. Makomoto's blood. She wiped at them weakly.

"I have to go see my husband," she told the agent.

"It'll be a little while before we can let you leave," the woman replied. "We have to get a report."

Within moments, Carrie was ushered into an airport office, where she answered questions in a daze. By the time the questioning was over, she had begun to feel normal again.

The female agent ushered Carrie to the door, promising to be in touch. Carrie focused on the warm brown eyes, once more seeking reassurance.

"Is it really over now?" Carrie asked.

The agent nodded and smiled.

Almost an hour later, still shaking, Carrie got into her rented car and headed for the Center, pulling off her pantyhose at one stop light and wriggling out of her suit at the next. She didn't care that everyone was watching her change her clothes while driving. She was home and safe and that meant she could once again allow herself the freedom to relax, a gift she would never again take for granted.

When she got to the Center, she practically ran down the corridor connecting the lobby to the private rooms and repeated to herself over and over again her wish that Alex would be in his room, that she wouldn't have to go searching for him. She needed him desperately, his arms around her, his strength and his understanding. She needed Alex to tell her everything was going to be all right.

Rounding the last corner, she stopped dead in her tracks. Right in front of her, walking with the help of two canes, one in each hand, was Alex. He wore a T-shirt which revealed his fully developed chest muscles and arms. Carrie's heart stopped and the feeling that captured her body was the same one she'd had when she'd first realized she was in love with him.

An incredibly proud smile lit up his handsome face. "Well, what do you think?" he asked, a catch in his voice.

She walked toward him slowly, swallowing hard and blinking her eyes. Nothing, nobody else in the world could make her feel like this, she realized. Nothing could replace her love for him, the love she'd denied for so long.

She held out her arms and walked more quickly, laughing and crying at the same time. Then she stood in front of him, not knowing whether to hug him or to marvel at the fact that he could walk again. Looking up into his face, she saw her love reflected in his clear blue eyes and said quietly, in a voice thick with emotion, "This is the best present you've ever given me."

He leaned on his canes and lowered his face. "I've got one better," he said, his lips touching hers. "I'm coming home tomorrow."

"Good," she answered as she returned his kiss eagerly and snaked her arms around his waist, "because it's mating season soon and the way I feel this year, it's going to last a long time."

YOU WON'T WANT TO READ
JUST ONE – KATHERINE STONE

ROOMMATES   (3355-9, $4.95)
No one could have prepared Carrie for the monumental
changes she would face when she met her new circle of
friends at Stanford University. Once their lives intertwined
and became woven into the tapestry of the times, they would
never be the same.

TWINS   (3492-X, $4.95)
Brook and Melanie Chandler were so different, it was hard
to believe they were sisters. One was a dark, serious, ambi-
tious New York attorney; the other, a golden, glamourous,
sophisticated supermodel. But they were more than sisters – they were twins and more alike than even they knew
. . .

THE CARLTON CLUB   (3614-0, $4.95)
It was the place to see and be seen, the only place to be. And
for those who frequented the playground of the very rich, it
was a way of life. Mark, Kathleen, Leslie and Janet – they
worked together, played together, and loved together, all behind exclusive gates of the *Carlton Club*.

*Available wherever paperbacks are sold, or order direct from the
Publisher. Send cover price plus 50¢ per copy for mailing and handling to Penguin USA, P.O. Box 999, c/o Dept. 17109, Bergen-
field, NJ 07621. Residents of New York and Tennessee must
include sales tax. DO NOT SEND CASH.*